THE
LIFE

The Russian Guns, Book Two

Bethany-Kris

Published by Bethany-Kris

www.bethanykris.com

ISBN 13: 978-1-988197-70-8

Cover Design © Jay Aheer
Editor: Elle Leigh

For anyone who believed in this. You're why I continued, and why it's here. Thank you.

CONTENTS

Chapter One

"I've narrowed it down to three, Mr. Avdonin."

Anton glanced up from the case displaying watches at the jeweler's voice. Richard, his usual jeweler, sent him to this particular place of business for the piece he was looking for.

After all, pearls were a speciality for some. For others, they were only a fancy.

"And?" Anton asked.

The jeweler produced three black velvet cases from under the counter. The first held a two stranded, white pearl design. A bit too simplistic for what Anton desired. He waved off the necklace, his gaze traveling to the second. Larger pearls with a pink sheen rested on a white gold strand of thin chain, each globe separated by a good inch of space. It was intended to hang low on the chest of the person wearing it.

"This is a bit long," Anton said.

"It's meant to draw attention to the clothes being worn, and not so much the pearls."

"I want to show off the woman, not her clothes."

"Ah, point taken." With a faint smirk, the jeweler waved at the third. "This may be more to your liking, then."

Anton went back to surveying the final piece with little interest. Much like the first one, it was a simple white design, only instead of two strands, there were four. Even with the simplicity of it, the jewelry still screamed flashy. It wasn't long enough to be called a necklace, in his opinion, as it looked short enough to be more of a choker.

Anton wasn't trying to brand his wife with a collar.

"No. None of these."

The jeweler seemed struck speechless. "None?"

"They're not to my wife's tastes or style. She wears the jewelry, not the other way around." With a sigh, Anton asked,

1

"What about gray pearls?"

"Gray?"

Anton shrugged. "Why not? If you have them, I'd like to see them."

"I do, but they're very ..."

"Expensive? I don't care, show me."

Money was the least of his concerns. People usually assumed the more expensive the jewelry, the flashier it was. That wasn't always the case. Sometimes the most costly pieces came in modest designs. It was about the quality, not the quantity.

As Anton said, his wife wore the jewelry, the jewelry didn't wear her. Viviana Avdonin didn't need accessories to class her up, she did that all on her own.

The jeweler wasn't gone but five seconds before a feminine form saddled up beside Anton at the counter. Slender fingers reached down to caress the rows of pearls left resting in their precious velvet. Each digit was adorned with rings that glittered off the lighting in the shop.

One of those rings in particular, Anton recognized.

The hackles on the back of his neck raised in his disgust and anger. "Tatiana."

"Anton." Tatiana purred his name, leaning on the counter with one arm. The low cut dress she wore showcased her cleavage, opening further as she stretched over the counter to snag the third case of pearls, dragging them towards her. "Funny meeting you here."

Anton beat back his scowl. "Yes, funny."

Tatiana Belov was the devil in a pretty package. Slender, tall, and curvaceous in all the places that mattered, she didn't lack male attention. Her blue eyes stung like steel, her blonde hair perfectly managed in waves, and an attitude that said she'd take all or nothing. Less than two years before, after Anton rejected her, she'd attempted to burn his club to the ground. Less than one year ago, the vile woman cornered his soon-to-be wife and verbally attacked her.

Being an old lover of his, Tatiana was due her jealousies.

Anton didn't deny her that, but he had thought he made it clear as to his lack of interest or desire to have her again. Especially now that he and Viviana were married.

"What are you doing here, Tatiana?"

"Visiting a friend," she said vaguely. "These are beautiful."

Anton rolled his eyes. She would think they were something, if the jewelry she wore was any indication. Beyond that, Anton knew Tatiana enjoyed the expensive things that came along with living in the mafia lifestyle. Clothes that were on the runway only weeks ago, gems the size of large marbles, and vehicles that were drool-worthy ... No, the girl didn't lack in her tastes.

Unfortunately, her father indulged her far too much. Spoiled, beautiful, and rich, Tatiana was every man's worst nightmare. She wasn't wife material, she spread her legs to get what she wanted, and her mean streak couldn't be contained. Anton didn't trust her in the least.

Speaking of which ... "I have a sit-down with your father later today. Is that why you're here?"

"Do you?" Tatiana at least had the decency to look surprised. "I didn't know. Should I call—"

"Cut the shit," Anton interrupted coldly. "What do you want, Tati?"

"Nothing. I told you, I'm visiting a friend."

The way she cooed the word twisted something in Anton's gut. Instincts or nerves, whatever someone wanted to call it, he had it in the gallons. When they acted up, Anton tended to take notice.

"I told you the last time we met up that you were not to come back here, Tati."

Tatiana tapped her manicured nail to the glass counter. "No, you told me to stay out of your territory. I've not been in Brighton Beach since. You don't own Brooklyn as a whole, Anton."

Fuck, he hated that was true.

"Why do I doubt this is just a random meeting?"

"Well, it is," Tatiana said, unbothered. "I noticed your car outside when I was leaving a shop across the street and came to say hello. Surely we can be friends, can't we?"

No, Anton thought.

Before he could respond, the jeweler was making his way towards them from the back of the shop. Only one case rested in his hands. The man didn't even acknowledge the girl now standing at his counter, as he seemed wholly focused on the velvet he held so carefully.

"Mr. Avdonin, these may be just what you're looking for. Three strands, gray pearls ranging from small to large going from the top of the strand to the bottom with a diamond studded clasp at the back. They stay in my vault, as they were purchased for a specific customer who changed his mind last minute. They are much too expensive to be out here with the others. I only bring them out on request. Please do not touch unless wearing gloves."

Anton liked this man. He was straightforward and blunt. There was something to be said for those qualities.

"The price?" Anton asked.

The pearls were placed to the glass in their case, and Anton knew instantly they were the ones.

"Eight," the jeweler answered.

"Thousand?" Tatiana asked.

The man across the counter snorted, causing Anton to smirk. "No, my dear. Eight-hundred thousand. Imported, specially designed, and meant for the proper woman."

With those words, the jeweler tossed Tatiana a baleful look. She was not the kind of woman he would expect to see toting pearls of these caliber. She couldn't hold the weight of them, so to speak.

"These will fit Viviana just fine, don't you think, Tatiana?" Anton asked, stating her name for the benefit of the jeweler.

Tatiana didn't bother to hide her glower. "Perfect, I'm sure."

Satisfied, Anton turned back to the counter. "My wife will be pleased, thank you. Ready them for me."

Again, the man seemed thunderstruck. "Just like that?"

"I like them. I think it's an appropriate gift for my wife for the birth of our child. Why not?"

At the word birth, Tatiana took an entire step back. The expression she sported could only be described as slapped. "Pregnant?"

"Mmhmm," Anton hummed, turning on his heel to face her. "Very pregnant, actually. We're having a little boy."

Tatiana swallowed a gulp of nothing. "Congratulations are in order, then."

Were they? The last thing this female seemed like she wanted to do was congratulate him or Viviana. Even so, Anton sincerely hoped whatever fancy Tatiana might have previously held for him disappeared with the knowledge that his wife was carrying his child, and he had no interest in her, now.

"I should go," Tatiana said softy, her brow furrowing. "My friend …"

Anton waved her off. "Sure. I do have a meeting to get to, after all."

"Tell Viviana I said hello, Anton."

Absolutely not.

● ● ●

"Vine?"

When Anton's wife didn't immediately answer his yell, he knew where he'd find her.

Wife.

Goddamn, he loved calling her that.

Anton quickly made his way to the back of the house. Passing the maid's room, he noticed Clarissa wasn't in her usual spot reading. The house didn't smell like food, either. That was the most unusual.

Viviana attended school three days a week, but they didn't miss an evening meal together. While Clarissa did most of the cooking in their home, his wife nearly always had her hands in the pot when it came to supper.

5

"Viviana?" Anton called out her name again when he came up to the sliding glass doors. The main door was opened, but the screen was shut tight. "You out there, baby?"

Sure enough, as he pushed open the door he found everyone lounging in the backyard. Clarissa, perched up on one of the benches, had a book in her hands. Rocco slept on his plush pillow. Viviana, the one Anton searched for first, was out in the middle of the backyard soaking up sunshine on a blanket.

Anton grinned at the sight. It was unusually warm for late April. A muggy heat was sweeping New York. Viviana, nearly seven months pregnant, couldn't stand the weather half of the time and then the other half she downright loved it. He couldn't keep up with his pregnant wife's moods. Not that he complained. There was no way in hell Anton would ever be able to understand the changes her body was going through for his child.

But he adored every fucking minute of it.

"Hey, baby."

Viviana's head turned to the side at his quiet greeting, her dark hair spilling to green grass as she smiled. "Hey."

The cellphone in his pocket buzzed with a gentle tune. Anton ignored it. Like hell was he about to take calls for the Bratva. Give him an hour with his wife. That was all he asked of his guys. Unfortunately, his job as a mafia boss never really ended. There was always some issue or opinion needing immediate attention. When the phone buzzed with its call again, Anton slipped his hand inside his slacks and silenced the offending device.

Nothing on earth was more important than the brown-eyed beauty resting on the lawn with her hand perched at the top of her rounded stomach. Viviana was life to Anton. She breathed it into him every moment of the day. Somehow, she managed to remind him that despite his occupation, he could still be him.

"How did the sit-down go?" Viviana asked.

She attempted to prop herself up, struggling in the cutest

way. Anton quickly crossed the porch and then the back lawn to help her. Standing upright, she offered him a sheepish smile.

Anton wrapped his arms around her shoulders and rested his lips to her forehead. "It didn't happen."

"No?"

"Nope," he replied with a shrug. "Clearly Sergei still hasn't forgiven me for breaking his face, not that I give a fuck."

Sergei Belov was a man, much like Anton, who ran his Bratva in his territory of New Jersey. Seven or so months earlier, the two men ended up in a disagreement of sorts when the Jersey boss slandered Viviana and Anton retaliated physically. It was only recently that they had attempted making peace again. Unfortunately, Sergei's tactic of setting up the sit-down and then not following through was as good as a shunning to Anton. It was, for all purposes, a signed death warrant.

"What's going to happen now?" Viviana asked.

Anton decided to evade the question. He wasn't entirely sure how he wanted to handle the situation with Sergei. And he certainly didn't want to bring up Tatiana's unexpected, unwanted presence and concern his wife.

"How was your day?"

"Long." Viviana frowned unhappily. "The air conditioner in the lecture hall was broken all morning. I managed to forget where the bathroom was in the third wing and nearly peed myself. Your son thinks my bladder is his personal soccer ball."

"He doesn't mean it."

Seemingly at the sound of his father's voice, the baby boy pressed some appendage against the heel of Anton's palm. By rolling his thumb over the spot, the baby finally relaxed inside his mother's womb. Viviana huffed a breath of relief. Every time he kicked or stretched that hard, she swore the child was trying to put her into early labor.

"Yeah, Papa's home, little man," Anton said, smiling.

"Still going with Papa, huh?"

"It's what I called my father, and what he called Nicoli. Call me whatever you want to him, but he's going to know me as Papa, Vine. Mark my words."

Viviana's beautiful face lit up with bliss. "I bet if he was a girl, it would have been Daddy all the way."

Maybe. There was something about his first child being a boy that had him twisted into a million and one little knots. Especially when one of his guys asked how the little prince was doing and Anton realized for the first time, they weren't asking about him. Oh, he'd been beyond ecstatic to find out they were having a boy. There weren't enough words for him to use to explain his excitement. Pride and love were the closest, though.

"Ouch!" Viviana made a miserable noise, her hand coming to press under her lower rib. Anton moved his hand accordingly. "Damn it, that one hurt."

"He doesn't mean it," he repeated, practically cooing the words. "He's just strong and impatient, like me."

"I know." Viviana's hand found his as the baby kicked again. "But he still has a couple of more months to go, so he can simmer Papa's attitude right down."

If only some of Anton's men could see him now. They probably wouldn't know what to think. Anton was known for being a hard-ass, cutthroat boss. One with a mighty fucking temper and little patience for nonsense. His behavior with Viviana was the complete opposite.

With Viviana's hand pressing to Anton's chest, she leaned closer into his embrace.

"Missed you today. No problems, right?"

Viviana shook her head. "Nope."

"Good."

"Did you see Daniil this morning?" she asked.

Anton flinched inwardly, fighting off the immediate rush of sadness that flushed his veins like poison. "Yeah, but he didn't talk much. Slept through most of my visit."

His father's sickness had progressed to its very final stages. At the most, the doctors gave him a couple of short months, which was better than what they had predicted before. Daniil was a fighter, and he wasn't about to miss his first grandchild's birth. Even if Daniil wouldn't admit it, Anton knew that was what his father was waiting for.

"And Sasha?"

"Tired."

Viviana didn't seem to have a reply, so he settled for holding her close as the warm April evening descended down. The gentle stillness settling between the couple had Anton sighing. This was his happiest time, the moments he waited and worked for every damned day. Between feds that tailed him and guys that constantly called, the only thing on his mind was his wife.

Seemingly sensing Anton's lingering sadness, Viviana fisted his shirt and pulled him down to meet her for a kiss. Her front pressed to his as their mouths connected with a slow building passion. Anton relished in the way her fingers curled tighter, the taste and heat of her parting lips that moved in sync with his. Allowing his hands to wander, he trailed his grip up her sides, feeling his wife shiver under his touch.

Slowly, Anton pulled away, letting her gentle pecks dot down to the line of his jaw. "Did you want to go out for supper?"

"Nope." Viviana smiled. "I was craving pizza something awful, so we ordered in. It should be here anytime."

Ah, well that explained the lack of food when he arrived home.

"Craving, huh? Nothing weird, I hope."

Anton was only half teasing. After the soup mess the week before, well, Viviana could have ordered something nasty to be put on the pizza. Of course, that was nothing compared to the vanilla ice-cream and ketchup topping concoction she had him making a month ago.

While it all led to funny situations, it was also disgusting.

He was more than happy to appease her strange desires, though.

"Pepperoni and cheese," Viviana said, bringing him from his musings.

"That sounds good." Actually, it sounded great. Anton barely ate a thing all day and his insides were now trying to feed on themselves. "So—"

A slight movement over Viviana's shoulder caught his eye. Just beyond the stone fence that surrounded their backyard, an unmarked, gray car sat on the back road. The window was rolled down. Anton could see the lens of the camera sticking out the window. There was no doubt in his mind it was a federal car, and his anger swelled at the sight.

What in the hell gave them the right to be taking pictures of him and his wife in their backyard? It wasn't like Anton was in the middle of a business meeting or brandishing a gun for the neighborhood to see. Being the head of his family, a family that dealt heavily in the world of organized crime, it wasn't unusual for the feds to be around. That didn't mean he liked it.

Instinctively, Anton's hand covered Viviana's stomach, wanting to somehow shield his pregnant wife from the photographs. He knew it was useless, but he still bared his teeth and openly glared at the camera.

Fuck them.

He hadn't been doing anything to warrant the feds following him, never mind picture taking. If they wanted to play that game anywhere else, Anton didn't care, but not as his house. Usually there was always a car parked near their home. Some idiots attempting to catch a bit of Russian mob action, but this was different.

It even felt different to Anton.

After Tatiana's appearance earlier in the day, and her father blowing Anton off later, the boss was two seconds away from losing his patience.

"Hey, what's wrong?"

Viviana's worried voice resounded above the rushing rage pulsing blood in Anton's ears. He hid the anger on his face with a tender smile. The deflection didn't work. It shouldn't

10

have been a surprise; Viviana knew him better than anyone. His wife was already trying to turn around to look in the direction of where his gaze had traveled. Anton diverted her attention with another kiss.

"Come on, let's go inside and get Rocco out of this heat," he murmured, his hand finding the small of her back.

The dog in question perked up at his name. With a low bark, it was all the animal offered. Anton assumed he must have been given his pain medication for the day. The German shepherd hadn't even gotten up to greet his master like he usually did. The meds always made the pup sleepy and weak.

"But—"

"No buts," Anton interrupted, glancing back at the car with its camera still trained on them. He didn't want whoever that was taking more pictures of them than they already had. God knew how long they'd been out there as it was before he returned home. "In the house, Vine."

"Okay."

Following his lead, Viviana chanced a glance behind them. Sure enough, her gaze narrowed and a slight pink reddened her cheeks.

"Anton, why are they photographing us?"

"I don't know," he said gruffly.

"Has that been happening a lot?" she asked as they started up the steps.

The Bratva boss sighed heavily. Bending down, he gathered the dog in his arms, being mindful of the sensitive areas that hurt Rocco when they were touched. He didn't know what to say to Viviana, honestly. Yes, they'd been following him a little more recently, but no one understood why.

"Yeah," he finally answered. "But don't worry about it, baby."

Her brown eyes met his as her bottom lip disappeared under her white teeth. "How can I not?"

How, indeed.

It was the ways and rules of their life, and no one played

fair.

• • •

Anton rested between Viviana's legs, his hands acting as a pillow on her stomach while he watched her read. The textbook in her hands barely received any attention at all. Whenever her husband was around, her mind wandered more than usual.

Tonight was no exception.

"Quit watching me," she whined behind the book.

"I can't." Anton offered nothing else as an explanation. Shifting his form a little, he moved up Viviana's rounded midsection. Pushing her maternity tank away from her flesh, he kissed and spoke in a language she still hadn't bothered to learn. Finally, his words turned to English again. "For God's sake, would you pick a name for this boy of mine already?"

The textbook was tossed to the sheets, forgotten. "Is that what you're muttering about down there? That he doesn't have a name yet?"

Anton shrugged his broad shoulders. "No."

"What do you say, then?"

"Things."

Viviana knew her lover wasn't one to be shy, so his change in demeanor had her curiosity perking. With another movement, Anton allowed her to sit up.

"Did you get anything out of that lecture this morning?" Anton asked.

Viviana didn't miss the deflection tactic for a second. "No, it was a waste of my time as usual. Did something happen that I didn't hear about on the news? Are you in trouble?"

Anton's eyes widened at her brazen question. "I'd tell you if there were."

"Would you? There are feds photographing me behind our home. At least I assume it's federal. Erik and Ivan are missing lately. If something is about to go down, I would appreciate getting a heads up about it. What's going on?"

"I really don't know," Anton said almost gently. The heated blue of his gaze bore into hers with an openness that told Viviana he was telling the truth the best he could. She knew sometimes Anton held things back from her, not because he wanted to, but because he knew she wouldn't want to hear it. "I swear to God if I did, I would tell you."

Nodding, Viviana reached for her textbook and whispered, "Okay."

"The moment we hear anything, you'll know. I wouldn't keep it from you if it was something terribly important or imminent."

"We?"

"Erik is doing his job, so is Ivan. *We* are all working on figuring it out. Maybe the guys haven't been around because we're trying not to bring more attention than what's already been here, Vine. I know it's tough, but ..."

Viviana didn't tune him out, but she didn't need to hear the same speech again, either. There was a certain level of faith she had to put into her husband. If he thought she had to worry, Viviana had to find trust that he would let her know. Because of his boss status in his crime family, the feds were always trying to take down the king pin before hacking away at the rest. Why only harm the outer shell when you can take out the jugular and go straight for the kill?

"You're going to be here, right? You say you don't know what's going on, and I'll take that for what it's worth as your word because it's you, Anton. But I need to know you're going to be here for this."

"What?" Anton turned back to her, his eyes sharp and his mouth set down into a frown. "For what, baby?"

"Him," Viviana said, pointing to her stomach. The baby always fell asleep whenever she was resting in their bed. She hoped he was as good about sleeping outside of the womb as he was inside. "I can't do all of this by myself."

Anton blinked back at her, emotions crossing his handsome features one after another, never settling down on one thing. He appeared torn, saddened, confused, and hurt all at once. Viviana didn't purposely set out of make him feel that way. Rarely did she bring up the prospects of his profession and their life, but she still knew there were things that had to be said.

"I just *can't*, Anton. We've only got a couple of months left before he's here."

When he didn't give her a response, Viviana sighed and opened her textbook again. Minutes passed by as she read. Silence covered the bedroom but for the rhythmic sounds of the couple's breathing. Fully engrossed in the study of biology, she nearly missed Anton's deep voice that turned uncharacteristically soft.

"I tell him his mother is pretty damned amazing. That she's beautiful and intelligent, but stubborn as hell." Viviana's breath caught as Anton's thumbs rolled around her navel, and he continued speaking. "I tell him there's a whole world of people just waiting to see his face, but no one more eager for his arrival than you and me. I say that I hope he's nothing like me in a lot of ways, but just the same in so many others. I tell him hopes and fears ... I have lots of those, Viviana."

The textbook dropped from her hands, resting to her chest. Viviana listened to her husband hum a sweet tune and trace loopy pathways over her exposed midsection with his fingers. To her, there was nothing better than seeing Anton at an honorably vulnerable place.

When doors closed, she still got him just the way she liked.

"But most of all ..." Anton said with a tender smile, "I tell him that I love him."

Viviana cleared her throat, forcing back the emotions and tears threatening to rise. "It has to be Russian? The name, I mean." Anton nodded silently. "I picked up a few books, but nothing caught my eye. It's just lists. Nothing seems to fit."

"I thought you'd go right for the namesake," he replied, chuckling.

"Anton did cross my mind for a second, but more for the middle." Viviana scrunched up her nose. "Is that what you want?"

"No. He has to have his own to make his way. You understand?"

"Yeah, I guess. Maybe Daniil?" Viviana suggested the name as she reached down to brush away the black wisps of his hair that had fallen over the eyes she wanted to see. "Your mom would really appreciate that."

"Again, making his own way," Anton said, lifting his shoulder dismissively.

"Does the meaning of the name have to be terribly important?"

Another graze of his hand over the unblemished plains of her stomach had Viviana's body turning into a puddle of want and desire. Starting in on her final months of the pregnancy had dimmed her sexual appetite, and she worried her lack of desire would send Anton off running to find it elsewhere. That didn't happen. Anton seemed to find the things to say or do to have her need for him flaring up with a power she simply couldn't ignore. Like now.

"Not if you don't want it to be," he said, laying a kiss below her breast. It wasn't long before he had her shirt pulled up and tossed away, the textbook pushed to the bed sheets. "It just ... has to sound strong—feel important. He has to be able to own it."

"Alexei means defender."

"That's nice. You're getting warmer."

A few random names that had managed to stick out in Viviana's memory were on the tip of her tongue. "Vadim?"

Anton made a face. "No."

"Marat?"

"No, Viviana," Anton mumbled, kissing the swell of her tender breast. Then, he leaned up and said, "It reminds me of something like Igor. I don't want to give him a name that doesn't fit in being said in English. There had to be one name you really liked."

Viviana pursed her lips, considering the many baby name books she'd read since finding out their baby was a boy. There had been one name, but she wasn't sure if it would fit well for a Russian Bratva child. Especially for theirs, considering the Avdonins seemed to really prefer their names to be wholly Russian and well suited to the child.

"Well, how about Demyan?" Viviana was thoroughly enjoying the view of Anton tugging off his shirt. Her husband froze, the action making her nerves grow. "I mean, I know it's the equivalent of Damien in a way, but it still has that Russian ring and style. It's strong and fits in. I kind of liked that one. But if you don't, then that's okay."

"Demyan." Anton tilted his head, his fingers drumming a tantalizing beat to her side. "And what about for the rest?"

"I think the middle names should reflect the footsteps he's following, because you can say he's making his own way all you want, but he's still an Avdonin. Your middle name is Daniil, and I really wanted your given name somewhere in there. So if we add in Daniil, it's almost a repeat of yours, anyway. You don't want that. So, Anton Nicoli for the middle, then."

"Say it for me, all of it. I want to hear it from you first."

"Demyan Anton Nicoli Avdonin," Viviana said, smiling nervously. Names were so important, especially for this boy she carried. After all, it would be his first title, and whether she wanted to admit it or not, so much was already expected for Anton's son. "What do you think?"

The flash of his movement as he leaned down over her, his face coming to stop just a millimeter from hers, was a flurry in her vision. The brilliant grin overtaking his features washed every worry she had down the drain. When his hands weaved into her hair, his thumbs sweeping along her neck, Viviana sighed into his touch. Instantly, she was relaxed again

"You like?" Viviana asked, breathless.

"*Love*," Anton said fiercely. "It's fucking perfect."

Chapter Two

Anton tossed a wrench hatefully to the floor. "I'd rather be shot in the face than deal with this crap."

He was completely exasperated. Every damned ounce of patience that was left in his body disappeared. Anton didn't think he could take another minute of this shit before he totally blew his top.

"Why does this have to be so hard?" Anton asked the empty room.

Well, he thought it was empty.

The snickering from the doorway drew in his narrowed, aggravated gaze to where his lawyer stood with half of a cookie shoved in his mouth. At the sight of Anton's growing anger, Ivan shrugged apologetically and took a step inside the room. Looking around at the mess scattered across the floor, the older man didn't seem to know what to say.

"You've built three of these goddamn things so come fix this for me," Anton barked.

"Nope."

"Ivan!"

"Nope, I did not build them," Ivan said, cocking his eyebrow. "I came home one day and they were already set up. Eva did it without a lick of my help and never fails to remind me."

Turning to glare at the offending wooden and metal pieces scattered over the floor, Anton had absolutely no idea how he managed to get himself in this predicament. Running guns, getting the narcotics past authorities, and keeping his business and guys in line was his thing, not *this*.

Even the fucking directions were in Chinese!

Not really, but they might as well have been.

Defeated, Anton heaved a sigh. "This is pointless."

Ivan swallowed the last bit of his sweet. "No, it isn't.

You're just pissed off because everything else comes easy for you and this hasn't."

That was a little bit true. Anton couldn't help it that he wasn't the kind of guy who had tools in the shed and the basic understanding of how to work a fucking wrench. That wasn't the values and life lessons he'd learned growing up. If Viviana walked in and saw him now, she'd probably laugh herself into labor.

"I feel like an idiot," Anton said, sitting down to the floor.

Sounding just as bleak, Ivan muttered, "I did, too."

"Eva did it for you, remember?"

A bitter laugh chimed in the room. The silence that followed the laughter felt awkward, and Anton wondered if maybe he crossed a line with his friend, but Ivan only shook his head and chuckled. Bending down, Ivan picked up a bolt and twirled it between his fingers.

"Yeah, she did, but not until after I tried to set one up myself. The damned thing was a deathtrap waiting to happen. My pride wouldn't let me call my father and say, "hey, can you come down here and teach me how to set up a baby's crib?" I mean, it's a fucking crib. Just wood and bolts." Ivan waved at the pieces of what should have been set up an hour ago if Anton knew anything about what he was doing. "It can't be that hard, right? Yeah, whatever. I spent a decade getting the education I have and a couple hundred grand making sure I got the best one, but not a lick of it got me ready for this shit, or parenthood."

"I wish I could call Daniil. He'd tell me to suck it the fuck up and get it done."

That was really all Anton needed; his father to say he was acting like a spoiled man, and to handle his stuff. Unfortunately, Daniil wouldn't be spending any time outside of the hospital unless it was in his casket. That only served to have Anton's sadness rising. Simply thinking about not having his father around for things like setting up his son's crib or a late night phone call when he didn't know what to do after Demyan was born was a dreary prospect. One that broke his heart to pieces.

Sure, he would still have his mother, but there was a whole different facet to the relationship Anton shared with Daniil. Be it the way his father raised Anton, the Bratva lifestyle, or the secrets each man carried for the other, their father and son relationship went a little deeper than others.

"Is this really about the crib?" Ivan asked. "Or is it something else, too?"

Anton blinked away the miserable expression he must have been sporting and slid on one of his usual masks. "What the fuck are you, my therapist?"

Ivan didn't bite onto the jibe. "No, I'm your friend, so quit with the attitude."

Fuck, Anton hated feeling shit. When it came to emotions, he would much rather just bottle it up and store it away for a rainy day when some asshole in the Bratva pushed the boss past his limits.

"Have you talked to Vine about whatever is going on with you?"

Glancing away with a grimace, Anton said, "A little."

"And?"

"And what? She's got enough going on, Ivan. I don't want to stress her out with nonsense right now. Between being pregnant, her classes at the university, trying to get ready for her final exams before the baby is born, and now last week with the feds suddenly photographing her? My wife has enough to deal with without me adding to it."

"Well, that's crap if I ever heard it."

"Fuck you."

"No, it is," Ivan said just as sharp. "Think about it, that girl knows you better than anyone, and you're telling me she's sitting back oblivious to the fact that you're clearly bothered by something. Absolute *crap*."

Not wanting to dwell on the elephant in the room, Anton began tinkering away with what little bit of the crib he already had set up. Purposely ignoring Ivan, he somehow managed to get the four walls of the crib to stay up long enough for him to loosely place the bolts where they needed to go along the bottom. Without saying a word, Ivan was suddenly kneeling down beside Anton, steadying the structure as the younger man began placing washers along threaded steel and tightening the nuts to the backs of the bolts.

"I'm really going to miss my father," Anton whispered, keeping his eyes on his work.

"Yeah, I know."

"It sucks even more right now because it'd be great to have my dad as just my dad for once, without all the other bullshit we usually had to deal with around it, you know?"

"Yep." Moving out of Anton's way so the younger man could start tightening the other side, Ivan said, "But I think you know as well as I do that you had a pretty great father in Daniil. It's not like you're going into this completely blind."

"Still scary as hell."

"Yep," Ivan repeated.

Twenty minutes later, the white crib rested in the spot Viviana had asked for Anton to place it. On either ends of the bed where they curved with high, rounded edges, a crown had been carved into the wood. From the ceiling to the floor hung sheer fabric to match the colors of the furniture, surrounding the crib in the billowy material. With the crib sitting opposite to the window, sunlight would grace the baby every morning he woke up.

Fit for a king but made for a little prince.

Despite Anton's earlier frustration over his lack of skills in the building department, the crib was as sturdy as it was going to get, and he was a little more than pleased at his work.

"Didn't you already have to put one of these together for your bedroom?" Ivan asked as Anton lowered the small mattress to the bottom of the crib.

"When were you in my bedroom?" The warning couldn't be hidden.

Ivan guffawed. "You are the worst, do you know that? I have never met a man as jealous as you. I don't know how Vine puts up with it."

"Shut up. That's my bedroom. I share it with my *wife*. No other man needs to be inside of it."

"I wasn't in your bedroom, asshole," Ivan said, laughing. "Vine told Eva about the bassinet she came home to. So, I assumed when you asked me to come help you today that you already knew what the fuck you were doing."

Anton refused to acknowledge the dig. The gift in question wasn't so much a bassinet as it was a miniature, circular crib. Carefully designed to match ornate carvings on Anton and Viviana's four poster bed, he meant for it to be something they could pass down to their children.

"I ordered that in from Russia. Cost me a pretty penny. It was all made by hand and it came put together. All I needed to do was take the damned thing out of the box."

"I heard she liked it."

"That she did." Anton grinned at the memory of Viviana's joy when she came home to find the little cubby in their bedroom furnished. It had been only one of his gifts to her, but it was the one she enjoyed the very most. So far. "Worth the cost, anyway."

"So ..." Ivan trailed off, grinning conspiratorially. "Did you two pick a name, yet?"

"Yep."

"And?"

Having already decided to keep the name to themselves until after Demyan was born, Anton warned Viviana their friends and family wouldn't leave them alone about it. His mother, in particular, had all but demanded she be told as soon as they picked it out.

"And?" Ivan demanded again.

Anton shrugged, striking out with a playful punch to his friend's arm. "And it's perfect."

● ● ●

Viviana rested into Anton's side as they strolled through Little Odessa at a leisurely pace. While she had always called the neighborhood Brighton Beach, after a few trips through the place, she had been quick to adopt the nickname that everyone else called it as well.

Brighton Beach Avenue was bustling with activity. Voices carried through the streets, laughter ringing out high or deep. The shopkeepers had their doors opened wide, allowing in the cool air from the breeze sweeping the area. Seagull squawks became louder the closer they came to the boardwalk. In the distance, the life of Coney Island was beginning to take shape in the background.

At first, Viviana was concerned she wouldn't fit into Brighton Beach as well as Anton did. Maybe it was due to the fact that growing up, she hadn't visited the area once. It wasn't as if that had been by choice, but it didn't make a difference to the end result. Not a soul made her feel out of place when she walked the streets with her husband, or even without him.

"Anton, my boy, come!" someone shouted. A single look to the side showed one of the many restaurant owners leaning in the doorway of his place, his hand waving at the couple. "Hurry, now."

With a questioning look down at Viviana, Anton conveyed his silent request. She nodded, and they crossed the road quickly, her hand still tucked into the warmth of his elbow. Drawing her closer into his side, Anton kissed Viviana's temple before tightening the belt on her tweed coat.

"Look at you." The man appraised Viviana, his voice heavily accented with his Georgian dialect. Giving only enough to pause to glance at Anton when his large hand came close to the roundness of her midsection, he asked, "May I?"

Anton shrugged. "Ask her, Gio."

It wasn't unusual for people in Brighton to want to be close to Viviana. It was as if communication between the residents fell somewhere in line with physical contact. It also wasn't strange for them to know her by name or face, even if she hadn't met them before. Little Odessa was a tight-knit community where everyone knew everyone else, and because of Anton's family, he was one of the most recognizable. He was also one of the most respected. However, whether that was attributed to fear, Viviana wasn't sure.

"May I, sweetheart?" Gio asked Viviana.

"Sure," she said, smiling.

When the shopkeeper's hand rested down to the top of her midsection, the baby boy inside seemed to wake up at the contact. The movement from the baby must have pleased Gio. His face lit up and his old, gray eyes wrinkled at the corners, causing Viviana to beam with happiness as well.

"Healthy, then?" Gio asked.

"From what we can tell," Anton said. "He's certainly more than big and strong enough."

"I had heard he was a boy. I'll have to spread word that it is indeed a fact. I'm sure Nicoli would have been so pleased."

Unsure if that had been said for her or Anton, Viviana chose to stay quiet. Anton, on the other hand, did not. "I hope so."

"Baruch dayan emet," Gio said, a frown tugging his mouth down.

She didn't understand the words, but Anton seemed to. A brief flicker of sadness crossed his handsome features. Viviana swallowed back her own rising sorrow at the sight. Sometimes that happened as well on their travels through Little Odessa. Someone was always remembering who had once walked before them, and while their words weren't meant to hurt, but rather console, at times they still did. At least for Anton, anyway.

"It's been a long time." Anton responded with a shaky exhale that took Viviana by surprise. "You don't have to recite that to me, now. You know I don't follow the religion, either."

"I know." Gio nodded, rubbing his hand once more along the top of Viviana's stomach. "But Nicoli did, my boy."

"Yes, well—"

"Oh! One minute," Gio interrupted Anton, pulling his

hand away and grinning conspiratorially at Viviana. "I have something for you, sweetheart. I think your palate will thank me for this later."

Only disappearing long enough for Anton to pull her back into his side and replace the empty spot on her swelled stomach with his own hand, Gio was back in the doorway once more. In his hand, he held something wrapped in white, wax paper. Passing it to her with a smile, Gio winked.

"Go on, open it."

Warm in her palm, Viviana opened the wax paper with her own smile. Inside the wrapping was one of her most favorite treats.

"Xachapuri."

The Georgian flat bread filled with cheese certainly wasn't the healthiest choice for an after supper snack, but she didn't care.

"Well done." Anton praised her with a kiss to her temple. "You said that perfectly, baby."

Viviana nudged him with her shoulder. "I do okay."

"That you do."

"You like?" Gio asked, seemingly delighted he'd found her weakness.

"Very much," Viviana replied. "Thank you, Gio."

"Okay, on with you. I have to get back to work. Take your wife home, Anton, and rest her feet."

Anton shook his head at Gio's wagging finger. "On it now, Boss."

With one more wink, Gio's hand reached out to touch the spot where Anton's was resting. Quiet words were whispered under the old shopkeeper's breath too low for Viviana to discern, even if they had been said in English. Removing his touch only long enough to reach up and pat Anton gently on the cheek with two fingers, Gio disappeared back into his shop.

Viviana allowed Anton to guide her further down the street before she said anything about Gio's odd gestures.

"What was that?" she asked softly.

"Hmm, what, baby?" The amusement in his gaze had her rolling her eyes.

"That, at the end. When he touched you."

Anton shrugged passively. "His way of greeting a Pakhan, I suppose. It doesn't matter how they do it, so long as it's respectful. If he was Bratva, it'd be a different story. I would have expected it from the beginning."

Sighing, Viviana poked at his side. "That's not what I meant."

"The baby?" Anton mused with a wry smile. She nodded. "Blessing him, and us. He bid him good aspirations for the duration of the pregnancy and beyond, and wished him great things in his life."

"And the one for us?"

Anton smiled softly, his fingers curving her waist tightening gently. While he spoke at a level too low for any of the passersby to hear and he didn't turn to look at her again, Viviana heard his words and saw his emotions nonetheless. "He was asking for the ones we've left behind to keep watch."

Viviana's stare turned down to the lights blinking in the distance. "Do you think they do?"

Neither of them were religious. They still didn't go to church, or the temple. They didn't live a devout life, but that didn't mean they had no faith.

Before Viviana realized it, a tear escaped the corner of her eye. She wiped it away before Anton would notice. The question wasn't meant to affect her or her silenced lover the way it had, but it still hung between them heavily.

So much blood had already spilled for them to be where they were together, and Viviana sometimes wished that didn't have to be so. More than anything, she so wanted to share the birth of their son with her dead parents, her brother, and Nicoli.

"Do you think they watch after us?" she asked again.

"I hope so."

• • •

Back at home, Viviana scowled at her blood glucose meter. Scribbling down the number that was too high, she knew her next appointment with the doctor would be filled with another lecture.

Anton leaned over her shoulder to check the number with a raised brow. "Too high."

"Thank you, Captain Obvious."

The bite in her tone didn't escape his notice. Anton backed away, raising his one free hand in surrender. "Hey, I'm not the one who will be needing to take insulin for the remainder of this pregnancy if you can't get it under control, baby."

Yes, because Viviana needed another reminder.

Willing her raging hormones to simmer for a moment so she could think before biting his head off, Viviana took a deep breath and counted back from ten. She had never been one to let her emotions rule, but sometimes it just took the littlest things with this pregnancy to set her off.

Viviana didn't want a repeat of one of those moments, so she forced herself to be calm and talk rationally. "I know my sugars are too high. I follow the diet, exercise, and whatever else. It's being stubborn."

Anton bit the inside of his cheek, glancing up at the ceiling with an amused expression. "I'm sure the xachapuri didn't help. It is bread and cheese, Vine."

Again, thank you, Captain Obvious, Viviana thought. "But I like it."

"Mmhmm. I like strawberries but I'm allergic to the seeds. You don't see me eating them."

"That's different."

"Not really," he argued, cocking that brow of his again. "You do know if he continues to grow at this rate, you're going to need a C-section, right?"

Oh God, that stopped her heart right up. "But—"

"He's already hitting the weight of a baby at nearly eight

months gestation and you just reached seven months last week," Anton interrupted quietly. "I'm not trying to give you a hard time, but you're the one who wants to be out of the hospital as quick as possible with an easy recovery. Surgery won't do that for you. C-section is surgery, Viviana."

She hated it when he did shit like that. "No more xachapuri, huh?"

The tender smile he sported had her air catching. "Nope, but I'll get you some the moment you ask for it after he's born."

Viviana suddenly felt embarrassed and a little more self-conscious than she was accustomed to, so she wrapped her arms around her middle. "So I must be getting huge, too, then."

Anton's blue eyes widened. "Uh …"

"Well, you said it!"

Anton shot a fleeting glance at the entryway to the kitchen like he wished it would swallow him whole.

"That's not what I said exactly," he said weakly. "And you look fine."

"Do I?"

"Of course!"

"But … but …"

Viviana didn't even get to finish her sentence before the coffee cup he held was placed to the island and she was wrapped in his embrace. Burying her face into his chest, she inhaled the spicy scent of his cologne, letting it calm the overwhelming feelings that washed through her like a tidal wave.

"You look fine." Anton punctuated each word with a kiss to the top of her head. "Fucking fantastic and it kind of drives me crazy, okay? You being pregnant is my own personal ecstasy. I want to kill every fucker who looks at you right now. I'm always hard and ready. If you were up to it, I'd have you morning, noon, and night, baby. You look fine."

"Fine?"

"Fine." Anton drawled the word out with a teasing leer.

Viviana tapped her fingers along the hemline of his jeans. At the suggestive touch, Anton pushed against her lower back, drawing her body in closer to his. The length of his erection beneath dark wash denim proved his point loud and clear.

"It's almost nighttime now."

"It is, isn't it?" Anton asked, grinning a wicked sight.

"Yep."

She didn't have to say it again.

Chapter Three

"Anton, we meet again."

Those words were as sweet as sugar and as poisonous as a snake.

A heavy weight settled inside Anton's churning gut as he turned in the direction of Tatiana Belov's voice. One random meeting he could overlook, but two chance encounters in less than two weeks? No, that didn't feel coincidental at all. Tatiana wasn't exactly a straightforward woman, either.

She liked her games.

Now, Anton was beginning to wonder if she was playing one with him.

"Tatiana," Anton greeted, turning his attention back to the coffee he was waiting for. "Did your father send you?"

Tatiana raised a blonde brow as she came to stand beside him. "No, I haven't spoken to Daddy in days. Did your meeting not go well?"

"It didn't go at all, though I'm sure you already knew that."

"I didn't," she said with an apologetic smile.

It didn't ring true. Nothing with Tatiana ever did.

"Are you going to tell me it's funny to meet up with me again?" Anton asked, not bothering to hide the sarcasm in his tone.

Tatiana waved at the workers behind the counter preparing coffees and specialty drinks. "I was told this was the best coffee shop in Brooklyn, Anton. That's all."

"The same coffee shop I buy every morning coffee from," he intoned dully.

"One in the same." The quip was light and heavy at the same time. Loaded with more than what she was saying. It was only punctuated more by the vicious curve of Tatiana's lips. "Surely I can grab a coffee without you being unnerved by my presence. Do I still have such an effect on you, old friend?"

Anton felt the bile rise in his throat at her suggestive implication. "The effect you had was the same effect any seventeen-year-old boy's cock would have for a girl willing to spread her thighs for him, Tati. Don't play coy with me. I hate a coy woman."

"Would you rather I be a little more clear?" she asked demurely.

"No, I'd rather you left me alone."

Tatiana sighed, eyeing Anton from the side, appearing frustrated. "You act like I'm chasing you. Is that what you want?"

That was a chain Anton refused to bite onto. What was it going to take for this girl to get the point and stay the fuck away from him?

"Does the thought of me killing you not scare you a bit, Tatiana? I was positive I made it clear that was exactly what would happen when you accosted my wife at my last birthday party."

"I'm not accosting your wife, Anton."

"But you are following me," he said low, daring her to deny it. "And I don't like it. Whatever you're playing at, quit it before it becomes annoying."

"Oh, but I'm just getting started," Tatiana murmured in response. "Besides, I'm following your rules, staying away from Brighton Beach, keeping my distance from your pretty little wife. What reason would you have to hurt me?"

Without another word, Tatiana simpered a smile before turning to leave. Anton watched her go, confusion and simmering anger growing. Not only was the woman's behavior strange, but erratic, too.

She was right, though. Anton couldn't do anything about her appearances or unwanted presence unless she did something threatening. So far, she hadn't. It was only two meetings, after all.

Viviana would have a fit if Anton told her about Tatiana.

Worrying his pregnant wife wasn't the best idea. She had enough stress as it was.

"Sir?"

Anton blinked away his thoughts as his coffee was handed over the counter. "Thank you."

The young man nodded towards the front where Tatiana had disappeared. "Did she not want anything, sir?"

Well, that was the question of the hour, wasn't it?

Tatiana hadn't bought that coffee she supposedly came in for, either.

• • •

An envelope was passed over the tabletop with a stealth meant to hide the package from being seen by any other eyes in the diner. Anton made quick work of sliding the brigadier's tribute into the inside pocket of his jacket as he resumed his meal like nothing had happened.

"How's the wife, Boss?" Boris asked as he slid into the booth.

"Pregnant," Anton answered.

There were a dozen other things Anton could have said about Viviana that were just as true and a great deal more heartfelt. Unfortunately Anton knew he needed to keep a distance built up between his wife and his guys. He didn't want them feeling as though they had some kind of connection to her that they didn't. Safety wise, it was better for Viviana, too.

"And the baby?"

Anton didn't bother to hide his forming smile as he said, "Getting there."

"I heard Sergei blew it," Boris noted, not taking his attention away from the menu in his hands. "Goddamn moron."

"Like a pro." He was still a little sore over the other Pakhan's refusal of their arranged sit-down. It certainly didn't help that everyone was waiting on Anton to make some kind of move about it. With Tatiana adding into the equation, he wasn't ready to strike without knowing more. "Unfortunately this isn't the best time for me to let my Bratva honor and pride control the situation."

"True enough. I'm sure Vine wouldn't appreciate being taken out of state while the issue was handled."

No, she certainly wouldn't, Anton thought. With her being pregnant, it would probably only serve to worry her more. "*Issues*, I think."

Boris's brow rose. "Come again?"

"Issues meaning there are more than one."

Noticing the couple in the next booth were finally readying to leave, Anton waited until they paid for their meal and had left the table before deciding it was safe to continue on the topic.

"All dealing with Sergei?" Boris twirled a butter knife between his fingers.

It was funny how the simplest of things looked the most dangerous when the brigadier had a hold of it. Boris was one of Anton's more brutal guys when it came to handling some of the violent aspects of their business.

"Maybe," Anton agreed quietly. "A little over a week ago I noticed a car behind my house. The driver was taking pictures."

"And?"

"And I assumed it was FBI."

"But?"

Anton shrugged as he took another bite of his meal, purposely wanting to keep his appearance as unbothered by the situation he was talking about. Frankly, he was horribly worried about it. The more time Anton had let pass by for him to consider the unknown photographer, the more unsettled it made him.

"Why would the feds be taking pictures of Viviana in our backyard while she was doing nothing more than sitting out in the sun?" Anton asked rhetorically. "I thought maybe they were attempting to catch me doing something, but I'd just arrived home. They would have been following me from the other side, not waiting out back."

Boris leaned forward. "Whoever it was had been taking pictures before you even returned home, then."

"Yeah, that's my thought. If it were the feds, we'd know. Someone is always blabbing about something concerning us. One of our insiders would have heard. There's been nothing from the federal side. That tells me it's not FBI."

Anton hated to even consider what that might mean for his wife. Who would be following her and why? Not to mention wanting pictures of her in situations that would show her without obvious protection. The bulls who kept a close watch while she was away from their home were instructed to close more of the gap Anton asked them to keep. He still hadn't brought up the possible threat to Viviana.

Unfortunately, Tatiana Belov raised a whole bunch of other questions. Anton despised the fact that she might be the answer to all the other ones, as well. Worse still was the fact there wasn't any proof. That was what Anton needed, now.

"And you believe this is Sergei?" Boris pursed his lips in contemplation. "That'd be an awfully stupid move if you found out. From his end, I mean."

"I know," Anton replied. "I don't want to risk thinking it is just the feds doing their usual nonsense if it isn't. This isn't exactly their deal, anyway. They'd be more adept to taking her picture when she was with me and we were in contact with someone connected to the Bratva. Not at home being happy and innocent. Not like that."

"Maybe you should get her out of state. Have you talked to Ivan or Erik about this, Boss?"

"I want to know everything before I do anything."

Making hurried decisions that could lead to messy situations later wasn't exactly Anton's forte. Finishing up the last bit of his parmesan risotto, Anton flicked his hand up as the waitress passed by his table to signal he was ready for the bill. Anton wanted to catch up with Boris about his trip to Vegas and what had come of it business-wise, but he promised to pick up Viviana from her study group.

"You have a good contact with a tracer. Is he worth his price, or what?"

"She," Boris corrected, his gaze meeting Anton's. "And yes, I'd say so. She's done great work for me. Who do you want checked up on?"

"Tatiana."

Instantly, Boris was sitting ramrod straight in his seat. "Oh, hell. That's a problem you don't need. Were you messing around with the Jersey girl again?"

Anton nearly choked on his tongue. "What the fuck?"

"I'm just saying, Boss. We all know how pregnant women can be sometimes. Well, it wouldn't be out of the ordinary—"

"For me it would," the boss interrupted coolly. Rage washed through his insides fast and hard, raising his pulse to a racing speed. "I don't fuck around on my wife."

The older man seemed struck speechless. Why was it that everyone seemed to find it hard to believe that Anton was faithful to his wife?

"Ever?"

"*Never*," Anton hissed.

"Well, why in the hell do you think Tati—"

"Because she's up to something," Anton interjected sharply. "Twice in less than two weeks she's cornered me at either a place I frequent, or a place she would have needed direct information about. She's acting like an annoying puppy sniffing at my heels, and my wife is being photographed in positions that make me rather uncomfortable. Both are odd."

"And you think Tati's involved."

"I don't *think* anything. What I know is even less, and I don't like that."

The brigadier looked uncomfortable. Anton could understand that. The Jersey Bratva family had always been good to their side of the brotherhood, minus the birthday incident. If Tatiana or Sergei were involved in something like trailing Viviana—a well-respected Pakhan's wife—no matter the reason, there would be hell to pay.

"Are you looking at this from her husband's perspective, or the boss?" Boris asked, suddenly interested in the white crescents of his fingernails.

Anton expected that question, especially since the person of interest just happened to be one of his old lovers. To others, it could look as if the Russian boss was simply trying to avoid issues with his wife by ridding the source of the problem under the guise of Tatiana being dangerous to Viviana.

Of course, Anton wasn't stupid, either.

"Tati was seen in my club a half a year ago causing her usual problems. More than one person heard the things she said to Viviana and any one of them would have construed it the very same way I have," Anton explained calmly. Drumming his fingernails to the tabletop, considering his next words carefully, he shrugged and added, "I've looked at every other option. Who would want to hurt her, why, and what would be gained from doing so. The Italians are out of the picture."

"Can you be sure?"

"Yes, I'm sure." Anton scoffed, almost offended that his opinion was being questioned. "She's cut all ties with the Cosa Nostra. I thought about possible enemies from the Bratva side, but the girl doesn't have any connections other than what she's made through me. It all leads me to the same conclusion."

"That whoever is doing it means to hurt you," Boris finished with a nod.

Anton hadn't once mentioned the baby boy Viviana was carrying, or her importance to him. In fact, he'd stuck to the facts he knew, the pertinent issues at hand that they needed to deal with for obvious reasons. He knew it wouldn't be missed by his brigadier.

"So," Anton said with a smirk, "I suppose you can say you're dealing with the boss."

"You really think it's the fire bug?"

Exhaling harshly, Anton stood from the table. He tossed a hundred dollar bill down. It would more than take care of his meal, whatever Boris would choose from the menu, and still have quite a generous tip left over for the waitress.

"Like I said, I want all the facts before I make any rash decisions. You can get the info the tracer needs, yeah?"

"Sure, but I don't know if it will get you your answers."

"No, but it'll get me one step closer to whoever, or whatever, it is if it isn't the Jersey scum," Anton said with the cold indifference of a Bratva boss. "I need to know if it's her, Sergei, or someone else following my wife. And I needed to know it yesterday. So get on it."

• • •

"Tell me what happened."

Viviana turned away from Anton's voice, not wanting him to see the tears gathering and fighting to fall. He'd found her sitting on the steps of the Long Island University's library, waiting for him. The saddened, ruffled appearance she sported was enough for her husband to figure out something had gone wrong at her study group. And did it ever.

A new girl had been invited into the group, Vanessa. She was smart and opinionated, but Viviana didn't mind that. It was someone else who was willing to have discussions worth having on the topics they were currently studying. Viviana liked to be challenged. She didn't think anything of the girl's uncomfortable stares or veiled comments, until they weren't so veiled anymore and the stares turned to accusatory, hateful glares.

"Vine." Anton leaned between their seats, his hand caressing the arm of her sweater. "I need to know if something happened so I can take care of it."

"You can't fix everything, Anton!"

His hand snapped away from her side as if he'd been burned. Even Viviana was surprised at her outburst. Anton could fix just about anything if he really wanted to. In one way or another, the issue would disappear. She didn't even want to consider what that might mean if she told him of her recently acquired enemy.

"Okay, so obviously something did happen," Anton said coldly. "Your bulls won't have anything to say because they were on the other side of the library out of earshot. I can send them around Brooklyn just as fast to find and question every single person who I know you were with until I do find out what happened. They will find out, Vine, and I don't care how they extract the information so long as I get it."

A lump formed in her throat, stopping the bubbling sob catching painfully in her chest. "But—"

"What?" her husband interrupted, canting his head to the side. "Did you think I wouldn't know who was in your study group? I absolutely fucking do. You're my *wife*—I wouldn't risk putting you in a situation with people I can't trust. Now, what happened?"

An aching rhythm kick started Viviana's heart. Something akin to embarrassment and anger swelled inside her stomach. This was exactly why she didn't want to tell him what had happened in her study group; his overprotectiveness would immediately send him into worry mode, not to mention prickle at his fury.

"No, Anton." Turning sharply, Viviana leveled him with a glare. "Shit happens, okay? If it was something for you to be worried about, I would tell you. That's not what this is."

"Viviana, do not make me—"

Viviana was out of their Mercedes-Benz M-Class before Anton could finish his sentence. It was a fight she didn't want to have with him. When she was acting like the normal woman she was, not the Russian mob boss's wife she sometimes needed to be, he didn't get to pull his Bratva cards and throw threats.

Threats she knew he would follow through with, unfortunately.

Viviana knew Anton had a lot going on behind the scenes

that he wasn't informing her about. She understood he was grieving for his sick father, that he was frightened about the changes in his life, like being a new husband and a soon-to-be new father. In the midst of all that, he was keeping it to himself, dealing with it how he saw fit. Viviana didn't think it was the best way for him to go about it, but she knew he would come to her when he was ready.

Well, this wasn't any different. It was something Viviana needed to deal with alone.

Leaving Anton stunned, she let the slam of their SUV's door say what she wouldn't. The sound of his fists hitting the steering wheel and a Russian curse answered her back. Viviana didn't turn around. She kept walking until she disappeared behind the front door.

A hot bath called to Viviana. In a dazed state, and with the heaviest heart, she moved silently through their home until she found herself in the master bath. Closing the door, she found it was exactly what she needed. To shut out the world and its judgment so she could pretend they didn't live a life no one else could possibly understand.

Sinking most of her body below hot water, Viviana finally let her tears fall. They rushed heavy and hot down her cheeks, undisturbed by her hands that itched to wipe the wetness away and hide proof of her fears and weaknesses.

When Vanessa had brought up the topic of organized crime in New York, something that certainly wasn't on their study group's agenda, Viviana knew she was in trouble. Most of the people who Viviana studied with knew who she was, or at least, they knew of her family. Most even knew her husband, despite the fact that she didn't wear her wedding and engagement rings during her classes or study group. The obvious extravagance of the pieces would cause distraction.

When the girl pointed out her earlier studies had been law, Viviana had closed her books and laptop, ready to leave the library and find her bulls. What she didn't want or need was to fight with someone whose opinions could only be based on the things they heard or read.

Needless to say, it hadn't gone well. The four other students had been much too shocked to step in and stop Vanessa's verbal attack. Sure, Viviana was able to deflect enough, stood her ground and kept her mouth shut when she needed to. Viviana refused to let the girl see even an ounce of the anger, awkwardness, or pain she caused by her spiteful words.

But when Vanessa's words had turned from Viviana's dead family to her current life, she had taken all she could. Vanessa had spewed on about Viviana's husband and unborn child, about how privileged they lived in their beautiful home, with an abundance of wealth that was smeared with the dishonor of greed and death.

No one had the right to judge Viviana. Certainly not Vanessa or anyone else.

For once, Viviana didn't want to be who she needed to be. She only wanted to act like what she was feeling. And she was feeling absolutely horrible—heartbroken and ashamed.

Maybe she should have expected it. Anton and Viviana weren't low profile in New York. People knew who she was, and Viviana should have had her guard up. It just hadn't been an issue before today.

An hour passed Viviana by in silence, other than the quiet noise of her hiccupping sobs. Long after the water had turned cool and most of the steam in the bathroom disappeared, she finally felt calm enough to get out of the tub.

The softest knock on the bathroom door stopped her. "Yeah?"

"Can I come in?" At least Anton sounded calmer.

Sighing, Viviana knew it was useless to refuse him. Whether she liked it or not, she needed to talk to him and have him closer. "Sure."

Less than a second later, her husband's presence in the bathroom soothed away a little of the sadness and remaining anxiety Viviana felt. Without a word, Anton crossed the bathroom and sticking a hand in the water, he unplugged the tub's drain before resting his arms to smooth porcelain.

Reaching out, she traced the tribal tattoos on his arm that led down to his elbow. Anton's eyes fluttered closed, his lashes fanning over his cheeks at her silent apology.

Viviana pulled herself up, deciding to give him a verbal one as well. "I'm sorry."

"Don't be," he replied. "But I wish you would have told me what happened. You left your purse in the car, your phone was in it. Your friend—George—he called to apologize for inviting Vanessa to the study group and to say she wouldn't be returning. When I asked, he explained some. It was enough for me to figure out the rest."

"I handled it."

"I know you did," Anton said, finally turning to look at her. Instead of the anger she expected to see, his blue gaze only held sadness and a sympathetic understanding. "You're the twenty-five-year-old wife of a mob boss, Vine. You're allowed to stick up for yourself when some *suka* hurts you, no matter how she's doing it. Did you think I was going to be pissed off because you told her to shove her opinion up her ass, or what?"

Reaching out with one hand, Viviana uncurled Anton's fingers that had tightened to the edge of the tub in a death grip. She rolled her thumb along his knuckles. Anton sighed and rested his head to her arm. Slowly, he intertwined their fingers and they stayed silent for a moment longer before Viviana felt okay with speaking again.

"I was okay with her cutting out at Roman with all her alleged comments. I let that shit roll right off me," she said angrily. "I wasn't fucking pleased about it, considering she wasn't the one who listened to her father be murdered. She wasn't the daughter who sat beside her mother the next day, watching news broadcasts, knowing exactly who pulled the trigger and knowing there wasn't a thing she could do about it. I handled all of that, Anton."

"But?" he pressed gently.

"It got worse." Viviana shook her head, rubbing her free hand over her stomach absently to soothe the sudden flurry of activity from the baby inside. "She asked where my rings were. How did my husband feel about me not wearing them? Did I know where you were tonight?

"There's no pretending we're innocent, okay? Like this house we live in is paid by money Nicoli got free and clear, or that my son is somehow going to escape the expectations of a mafia child."

"We talked about this, baby," he said calmly.

Viviana nodded jerkily, not wanting to go into all that again with him. The first time was more than enough emotionally. "I know what you do, Anton. I watch the goddamn news. I've been reading about your family ever since I was old enough to have private access to the internet. I am not a stupid woman, and locking myself into a marriage with a man I didn't know a thing about wasn't okay with me. So yeah, I know. Alleged this and supposed that, I really don't care. What I do care about is when shit starts to turn personal.

"She didn't just attack me on a level where I could shove her opinions off. She came at me as a woman, too. She cut out at the *life* I live—my husband and baby. She might as well have called me a paid whore. *How fucking proud you are*, she said. *Why was I even there*, she asked. I don't need to go to university; did I even have to get accepted in or did my husband just pay my way?"

"Vine—"

"It was horrible," she cried low.

The water had all drained from the tub and Viviana shivered from the cold air surrounding her. Anton grabbed one of the large towels from the rack and wrapped her shaking frame with it. He lifted her up out of the bath like she hadn't put on a good thirty extra pounds of weight. Cradled in his quiet, strong embrace, she barely noticed the tears streaming down her cheeks again.

In their bedroom, Anton placed her to the bottom of the bed. Then, he unwrapped the towel, drying the ends of her hair and wiping away the wetness on her face. Tugging over the Afghan throw that rested at the edge of their bed, he draped it around her shoulders before his warm hands framed her face.

"Thank you for defending me, Vine. But you know you don't need to, nor do I deserve it half of the time. I probably earned whatever she had to say and more."

"How did you—"

Anton shrugged as he bent down to one knee. "George. Like I said, he explained some."

"You can't do anything." Viviana pleaded with her watery gaze for him to understand. "Just leave it."

"I think," Anton said with a wry smile, "that my wife handled it fine from her end. When business turned personal, she stopped gritting her teeth and used her mouth like she should."

"So you won't—"

"Oh, I didn't say that," he interjected grimly.

"Anton, *please*."

Suddenly, Viviana found herself pushed back to the bed, the Afghan throw opened to expose her pebbling flesh. Anton crawled between her legs with a predator's grace and an intense stare that seemed to be soaking up every inch of her body that he could see. Viviana exhaled shakily. His hands under her arms lifted her further onto the bed, his mouth coming down to kiss, suck, and nip at her sensitive skin.

"Jesus." She gasped when his teeth found her taut nipple, biting down sharper than she expected him to. "Anton, wait, we need to talk—"

"No talking."

His answer was so simple and sure. The words melted away whatever else it was she wanted to say before Viviana relaxed into the bed, her body calming under his skillful hands.

"You're wrinkly." Anton shook his head and kissed the tips of her fingers where water had puckered her skin, warming them instantly. "And cold." His lips trailed a hot path down the side of her rounded midsection, his grip loosening from her wrists only to find her thighs and spread them opened further. The closer he came to her throbbing sex, the more her nerves grew. "Shh, stop shaking, baby. Let me in."

Viviana hadn't realized she'd been unknowingly trying to close her legs on him. Propping herself up on her elbows, she bit the corner of her lip. Something about being pregnant had made her slightly uncomfortable with oral sex. She purposely diverted Anton's attention every damned time he made his way down there.

Now, though, she was aching to see and feel him like that. To see his mouth love her into oblivion. To know he was tasting her pussy when she was so full of the life he had given her. To feel him owning her body beautifully.

"Let me in." When his hands pushed at her thighs to widen them again, Viviana felt her knees fall open under his want. Soothing and sweet, Anton's voice echoed in the darkened bedroom when he said, "There you go, baby."

When the tip of his thumb slid between the fleshy folds of her swollen, wet sex, Viviana yelped in surprise. She hadn't been expecting that, and the swell of her midsection made it a bit difficult to see everything he was doing. Chuckling darkly at her response, Anton kissed the inside of her thigh before laying a gentle bite down to the same spot.

"You know what makes me proud?" he asked, that thumb of his pressing with just enough pressure to stretch the entrance of her pussy. The teasing contact had her rocking into his hand, wanting so much more.

"What's that?"

"I have an amazing wife. Strong, brave, and smart. You could have just as easily turned around and left, found your bulls and let them get you away, but instead you stood your ground. It doesn't matter if what she said hurt, you couldn't let it be said without proper justification. Not for the Bratva, or Cosa Nostra, or even you, just for us. For who we are.

That's honor, baby, in a way a lot of people can't begin to understand."

When his thumb slid into her soaked, clenching pussy, Viviana moaned.

"And you're beautiful," Anton added, drawing her gaze in to watch him focus his attention between her thighs. "So goddamn beautiful. Lighting up my fucking life every day you breathe, Viviana. Always."

It wasn't a moment later before his mouth was covering her sex, too, that skillfully quick tongue of his striking out to spear her aching clit with a force to make her shake. The cry that bubbled its way up from her middle resounded above her shuddering pants and his approving growl. From the tips of her toes to the top of her head, she felt electrified.

With her fingers finding purchase tangled in her husband's hair, Viviana rested back on her one elbow and simply *felt* him. Felt the way his tongue lavished a slow, tantalizing beat to her sex and how his thumb caressed her tightening passage.

Her blood rushed through expanding veins, pounding in her ear drums as her legs widened further and air sucked through her clenched teeth. The sounds of his tongue lapping at her pussy, sweeping away her arousal with every lick and suck had her peaking quicker than she thought possible. There was something beautifully harsh coiling around her beating heart, burning bright colors behind her closed eyelids.

Viviana didn't even care what the man touching her had done is his life to get where he was. She just didn't—he was *hers*. Anton could be as bad as he wanted, washed in his own fucking sin, but he'd always be hers.

When his teeth nipped into the tender flesh of her sex, mouth encasing to suck hard against her clit, Viviana felt every nerve in her body snap awake with life. The pleasure of ecstasy sung through her senses with the sweet bite of the pain chasing behind. She thought he would release his hold and remove his mouth, but Anton didn't. Instead, his thumb was replaced by two fingers, curling up into the walls of her

THE LIFE

pussy to seek and find that fleshy spot that would have her shaking as tart smelling fluid soaked his hand further.

With her body burning with the aftershocks of one orgasm, she didn't think she could work up to another one without taking a pause first. But her fingers tightened their grip on his hair as her heart skipped a beat, feeling him press a little harder on her g-spot as his fingers thrust inside her pussy once more. Trembling and weak, she shook her head frantically, the oddest sensations traveling from her sex to her midsection.

"Anton, I *can't*—"

It was only then that he spoke, all dark and husky in the quiet room. "Fucking right you can."

Sure enough, with his mouth back on her sex, his tongue joining the assault on her clit once more, Viviana was lost. Coming hard and fast, her head fell back as she blew through a second orgasm that ached just as much as it relieved.

Painfully slow, Anton was crawling back up the bed again, over her body. Her trembling hands pulled at his shirt to remove the offending fabric. Viviana wanted him closer, his muscled frame covering hers, and their skin pressed together.

She wanted to feel *them*.

"Please …"

"Shh." He soothed away her trembling, kissing her jaw as his hand cradled the side of her cheek. "Breathe, baby."

The wetness of her arousal on his thumb grazed the apple of her cheek and she caught the digit as it came closer to her mouth. The tartly sweet fluid swept along her bottom lip. Viviana calmed as their gazes met.

"I always will, Anton."

"What's that?" he asked, leaning down to brush his nose against hers.

"Defend you."

As his eyes flicked away from hers, Anton murmured, "I know."

"It's not honor," she said quieter. "It's *love*."

"Yeah, I know that, too."

Chapter Four

"Why on earth am I here?" Erik asked, not bothering to hide the disdain in his voice.

Anton didn't pay any mind. Where Ivan's job in their business where the boss was concerned was an obvious one, Erik's was a little more complicated. Known for his ability to talk himself through any situation, the man could get close to anyone, find their weaknesses, and play them like dice. He also had personal access to the Bratva's money for even more complicated reasons.

Enticements that were. Or bribes, as some preferred.

Erik whined his impatience. "Anton."

Anton shot the older man a look to silence him. "To do your job."

"In a *gym*?"

"Does it really fucking matter where you have to do it?"

Erik said nothing as Anton hit the speed button on the treadmill he was currently jogging on. Turning it to go faster, he kept up the speed easily. There was nothing like getting out some aggression through a decent run.

Usually he'd work out in his basement, but Anton had a need for being at this particular gym today. He also had a need for Erik being there. That reason just happened to be thirty feet away doing stretches against a wall lined with mirrors.

Tall and curvy, with her red hair pulled back into a high ponytail, the woman was pretty. Vanessa Macey didn't lack attention in the male department if the way some of the men's eyes in the room were following her was any indication. It took Anton all of two days to get the information he needed on the girl, and now he was going to use it.

Tugging up the hood on his hoodie, Anton hid his face.

"Go find something to do," he told Erik.

The older gentleman cursed under his breath. "Like what?"

"It's a gym, Erik, you figure it out."

"Do I look like I'm dressed for this shit?" Erik asked sarcastically. Anton had to admit his Obshchak appeared completely out of place standing in a suit that likely cost more than the treadmill. "This is ridiculous."

"Tell that to your pretty wife when you have a heart attack, old friend."

Sure enough, that did it. Erik turned on his heel and walked away, grumbling. Anton disregarded him as he slid the iPod out of his pocket, and put the ear buds in before turning on the device. The loud, harsh bang of heavy metal thrummed in his eardrums as he continued jogging. Less than five minutes later, a female form joined the pace on the machine next to his. Anton smirked under the cloak of his hood, but said nothing while Vanessa Macey began her workout.

As per his information, the girl lived four blocks away from the gym. Working a part-time job in a bar across the street as a waitress, she showed up to the gym three times a week before her work shifts. She attended Long Island University full time, intent on getting her degree in Education. Born and raised in Long Island, New York, she likely had the usual expectations and naive understanding of the crime world that revolved around her home state.

With a sick father at home and no mother, Vanessa had yet to move out on her own and took on a great deal of her diabetic father's care by herself. Add that in to everything else she had going on, and she was a busy woman.

For all purposes, she was a good girl. One who seemed nice enough on the outside, and probably was just as sweet on the inside. But, she'd also hurt his wife—the only thing on the earth Anton would move heaven and hell for. It didn't make much of a difference that Viviana moved on from the situation, determined to brush the girl's comments and opinions off. Anton couldn't let it go.

After all, he hadn't promised his wife a thing when it came to Vanessa.

That didn't mean he had to tell Viviana, of course.

Ten minutes into Vanessa's run, Anton pulled a single ear bud out of his ear. Letting the wire dangle freely, the loud music hummed from the tiny speaker, drawing in the girl's attention. Watching her from the corners of his eyes, Anton said nothing as she reached out to hit the speed button on her machine. Just as quickly, he stopped his altogether.

Placing both of his hands to the treadmill's top, he rolled his shoulders and took a breath. With his face still covered by the hood of his sweater, Anton knew Vanessa didn't have a fucking clue of just who was beside her or how close to death she had come two nights before when his wife had cried herself to sleep.

There were things Anton knew he and Viviana couldn't ever get away from—judgment from others for one, but that didn't mean he had to turn cheek, either.

"I suppose you switched from law to education because it wouldn't take as long to get your degree, huh?"

The girl missed a step on her run, nearly slipping off the treadmill but she managed to catch herself just in time. "Excuse me?"

"University," Anton clarified, keeping his head down. "You were studying law, but it was going to take you a good seven years at least to get there and a hell of a lot of study time in between. What with your father being sick like he is and his retirement not paying out as good as it should, you were stuck. He needed you, and you wanted to continue school. With the credits you already had, education was the quickest endgame. I bet you would have made one hell of a good D.A. God knows they could use a few more opinionated bitches like you on their docket."

That seemed to have its desired effect. Vanessa reached up with a shaky hand to hit the off button on her machine before attempting to step off. Anton didn't let her. In a flash of movement, he was off his treadmill and beside hers. His hand grasped her wrist with a pressure he knew would have been painful to a man of his size, let alone a woman of hers.

Finally, he tilted his head up to regard her blatantly, unbothered by the wide, frightened green eyes that stared back. To anyone else, it might have looked like he was approaching the woman as a friend, but if someone came close enough, Anton knew they would see the fear written all over her features.

"I'd say you know who I am, then," he said, sneering.

"Let—"

"Scream, I dare you. I'll have someone outside of your place of work at the end of your shift. Or maybe I'll wait to have them catch you tomorrow morning on your trek to the university. Hell, how do you know I don't already have a man standing outside your father's apartment waiting for my call? I very well could."

"You wouldn't," Vanessa spat.

Anton cocked a brow, challenging the girl. "You don't know for sure, though, do you? The only thing you really know about me, or my wife, is what you've been told. Don't let me sully your opinion or anything, because most of what you've heard about me is likely true. Viviana is a completely different matter."

More than once, Anton had been told when he leveled on someone, he did so with a predator's graceful composure. Swathed in calm and unbothered by any and all of the activity around him, when the boss moved in, he went straight for the kill and didn't give a second glance back. Striking with a gaze that could burn in a single look, and terrorizing with a voice that rolled and coated like sweetened molasses, he was frightening.

Anton preferred *dangerous*.

The girl didn't seem to know what to say, so Anton continued with his same cool, quiet tenor. "If you had considered to think about the things you said to my wife, you would have known just why it was a stupid choice and you wouldn't have done it at all. I'm not just affiliated with the Russian Mafia in New York, Vanessa, I fucking *am* it. You'd disappear, sweetheart—just like that. *Poof*, gone. Did you realize that when you told Viviana her hands were just as filthy as mine? Did you consider I could have blown your brains out and still made it home to wake my wife the next morning with a smile on my face when you called my unborn son a *criminal's* bastard?"

"I—"

"Shut the fuck up." Anton's grip on her wrist squeezed tighter again. "You had your chance to speak, and now I'm going to have mine."

The girl swallowed nervously, her gaze flickering somewhere behind him. With a simple tug on her arm, Anton had her attention back on him. "What, did she run home and cry to the criminal who shares her bed that some nasty girl made her cry?"

Anton scoffed. "Oh, no. My wife has a hell of a lot more intelligence than that. In fact, she told me very little about your encounter. What I learned, I heard from your friend George. Nice guy, but trust he knows which is the safer side for him to be on, Vanessa. That was probably a better outcome for you. If I had heard it from my wife, I would have shoved my gun so far down your throat that when I pulled the trigger, you'd have felt the bullet rip through your esophagus before it killed you."

Water formed behind Vanessa's eyes as she breathed shakily. "Please ..."

"Yeah, now is the time you'd want to beg, girl. Unfortunately, my patience for you is already worn terribly thin. I think it'd make my wife awfully upset to wake up tomorrow morning to a broadcast about a Long Island University student who went missing the night before."

"You're not going to—"

"No," Anton said, his gaze narrowing. "And you're fucking lucky. It wouldn't have bothered me a bit to end someone's life who made my wife unhappy. But, I will tell you what *you're* going to do, Vanessa."

Swallowing audibly once more, she asked quietly, "What's that?"

Anton nodded his head to Erik who was watching their encounter ten feet away with a bored fascination. Now, with Erik being so close to the quiet conversation, Anton knew he understood exactly why he had been asked to meet his boss at the gym.

"See him?" Anton asked.

"Yes."

"His name is Erik, and he's a very good friend of mine. When I leave, you're going to have a nice conversation with him. I'm sure the little chat you two will have should clear up any confusion regarding what I'm about to say."

Taking a deep breath, Anton sighed. "Tonight, you will go to work. It'll be your last shift. Then, you'll go home to your father and tell him you both are moving out of state. I don't care what excuse you use, or how much he argues, you're to make him understand without bringing up my name. There isn't a soul who would believe you if you did, anyway. Tomorrow afternoon, you'll go to the university and unregister from your classes. I want you gone. I don't give a fuck if it's the next state over so long as it isn't New York. That man over there will write you a check. Name your price. Everyone has one."

"I can't leave," Vanessa said feebly. The slight sniff at the end of her words mixed with the tremble in her hands told Anton she was terrified. That was good. It was exactly how he wanted her. "You can't just make me—"

"What's the price of your life worth? One million? Two? Believe me, there isn't a number big enough that I won't pay so I can feel assured you will never look in the direction of Viviana Avdonin again. Say it, and I will have it paid by tomorrow night."

Vanessa's mouth popped open. "You're serious."

"You're goddamn right. Name your price."

. . .

"Boss, we've got a major problem right now."

Anton cursed as he zipped up his leather jacket. He hadn't even made it out of the gym and already there was something else going wrong. Why did his life have to be so stressful?

"What is it?" he asked Joe as he walked out of the locker room. "Surely it can't be that bad. Isn't Viviana with Sasha visiting Daniil?"

At least, that's where his wife should have been. There wasn't much trouble to be had in a hospital.

"Yeah. But, uh … well, maybe you should get over here to the hospital, Boss. And hurry up about it."

Anton's heart leaped into his throat. "Is Dad …?"

"Not that I know of. He seemed okay when I was up there a few minutes ago. Tired and groggy because of all that Demerol they've got him high with."

"Well, what the fuck is it, then?"

"Boss, really—"

"Let me talk to Rory," he interrupted angrily.

Joe swore severely. "Can't, Boss. He's in the hospital with Vine."

Anton's mind stuttered over what his wife's bull was telling him. "Do you mean to say neither one of you were outside watching her car?"

After the bomb incident that nearly killed his wife, unsupervised vehicles only served to make Anton nervous. It wasn't hard to check if they'd been tampered with, but it was dangerous. He made sure his guys knew to never leave Viviana's car unattended when it wasn't parked in their secured garage.

"Shit, I'm sorry, Boss. Rory's phone must have died. I couldn't get a hold of him so I went upstairs. You need to get here and fix this before Vine comes down here and sees it first."

"What happened?" Anton asked. It'd be the last time he

did or Joe wouldn't like the consequences.

"Somebody slashed her tires," the bull replied quietly. "Every damned one of them."

It took Anton half the time it normally would for him to make it to the hospital. In the underground garage, he found Joe standing next to Viviana's new black Bentley. Sure enough, every white-letter tire had a large gash and the car was resting on nothing but useless rubber and five-thousand dollar rims.

It wasn't that Viviana would have a freak out over the damage, but more so that someone had done it at all. That was Anton's problem, too. How likely could it be that someone randomly chose her tires to slash out of all the cars in the hospital's parking garage, never mind that it just happened to occur when her bull left the vehicle for a few moments?

Not likely at all, Anton thought.

The remnants of Tatiana's previous appearances still left a bitter taste on the back of Anton's tongue. This kind of nastiness screamed guilty with ten fingers pointing straight at her. Because he still didn't have any proof about whatever plans the Jersey bitch might have had, Anton wasn't comfortable bringing it up and causing issues that might not be there. He hated feeling out of the loop.

"Why the fuck would somebody do this?" Anton asked as he surveyed the damage.

The tires were completely ruined but he had two spare sets in a warehouse not far from his club in Brighton, and a set of rims. He knew he had to get the tires changed before his wife noticed what happened. Anton couldn't have Viviana worried and frightened while she was pregnant. This would definitely do that to her, but it was also seriously screwing with his head, too.

What with the unknown photographer and his suspicions about Tatiana, this act screamed with alarm bells that it was probably related. Anton had to put a stop to this shit before it escalated anymore. Slashing tires wasn't as irksome as a photographer, but it was just as personal and twice as threatening.

He also had to consider what Boris said during their private meeting. Maybe this did have something to do with the Italians. The Cosa Nostra crime family in Long Island was known to drop dangerous hints until someone got the point and called a sit-down to resolve the issue. Anton couldn't figure out what the issue would be, though, if there even was one.

After all, Anton killing their old boss wasn't just to his benefit. The cousin of Sonny Carducci—Conrad—the man who helped them and gave them information on the side had taken over the family's head without much trouble at all. So, Sonny's murder at Anton's hand had been a win-win all the way around for Conrad.

Regardless, Anton needed to find out if the Italians were involved and why. If they weren't, which he thought was more likely, maybe they'd have some information he didn't as to who possibly was.

"Boss, I'm so so—"

"Shut up," Anton barked, glaring at Joe. "You know the rules. You don't ever leave her car unattended. Remember what happened the last time?"

Joe averted his eyes and dipped his chin down. "Yeah."

"Call that tow company we use. You know where the extra tires are, so get on it. I want her car back in our driveway within the next two hours. Don't say a goddamned thing to Vine about it. Understood?"

"Yeah. I'll call Rory right now. Get him down here to help."

Anton frowned. Hadn't Joe said Rory's phone was dead?

Not important, he thought.

What was important was keeping his wife calm. Anton turned and left the bull without another word. If he stayed in the man's presence for too much longer, he might blow his fucking top. It wouldn't be unusual for Anton to pick up Viviana somewhere and get her bulls to drive her car home, so she wouldn't question his sudden presence. Keeping what happened away from her was an easy feat.

He wondered if that had been the perpetrator's point.

Again, he considered the Italians. With the cell phone in his hand, Anton dialed Ivan's number. The lawyer picked up on the third ring.

"Yeah?"

"Call the Italians," Anton said immediately. There was no point in pleasantries. "Request a meeting with the Don as soon as we can get it."

• • •

"What in the actual *fuck*, Anton? Where do you get off—"

Viviana's rant stopped short at the sight staring back at her. Dread washed the color from her face as the silence answering back only seemed to grow, making her even more uncomfortable than she was.

She hadn't bothered to knock before entering her husband's office at Seven Lights. Maybe she should have, considering there were four other men inside the room, two of which she didn't recognize at all. The other two, Ivan and Erik, sported matching expressions of shock and amusement.

Anton's eyes flitted over to her spot, surprise and anger registering in the blue of his irises before one of his usual masks replaced the emotions. "Excuse me?"

"Um ..."

Viviana tittered, unnerved by all the stares currently leveling on her. One of the older gentlemen coughed under his breath, hiding his laughter poorly. Another man, younger than the first but older than Anton, scowled back over his shoulder at her. His obvious disdain of having a woman walk in on business was obvious.

"I'll uh ... just wait, yeah, outside."

Coldly, Anton responded with, "Please do."

Outside in the hallway, with the office door shut tight behind her, Viviana groaned. Squeezing her eyes shut and pressing the heels of both her palms to her forehead, she resisted the urge to bang her head repeatedly against the nearest wall. Embarrassment welled up in her heart.

She should have known better than to just storm in like that. Hell, she *did* know better.

Sure, Anton would apologize for her rude interruption of his meeting—likely a Bratva meeting—and blame it on the pregnancy hormones. Viviana knew she'd have to apologize to him, as well.

When things like that happened, no matter if it was a mistake or not, it only served to make Anton look positively ridiculous. As if he couldn't control his wife, her actions, and her temperaments. Not that he did try to control Viviana, because Anton didn't. But, there were certain appearances they had to keep up outside of their home for the obvious reasons related to his status, and this was one of them.

Viviana screwed that up royally, *again.*

Regrettably, she didn't miss the question being asked inside the office, either.

"How much tighter do you have to yank on your wife's leash before she understands her place, Boss?"

Scowling, Viviana fought off the urge to walk back into the room and give the man a piece of her mind. She couldn't. It would only make Anton look more like an idiot. She would feel horrible afterwards when her husband was left either explaining, or hiding a pile of bodies because she couldn't keep her opinions to herself.

"Mind your fucking wife and I'll mind mine," Anton replied, his voice clipped.

"Yes, because you're doing such a superb job as it is."

Goddamn it, way to go, Viviana thought miserably.

Yeah, Viviana definitely owed Anton an apology. Right after she got hers, of course. Because he owed her a big one after the crap she learned today. Sometimes being Anton's wife had a million and one benefits, and other times she had to excuse or ignore his decisions and behaviors a lot more than she liked.

Fucking Anton and his lack of a moral compass.

Deciding it would be better for her to be far away from the office when the men left, Viviana made her way down to the main floor of the club. In the kitchen, she found Jen bent over the counter reading papers. At Viviana's sheepish appearance, the older woman smiled knowingly and snorted under her breath.

"Honey, I told you not to go up there," Jen said, laughing.

Viviana stuck out her tongue. "You didn't say *why*."

"By now, I shouldn't have to."

That was true enough. Sighing, Viviana rested herself up on a stool, crossing her fingers over her rounded stomach as she considered her course of action when Anton was done with his meeting. Lost in her thoughts, she barely noticed Jen coming over to rub her hand over Viviana's bump with a sentimental smile.

"How'd your appointment go with the doctor yesterday?" Jen asked.

Viviana frowned. "My sugars are out of control. He wants me to start taking insulin the moment I can have the prescription he wrote filled. I just ... ugh."

"Needles, huh?"

"Yeah, that and I'd have to listen to Anton tell me I told you so again," Viviana explained with a roll of her brown eyes. "I know he will."

Jen looked flabbergasted. "You haven't told Anton, yet?"

"Yeah, no. He's going to make a big deal out of it. I was just going to send him out on an errand and hope he figured it out on his own when he got to the pharmacy. Then, by the time he got home, he'd be over it."

Laughing loudly, Jen said, "That is the stupidest thing I have ever heard."

Even Viviana had to admit she hadn't thought out her plan well enough. "I know."

"He only worries because he loves you."

That was exactly the problem. If every little thing Anton

did could be explained or excused away simply because he loved Viviana, then everybody would be happy. A lot of his decisions were attributed to his intense feelings for her. More often than not, he didn't think things out when it came to her because his first reaction was to fix the problem and make whatever it was go away.

Unfortunately, sometimes it backfired.

God knew Viviana loved Anton. She *did*, more than anything. What she didn't want to do was overlook things because she loved him. Beyond the mob boss suit he wore, he was her husband first. He was damn well going to act the part whether he liked it or not.

"Vine, you can go upstairs now."

Viviana jumped in surprise at the new voice. She'd expected Anton to come down and find her, not Ivan. That didn't bode well for her husband's mood. Sighing heavily, she pushed herself off the stool and frowned at her lawyer.

"Is he terribly mad at me?" she asked.

Ivan shot her a look. "Does that man ever really get mad at you? I don't mean frustrated, or annoyed, no I mean *mad*. We've all seen Anton get pissed off at one point or another, but is it ever at *you*, particularly?"

Point taken, she thought.

"Thank you for letting me know the meeting was done."

Ivan disappeared with a wave and nothing else.

With a quiet goodbye to Jen, Viviana made her way back through the club. Biding her time, she made her way up to Anton's office with a slowness she hoped gave him the same kind of time she needed to think through what she wanted to say to him. Sure, Ivan had been right. Anton never got angry with her directly, but sometimes his fury with others bled off onto the people surrounding him when he didn't mean for it to.

She didn't want this to be one of those times.

Knocking on the office door with two of her knuckles, Viviana asked, "Can I come in?"

"Yep."

There was no missing the bite in his tone as she slipped inside the office and closed the door behind her. "First things first," Viviana rushed to say, "I'm sorry for earlier."

Anton said nothing, his head still bent down over the papers he was reading. Viviana scowled at her husband's blatant attempt to ignore her.

"Anton?" Again, nothing. Irritation bubbled through her blood. "Funny, Ivan said you weren't angry with me."

"I'm not. I'm terribly pissed off that I just let Kalvin walk out of here alive, though."

"He said something nastier about me than just the leash comment, I assume?" she asked softly. It was the slightest tick of his strong jaw that gave her the answer. "I am sorry for barging in on your business. I know better than to be doing crap like that during your work hours, and I didn't mean to cause problems."

Sighing, Anton raised his hand in the air, waving at his wife. "Come here."

Viviana didn't waste any time. Crossing the distance of the office floor, she sunk into his opened embrace before either of them had blinked. Anton had her body curled up on his lap without saying a word before he buried his face into her neck and inhaled deeply. Then, his warm hand rolled along the base of her stomach, gliding carefully under the waistband of her black skirt until it came to rest on her public bone.

"He's an asshole," he mumbled against her flesh. "He told me that maybe—*maybe*—if I could learn to spend less time at home, and more time having fun elsewhere, that my wife would become accustomed to not needing me around so much. Perhaps then, he said, she would find more respect for her husband if he wasn't at her every beck and call. I'd just … fucking kill him."

"Did you tell him to go screw himself?" Viviana asked.

"Maybe," he replied in a breath.

"It's a good thing you're the boss, Anton."

"Don't I already fucking know it, baby."

Lifting his head, Anton rested his cheek to Viviana's and blew out a harsh sound. She knew her husband was about done with the day and wanting to go home. Slowly, Viviana turned her head, letting her lips ghost along the dusting of his five o'clock shadow, the sandpaper feel tickling tantalizingly to her mouth.

"I'm sorry."

His arms tightened around her frame. "Hmm, don't be."

"I like having access to you whenever I need you, Anton."

"I know."

Swallowing the lump forming in her throat, Viviana asked, "I'm going to have to steer clear of the club, huh?"

That was usually his request of her when something like this happened. At least then it looked like she'd been properly chastised for her behavior to someone on the outside looking in. Viviana understood, and followed along with it for Anton's benefit, but that didn't mean she had to like it.

"Yeah, for a little while, anyway," Anton said sadly. "Kiss me?"

Damn, he didn't have to ask a second time. Seeking out the heat of his mouth, Viviana let her body melt into his as Anton's fingers traced up her sides to find her cheeks. Holding his gaze, she lost herself in the wide open blue of his eyes locked onto hers as his tongue swept over the seam of her lips, wanting entrance to her mouth.

Like this, their kisses were always so slow. Tantalizing enough to feel every swipe of his tongue exploring her mouth. Sweet enough to taste the coffee he'd been sipping on. Gentle enough to know he was apologizing for things he wouldn't say out loud.

Pulling away, Anton cleared his throat sexily, smirking as he bumped his nose to hers.

"So, why aren't you in class?" Anton asked.

"Yeah, about that," Viviana said bitingly. Poking a finger into his chest, and enjoying the look of shock he wore, she scowled at her husband. "We need to talk."

Chapter Five

"And our best conversations always come from those words."

Viviana frowned at him again. "I'm serious, Anton."

"Me, too," he grumbled under his breath.

Anton had been so worried when Viviana flew into his office unannounced. Usually one of her bulls called ahead of time to say she was on her way over to the club. They hadn't this time, for whatever reason.

With that finger of hers still pointed at his chest like a gun ready to blow, Viviana spoke through clenched teeth as she asked, "What did you do?"

Anton blinked, surprised at the venom in his wife's tone. "Me?"

"Well who the hell else am I asking, Anton?"

"I'm confu—"

"*Vanessa*," she interrupted with a cock of her brow.

"Oh."

From Erik's accounts, the girl in question was readying to leave New York. It had only been three days before that Anton had approached her. He was satisfied with that result.

"Yeah, *oh*."

Keeping his face blank, Anton said, "I didn't hurt that girl."

"Obviously," Viviana replied shortly. "She was very much alive when I visited her apartment earlier. So unless something happened between an hour ago and now, then she's probably on her way out of town as we speak, frightened she might not make it out alive otherwise."

"You did *what*?"

Viviana refused to meet his stare, but her next words were enough to say exactly what she felt about his choice in actions regarding Vanessa Macey. "You can't just go around doing whatever it was that you did, Anton."

"I didn't *do* anything," he argued, annoyance seeping into his tone.

"Right."

"Okay," Anton said with a roll of his eyes. "So, let me rephrase. I didn't do anything that wasn't to her benefit. Does that make you feel better?"

"No."

The word was suspiciously whiney. That wasn't like Viviana at all. Forcing his wife to look at him, Anton searched her gaze for some kind of hint as to what was going on inside that crazy beautiful mind of hers. Instead, he got nothing but the bat of her long lashes and confused brown eyes staring back.

"I won't say I'm sorry," he finally said quietly. "But, I would love to know how you found out anything."

Viviana shrugged, but even the action looked weak. "I didn't find out very much from her. She wouldn't even speak to me when I visited her place, just shut the door on me and said I wasn't supposed to be there. Something about her promise to you and I had to go immediately. I didn't understand what in hell she was talking about, but her apartment was filled with boxes—packing boxes."

"That's not what I asked."

"When she didn't show up for class today, I thought it was odd. She doesn't miss class. I asked George, and all he had to say was that she wasn't answering his calls. He didn't seem all too worried, but he's not me, Anton."

Biting the inside of his cheek, Anton understood what she was getting at. "You assumed I had the girl killed."

"Would you blame me?"

"Is that the first place your mind goes whenever you think about how I handle issues?"

Viviana snapped back away from him as if she'd been burned. "No, of course not."

"Then why did you automatically think that would be my solution with her?"

The silence that followed his question felt wrought with tension. Those expressive eyes of Viviana's didn't waver from the stare he was leveling on her. Sometimes their arguments were loud and fueled with heavy emotions, and other times, like now, they were silent and pushing against invisible barriers. Regardless, they all ended the same, and it hurt just as much. Perhaps Anton had crossed a line with his wife, but if that was really how she felt in regards to him, he wanted to know.

"I'm so—"

Viviana raised a hand, stopping him. "If you don't mean it, I don't want to hear it."

Anton leaned back in his seat, allowing her to move off his lap. Seated at the edge of his desk, she crossed her ankles and stared up at the ceiling. "Christ, you've got to let me finish a sentence," he said into the palm of his hand. "I certainly don't mean to apologize for handling Vanessa how I felt comfortable with. *Nevertheless*, I am sorry that you must think I am so much of a monster that the first thing you consider above all else is that I had her whacked."

"I didn't say that exactly."

"You didn't have to," he replied.

The next words she spoke were barely breathed above a whisper, and they all but slithered to his spot like a snake in cold grass. "Did you want to kill her? Would you have done it if you thought I wouldn't have been hurt and angry?"

Anton froze, the arms crossed over his chest falling limply to the chair. Did Viviana really want the answer to that? He supposed if she asked, she did. After all, she knew better than to ask things when they were in private, as the words he spoke to her then were safe should she invoke spousal privilege in any trial.

And his wife would invoke the privilege; she loved him.

When Viviana asked for honesty, he gave it back to her tenfold.

"Yes."

"Why?"

Viviana all but spat the question out as she finally regarded him again. The intense expression that had taken over her features weakened Anton's emotions for a moment. Sometimes he hated that his wife had such a profound effect on his soul—a soul that was never meant to feel. All at once, with just one of those blinks of hers, every feeling running through her heart and veins seemed to flit over her face.

"*Why*, Anton?"

The shock that had previously taken hold of his body and emotions left in one fell swoop. In a flash, Anton was off his chair and standing in front of his wife, hands on either side of her hips as he leaned in close enough to her face that their noses touched. This time, Viviana didn't shy away from the sudden change in his temperament or demeanor.

"Because I can," he said.

"You're lying."

She was right.

"How could you possibly know that?"

Viviana's tongue peeked out to wet her lips before she said, "Your pupils. They dilate when you lie."

Anton forced back the frown threatening to form, replacing it with yet another sneer. "That would have been a great little tidbit of information to know a decade ago when I had Roman Carducci's fist in my face while he asked me if I had fucked his daughter."

"And your voice," Viviana continued, ignoring the scorn coating his words that were only meant to deflect. "When you lie to me, and only me, it shakes. Tell me why you wanted to kill her, Anton."

His palms slammed down to the desk hard, rattling the items setting atop the precious, antique oak. Goddamn it, this was not the conversation he wanted to have with his wife. If there was any time he wished she would turn her cheek to something he'd done, it was now. It certainly wasn't because he was ashamed of his actions, but because he was feeling enough shit as it was and this was something he simply didn't want to dredge up.

"Don't—"

"Why?" Viviana interjected, softer, her eyes kinder.

"Because!" Anton swore he felt every nerve in his body snap, tension building to the point of no return. "Because she doesn't have a fucking clue about you, or me, or *us*, okay? She doesn't know that I love to kiss the spot over your heart just because it beats. She doesn't know that every part of my world revolves around you. She doesn't know that the best gift you ever gave me was *life*, Vine."

"Anton—"

"What does she know?" he asked, knowing very well he sounded cruel. "Does she know that every day you're with me is dangerous? That having my last name makes you a target in more ways than one? That sometimes loving me hurts? No, and she sure as *fuck* doesn't get the goddamn right to, either."

"Okay," Viviana said, her hands coming down to rest atop his.

"So yeah," Anton murmured, nodding once. "Yeah, baby, I'd have killed her if I thought you wouldn't have cared. I would have because despite the fact that you're strong enough to handle it yourself, and I know that you did, she still hurt the *only* thing I protect with *everything* I am. I'd have done it for the simple fact that she made you cry and it made me *ache*. In a roundabout way, it was really me who made you do it, if you think about it, and that shit isn't okay."

"But you didn't kill her," his wife added.

"No."

"For me."

"No," Anton repeated.

Surprise blinked back in her wide eyes as she asked, "What?"

"I said *no*. One way or another, you would have forgiven me. That's how we work. We fight hard, fuck harder, and love like crazy. We're predictable that way, and I love it like you don't even know. You can't hate the things you love,

Viviana, even if you wish you could. So, no, I didn't spare the girl's life simply because I knew it would make you angry with me for a little while."

Swallowing audibly, Anton said, "I didn't kill her because she's just a *girl*. Nothing to me, or you, or *us*. She didn't know and I couldn't expect her to. Something wholly irrelevant and stupidly unimportant to the things we share. So, I took her haughty fucking attitude and her arrogant fucking morals and made her *choke* on them."

"Excuse me?"

"You heard me. She didn't blink a lash at cutting out at our life; at the money she called filth; at the innocent child you carry. No, she didn't have a problem with thinking she was above that at all. I put that girl in her place, and all it took was a little bit of my *filth* to do it. There isn't a soul on this earth that can't be bought away, regardless of where the money comes from or how it was made. Vanessa Macey isn't any different than one of my girls who work the poles across town. She'll do anything for a price, just like them."

"You bought her off."

Anton nodded, shrugging his shoulders like it didn't matter. "Absolutely. Her father is in a wheelchair; he needs a lot more care than she is able to give. What he doesn't need is to be on the fourth floor of an apartment building with an elevator that doesn't work. The girl is intelligent, dean's list all the way, and she's going to make one hell of a lawyer someday—I guarantee now she'll be a first-rate defense attorney, though. Let her have whatever opinion she wants to spit, baby, because I stripped every bit of pride she had left away.

"And I'd do it again, too," Anton said, finishing with a smirk. "So I repeat, I didn't do a thing that wasn't to that girl's benefit, even if that meant I had to scare the hell out of her and beat down her ego while I was at it."

• • •

"Now, I answered your questions, so I'd love to have you answer mine," Anton said, canting his head. "Why did my wife automatically assume I would have had that girl killed?"

With Viviana's hands still resting on top of her husband's, she almost felt as though he grounded her. Taking the moment he gave her, she gathered her thoughts, took his frank honesty about the situation for what it was, and steeled herself to give him exactly the same.

Anton didn't give her the chance. "Have I ever given you that idea before?"

"No," she said instantly.

There was the issue of her uncle Sonny, but she didn't lump that into the same category.

"Do you get a front row seat to the business on a daily basis?"

"No."

"Do I come home with blood on my hands, wake you up with late night issues, or worry your mind when it's unfounded?" Anton asked.

Blowing out a heavy sigh of resignation, Viviana knew he was right. "No."

"So, *why*, baby? Why, when I've never given you the impression before, do you think I am that much of a monster, huh?"

"Because I'm me." Viviana's fingers curling around his hands and squeezed tightly. "I'm not like every other person to you, and we both know it. Vanessa might not be one of the guys you're running, or some man getting a little too close to your wife, but she can hurt me all the same."

Anton tried to take a step away, but her grip rooted him in place. "And when I hurt, you hurt. You don't like to hurt, Anton."

"I don't like you to hurt," he corrected.

"Call a spade a spade. If this was anyone else, you wouldn't have blinked twice about it, but it's not, so you reacted. I never called you a monster—wouldn't *ever*. Are you going to be like this for him, too?" Viviana asked, finally releasing one of his hands to wave hers over her midsection.

Anton cringed away from her view. "Maybe."

"Until he can do it for himself," she said, knowing he wouldn't.

Again, a silence overtook the office, surrounding the couple in its smothering grip. At least Anton hadn't shut her out like she assumed he would when the discussion went a little deeper than he would normally let it. Even so, Viviana could tell by the tightness in his clenching jaw, and the fire burning behind his eyes that he was unhappy about her way of confronting him.

Viviana wasn't sorry in the least.

"You know girls can't join, right?" Viviana asked, smiling just a little when Anton's gaze narrowed at the wall. "So if we ever have a daughter, you can't expect there's going to come a day when she's been hardened enough to turn her emotions off. She's going to come home crying to her daddy when some mean girl takes a bite out of her. What's her daddy going to do, pay off a child with dolls and makeup?"

Anton didn't say anything, but the slight curve of his lips told his wife he was listening.

"Take Roman, for example. A girl in third grade took scissors to my braid because I wouldn't give her my sparkle pen. His fix was to tell me to go to school the next day and do the same to her. The school didn't like that, but his eye for an eye thing was bred as deep as it could get.

"That goes for your wife, too," she said, meeting his gaze. "You can't expect me to turn off everything because you might go ballistic over the fact that I shed a few tears. I don't want to, either. Newsflash, Vanessa isn't the first girl I've gone toe to toe with about the way I was raised or live. Girls in high school, particularly, were hell. Privileged little bitches who thought their daddies weren't fucking around on their mommies with high priced escorts, or that their mommies weren't snorting scripts behind their daddies' backs. But oh, because *my* daddy had a rap sheet, that made me something else entirely."

Viviana scoffed. "Fuck them. Girls aren't like boys, Anton. We can't go a couple of rounds in the dirt, bloody up a nose, and be done with it like you can. There's a whole different set of rules in a woman's world and you …" she said pointedly, her hand reaching up to tap his jaw, "have to learn to play by them, too."

"And you considered what happened with Vanessa a battle won, then?" he asked, appearing skeptical.

"Sure. I didn't run away. She didn't see me cry. There was no satisfaction in it for her, even if she thought there was. After all, I would be the one attending the next study group and she wouldn't have the balls to show, regardless if she was invited back or not. Yes, Anton, that is a battle won. Without threats and bribery."

Anton's lips curved with one of his wicked grins. "I didn't threaten her. I simply admitted what I could have done."

Rolling her eyes, Viviana guffawed at his genuine enjoyment over the situation. "You're horrible, you know that?"

"You love it."

Viviana leaned forward and tilted her head up to kiss the line of Anton's cheek before resting her head into the crook of his neck. Immediately, his arms wrapped around Viviana's shoulders in response. They stayed locked in that comfortable, quiet embrace.

"So, a daughter, huh?" Anton asked with a dark chuckle.

"That's what you got from all of that?"

"No, but that's what I liked the most," he confessed. "Well, minus the whole girls making her cry thing. I promise nothing on that front, by the way. She'd be little, and cute as hell, and mine, and … *fuck*. I would kill somebody, I know it."

Giggling lightly, Viviana poked at his midsection with her fingers. The truth of the matter was he hadn't promised her a damned thing when it came to Vanessa. Regardless, she was sure the next time something like this happened, Anton might actually consider how she handled the situation first before he jumped in. But, who was to say? Her husband was a fickle man with constantly changing temperaments. Loving her only made it worse, not that he complained.

"Can we at least wait until this one is out of my body before we start talking about more, Anton?"

"But you are guaranteeing Demyan a sibling?"

"I'm guaranteeing that it's a definite maybe."

"We're not … *hardened*, not like you think," Anton said after a moment, his tone growing softer. At her confused stare, he shrugged. "The boys—ones who join the brotherhood or don't. We're not little machines, baby. But at some point, there comes a time where you're not facing kids on the playground anymore. You're standing up against a whole different set of issues. It kind of jumps out on you, then. Emotions fuel us when we're younger, sure, but then it changes and a boy has to realize that it's better if emotions don't get brought into it at all. That way, no one knows where to hit out at next."

"Like me for you?"

Anton leaned down to catch her frown with his mouth in the softest kiss. "Just like that. Unfortunately, I've been failing at times, hence my earlier disagreement with Kalvin. You do the worst kinds of things to me, Vine."

"You love it."

"Damn right. Even if it kills me."

Anton realized the mistake in his words quickly. That, or Viviana's fear must have been written all over her torn expression. It wasn't a heartbeat later before his mouth was pressing down gently to hers. Her fingers fisted into the shirt he wore, drawing him in closer, needed him safer. Falling into the kiss, her stress eased slightly, but it still wasn't enough.

"You know I wouldn't ever let that happen, right?" Anton asked, his breath tickling along the line of her tightly drawn lips.

Viviana's heart was beating a staccato rhythm, hard, fast, and skipping beats by the second. Where his earlier words had been harsh and scarily honest, so were those. Horribly so. And hell, she would take her husband being locked up for a quarter of a century so long as she could fucking speak to him, even see him.

Death didn't offer that.

"Sometimes I think it's better if I don't wonder at all," Viviana whispered.

Giving her an understanding nod, Anton smiled grimly. "For the record, if the next time something like this occurs and it happens to be a man who makes my pretty wife cry, all bets are off, baby."

Well, Viviana knew it was pointless to argue with him over that one. Instead, she settled for tapping her palm to his chest and pretending like he was spewing his usual nonsense. Unfortunately, there was no hiding the shiver crawling up her spine at the knowledge that Anton absolutely would follow through on his promise.

Needing to distract them both, and wanting to lighten up the situation, she managed to say, "And anyway, we can't afford for you to be running around the city bribing every girl who pisses me off to move away, Anton."

"It wasn't that much. Morals, remember? I think Vanessa thought the less she took, the easier on her conscious it would be."

"How much?"

Anton's body loomed over Viviana. She leaned back using her palms to keep her balance. While his mouth did the sweetest exploration of her pulse point, his tongue striking out to lick every few inches, she mewled. It was clear he was trying to deflect her attention to something different, and it was working.

"Stop it," Viviana whined. "Tell me."

With Anton's lips brushing up to her jaw, he said, "It was a bit. Seven figures."

"Jesus!" Viviana gaped for a minute, not even wanting to know the number that rested in front of all the zeros. "Again, we can't afford for you to be paying off every person I dislike. Not that it isn't a nice sentiment or what—*no*," she muttered, cutting herself off abruptly with a shake of her head. Obviously his mouth on her skin was making her lose sanity, considering now she was seeing his bribery tricks as sweet. Something wonderful pulsed between her thighs as his hands danced up under her skirt. "It's not a nice sentiment at all. That's like, three and a half of my new Bentleys."

Because he just had to buy her yet another one after her first was ruined by a bomb.

Anton cleared his throat. "Try about six."

Every muscle in her body froze. Anton made a noise of discontent as he removed his wandering hands before placing them to the desk and leveling her with a stare that challenged, chastised, and apologised all at once. She didn't quite understand how her husband was able to do that shit, but he did.

"Viviana …"

"Th-that's—"

"A lot of money. I'd pay it again."

Behind his words, she knew he was telling her something else, too. Money. It was a topic neither of them brought up very often because they didn't have to. Between her parents' estate after their deaths and the money Nicoli had left for Viviana in trust, she sported a cool thirty-two-point-two mil, half of which was tied up in stock.

Did she need to go to university? No, but she wanted to.

Could she do practically whatever she wanted with her money and life? Sure, but Viviana hadn't figured out what it was that she wanted to do, yet. Her having wealth gave her the time to work it all out. Anton kept his exact figures quiet.

"How much money do you have?" Viviana asked. "You know, so I can be sure when I divorce your ass in the future."

Anton's eyes widened before he scowled at her playfully. Viviana knew she was in trouble, but she bet it'd be terribly fun for her. Again, she found herself bent back to the desk as his frame hung over hers, his head tipping to the side in that hunter's way of his.

"Divorce me, huh?"

Anton's hands slipped back up her skirt, his palm lying flat to the seam of her sex, making Viviana gasp in a lungful of hot air. "Here?"

"We fight hard and fuck harder, remember? Let me, let me, let me," Anton chanted, coming down to nip at her bottom lip. He glanced down at furniture she rested on. "How long has it been since I fucked you on my desk?"

Viviana couldn't remember, actually. "Um ..."

"Too long, then," he stated.

As he skimmed her cotton panties down around her thighs before pulling them off her ankles, Viviana asked, "You're not going to tell me how much money you have, are you?"

Anton grinned sinfully. "A lot."

"Wait," she pleaded when his hands spread her legs wide. "Just ... wait for a minute."

"My God, what?" Anton growled low, the stress echoing loud and clear. "I want to be buried balls fucking deep in you right now, not chatting about my money."

"You brought it up."

"Forget that I did."

"But ... but ... shit." Viviana moaned, letting his fingers stroke the seam of her pussy. "That feels fantastic."

"Mmhmm." Anton hummed throatily, teasing the entrance of her sex with those skillful fingers of his. "I'll get it feeling even better if you just zip those lips."

"But—"

Anton's fingers stopped and his gaze burned with impatient desire. "What do you want, baby? Fuck, or talk—your choice. I've got about ten minutes before that idiot comes back here to apologize."

"How do you know he'll be back?"

Viviana let him slide her hands back further on the desk before he popped open all the buttons on the blouse she wore. The black satin bra was pushed to the side as Anton cupped her tender breast, his thumb rolling over her peaking nipple until her blood sang.

"This is nice," Anton told her, gazing down on her exposed body. "All on display, baby. Every fucking inch of you."

"How do you know—"

"Because Kalvin is not an idiot, and he's afraid of me."

"Huh."

"Your choice," he said, sporting a suggestive smirk. "Fuck or talk."

Chapter Six

The cell phone inside the desk buzzed with a pre-set tune that told Anton the caller was the brigadier who had barely made it out of his office alive. At the raise of his wife's brow, he rolled his eyes and decided to take the call.

"Both," Anton heard Viviana say as he reached to open the top drawer on his desk.

"Both?"

Yep, he thought, *fuck the call.*

Kalvin could make his way back to apologize in person, as he should have done in the first place.

"I know you're a man and everything, but surely you can do two things at once."

Halting the slow thrusts of his one finger inside the wet walls of her pussy, Anton groaned appreciatively under his breath. He could feel the sensitive tissues flexing around the intrusion of his digits as he turned sharp on her and slammed a second finger in without warning. The lovely, heady scent of her juices teased him. Already, he wanted to be on his knees for her, tasting the sweet fluids of her sex as she came from his touch.

No other person on earth could make Anton get down on his knees.

"Fuck." Viviana moaned a sound that reverberated straight to his gut and cock. "Is that a no to multitasking, then?"

More than anything, he loved when his wife turned a little sarcastic and combative. It turned him on like nothing else. Just his cock alone was throbbing under the black slacks he wore, but every other inch of his body thrummed with the need and want to take her hard and fast.

Viviana knew what she was doing to him, no doubt about it.

"What happened to my wife today?" Anton asked, teasing the words along the line of his wife's throat as she tilted her head back. The taste of her flesh on his tongue was positively immoral. Sweet as heaven and as tantalizing as sin. "Barging into my office like she owns the place. Throwing a tantrum. Demanding answers. Questioning what I do with *my* money. Testing my patience every step of the way, Viviana. Being a goddamn little *brat*."

To punctuate his words, he added another finger to Viviana's soaked core, allowing his thumb to flick up and press harshly along the hood of her clit. Spreading his fingers on the withdrawal, Anton stretched her sex, wanting to make her feel full and opened for only him. Shuddering with the sexiest cry, Viviana clenched around his digits.

"An-Anton." Viviana stuttered over her words and air. When her legs opened so fucking wide, giving him the sexiest view of his fingers sinking into the slick flesh of her sex, he knew she was close. "Oh, God, please …" Without warning, he pulled away, withdrawing his fingers completely from Viviana's pulsing pussy. *"No!"*

Chuckling, Anton hooked her shaking legs around his hips as he took in her frustrated, flustered appearance.

"Being a brat," he repeated darkly. "Perhaps my brigadier was right, baby."

"W-what?"

"Maybe I should yank on your leash a bit harder."

Anton didn't miss the sound of her fingernails scratching against the oak wood of the desk as her tiny hands balled into fists. Indignant, Viviana huffed as she glared at him with her teeth bared.

"Would you like that?" Anton asked mischievously, lifting a brow in contemplation. "If I put you in your place a little more and made you understand who the boss really was here?"

"Oh …" Viviana drawled the word out coyly, her pretty pink lips curving into a sneer. "I think we both know who that is, *Boss*."

Anton couldn't hide the satisfied grin overtaking his features. "We do, huh?"

"Yep, and she goes by *Mrs.* Viviana Avdonin, now."

"Oh, you evil—"

Anton's words were cut off by something silver catching the line of his peripherals. Glinting under the lights in his office, the smooth metal had his more wicked desires raging. Those handcuffs represented something entirely different to Anton.

Like freedom and the loss of it. The very first time he'd experienced it had been in those cuffs. Locking his wife down with the same restraints that had once been used on him had Anton's dick twitching.

Anton said nothing as Viviana worked the button and zipper on his slacks, tugging down the fabric around his thighs before her hand slipped into his boxer-briefs. She pumped his shaft with a rhythm that was sure to make him ache if she kept it up. A smile played at the edges of her mouth.

"You're thinking a little too hard about something up there. I can smell the smoke."

Whatever worries Anton might have had about trying the handcuffs on his smartass wife disappeared out the window. When he reached for the restraints dangling off the side of a lamp on the desk, Anton heard Viviana's breath hitch. "I won't if you—"

"I know. I just haven't ever noticed them before."

Anton laughed deeply. "Sentimental, baby. They were from my very first arrest."

Viviana stared at him before she burst into giggles. "That's so inappropriate it shouldn't even be cute."

"Cute?"

"Very," Viviana said.

Anton felt his nerves grow under her attention. "Fuck, stop looking at me like that. Like I said, it's sentimental, baby. A part of my history, okay?"

"So you kept them on your desk?"

Anton rolled his eyes. "Stop judging me. Besides, they're about to come in real fucking handy to fix up that attitude of yours."

Viviana's bottom lip was drawn in between her teeth. Desire swam in brown eyes as she hooked her legs around his hips and dug her heels into his back. When her hand squeezed painfully snug around his cock, Anton nearly came on the spot.

"Get on with it, then. Teach me a lesson, Boss."

"You asked for it, baby."

Catching her wrist with his one hand and pulling the other from within the confines of his boxer-briefs, Anton pinned Viviana's arms behind her back. He forced her to lean backwards as he inclined over her beautiful body. With her hands secured tightly in one of his, he grasped at the handcuffs as he kissed a line up her jaw to her mouth.

"Tell me you have keys for those," she mumbled against his mouth.

Anton chuckled. "And if I don't?"

Viviana blanched. "But—"

"Of course I do. Relax." When she did, he kissed the corner of her mouth noisily. "Thank you. Now, let me finish here."

The desk was made in the old fashioned style with drawers on either end for maximum capacity, though Anton rarely used any. Mostly, the piece of furniture rested in the office for the significance of its age and the people who used it before him. Those unused drawers were about to come in handy.

Hooking the chain that connected the cuffs together around a knob, Anton went about sliding the shackles around each of his wife's wrists. Tightening the restraints so they hung loose but still snug enough that she'd feel the metal bite against her flesh should she pull forward, Anton was satisfied with his work.

Standing straight, Anton admired the view of Viviana

restrained. Her thighs opened, her skirt up, and sex exposed. Glistening folds that were pink and swollen, her flesh flushed from top to toe, black hair fanned out over her trembling shoulders ... Hell, she was downright fucking beautiful.

Viviana squirmed under his gaze. "Jesus, you're just ..."

"What?" Anton asked, surprised at the throaty tone his voice had taken on.

"Looking at me."

Because Viviana was rounded with the life of his child, Anton knew she sometimes felt awkward about her appearance. He completely fucking refused to feed into that nonsense. Her hips had widened, her midsection swelled, and she wore her dresses a little longer than he liked sometimes. She had the best damned legs he'd ever seen. But it only served to fuel his yearning for her more. What Viviana's body could do for him—what it *did* do—drove Anton crazy every single moment he was near her.

"Yeah." Anton let his stare travel up her figure once more. "But there's something missing, baby."

Viviana recoiled, seeming hurt. "I—"

"No way. I don't want to hear a bad thing come out of that mouth. I just want to see all of you."

Popping open the clasp holding her bra together between the cups, Anton freed Viviana's breasts. With both hands, he cupped the mounds that were so heavy and hot from her pregnancy. Viviana arched into his hands, a whimper falling from her lips as he tweaked her reddened nipples between his forefingers and thumbs.

"Easy," he warned.

"I shouldn't have agreed to this."

Anton smirked, enjoying the dirty look she shot him with.

"Oh, but this is great for me, Vine. Otherwise, you'd be up against me, and he ..." Anton said with his hand rolling over her midsection, "would be in the way. That's not fair to me. I want to see your pussy when I fuck you, watch your eyes roll, and your toes curl. This is *so* much better."

"Well hurry up with it, then. After all, you're going to have an apology to accept, remember, Boss?"

Fuck, he loved that word in her mouth, all demure and sweet.

"Who's to say he's not already downstairs waiting?" Anton asked.

Viviana stilled and he took the chance to slide his boxer-briefs down enough to free the steel-hard length of his cock into a waiting palm. Sliding the tip of his cock along her wet slit, Anton watched as his wife attempted to roll her hips towards his body. The restraints keeping her wrists looked tight stopped her from moving very far without metal biting against her skin and tugging at her pulled back shoulders.

"He probably is." Anton grinned with a lift of his eyebrow. Loud noises in his office tended to travel over the empty floor of the club, and Viviana wasn't one to be quiet when he fucked her. "He likely assumes I'm up here making sure my wife understands her place, giving her a proper chitchat about it all. So, do both of us a favor, Viviana, and make sure he hears me doing just that loud and fucking clear, huh?"

Mischief glinted in her eyes when they met his. "Will do, Boss."

• • •

With her palms resting precariously close to the edge of the desk, Viviana curled her fingers around the smooth side of the wood to get a decent grip. Anticipation twisted her stomach into knots, her heart beating like a wild drum out of control. Anton's smooth as velvet voice carried through the room to caress her senses while he rubbed the length of his erection through the lips of her soaked pussy once more.

"Are you okay?" Anton asked, eyeing her shoulders.

She could feel the strain the position was putting on her back, arms, and shoulders. The sweetest burn licked at her joints, the lovely bite of metal against her wrists as she shifted with a shrug left her feeling slightly out of control and entirely vulnerable. She didn't mind being at her husband's mercy—the only mercy he did grant was to her, anyway.

"Great. Promise." By the grin he sported, Viviana thought it'd be safe to work his nerves a little more. Nothing made her husband hotter than when she irked his jealous tendencies. "Hurry up and fuck me before I get serious about that future divorce."

"Vine," he growled, the noise originating from somewhere deep in his chest.

She tried to look innocent when she blinked back at him. But, the warning in Anton's grip that was suddenly stretching her thighs wider apart, his fingers digging deliciously rough into her tender skin to make her feel the sting and want in that grasp ...

"You couldn't fucking divorce me if you tried, baby. I wouldn't *let* you."

Her heartbeat pulsed between her legs. The fake innocence was lost. She smirked up at him instead. "What kind of husband refuses to discuss money with his wife? That's sure to lead us right off a cliff eventually, Anton. Doomed from the start."

"Nuh-uh," he replied indifferently.

She opened her mouth to speak, to poke at his green monster that was never hidden quite as well as he thought it was. Her words were cut off by a sharp inhale of air slicing through her throat as the tip of his cock finally found heaven and home. With three short, sharp thrusts, each one stretching Viviana's sensitive tissues, causing her inner muscles to flex and shudder to accept his swift intrusion, he was seated inside her sex.

There was nothing quite like the way Anton filled her fully, how he took her so easily. Their bodies molded together like puzzle pieces separated from counterparts for far too long. It was a sweetened mix of delirious and perilous. The way every inch of her skin seemed to hum with electricity and life, how her nerves snapped and burned. Everything seemed to blink away, lights faded, and worries disappeared when they loved.

Viviana's voice was a whine pushing through thickened air. *"Oh."*

Saying anything else was impossible. Her throat constricted around something building. The throbbing in his shaft responded to every beat of Viviana's stuttering heart. Squirming against the handcuffs keeping her in place, she wanted him to move so she could think again.

"Please, you've got to … I need you to … move, Anton, *please.*"

The low whisper of his soothing shush did nothing to help the ache and need clawing through her chest, piercing at her skin like a cloying want that she could almost taste. Viviana whimpered, her legs moving under his guidance to wrap around his waist again.

"Holy fuck … *yeah.*" Anton groaned.

For a brief moment, he simply held them connected. Bodies tight, his hand running over the inside of her thigh to soothe the ache where he'd previously grabbed, and their gazes meeting to watch emotions flicker on past with words unsaid.

Wave after wave of surprise fueled desire washed over Viviana's suddenly hazy senses. Her entire body felt like one long, melting sigh as Anton finally began to pull out. Slowly—painfully fucking so—he began a quiet, gentle rhythm of long, smooth thrusts that filled her clenching channel with every flex of his hips.

Viviana wanted him harder, so much faster. She wanted to beg, to cry, and *need.*

"Breathe, baby, you gotta—"

Fuck, wasn't she?

Everything was lost when Anton touched her, even the most basic of instincts—*fucking everything.*

A cattish whine clawed at her throat. Viviana felt her fingers curl tighter around the edge of the desk, nails scoring into precious wood as those slow strokes of his began coming faster, sharper, and *harder.*

"There, huh? That's what you wanted. Feel me, baby."

Viviana couldn't respond behind her gritting teeth. The mewling whines crawling from her throat were growing by the second. Anton answered each one with a stronger thrust than the one that came before.

With the departure of his cock, her inner muscles grasped at his length, wanting him back, needing him there. She was so wet, the scent of her arousal clinging to the air and edging at the tip of her tongue. The echoing noise of their fucking resounded at the very base of her mind.

Eventually, the haziness saturating her vision and wits cleared. Instead of simply feeling him everywhere, Viviana could see her husband, too. The blue in his irises burned with its raging desire, that predatory gaze of his locked onto the spot where their bodies connected. His lips, parted, trembling. Both of Anton's hands rested to her hips, holding tight as his fingers dug beautifully rough into her skin. Like he wanted her—only her. And he fucked her like he owned her. Viviana loved it.

"Fuck, I needed this," Anton ground out through his teeth.

"Needed *me*."

The flick of his eyes raising to meet hers was instant. The impact of his stare was like a shock straight to her sex and heart, as if every single inch of her nervous system was reflected from his.

"Only you."

The scratching whines in her throat were building into a crescendo of high cries and moans that tumbled over her lips with every thrust of his cock. The controlled snaps of his body meeting hers had sent anything weighing less than a paperweight dropping off the desk. Viviana could feel the muscles in his lower back where her heels were pressed flexing with every movement.

With a shift of hips, Anton seemed to be searching her gaze for something. Another flex of his body into hers, the angle changing once more, and Viviana's eyes flew wide as the tip of his cock grazed her g-spot before his shaft stroked the fleshy spot entirely. Every time he filled her, Anton had her body totally aware, her legs shaking, and her mind screaming.

"There we go," Anton said as Viviana reacted to the change in his thrusts by tossing her head back. "Mmhmm, you love that. Holding onto me so damned tight, Viviana. You're ready to fucking blow—I want your sweet come all over my fucking desk, baby."

"Anton ... Jesus. Oh fucking God—*almost.*"

There was a pressure building in the base of Viviana's spine. Strong and foreign, it coiled like a tightening spring ready to snap. Now, she wanted him closer, to feel him as her body released and fell from his high spun web. Jerking at the restraints still holding tight, she was reminded that she couldn't just touch him if she wanted.

"Closer, please," she managed to plead.

Those warm, strong hands of his trailed up her sides, roaming over her breasts, up her collarbones and neck until they grasped each side of her face to hold her head still. When she came, the orgasm rushed her blood with a soaking flood of euphoria. Frantically trying to keep the slipping grip she had on the desk, Viviana curled her fingers tighter around the edge. With Anton's mouth seeking hers, she cried his name so brokenly, surprised to find his movements had slowed enough to draw out the constricting waves of her orgasm for himself.

Jerky and praying Viviana's name, Anton buried his face into the crook of her neck as he worked his way into his own orgasm a few thrusts after hers had finished. While she caught her breath, Anton pulled away from her body. A trickle of fluids leaked between her thighs to the desk and she felt him hum his approval along her collarbones. Stopping to bite and suck at her skin, her husband sighed a happy noise.

Dammit, she still just wanted to *hold* him.

Viviana whined. "Get these fucking things off."

Anton grinned against the swell of her breast. "Okay, chill

out."

A small set of metal keys were produced from a drawer. Taking the time to readjust his softening cock inside his boxer-briefs and to pull up his pants before zipping them up, Anton winked at his wife. Finally, he unlocked the cuffs from her wrists one at a time, much too slow for Viviana's liking. Feeling terribly sticky with sweat, she couldn't help but notice the heavy scent of their fucking hanging in the air.

"I'm a mess," she said as Anton clipped her bra back in pace and began the work of buttoning up her blouse. "And your office smells like sex."

"I love it," he replied, smirking up through his lashes. "Love that you'll walk out of here looking like I just fucked you, because I did. Love that you made my office smell like us and anyone with two brain cells to rub together will know it."

Heat crawled over Viviana's cheeks. "You *are* horrible."

"Never denied it."

As he wrapped his arms around her shoulders, laying a soft kiss to her temple, Viviana sunk into the embrace willingly.

"You know I was kidding about the money, right?" she asked.

"I never thought it mattered. It wasn't like you asked before. Don't you know how successful you are, Viviana?"

"Excuse me?"

"Your businesses, baby," he clarified, leaning back to raise his brow at her. "What is it, five clubs, seven restaurants, and two strip clubs spread out across Brooklyn? Something like that. You're a very successful entrepreneur. I just work under you, technically. On paper, anyway."

Viviana had to let his words absorb to understand what he was telling her. Shocked was an understatement.

"Do you mean—"

"Yes," Anton interrupted with a single nod. "When Ivan transferred all my assets into my wife's name, he transferred *all of them*. I don't know if you read the fine print in our prenuptial agreement or not, but you never have to worry about money again. Everything that's mine is yours and it always will be, even if I'm not. Legally, you bring in anywhere in the range of nine to twelve million in profit a year. Your financial profile is all handled by Ivan's offices."

"And you?" she dared to ask, not even sure she wanted to know.

Anton licked his lips, glancing away from her gaze as he admitted, "Our trade is a multibillion dollar a year business. Am I taking that big of a slice? Hell no. I am taking a hefty enough chunk of it to make me a competitor amongst many, however."

Viviana didn't know what to say. She'd previously thought he was ignoring the discussion of money, but now she knew he just simply didn't care because it was either hers, or it was money she wouldn't want to touch, anyway.

Static crackled in the air, surprising Viviana out of her internal thoughts. "Anton, are you two finished up there, yet?"

Ivan's voice coming through the conference speaker not only seemed slightly annoyed, but a little bit flustered as well. Viviana couldn't hide the embarrassment that had her inappropriate giggles building at Ivan's attempt at an innocent question.

Anton sighed, reaching over to hit the reply button. "Finished doing *what* exactly?"

Ivan spluttered. "Uh ... Well, you know ... Christ, why do you have to make this so awkward?"

"Did Kalvin come back?" Anton asked.

"Yes," Ivan replied, "and he's been waiting at least ten minutes for you."

The conference phone was clicked off. Anton's smug grin grew a little more as he leaned forward to kiss his wife all slow and sweet. "Thank you for taking your punishment so well. Smile pretty when you go downstairs, huh?"

Viviana huffed in mock offence, her hand coming up to smack at his chest. "Can I at least have my panties back?"

"Nope, they're mine, now."

Chapter Seven

"That was fast," Anton said, sitting down in the booth. It'd been exactly a week and a half since his wife's tires were slashed. He expected the sit-down with the Italian mafia boss to take at least a month to set up properly. "I appreciate it."

Conrad Carducci sipped from his to-go cup of coffee and said nothing long enough for Anton to order his own cup. "This is me extending trust," he replied, tossing a glance across the booth. "We've worked together before—"

"I paid you off, once," Anton corrected. "I killed your cousin and you took his spot after I did so. I wouldn't call that working together, but more like circumstances that fell into place for you thanks to me."

"I knew you were going to do it. I could have stopped you, or ordered someone to."

"But you didn't. Did you even have to fight for Sonny's throne?"

Conrad barked a spiteful laugh. "Fuck no. They wanted him gone. I was the next logical choice. Some were already trying to plan it, but the feds were so far down our throats over Roman's death it was ridiculous. I think they were close to coming down on Sonny for that—they just needed something else."

"Better they didn't. He still would have been running it from behind bars."

"Truth." Conrad offered the admittance without shame. "So, extending you my trust, Russian. A quick meeting, no pre-planning. I don't own this place, but it's safe, and my guys are outside out of earshot. Yours are three tables down."

Actually, just Ivan was there, and he was too far away to hear the conversation. They both handed over their guns before coming in to the café. Whether or not Anton considered that to be a show of trust was something entirely different.

"My wife's tires were slashed," Anton said as a cup of coffee was placed in front of him. "Every one of 'em right down to the rim. I managed to get it fixed and have her car brought back home before she noticed a thing out of place. Also, a photographer was seen behind our home taking pictures of Viviana. Do you happen to know anything about that nonsense, Conrad?"

The Italian's eyebrows flew up to his hairline. "I haven't any need to be bothering Viviana. And I don't think my new wife would appreciate me doing any harm to her niece."

Anton didn't realize Conrad married Sonny's widow. Then again, both he and Viviana stayed far away from her family.

"Funny, it seems like something one of your younger guys might do for some enjoyment. I don't mean to say you would order it done, but maybe they thought it would catch your attention given whose tires it was."

Conrad drummed his fingers to the table, glancing out the window to where his men stood beside a black car. "No, someone would have bragged about it, surely. Even if they were young and not yet made. They can't help but talk, the fucking idiots."

Strangely, Anton believed Conrad. The man never lied to him before, and Conrad said it himself, he had allowed the Russian boss to practically do as he pleased in regards to Sonny. There was no backlash from the Italians, thankfully. He had a sneaking suspicion the Don had his hand in that pot, too.

Well, shit. If it wasn't from Conrad's side, then Anton had done nothing but waste his time. On the better side of things, that took away one more person who wasn't fucking Anton around and each man would walk out of the meeting alive. No issues and no attitude was good for business.

"Thanks for this," Anton started to say, waving his cup and standing.

"Wait …" Conrad cleared his throat as glanced down at the table as Anton sat again. "There might be something, but

I don't think it's related at all to this. Or at least it doesn't seem like it."

"All right."

"A couple of months back there was a little talk, but it wasn't about Viviana."

Anton cocked a brow. "About me?"

"I don't know for sure," Conrad said pointedly. "It was just in general. Since it really wasn't about me, or for me, I kept my nose out of it. I figured nothing was going to come of it, either. Considering how long it's been, well, I thought nothing had come of it."

Anton was growing frustrated with the useless chatter. "And?"

"Like I said, there was talk, but it was small and no one really knew where it came from to start with. Apparently there was expected to be … *changes* … in the Russian leadership soon. Or, that's what they took it as."

Anton froze, the hot coffee he sipped burned his tongue. Changes in leadership only meant one thing. Death. "They being who?"

"Again, I don't know. Word spreads and it turns into more gossip than fact, you know that. Like I said, I didn't think much of it at the time. I still don't, Anton, even with this tire issue you mentioned. That's a bit petty, if you think about it."

"Jersey Bratva family or my Bratva?" he asked, surprised at the threatening tone he took on.

"Fuck, I wish I knew. I'll ask around, but it's likely been too long now. But if it is yours, you know as well as I do, it comes from the inside first."

That it did.

Standing from the table once more, Anton said, "Thank you for meeting me."

Conrad shrugged, offering a thin smile that held reluctance. "Forgive me, but I hope we don't need to have another one. My family has mixed with the Russians long enough, I believe."

Anton wholeheartedly agreed. The one Italian he mixed well with was his wife, and she was only half. "To keeping to our own territories, then?"

Conrad nodded and bumped his cup against the one held out to him without hesitating. "To territory."

• • •

"This is damned good." Ivan moaned, tapping his fork to a Tupperware container.

Anton grinned as Erik nodded his agreement, his mouth too full with pie to speak. Sucking the bit of sweetened pasty off the tip of his thumb, the mob boss didn't even bother to hide his smug pride at the simple gesture of other men fawning over his wife's cooking.

It might have been a little primal, but Anton didn't give a fuck.

There was no doubt about it, his wife could cook her ass off. Viviana had skills in the kitchen. She also had a tendency to make homemade pastries and sweets to decorate their kitchen with the scent of sugar and its accompanying goodness. There was nothing quite like him coming home to find their house saturated in the smell of fresh apple pie with cinnamon drifting along the edges of the wafting aroma.

It wasn't like Viviana was Suzy Fucking Homemaker. Her plans for their life didn't include a dozen children and her staying home with his kids while she was barefoot in the kitchen. But it was clear she'd picked up one hell of a thing or two from her Italian born and raised mother.

Anton was grateful for that.

Well, grateful that was if his wife didn't have gestational diabetes.

Viviana hadn't been out of his office for twenty minutes a week and a half ago before her doctor's office had put in a call to his cell phone wanting confirmation that she filled her prescriptions. Apparently Viviana wasn't answering their calls, so they assumed her husband would have the answer. If their fight about Vanessa when she showed up at his office had been bad, the one that ensued when he got home was something far worse.

Pissed off would be an understatement.

Anton didn't get pissed off at Viviana. It had been just as much unexpected as it had been hard. It was the first time in their marriage that he felt like she was purposely hiding something from him—something *important*. She should have told him immediately. That was her body and his son and he goddamn well deserved to know the moment she did.

Anton loved his wife no matter what, even when she was being particularly difficult.

But sometimes she made it hard.

Anton had cut his meeting with Kalvin short, giving the brigadier his forgiveness without an explanation, and then made his way home before the day was officially done for work. He didn't even care; he had more important things to handle at home. Like his wife and unborn son and her ridiculous need to pretend as if he wouldn't find out that shit.

Bottom line, Viviana couldn't eat what she cooked anymore.

So, when he arrived home earlier today after his sit-down with Conrad, those familiar, lovely aromas were rolling through their house. He got a tad bit worried. Anton didn't have to worry for long. Viviana snapped a Tupperware container at him and told him to get the fuck out of her house with it. Apparently those hormones of hers were making an appearance again.

The pie and all its sugary poison that Viviana couldn't enjoy anymore had remained untouched in its container.

"*Gonvo*," Erik muttered, the Russian curse coming off a whole hell of a lot like approval. "My God, Larisa is going to skin you alive if you keep feeding me this sugary crap, Anton. She's convinced *I'm* going to be the next one with diabetes."

"Well, no offence, but you're looking a little pudgy," Ivan said, side-eyeing his friend with a leer.

"Fuck you, you *govnuik*. I have the body of a God."

Anton snorted as Ivan retorted with, "A well-worn one, maybe. Don't call me a shit—"

"Stop it or no more pie." Anton hid his smirk with a turn of his head. "Just like fucking children, I swear to *God*. The both of you could use a good gym membership and twenty less pounds. Clogging up your hearts like you do, honestly. Now, shut up."

"The both of us." Erik jeered, tipping his chin at his boss. "Listen to you, prince."

"King," Ivan corrected. "The little prince grew up and knocked up a half-blood, didn't you hear?"

The oldest gentleman's hands flew up in the air, his head nodding. "My apologies—*King*."

Anton laughed deeply, rolling his eyes in amusement. These were probably the only two men on earth still alive that could tease him with all that junk and get away with it unscathed. Really, he fucking needed the lighthearted conversation and distraction anyway. There surely wouldn't be an easy thing about the conversation he was going to have with his guys once Boris finished up his business with the girls on stage.

In all truth, Anton loved sitting there listening to the friendly banter between his two spies. Rarely did they all get to sit down and enjoy one another's company privately without business or other people mucking it up with whatever nonsense. There would be business at this meeting to be sure, but it was private business he wanted to handle with them and them alone.

Viviana's surprise pastry had simply given him a reason to have Erik and Ivan meet him—one they wouldn't deny.

"Speaking of which, quit it with the prince comments around Viviana," Anton said, his tone turning a little somber. "It's making her edgy. Her being edgy makes me fucking twitchy. It's like wading through a kiddie pool and trying not to get pissed on."

"That's pregnancy. The piss is unavoidable."

"Truth." Ivan's agreement followed the jerk of his thumb at Erik who smirked.

Anton flipped them both off. "Just knock it off when she can hear, would you?"

"She does *know*, doesn't she?" Ivan leaned back in his seat, eyes sweeping the strip club's floor with boredom.

In another twenty minutes, it'd be opened for business, but as of then, it was just beginning to thrum with life. Anton owned the club, but his brigadier took all the responsibility of running the place.

"Because otherwise ..." Ivan continued, turning to face his boss, "she's going to be one pissed off woman when she's got hordes of Bratva making rounds to her house after the baby is born to say hello."

"She gets it," Anton said, frowning. "That doesn't mean she has to like it, though. Can we drop it?"

Both men nodded their agreement, settling into silence as the Tupperware container and forks were shoved off to the side. Anton looked down at the pup sniffing around his heels.

A good portion of Rocco's coat had grown back, although he still had large patches that would never produce thick hair again, but instead thin, straggly peach fuzz. The tip of his left ear was gone, no longer standing up straight and proud like it used to, only hanging limp. The pup couldn't scent like he once had, never mind seeing and hearing with the sharpness canines were known for.

Poor old Rocco, Anton mused sadly.

It didn't even matter about his issues, or the upcoming surgery to remove a bit of shrapnel still lodged in his aching hip, because Anton loved the fucking animal. Loved him to goddamn death and back. He always would. Rocco had given the boss more than anyone else ever had—next to Viviana, of course.

"Bored?" he asked the animal quietly.

A quiet chuff answered back. With what seemed like great effort, the pup rested back to its haunches and blinked at the flashing lights near the stage. The lupine cant of his head amused Anton as the pup watched the girl sway on stage with the music pumping at the floors. Even with the activity to distract him, Rocco wasn't settled.

"Viviana?" Anton asked, cocking a brow down at his pup. That worked. All attention was back on his master, a lazy tail sweeping the floor with gentle thumps. "Go get your pillow."

When the pup disappeared in search for his portable bed, Ivan laughed. "I'm surprised he's responding to you in English, now."

"Viviana refuses to talk to him in Italian and she won't learn Russian. Rocco's a quick study when he wants something—and he really wants her to talk to him whenever she's near."

"Amazing animal. Odd, though," Erik said, his fingers drumming to the table.

Anton grinned in the direction Rocco had gone. "He keeps me amused."

That was about as much as anyone got when it came to his pup and his feelings. There were some things Anton wanted to keep locked up as tight as he could get them. Someday— maybe sooner than he'd like—the pup would have to be put down. Especially if a surgery didn't go well, or his bladder let go because of stress. The variables were still up in the air when it came to Rocco.

Out of the corners of his eyes, Anton watched his two spies chat quietly. The private joke they shared had both Erik and Ivan laughing, their amusement echoing above the music pumping through the club. It bothered Anton that while he sat there, watching them, he had to consider things—consider *them*. If what Conrad had told him at their meeting had any merit about changes in leadership, maybe it was his closest guys who were causing the Russian boss problems. Whenever changes happened, that was almost always the case. Maybe it was them creating the personal attacks on Viviana because they knew how much that would bother Anton—they knew how much he loved her, unlike so many others.

He hated even thinking about it. It literally made him sick to his stomach.

Frustrated at his own thoughts, Anton settled in his seat as Rocco made his way back. The pup dropped the pillow beside Anton's feet and plopped onto the cushion with big brown eyes looking up at his master pleadingly.

"Just a little while longer, buddy," Anton promised the pup.

"Vine isn't going to like you hanging out here for too long," Ivan said, bringing Anton's attention back to his two spies.

Erik snorted under his breath. "The way you spoil that wife of yours, man."

Anton swallowed his irritation. There was no doubt Viviana would have a right fit about him being at the strip joint, even if it was for business, but he wasn't in the mood to discuss it. He'd had a difficult enough week as it was.

"I'm not here for pleasure. Besides, if I fucked around on her, it's the only time you'd have permission to knock my teeth down my throat."

Ivan smirked. "Good to know."

"Me, too?" Erik asked, winking.

Anton cocked a brow challengingly. "You'd have to lose those twenty pounds before I even considered you worthy to raise your fist."

Erik shook his head. "Christ, listen to you. I wish Daniil was here; bet he'd smack that attitude right out of you, prince."

"And he'd somehow make you feel like he was doing it for your mother, too," Boris said, clearly having heard the end of the conversation as he made his way over to the table. The brigadier pulled up a seat and sat down, picking up his glass without having missed a beat. "Daniil was fucking golden for pulling that nonsense on you when you were younger. Guilt tripped you like nothing else about how disappointed your Ma would be. Worked every time."

They snickered at their boss's expense. Anton let the men

have their moment. It was one of their ways of grieving for his father. Remembering the good times just as much as the bad were all a part of the Bratva way. There would be a lot more of that to be spread before it was over and Daniil was gone.

"Yeah, ha fucking ha," Anton said. "Deny you all loved your mothers like nothing else, too."

None of the men would.

Eventually, Ivan glanced down at his watch. "Opening in ten, boys."

"Best get it done before the clients get in, then," Erik agreed.

Anton went about explaining his theory regarding the unknown photographer from last month, and the suspicions that followed. At the mention of Tatiana, all the men wore equal expressions doused with a heavy layer of disgust. He also tacked on the slashed tires incident for Erik and Boris, seeing as how they didn't know about that or the sit-down with the Cosa Nostra boss that followed.

There were a few things Anton kept quiet about. Things like how word had been passed that maybe there would be new leadership. Because he didn't know where those words had come from, except that they'd made their way to the Italians. Anton didn't know who to trust, and he hated that it might have come from one of his closest guys.

When Anton was finished, Erik scowled. "I hate that my informants on the federal side have suddenly clammed up like they have. Something's going on there, I'm sure of it."

"Nobody's contacted me," Ivan added, giving Anton a pointed look.

There hadn't been a single backlash from the Sonny episode. Not one. It was odd considering Viviana was Anton's wife, and there had been some obvious tension between the Avdonin Bratva and Carducci Cosa Nostra families before Sonny's murder. At the very least, he should have been questioned by an agent with his lawyer present.

"I don't think it is Tatiana Belov, Boss," Boris said as he

tipped up his straight vodka and downed the rest of the glass. "The tracer checked up on her records, watched her cards for a while. Burner phones, like us, so there's nothing coming from that end. Maybe Tati is just trying to make a point with you for something different, like a crazy woman does, but it doesn't look like she's related to the photographer. That was about all she got, so she went a little deeper elsewhere, you know ... with Sergei."

"And?" Anton asked.

Boris set his glass to the table. "Seems like he had to get his daughter out of a pinch a couple of months ago. Drank herself stupid and caused a ruckus in some club over in Jersey. Surprise, surprise," he muttered dully. "If that were my daughter, I'd want her out of town getting her shit straight."

"That's likely what he did," Ivan said.

Erik rolled his eyes. "If she were my daughter, I'd beat her ass black and blue and then ship her off to rehab."

"She's twenty-seven," Anton said. "If he hasn't gotten her under control yet, it isn't going to happen."

Despite his outwardly calm appearance, Anton was infuriated. This wasn't how he wanted the conversation to go. If Tatiana was seemingly staying away from Anton's business on the mafia side of things, and his wife on a personal level, then it left him more confused than ever and still wondering who in the hell was behind the tires and pictures. That led Anton straight to a worried place that he didn't want to be.

Now, he didn't even want to be here. His wife was at home—with two bulls outside, sure—without him. Anxiety was eating away at his insides.

"I have got to get home. Thanks, Boris."

"Wait, Boss," the brigadier said, looking a little bothered. "I may have made a few calls myself, also." Anton's attention wasn't on the conversation any more, but he waited for the man to continue, anyway. "That trouble she was in ..."

"What about it?" Anton asked.

"Russian, apparently. A boy, specifically. Nobody wanted to name names, or they simply didn't know who it was. Sergei might have found out I was asking around, too. Sorry about that."

Anton beat back his irritation. Was that the friend Tatiana mentioned during their first encounter? "Ivan, call that bastard and set up one more fucking sit-down. If he doesn't show ... No forgiveness this time. We take him out."

Chapter Eight

Anton's fist slammed into the dead weight.

Fucking hell, it felt good to hit something.

Stepping back to adjust his stance, his knuckles slammed out and cracked into the red bag again. He'd been working out his aggression and frustrations for a little over an hour. Sweat had dampened his hair and slicked his skin. The T-shirt he previously wore had long been tossed off, the fabric only serving to make him feel restricted.

With a grunt, he stepped back and struck out again, feeling a faint sting radiate through his muscles with a burn that said his body was finally starting to tire. After his meeting earlier in the day with his guys, Anton really needed a moment to decompress and relax.

Hitting things made him relax.

So did shooting shit, but beating the hell out of the punching bag in his basement and running himself dead on the treadmill seemed like a less illegal option. At least he wouldn't get locked up for a night in jail for shooting off a gun.

It was a win all the way around.

So, he hit the fucking bag with unprotected knuckles. Anton let the pain register instead of allowing the feelings to roll off his body like it usually would. Letting the natural adrenaline pump through his blood, he was revving and ready to go, but he was finally starting to calm, too. His teeth clenched, and his gaze narrowed in on the swinging bag as he fought back against the stress running his life.

Fuck, Anton wished he knew what in the hell was going on around him. He hated not knowing things. Between the photographer, the slashed tires, and his wife's diabetes ... add in a sick father, the changes in his life, and everything else surrounding those issues, it was just ...

Too damned much.

Anton didn't know who to trust. The meeting with the Cosa Nostra boss had only served to make him think about the people around *him*. It took his mind off the people he thought had been involved, and made him look at his own. People he was close to, who would have never been a thought in his mind before. Was it possible that one of his guys were planning to make a move on him?

Something tasting a fuck lot like betrayal stung on his tongue.

Viviana's quiet sigh barely broke through his concentration. "Rocco has been whining at the top of the stairs for the last hour. He wants to be down here with you."

Another punch landed to the hard, red fabric. "He needs to get down the stairs by himself. That physical therapy I pay for twice a week isn't for nothing, Vine. The pup knows he can do it, he just doesn't like the pain that comes with it. You know he needs to learn to work through it."

"Or you could just go up there, pick him up, and carry him down the fucking stairs like you usually would," she argued.

Anton scowled, turning his head just enough to see his wife in the corners of his eyes. Her long, black hair had been pulled up in a high ponytail, the scar above her eyebrow more pronounced as she cocked a brow back at her husband. Wearing tiny shorts and one of his old high school baseball hoodies, she seemed smaller than normal.

"I had him with me all day, baby."

"I know that," Viviana said, rather shortly.

"No, clearly you don't. I had him with me all day." Frustration ran rampant as Anton stopped his workout with the punching bag. "I didn't carry him once and he did just fine. Rocco can walk down those goddamned stairs without my help. Stop babying him—he needs this, Viviana. You're not helping him, not like you think. That dog needs us to challenge him more or he'll do nothing but lay around and wait for everyone else to do everything for him. We can't keep relying on his meds to handle the pain. He'll become *dependent*."

Viviana gasped sharply. Where had all that come from, anyway? Hell, he never raised his voice to his wife, never mind reprimanding her like she was a child. The water blinking back in her gaze told him he'd crossed a line ... or two. Damn, he might as well have just jumped over the whole invisible fence.

Confused and hurting, Anton rubbed his hands over his face, wiping away the sweat that had gathered above his brow. "Ivan and Erik said thank you for the pie, by the way."

Viviana said nothing in response, instead staring back at him blankly.

"Did you do okay with your insulin to—"

"Hit the bag, Anton."

"What?" he asked turning on her.

Viviana waved at the punching bag. "Hit it. Isn't that what you want?"

Yes and no, he thought. The adrenaline was beginning to ebb away. "I don't know."

While his body was working on overtime, his mind was starting to shut the fuck down. Anton could feel that familiar coldness seeping into his veins, the desire to shut off his emotions banging through like a drug. It was what the boss did whenever he couldn't, or didn't want to, deal. This was one of those times.

But, this was his wife, his life, and his home.

It wasn't the same.

"Come here," he demanded, jerking his head at his wife.

Viviana didn't move. "No."

"What?"

"I'm not a puppy, or one of your men. You can't order me around like one, either. Hit your bag, Anton. I'm going to bed."

It wasn't a second later that his wife had disappeared, her soft footfalls echoing up the staircase to the first floor. Anton was left stunned and more befuddled than ever. Shit, why did being married have to be so difficult at times?

Anton made his way across the room before taking the stairs two at a time. Following the path Viviana would have taken to their bedroom, he had plenty of time to gather his thoughts about what had just occurred between them and where he went wrong. It probably started with the fact that he knew she had been standing in their basement watching him for over an hour and she didn't say a thing. He also hadn't spoken to her during that time. That, for the most part, had been their week in a nutshell.

Anton was still pissed about her hiding the need to start insulin, resulting in his self-imposed silent treatment to his wife. Sure, they spoke here and there, sharing the occasional good morning or kiss goodnight, but it hadn't gone further than that. In fact, he hadn't been truly close to his wife all week. Damn, he hadn't loved her physically once all week, either. That was the longest time since Anton had gotten Viviana back that they hadn't had some kind of physical intimacy.

Leaning in their bedroom doorway, he took note of the fact that a basket of baby clothes was sitting at the edge of their bed. Cleaned, folded, and waiting to be put away, it looked like Viviana had made herself busy during his time away from the house, anyway.

"Listen, I'm sorry," Anton said, flinching when the quiet whine of Rocco downstairs said the dog wanted to be brought up with his masters.

"Goodnight, Anton."

"Viviana—"

"I said goodnight."

The clipped bite in her words stung his skin like they were exposed nerve endings.

Swallowing his instant mean reply, he brushed off the anger at her rejection. "Why didn't you tell me about the gestational diabetes the moment you found out? Why, huh? All you had to do was call me, baby. That was it. Just pick up your fucking phone and *dial*."

"Is that what all of this is about?" Turning on her heel, Viviana pressed her fists into her hips and glared at him. "Are you still angry with me over that?"

"I'm not angry—" Anton stopped abruptly, because yeah, he was mad. If he considered it, even during their previous argument, he hadn't once told Viviana he was angry with her for hiding it. He'd said a lot of things, but not that. "Yes. God, yes, I'm so angry with you over that. It's not a real great thing, Vine. It worries the hell out of me. Do you realize the shit I've got going on right now? I blink all of that away when you come into the picture, but when you pull crap like this, I just … it only adds to it."

"No!" Viviana barked.

Anton felt his spine crack as he stood ramrod straight. "Excuse me?"

"*No.* I haven't a clue what you've got going on. You haven't told me anything. You don't tell me, so how can I?"

Speechless would be an understatement. Anton tried to speak but the words just wouldn't form. Instead, they lodged in his clenching throat like the proverbial knife twisting in his heart. It certainly didn't help that Anton suddenly felt like a giant hypocrite. He was frustrated with her for not telling him something important, but wasn't he doing the exact same thing?

"Say something," Viviana whispered. "My God, Anton, just talk to me. If you want to yell because I made a shitty choice, do it. Just please stop ignoring me. It *hurts.*"

Anton released the air he didn't realize he was holding in. "Daniil is dying."

Viviana blinked and wet her lips. "That's not news, babe."

Her words weren't meant to hurt, he knew, but they did nonetheless. "No, Vine. Dad—my *Papa*—is dying. Not my brigadier, or the Bratva's man, *my* Papa. I'm going out of my mind over it. I don't know how to comfort my mother. I want him to know my son and he *won't.* I can't seem to even cry. It aches.

"There's people photographing you in our backyard and I don't know who the fuck it is," Anton continued, fisting his hands at his sides. The pain of his fingernails cutting into his flesh barely even registered. "I thought it was the feds, but it probably isn't. There's other crap happening, too, but I don't want to worry you right now when you're pregnant. Then, I thought Tati was pulling a stunt, but that's coming to a dead end, too."

"That's why my bulls have been sticking closer, huh?" she asked, frowning.

"Partially," Anton said. It was a bit of a relief to get some of it off his chest. "I didn't want to worry you, but it's starting to worry me. I want you out of state next week. I'm hoping to have a sit-down coming up with Sergei, and I don't want you within a hundred miles of it."

Viviana didn't look pleased but she nodded. "Okay." Then, she looked up at him, her brown eyes filled with tears and beginning to spill over. "Anything else?"

"Yeah, I'm freaking out."

Her laughter was a sweet balm to his hardened soul. "About what?"

"This," he said with a wave between them. "I can handle you, being a husband, whatever, but this baby ..."

"You're going to be a great dad." Viviana smiled to tell him she was being truthful. "I'm sorry Daniil isn't going to see the payoff of his hard work with his own son, but you know everything is going to be fine, Anton. He raised an intelligent, charming, reliable man. You work loyalty, pride, and love like it's a second job. He taught you that and Christ, there's nothing wrong with feeling exposed sometimes. All you have to do is talk to me."

"I don't like being angry with you. I don't get angry with you, Viviana, and now I know why. This week just sucked in a whole bunch of ways."

She traced the silver comforter on their bed with a single finger, sighing softly. "For me, too."

• • •

Letting his words and confessions sink in, Viviana felt an invisible weight fall from her shoulders. All week she'd been tied up in knots because she couldn't get him past a simple hello, not without that fire in his gaze and heat in his tone. Now, she understood why.

"Where'd you meet up with Ivan and Erik?" she asked, wanting to cool their conversation from the difficult topics a bit.

Anton cleared his throat, shifting on his feet and looking guiltier than she expected. "Velvet Ropes."

Jealousy raged through her emotions like a wrecking ball, but Viviana forced herself to stay calm. In all truth, her husband never gave her a reason to believe he strayed from their marriage. Anton loved her—she knew it. That didn't mean she liked him in a place where women took off their clothes for a living.

"Your strip club in Brighton Beach?"

"Yeah, shit, I know you don't—"

"Did you go there because you were pissed off at me, or what?" Viviana asked, letting the coolness seep into her tenor. She couldn't hide the hurting shake in her words, either. "God, that's fucking ridiculous, Anton."

"No," he stated, shaking his head. "I had to meet up with Boris about whatever he found out regarding Jersey. The club was closed, so no one was going to be stepping in on the discussion that didn't need to overhead, okay?"

"But the girls were there?"

Anton's confusion furrowed his brow. "It was close to opening time, so yeah, of course."

"Of course," she mocked. "What, a random restaurant wouldn't have worked just as well?"

"I needed to speak with Boris. He was *working*."

Viviana didn't even want to hear it. "And I bet you got a nice show all the while huh?"

Anton choked on nothing, his eyes flying wide at her

veiled accusation. "What? No, it's not like that at all."

When Anton moved forward, Viviana stumbled a full step back. A pained grimace took hold of his features when she said, "I don't even want to know, Anton. Don't bother lying, I'd rather you didn't say anything at all."

"Oh my God, will you shut up?" he growled. "Chill out with the sensitivity. Why would you assume that I'm going to find the closest pair of tits or pussy that I can and take the girl to bed?"

"Maybe because I'm pregnant, bitchy, and horrible right now?"

Anton was goddamned gorgeous. Six feet tall, built like a brick house, and looks any woman would die over. It wasn't that Viviana thought girls didn't notice her husband, but she didn't like to think about him noticing them.

"We've had the worst week together—the hardest since we married. Would it be so crazy for me to think you're sick and tired of this if you can't even be bothered to open your mouth and speak to me? You wonder why, Anton? *Really*?"

Apparently that was the wrong thing to say, because he crossed the space between them in three long strides. His hand fisted into the sweater she wore, tugging her into his chest as a sob caught in her throat.

"Just … stop it. That's not what it was. I love *you*. I only want *you*." The words were spoken into her hair so strong and sure. When Viviana didn't say anything, Anton squeezed her tighter. "Come on. Let's get out of here."

"It's ten at night."

"I know, but I need to do something. I'd really like it if my wife was there with me."

Viviana didn't even hesitate. "Okay. Let's go."

"Pack a bag."

"A bag?" she asked, feeling his smile curve against her hair.

"Yeah. Whatever we need for a few days."

Viviana could have argued that he had work to do, that

people here needed them, not to mention her classes. They couldn't simply upheave everything and forget about it just so they could take a minor vacation away from stress and life. Or, could they? She could have just as easily denied the request, but she didn't want to. Anton hadn't been hers all week, not like he usually was. If he was offering to give that back to her, however it was that he wanted to do so, she wouldn't refuse it.

Releasing his hold on her, Anton said, "I have to make a couple of calls, but I'll meet you downstairs."

"Where are we going?"

Anton shrugged before tugging her closer once more. "Somewhere quiet."

• • •

"Anton?"

"Ma, hey." Anton's throat felt sore, like someone was tugging an invisible noose tighter and tighter around his windpipe. He barely noticed the cars he passed on the highway, but the sleeping form beside him in the passenger seat had every damned bit of his attention. "Is Daniil awake?"

"Not really," Sasha said. "He's in and out mostly. They just administered more of his pain medication an hour ago."

"Will he talk, though?"

"For you, always. You know that. But I don't want to wake him, he had a rough day."

"Dial the meds back. Please, you know I wouldn't ask otherwise. Just enough for him to get on the phone. I need to talk to him for a minute."

Sasha seemed like she was going to argue but then agreed instead. Maybe the desperation Anton was feeling had been manifesting in his voice. The quieter things grew around him, the louder he could hear his thoughts beginning to scream. He had too much time to think about the things happening in his life on this drive. Viviana had fallen asleep within thirty minutes of pulling out of their driveway, so he didn't have her to distract him.

The only person he figured he could talk to was his father. Daniil would understand; he always had.

"I'll call you back," Sasha said. "I don't know what's wrong, but don't make him fret, Anton. I know you think he doesn't worry, but right now, that's all he ever does."

His mother hung up without another word. Overwhelmed, Anton tugged the Bluetooth out of his ear and dropped it to his lap. Without his mother's voice in his ear, the car had turned silent again except for Rocco's gentle huffs from the back seat and Viviana's occasional mumble. There was another three hours of driving before he reached his destination, so Anton could wait for his father to get up and around.

He also didn't know why he chose the lodge in Vermont, but it had been the first thing that popped into his head when he asked his wife to leave with him. It was always a safe place for his family. They had made some of the best memories there, especially when he was growing up.

Maybe that's what he was chasing, or it could have just been what he needed.

Forty silent minutes later, the cell and Bluetooth in Anton's lap began vibrating with a call. Placing the earphone back in his ear, he switched the call on but couldn't bring himself to speak as he listened to the shallow, painful breaths of his father on the other end of the receiver.

Anton didn't have to say a thing, anyway. Daniil just seemed to know. "Ant, whatever it is, it'll be okay."

The tears in his eyes made the road in front of him bleed together in the shine of the headlights. "Papa ..."

"Jesus, you haven't called me that in years," Daniil coughed out.

"I know. I'm sorry I stopped. I just—"

"Grew up," his father interrupted with a stronger voice than before. "You grew up, Anton, like every boy does. It just so happened you grew up a little quicker than others. I didn't mind; it was amazing to watch you do it. My son became a

110

great man—strong inside and out. Would I have given up who you are now to have you see me as your daddy for a few more years? No. Your mother always thought we made you like this, but we didn't. You did it all by your own choice, and I just *let* you while the rest of us watched. It's okay, son. Everything is *fine*."

No, no it isn't, Anton thought anxiously.

"I think someone is planning to come in on me." Anton's gaze slid to the sleeping girl beside him. The last thing he needed was for Viviana to hear him confessing his worries that someone was going to make an attempt on his life. "Someone close to me. That's how it always is, Dad. It has to be somebody close, I just can't figure out who. Or maybe I don't want to. It's probably staring me right in the face but I'm too fucking close to these guys so I can't see it objectively."

"Whoa, slow down," Daniil whispered.

Even the words felt painful and Anton immediately felt guilty for waking his father up for this. The cancer his father was suffering from was constantly eating away at his body and strength. Anton didn't want to take any more from his father than what the sickness already had.

"Someone's going to make a move on me. I know it. They're screwing around with my wife but only in ways that I see it so that it bothers me because it's personal shit. Slashed her tires, Dad. Taking pictures of her when she's at home. Tatiana has been around, but I think she's just playing her old tricks. Even those fucking Italian scum heard things might be changing in the brotherhood soon. It's messing with my head."

For a long while, Daniil was silent. "What did Nicoli always tell you about this?"

"I don't know. I can't even think right now."

"Goddamn it, Anton, yes you do."

"It's always somebody close," Anton replied, forcing himself to say it. He didn't want to think what that meant, honestly. His spies were the closest anyone was ever going to get to him, next to his own wife, of course. "That's what Nicoli would have said. To look at your sides first and then go outward. I was with them today, Daniil. Ivan and Erik ... I can't see it. It's because I'm too close to them, isn't it?"

"No. That's not it at all. You're not seeing it because it isn't there."

"It is!"

Viviana mumbled unhappily in her sleep, and Anton cursed himself silently. When his wife was settled, he sighed in both relief and worry and went back to his call.

"It's there, Dad. I can feel it. Something is coming."

"I'm not saying it's not happening at all, I'm just saying it's not there with your spies, boy."

Now, Anton was just confused. "But—"

"Erik is a complacent fucker," Daniil said sharply. "He likes access to the money and he works the cash well. What he doesn't want is the responsibility of making it, Anton. He's also loyal to a damned fault, ask anybody. You just happen to be the one he's loyal to. There isn't enough money in this world to make him bite the hand that feeds him, not when he likes that hand."

"And Ivan?"

Daniil barked a sour laugh. "Really, Ant? You have to think about that at all? My God, that man is only in the Bratva for *you*. Saved his fucking life when you were just fourteen. I would have blown his brains out the night he screwed up my guys' steal on that truck had you not been there. He owed you then and he owes you now. Give him the chance to save your life too someday, huh?"

That much was true. It was also the exact reason why Anton couldn't see the possibility of his two spies being the ones who were planning to off him.

"Am I making a big deal out of this?" Anton asked. "Am I just paranoid because Vine's pregnant and life is changing for me, or what?"

"No," Daniil said softly. "Absolutely not. You don't get

paranoid. Nicoli practically culled all of that nonsense right out of you growing up. If you worry, you have a reason to. He taught you to think logically first. Made you look around and consider everything before you chose your path. This isn't any different. He gave you Ivan and Erik because they were the best for you. Look outward from your sides, Anton, that's what you have to do now. It's not them, I'm sure of it."

Anton's mind was already starting to drift to the next possibilities. His brigadiers, their issues, if there were any, and why. After all, that was the next valid choice to who was the closest, who had access, means, and mode. There weren't a whole lot to consider as they were all on a pretty tight leash and there hadn't been any problems. Well, except for Viktor, the brigadier who had his fingers and jaw broken for hurting Viviana when Anton sent for her the year before. But even that seemed unlikely as Viktor was another one, complacent in his place, unfit for the job of Pakhan, and happy to stay where he was.

"It really messed me up today," Anton said as his grasp on the steering wheel tightened. "I was dealing with crap from Viviana but on the side, I couldn't get this out of my head. I was sitting there with Ivan and Erik, just laughing like we do, and I couldn't help but wonder, Dad. What if they were coming in on me and I didn't know it? What if, right? I *couldn't* ..."

"Stop looking at them."

"I am. I just needed you to tell me to do it, too."

Daniil wheezed into the phone before asking, "What are you doing right now?"

"Driving out to the lodge," Anton said with a chuckle. "It was the only place I could think to find some peace from this crap. Take a week to think, maybe."

"Take a week," Daniil repeated. "Don't be Pakhan, Ant. You said you were dealing with Vine, too, so ..."

"This husband job is something else. Ten times more stressful than being a mob boss. Sometimes I swear she's just being difficult because she can, or because she wants to push my buttons. She hid stuff from me and I couldn't believe it. Ate at me all damned week."

Anton swore he could see his father smiling as Daniil laughed. "The diabetes?"

"Yeah, how'd you know?"

"Your mother mentioned something about it. You know she's chatty when she's bored. And about Vine … She's a woman—yours, actually—so did you think it was going to always be easy? Marriage is tough, son. Take this week and work on loving your wife like she needs you to right now. It'll clear your head a little more about the rest if you focus on her for a while, trust me. Nicoli taught you about being a boss. I taught you how to be a man. Vine is teaching you how to be hers. Everything else in your life has worked out, why wouldn't this, too? Have a little faith."

Faith wasn't going to save his father.

"What am I going to do without you, huh?" Anton asked brokenly.

"You'll go on with your life." Daniil's words held that confident knowing he always seemed to have. "You'll raise that boy of yours like I did you because that's how you'll remember me and our life. You'll smile a little less for a while, but it'll get better. I'm not leaving you, Ant, I'm just leaving here."

"But—"

"But nothing. Don't be afraid of losing me, Anton."

"How can I not?"

"Because you'll always have me, somewhere. That's life. It's how we continue beyond beating hearts and breathing lungs. Things live, they die, and then memories take over."

"He's never going to know you, though. My son, I mean. Not like I do."

Once more, Daniil laughed, but it was more distant than before. "I'll see him once, I have to. After that, you'll tell him the rest. I have no worries there."

"Promise?"

"Yeah, son. I promise."

• • •

A breeze of air skimmed Viviana's naked shoulder. From the curve of her neck down to her arm, the draft followed the softest touch trailing her skin. In the background of her hazy senses, bleary from just beginning to wake up, she could hear a throaty hum building with desire.

Oh, yes, she could feel that desire growing hard against her backside pressed tight to Anton's groin under the sheets. His fingers curved into her hip grabbed tighter, pulling her closer into his heat and want.

Blinking away the sleep from her eyes, Viviana sighed into the warm body of her husband. Had daylight come already? She barely remembered the night before. It was only vague flashes of them leaving the house, toting a sleepy Rocco along for the ride. She hadn't been in their SUV for more than five minutes before Viviana passed out. Apparently she had been more tired than she thought.

Actually, she couldn't even recall where it was that they had ended up.

"Morning," she mumbled sleepily.

Anton shook his head behind her. "It's only like four in the morning. I just ..."

As he trailed off, she realized he was right. The room they slept in was still dark, and the window she was staring out of still blinked stars brightly in the sky.

"You just what?"

Anton breathed heavily, his face burying into her neck as his palm rolled over her side to lay flat against the hard roundness of her stomach. "Needed you," he said darkly. "Just need you, Vine. Right now. I haven't been close to you all week, and I can't fucking sleep because I haven't touched you or tasted you on my mouth in way too long. *I need you.*"

The desperation echoing in his strong tenor had Viviana's insides reacting instantly. It was like every inch of her soul was suddenly clawing to get out, to reach him. Already, her blood was singing as tendrils of lust and love swarm in her veins. Her lungs expanded as his hand roamed lower, spreading her legs gently as deftly talented fingers slipped and pressed between the folds of her sex with no hesitation.

"I love the feel of you like *this*. Warm and soft and wet." Anton's two fingers were slipping into her throbbing core. The groan he hid in the side of her throat reverberated to her heart. Nothing would ever dim the sound enough that she wouldn't hear it. It was his approval doused with a heavy mixture of need. "So fucking hot for me, baby. Always soaking me with that sweet honey of yours. I want you twisting in these sheets, screaming my name. I just ... fuck, I need to feel you."

Viviana whimpered, turning her face into the heated flesh of his arm that she had been using as a pillow. Her hips rolled involuntarily into the hand fucking her as her toes curled into soft sheets. When his teeth nipped along the tender spot behind her ear, she shuddered and turned again to find his lips ghosting over her cheek.

"I'm sorry for this week," she said, wanting him to know while she could still think to speak. Anton hummed a dark sound that had her lust spiking higher before he kissed the corner of her mouth. Maybe he didn't want to hear it, she didn't really know, but Viviana didn't feel like she had a choice, either. "So sorry, Anton."

"God, none of that, please." Anton dotted kisses along Viviana's cheek, his fingers taking on a deeper, harder rhythm. The tone of his voice seemed to come from inside his chest, forcing its way out from the back of his throat. Her sex's juices were smearing between her thighs, the sticky fluid coating her mound, slicking up her skin. "Not now, maybe tomorrow ... I don't *care*."

Viviana shook her head, feeling wildly out of control. That burning coil in her middle was beginning to twist so deliciously, a pressure already building in the base of her spine. How her husband always managed to get her body reacting so quickly, rising to beautiful, blissful heights so easily, she would never understand.

"Screw all of that," Anton said forcefully. "I only want to feel *this*."

"Jesus. I'm s-so, so close." Another shudder wracked her shoulders. His teeth bit into her jaw as a thick cry rolled over her trembling lips. "*Anton ...*"

"There we go. That's what I needed, baby."

It was whispered over her skin like a prayer, soothed into her rushing ears as the orgasm threw her off the waiting precipice without abandon. Repeating his words throatily into her mouth as he turned her body in his embrace, Viviana immediately felt the loss of his fingers. Their kiss deepened as she drowned in the safety and warmth of Anton's strong hold. Allowing him to dominate the kiss, to hold her tighter because she knew he needed to, she finally felt okay for the first time in a week.

"More." Already, Viviana wanted to beg. "Please."

Anton shook his head under her jaw, tilting his head up enough to kiss her chin. "Sleep, Vine. That's what I wanted the most, to feel you, hear you. Sleep for me."

"But—"

A soft click of his tongue stopped her argument up short. "You're tired and I know it."

The sudden flurry of activity from her midsection had Anton chuckling darkly in the room. The baby gave a sharp kick to the spot under her ribs and she whined low. Demyan was a strong little thing for having such a tiny presence. Without a word, Anton pushed the sheets from her body, moving down to roll hot hands over the baby that didn't seem to appreciate the surprise wake-up from his father. Near silently, he kissed and soothed with words Viviana couldn't hear let alone understand, but the familiarity and love in his actions rang loud and clear. Eventually, the baby boy's movements calmed enough for Viviana to be comfortable again.

"Sleep for me?"

"Love me so good in the morning?" Viviana asked.

Anton smiled lazily. "Like crazy."

Chapter Nine

Anton's breaths came out shallow and ragged. The constant throb in his cock as it found heaven and home inside of Viviana's pussy was a beat out of control. Tension had his muscles locking up tight like nothing else. Hot, overworked, and ready to blow, he reveled in the teasing bliss just beyond his grasp—he was nearly fucking there.

The faint sting of pain felt like heaven as his wife's fingernails scored lines from the top of his chest to the clenching abs of his midsection. There were sure to be marks left as her hands curled into balled fists, her shaking legs resting to either side of his body tightening as her walls clamped down on his cock hard and hot and sweet.

The smell of their sex saturated the room, and Anton was pretty fucking sure that was his favorite aroma in the entire world right then. He'd had access to the most expensive wines and perfumes in the world, but not a damned one of them compared to this right here. Nothing could seep into his senses, take over his heart, and creep around the edges of his mind for the rest of the day like he and his wife.

Above all else, Viviana was still *life* to Anton.

Golden, beautiful, and true.

Ripe with pregnancy, flushed with love, and her body burning up to a fever, Anton couldn't take his gaze off his wife if he tried. With her head tossed back and tendrils of wavy, raven colored locks fanned over her naked shoulders, she was so fucking sexy it hurt.

After all, every king needed his queen.

Her rolling cries had reached a gasping octave. Tiny beads of perspiration gathered between the valleys of her heavy breasts that he had cupped in each of his hands. She rode him slow and lazy, soaking up every inch of his body, taking in every inch of his length. Her pace was tantalizing and her concentration strong, determination and want for that ecstasy writing lines over her face.

Anton couldn't help but remember an earlier time—one when they both were young, stupid, and new to *them*. She'd been so nervous taking him like this, then. Worried how her sweet sixteen looked to his older eighteen. Embarrassed because she didn't know what to do, or how to move. Shocked and awed when it felt so good when she finally did find that rhythm.

It surely wasn't the same, now, but it was still so much better.

Wetter than ever and working on her fourth orgasm of the morning, Viviana seemed to have found that previous lustful drive her pregnancy had hidden from her for a while. While the start of her condition had left his wife insatiable for sex, touch, and love in any physical capacity, he hated seeing it dim like it had in the last couple of months.

Anton sure as fuck wasn't about to complain.

He needed his wife like lungs needed air.

She made his heart beat so fast it ached.

Slicked with arousal, fist-tight, and hot like a fire, Viviana's sex was heaven as it took in his cock, letting it fill and stretch her. Anton had the very best view of his member sinking in with every rise and lower of her body on top of his.

He was soaked from tip to hilt with her.

Holy fucking hell, his whole nervous system felt covered in *her*.

Pinching her nipples between his thumb and finger, it earned Anton one of Viviana's quiet gasps. Taking his cock in again, she rolled her hips roughly, her walls flexing with the movements in a way that had Anton's air catching in his throat like a choke hold.

"Shit," he hissed, feeling that familiar built up of pressure starting to release. "Holy hell, slow down for a second."

Viviana's pretty, pink lips curved with a slow, sly smile as she shook her head above him. When her hips came down, rolling a circle over his groin, taking his cock so fucking deep,

Anton couldn't ignore the tension building in his stomach at a rapidly surprising pace. She fit him like a glove. There was no chance of him beating the orgasm back. None at all.

"Vine, Vine, Vine …" Anton felt suffocated by the singing release that was edging around his wits. Losing it, he was so fucking close to losing it all. "Baby … Viviana, you've *got* to stop … you need to or I'm gonna—"

"Come," she said on a high sigh.

Yeah, that did it. Anton dug his fingers into the soft flesh of her ass, wanting to hold her still and tight as he groaned a low, throaty noise. Those hands of hers laid flat to his stomach, her thumbs sweeping from side to side as he came deep inside of her pussy, his seed filling her in thick, ropey streams.

This time it was Viviana above him with her voice quiet and shushing soothingly as her hands traveled upwards to his jaw. Anton didn't realize how fiercely he'd clenched his teeth, how tight his jaw had turned, until her fingers were dancing over his face to calm and hold.

Slowly, he released his grip on her backside, rubbing over the spots to help aid any ache he may have caused. Viviana didn't seem to mind as she hummed above him. Anton breathed a sigh through his nose, blinking up at his wife with a shake of his head. She grinned, her tongue peeking out between her teeth.

"Love you."

"Like crazy," he said, surprised at the hoarseness of his tone. "Jesus, you could have given me a moment to think, baby."

She shrugged her dainty shoulders. "That was kind of nice." Anton's confusion must have shown on his face, because she added, "Seeing you lose all that control. I never get to see that. I loved it."

Damn, his cock sure as hell loved it, too.

Leaning down over his form, Viviana snuggled tight to Anton's chest. Holding her tight, he brushed the black hair off her shoulders, exposing skin so he could kiss away the damp sweat that had gathered. In his ear, her voice was muted and soft, her lips brushing over his chest as she spoke.

"About Velvet Ropes yesterday."

Anton froze. "What about it?"

"I overreacted a little, huh?"

"A little," Anton said. "I had to meet Boris there because he had things to do at the club on the work side of things. I was telling the truth."

"And?"

"And nothing. I know you don't like it, but I'm not there for the show, baby."

Anton really wished they weren't having the conversation in bed, but Viviana seemed to be taking it well. While he was known for his jealousy when it came to his wife, he didn't think she realized how strongly her emotions burned when she thought another woman was in the picture, either.

Viviana cleared her throat, pushing up out of his embrace. Something unknown flashed in her brown eyes, something worrisome. "I really don't want to ask. I shouldn't have to." Viviana frowned, not meeting Anton's gaze. "I *know* I shouldn't. It's not even a possibility, and I know it inside …"

"Ask what?"

"If you're finding something elsewhere," she said.

Anton's first instinct was to deny that statement. To correct what he considered to be totally ridiculous assumptions, but he heard what she had said, too. There was no doubt Viviana's insecurities reared their ugly heads because of her pregnancy and the hormonal shifts were something her husband was only now starting to learn to roll with.

He lived a tricky life. Drugs, dangerous situations, and women made a daily appearance. And if he really thought about it, more than anything, Viviana believed what she had seen and what she was told because that's what she knew. He also knew she was a different kind of woman because she would ask when others wouldn't.

"I'm only *yours*," he said strongly, reaching up to grab her face and force her to look at him.

"I know," she said, blinking away tears. "I feel so crazy thinking about it because I know it's not even a thought in your head. I worry, though. I hate some of the places you do business, Anton. If I own that business, I should sell it out from under you. That'd make me feel better. I'm just saying."

He hid his amusement at her rant with kiss. "You're terribly cute when you're jealous, baby."

"I'm not—"

Anton didn't allow her to finish the sentence before he had her lifted from his body and her back falling to the bed. Viviana hit the mattress with wide eyes, flowing hair, and an oomph falling from her pretty mouth. Looming over her, he barricaded her body under his, feeling the gentle kicks of his son between their forms

"You are jealous, admit it." Anton kept his tone teasing and light.

Viviana drew her plump bottom lip between her teeth. "Okay, I'm jealous as hell."

"Kind of like when I want to throttle any man who glances your way for longer than a second, right?" When Viviana didn't answer, Anton heaved a sigh. "Not that you need to worry. I don't even need to tell you, really. I love waking up beside you in the morning, hearing you hum in the shower, watching you baby the shit out of our dog even when I tell you not to.

"Speaking of which," he said, tilting his head towards he closed door. "I should get up and get him outside for a walk. You should get some chow, check your sugars, and take your insulin, yeah?"

Viviana nodded, but it didn't look so sure. "Where are we, anyway?"

Anton coughed out a laugh. "I practically carried you in from the car last night."

"That doesn't answer my question."

"Out of state."

"Oh," she said, dimly.

"Yeah, that's about all I want to say. Just know that if I have to go for that meeting with Jersey in a few days, you'll be safe. It might be a little earlier than what I would have brought you out here, but it worked just as well. Our stuff is handled for a few days and the bulls are sleeping downstairs," Anton explained, assuming Rory and Joe were still snoring off the late night drive. "Just us, and they shouldn't be too much of a bother, so let's relax, baby."

"Relax," she repeated quietly.

Anton grinned. "Sounds like heaven, huh?"

Looking a little brighter than before, Viviana winked. "Sounds fantastic."

• • •

Viviana stared out the large bay window, absently rubbing her hand over her stomach. Her baby was being particularly restless, and whenever she sat down, he became even more troublesome to her insides. She couldn't help but wonder if Demyan was trying to tell her he was getting bored with his comfortable, safe home.

It also didn't escape her notice that she had the strangest ache in her back and Braxton Hicks contractions. Nearly eight months pregnant, Viviana should have been expecting the late pregnancy symptoms, but they still came as a surprise.

The beautiful, large lake the front of the lodge led to didn't give her a single clue about where they were. With its sparkling water and quiet atmosphere, it was a peaceful sight. Sure enough, it didn't seem to be a very populated place, wherever it was. Across the lake, there was a smaller cabin, but it didn't appear to be inhabited.

"Hey, Vine."

Viviana turned at Rory's voice, offering her bull a smile as his bleary one met hers. The sounds of footsteps echoing in the back hallway of the lodge followed a door closing. That must have been Joe making his way to the bathroom.

"Morning, Rory."

"Where's Boss?"

With a wave at the window, she said, "With Rocco."

When her stomach tightened, Viviana grimaced. Rory took note immediately. "You okay?"

Viviana didn't want to worry anyone, but the fake contractions were annoying. Random and varying in their length and intensity, they mostly felt like moderate cramps. Huffing uncomfortably, she rolled the heel of her palm against her side, wishing it would just stop.

"Yeah, but could you go find Anton for me?" Anton would want to know if she was in pain, or if something was happening with the baby that worried her. "Tell him not to rush, or whatever."

Rory sported a panicked frown. "Vine, is the baby—"

"Just fake contractions," she interjected quickly. "Please let me tell him that, though. It's important that I do it."

Viviana didn't want Anton to think she was hiding something from him again.

"Listen, if it's important, like baby-wise, we'll need to leave ASAP."

Viviana furrowed her brow. "What, why?"

"We're a couple of hours away from a decent hospital." Rory clamped his mouth shut instantly. "Oh, shit. Boss is going to have a conniption fit I told you that."

"You didn't tell me where exactly," Viviana said, lifting her shoulder dismissively. "Besides, this isn't the real deal. Trust me, Rory. Just go and find Anton and ask him to come back as soon as Rocco is ready."

Rory literally tittered on the spot. Like he was a fucking girl or something. What was it with men and the thought of labor, anyway? Suddenly they turned into worried, nervous little boys who couldn't handle a bit of pain.

"Go get my husband," Viviana said, turning away to hide her smile.

Rory didn't have to be told again. When the bull was gone and the front door shut, Viviana let out the breath she'd been holding in. The baby inside stretched, hell bent on repositioning himself. Placing both of her hands over her midsection, she closed her eyes and shook, the worried feeling settling in her middle.

"Come on, Demyan. Be good for mommy, please."

Asking the baby to do anything was probably useless, but Viviana also knew he could hear her. Maybe all he wanted was to hear something, or perhaps he was missing the comforting tenor of his father. After all, she'd spent all morning wrapped in her husband's arms, listening to that voice of his, feeling him love her like only he could.

Feeling the odd cramping sensation subside for a moment, Viviana wondered she should call someone and get their opinion on the false labor. Sometimes it was better to hear the voice of another who had experienced it, too.

Noticing Anton's cell phone sitting on a side table next to the couch, Viviana was quick to grab the device up and dial a familiar number. Not three rings later, Sasha's tired voice picked up on her end. Because her mother-in-law had her degree in nursing, Viviana thought she was just as good of a person to talk to about it as anyone.

"Anton," her husband's mother said, a smile in her voice. "I thought you were taking Vine out of town for a while?"

"It's just me," Viviana replied. "Anton forgot his phone when he took Rocco out. We are out of town, but I don't know where."

"Hey, Vine." The sound of a door shutting echoed over the receiver. "Is everything okay?"

"Yeah, just fine. How's Daniil?"

"He had a hard night, but he's sleeping fine this morning. Demanded I go get him some chocolate, so that's a good sign if he wants to eat. Enough about us, though. How's the lodge?"

Viviana snorted under her breath. "You know exactly where I am, don't you?"

"Just about. I spent enough time vacationing there myself. Well, they like to call it a vacation. It makes them feel less guilty about locking us away from the world for a week."

"I'm really liking it so far."

"That's good, sweetheart. It holds a lot of memories for our family, so it's nice you're finally able to see it, also. Why the early morning call?"

As if on cue, the baby boy decided to do another acrobatic move. The long stretch had Viviana cramping all over again and the ache in her back starting up, too. Sighing, she went about explaining her symptoms to her mother-in-law. Sasha listened patiently, occasionally voicing her understanding.

"Nothing to worry about, right?" Viviana asked.

Sasha hummed noncommittally. "It certainly sounds like false labor."

There was an unhidden *but* at the end of Sasha's sentence. Viviana didn't like that at all. Panic welled in her stomach like a poison. "What, it is just fake, right? It's too soon, otherwise."

"Well, the back pain is a little bothersome. I had that same kind of ache for a week before Anton was born. There's no blood or water?"

"No, none."

"I'd say it's just false labor, then, and try to get the little man to calm down a bit. Seems like something worked him up is all and he's awake and playing in there. Did you exercise this morning when you woke up? That'll do it, Viviana."

Viviana forced herself to stay quiet. No, she certainly hadn't exercised, not in the way Sasha was assuming. The last thing she wanted to blurt out was the wake-up she'd received from Anton the night before and then the nearly two hour long session that took over them in the morning. Unable to hide the embarrassment creeping over her cheeks, she make a noise that was supposed to sound dismissive.

Apparently, it didn't.

"But I thought you were supposed to exercise because of your sugars. If that's not what did it ..." Sasha trailed off before clearing her throat. "Oh. *Oh*, did I just make this awkward?"

"Um, no," Viviana said, cursing herself all the while. "Can

we not talk about that?"

"Okay, we can do that. Or not, I mean. But that will do it, sweetheart. Orgas—"

"No, oh my God, *don't.*" Viviana gasped into the phone, mortified. "Please don't. That would not be okay with me, never mind Anton."

Sasha made an uncomfortable noise. "I'm sorry, I'm sorry. But I want you to know, you're getting close to eight months. Your cervix is softening, Vine. It won't be unusual if you do notice a spot of blood or two anywhere from a half hour and beyond ... those activities. Okay?"

Viviana took some time to gather her bearings, and swallowed the lump in her throat. There wasn't anything to be embarrassed about, as her mother-in-law wouldn't take their conversation anywhere.

"Sex can bring on false labor symptoms?"

"Sure," Sasha said. "Well, the orgasm does, I suppose. The contractions of the orgasm mimics the contractions of the labor. The baby counters accordingly, some like it, some find it annoying. Funny how a great deal of women seem to want sex more near the end, isn't it? Don't be worried about that, for God's sake. Enjoy it, if anything. Once he's here, there won't be nearly enough time for you to find connection like that as often as you do now."

"Thank you," Viviana managed to say.

"No problem."

Viviana glanced out the window, noticing from the corner of her eye that Anton was finally returning back with Rocco walking along beside him at a leisurely pace. Rory was also there. At least her husband didn't seem to be in a panic, so her bull must have followed her instructions about letting her be the one to tell him of the false labor. Thank God for the little things.

"What did you do the first time they called him the little prince?" Viviana asked.

Sasha exhaled heavily into the receiver. The sound was as foreboding and sad as her answer. "Nothing. I couldn't. And neither can you."

Chapter Ten

"Any better?" Anton asked, rubbing a hand over his wife's stomach.

Settled into the large couch, Viviana's legs up in his lap, he watched her face carefully to see if he could notice any signs of discomfort or pain. It had taken a long, warm bath, and then a short nap before she admitted the cramping was easing up.

"A little," Viviana said. "Really freaked me out for a minute, though."

Anton massaged her left ankle before moving to the right. More than anything, he wanted to soothe Viviana, but he knew his worry was coming through strong and she wasn't missing it. His concern was forefront. It was too soon for his boy to be born. The doctors had already confirmed if he continued to grow much bigger because of the sugar issue, they'd induce her at thirty-eight weeks gestation. Demyan would be considered full-term then, anyway.

But, that was still three weeks away.

"Are you scared of what comes during the birth?" Anton asked quietly, trying to get his thoughts in order.

Viviana turned to look at her husband, smiling slyly. "Why, are you?"

"Yes. I can't stand to watch you cry. How do you think I'll fair through this? It'd be so much easier if this was years ago when men didn't have to go to the hospital until after the child was born."

"Oh my God, you are going to be inside that room with me." Viviana chirped out a laugh. "With a gun to your head if need be, I don't care. Lord knows if someone else cuts his cord, you'll regret it every day of your life."

Anton glared playfully, tickling up the side of her smooth calf. "I know, I'm just saying it made sense, that's all.

Seriously, though, are you worried?"

"I don't know. Right now I'm sort of complacent about it all. It's going to happen whether I'm ready for it or not. Of course, ask me that again when I'm in the middle of labor and I really have no choice, and I'll probably have a different answer."

Then, Viviana pushed herself up and stared at him intently. "Also, I don't want pain medication, so it's your responsibility to convince me not to take it when I'm seconding guessing that choice."

"Awesome," Anton muttered dryly. "I'll get right on that."

"I don't know about you, but I don't want a needle being shoved in my *spine*. Morphine makes me nervous after the accident, so that's a no-go. The other things offered just don't sit well with me. It's mind over matter, Anton. That's all pain is."

Well, he didn't totally disagree with her there, but if she started asking for pain relief, he guaranteed nothing.

"Whatever you say, baby. I'm not the one doing it."

Settling herself back down into the mess of cushiony pillows, Viviana sighed happily. "I think he's finally resting."

Small miracles, Anton thought. Reaching over once more, his hand found its way under her shirt to rub back and forth below her navel. Viviana hummed contentedly at the affectionate touch and Anton smiled, watching her watch him under her thick lashes.

Viviana was a crazy kind of beautiful. Thanks to that cocoa butter and oil concoction that she lavished on her midsection, her skin was as unblemished as it always was. She glowed when she smiled. Maybe Anton hadn't been telling or showing her just how beautiful he thought she was if her recent insecurities were any indication. Or, maybe that was just an awful by-product of pregnancy, too.

"You're beautiful, Vine," he said offhandedly.

Viviana blinked up at him with a slow smile creeping over her lips. "Come here."

Not wanting to make her ask again, Anton was quick to

move Viviana's legs from his lap and lean over her figure. With two fingers, he stroked her cheek, catching her bottom lip with his thumb. When her hand fisted into his white T-shirt, Viviana pulled him down to meet her kiss. Long enough to have his body aching and his cock waking up all over again, Anton pulled away from his wife's mouth sooner than he wanted to. Desire glittered in her hooded eyes.

"Too much of that and we'll be another two hours getting him calmed down."

Anton nodded his agreement and slipped back into his spot on the other side of the couch. "Is that a no to later, too?"

"Oh, definitely not," Viviana replied, her hand searching out his.

Intertwining their fingers, Anton brought her hand up to his mouth and laid his lips against each of her knuckles. The comfortable silence that ensued lulled Anton into a peaceful state. This last minute getaway was what they needed. Sure, the idea of the lodge worked out well for needing to get Viviana out of state, but it was more than just that. Very rarely did they get enough time for them together, and in a few short weeks, something beautifully new and already loved would be adding himself to the picture as well.

Were they ready for that?

• • •

Viviana rested on the swinging bench. Using the tip of her foot, she rocked the swing back and forth, enjoying the sun peeking through the trees. Below her on the ground, resting his large head on a pillow was Rocco.

She hated to admit it, but Anton was right when it came to their pup. He'd been following her around the trails leading into the forest surrounding the lake and lodge all morning without a single complaint. Rocco had started limping a bit, but that was fixed when Viviana decided to take a rest on the bench beside the lake.

Rocco was more than capable of handling the pain he was in, but the moment she or Anton gave any indication they noticed he was uncomfortable, the dog instantly turned into a whining baby. But, that whiny pup also saved her life, so she wasn't against giving him all the love and affection he wanted.

Enjoying the quiet hum of the forest, Viviana watched as Anton's form caught her gaze. Jogging around the lake had replaced his usual morning workout routine. It was their fourth morning at the unknown place, and this was the third time she had been able to sit down and enjoy the view of her husband. She purposely made a point of coming out to watch him run, even if that meant getting out of that warm, comfortable bed in the upstairs loft of the two floor lodge.

Wearing nothing but a pair of knee length track shorts, listening to an iPod, and his head down, Anton was lost in whatever zone he found.

The closer Anton got to her spot during his jog, the more Viviana watched him. The fast stride he kept was strong and sure, his skin damp with perspiration. The dangling cord of the ear buds stuck in his ears drew her eyes downward over the chiseled plains of his chest down to the definition of a solid abdomen lined with a railroad track path of muscles. The black licks of his tribal tattoos swayed with the movements of his body like living artwork. Strength wrote lines over every inch of his physique. Discipline colored his physical power.

Observing Anton in his concentration was near memorizing. If she had to guess, he was likely on his fourth or fifth trip around the lake, but his breaths came at an easy pace. He wasn't tiring in the least.

Glancing down at Rocco who had also noticed his other master getting nearer to their spot, Viviana smiled at the sight of his excitement forming in the thumps of his thick tail to the ground. Before the bomb, the pup loved to run with Anton, even if it was on a treadmill beside the one his master was using. Now, he simply didn't have the strength in his hind legs to keep up the pace. Sadly, she knew it bothered her husband that the pup couldn't be his running partner any longer, too.

Sighing away the inner melancholy, Viviana looked back up only to find Anton staring back at her. With that heated blue gaze of his trailing over the button down shirt of his she wore and the stretchy yoga shorts, the faintest hint of a smirk tugged at those full lips. It was the simple cock of his dark eyebrow and the baring of his teeth that had her pulse picking up. The want behind his eyes was clear to see; the throbbing at the apex of her thighs reacting accordingly to the unvoiced suggestion.

Close enough to her spot that she could make out the marks of her scratches on his forearms, she knew there was likely a few lines across his back, too. She wouldn't deny for a second how much she loved that he didn't hide the proof of their passion. It didn't seem to bother Anton a bit to allow the two men staying with them a view of the marks his wife left every time they fucked.

She woke up earlier that morning to colorful wildflowers scattered throughout the bedroom and the sweet smell of hot breakfast and raspberry tea. Viviana managed to get half way through the meal before a hunger of a whole different sort had taken over as she simply watched her husband check his emails.

It had been overpowering. The urge to feel him, to have him hold and kiss and *need* her.

There hadn't been many words spoken, only hands that roamed soft and sweet while lips fluttered down to taste and suck. On her knees with her back fitted snug to his chest, she could practically still feel him holding her, a hand between her thighs working quickly with fingers to her sex. The slow stokes of his cock hadn't taken her too hard, but they still reached her deep, hitting the spots to make her shake and shudder with broken, high cries.

Oh yes, Viviana's desire for sex, touch, and bliss had surely come back with a vengeance. Thankfully, the false labor didn't make its unwanted appearance every time they made love, otherwise it would have put a serious damper on the mood. She hadn't realized just how much she missed the intimate communication they somehow shared when they joined like that.

Viviana's insides were having the oddest reaction seeing her husband close in. With short breaths, electricity humming over her nerves, and trembling hands hiding in her lap, she knew she was in trouble.

Somewhere along the last four days since their arrival to the lodge, Viviana had stopped letting those pesky hormones and insecurities rule her. She stopped questioning Anton. She didn't need to ask or worry, and while Anton professed how beautiful she was and how much he loved her every chance he got, he didn't need to. More often than not, the way he showed her was enough. Words weren't needed.

Willing the lust she felt to stay out of her voice, Viviana offered Anton a smile as she said, "Hey."

The ear buds were tugged out of his ears, the speakers still buzzing with music.

"Enjoying the view, baby?" he asked with a smug grin.

"You know it. The lake is incredible."

Anton guffawed, but he didn't call her on the lie as he reached down to pet their pup. "How'd Rocco do on the walk?"

"Great. Limped a bit at the end, but I think I was, too." The worried frown that she got in response had Viviana rushing to reassure her husband. "Everything's fine, Anton. No pain, no show, no water. The baby is going to be inside of me for a few more weeks, anyway. I didn't realize how far we had walked, that was all."

"But it was quite bad last night, huh?"

Viviana made a face. "More pressure than anything."

"Did you call Sasha about it?"

"Yep."

Anton joined her on the bench and Viviana rested into his side as he slung an arm protectively around her shoulders. She didn't even care that he was sweaty and in serious need of another shower—him being closer was better. With her head tilted down to lay on his shoulder, she allowed him to rock the swing back and forth, tracing circles with the tip of her finger to her swelled stomach.

"Where are Rory and Joe, anyway?" Viviana asked.

The bulls in question had been missing all morning. At first Viviana thought they were just hiking, but they'd been gone far too long for that.

"Picking up something for me."

Viviana scowled. "It better not be business-wise."

The rumble of laughter he released shook their bodies. "Nope. A surprise for my beautiful wife, actually."

"What?"

Anton nodded, his arm squeezing her tighter. "Yeah, should be here soon, so you might want to go take a shower …"

"*You* might want to go take a shower. Stinky."

The desire shining in Anton's eyes and he looked down on her had Viviana shivering all over again.

"Care to join me? I promise to make it worth your while."

Viviana didn't doubt it, nor did she have the will or want to refuse.

• • •

"No way."

Anton huffed a breath and rolled his eyes.

"Yes way," he mocked, poking his wife's side gently. "Come on, baby—you talked about wanting to do this. Now would be the perfect time. The scenery of this place is amazing. I paid for it already. What's the problem?"

The question is more like what isn't the problem, Viviana thought.

The biggest of all the problems was twenty feet away chatting up a storm with Rory. The female photographer had been a shocker to Viviana, never mind a sudden stress she didn't want or need. Sure, she'd chatted offhandedly about getting maternity photos done, both private and couple shots, but that was months ago.

Seemingly deciding to try to appease his silent wife, Anton continued speaking. "She's a good friend of Eva's, so I trust her. She was more than willing to accommodate my demand to have the guys bring her here without notice or direction as to where she was going, so she trusts us. It's a woman, so I'm not going to be an asshole with my jealousy. I've seen a great deal of her work, and she takes amazing photographs, especially when the subject is a woman, or a couple."

When Viviana still didn't respond, Anton shook his head and left her side. He gave a quick word to Rory, and both the bull and her husband disappeared back inside the lodge, leaving her alone with the photographer.

The woman cleared her throat and offered a wave as walked over to meet Viviana. "Hi, I'm Scarlett. It's Viviana, right?"

Viviana offered her a tentative smile, but it didn't ring true. "Or Vine, either one will work. I'm really sorry he dragged you all the way out here for nothing."

Scarlett shrugged, keeping her face passive. "Maybe not for nothing. Can we chat frankly for a moment?" Viviana conceded with a nod. Scarlett leaned against the railing and looked out at the lake. "A lot of women freak out about maternity shots, especially if they're in their final months. Things don't look like they used to, they feel like crap, they're nervous about being naked, or whatever else. All valid excuses, and I can usually calm the fears or edit the photo a little to boost a woman's confidence. Can I ask what your excuses are?"

"Pardon?" Viviana asked, shocked at the brazenness in the question. "I'm—"

"You're quite beautiful," Scarlett interrupted, turning back on Viviana with an appraising stare. "Stunning, actually, and it's not a big surprise why your husband would want to have this time in your life and marriage memorialized for you both. Your skin is clear, your eyes are bright, you don't look the least bit tired, and your body is extremely fit for being nearly eight months pregnant. Tall, shapely, and model worthy. Trust that I've had the amazing opportunity to photograph many beautiful women before, pregnant or not, so I have some instinct about natural beauty."

Stunned, Viviana didn't know how to respond. "Why?"

"Why, what?"

"Why women? Anton mentioned you preferred taking photographs of women or couples."

Scarlett smiled, the sight bright and genuine. "Women are beautiful at all stages of their life. They are grace in motion—magnificence in curves and color. I enjoy photographing women because they deserve to see their honest beauty, however it is that I manage to catch it."

"And couples?" Viviana asked.

"Isn't that one obvious?"

"I'm not the photographer."

"True." Scarlett laughed breezily. "Beyond the career title, I'm an artist. What I want most in life is to capture things that capture me. Affection, for one. Your husband was correct, to a point. I do prefer women *and* couples, but not just any couple. *Specific* couples. The ones your eyes are drawn to because they don't notice the world around them when they're near one another. The lovers who need to touch or they're not complete."

"The ones in love."

"Exactly." Scarlett smiled once more, lifting her shoulders beneath the cashmere cardigan she wore. She seemed pleased Viviana caught on so quickly. "I would be honored to capture yours, Vine, if you'll let me."

It was only then that Viviana noticed Anton had come back to the front door, resting against the entrance with his arms crossed and waiting patiently. She understood why he wanted her to do the photographs, and Viviana had the distinct feeling if she didn't take Scarlett up on her offer, she would surely regret it.

Also, it was a pretty amazing gift Anton had given her. It

couldn't have been easy for him to set it up without her knowing, not to mention the expense. She had to admit it had her heart swelling, though her nerves were growing. She suddenly wanted to thank him for the surprise, despite her earlier hesitation.

With her decision made, Viviana nodded her agreement. "Did you have a spot in mind, Anton?"

"Of course, baby."

• • •

Viviana sighed when Anton's lips ghosted along the curve in her neck. The tips of her hair dipped into the water of the small creek that eventually led to the lake a half a mile away. She wore nothing but a pair of white lace boy-shorts and with her legs drawn up tight to his side, it probably appeared as if Anton was wearing nothing at all, though he did have boxer-briefs on.

Anton was kneeling between Viviana's opened legs, and his chest pressed to hers, effectively covering the nakedness of her breasts. One of his hands held the small of her back while the other was splayed wide open to the side of her stomach. With a simple sweep of his thumb over her hyperaware flesh, Viviana's desire waged an internal war, and love flooded.

It was intimate and sensual.

The faint click of a shutter in the background barely registered to her ears.

While Viviana's private shoot was done without Anton's presence, the photos being something she wanted to share privately with him, their couple session was almost as easy as breathing. Scarlett didn't say much. She simply allowed the pair to do what they wanted, to move how they felt comfortable, and to let their natural connection and love shine through.

Apparently, it did just that.

Lifting his head to stare at her, Anton watched her

through the honest emotions flickering behind his eyes. Viviana leaned up just enough to press her lips to the underside of his chin, raising her right hand from the ground to cover the one still opened to touch over the squirming movement coming from inside her midsection.

Another click of the shutter echoed in the quiet space.

Anton didn't seem to mind the woman just feet away with her gaze trained on them through the lens of a camera. Neither did Viviana, really. Even with the other presence, their need to have closeness wasn't in any way impacted. If anything, Viviana found she wanted these moments captured in still-life.

The perfection of them at one moment in time frozen forever.

"Thank you for doing this," she whispered into Anton's ear.

The feeling of his mouth curving a smile against her jaw as he ran his hand up the length of her spine had her own grin building. "I love you, Viviana. So, so much. There's not a thing I wouldn't do to show you, baby."

Viviana suddenly felt choked by the emotions rolling around in her heart and soul. The sentiments only seemed to swell as air caught in her throat and Anton brushed his nose along the line of her cheekbone before lifting himself slightly away from her form. Viviana was quick to use her arm to cover her breasts as he laid the softest kiss to the spot above her navel.

Viviana didn't hear the click of the shutter that time, but that could have been because her thundering heartbeat overtook all other noise. Laying another kiss a little higher down to her skin, and then another, Anton came to a stop just below where her arm was still covering for the sake of modesty. He looked up from her body, his lips still resting on her flesh, and their stares met. Behind his gaze there was a sure clarity of worship shining brightly back.

Good God, she was so in love with this man. The feeling was growing stronger by the second. Viviana didn't realize her vision had blurred with unshed tears until she felt the wetness slide down her cheek.

The camera's shutter clicked down one last time.

Chapter Eleven

Anton swiped his thumbs under his wife's eye to wipe away the silent flood of tears she couldn't seem to stop. His rules about Viviana and tears were pretty simple: if she was crying, someone had made her do it, and it wouldn't end well.

This was not at all the same. It wasn't so simple.

Anton made her cry … and it was for a good thing.

At least he thought it was.

Sometimes being a man who made it his job to hide emotional vulnerabilities was a double-edged sword. What Anton didn't understand from his own self, he could usually look to Viviana for an explanation. She was so reflective of him and their passionate waves together. Unfortunately, he knew exactly what he was feeling and why; love, contentedness, desire, and worry. Those things always seemed to revolve in his insides where Viviana was concerned.

So, why the tears?

Anton didn't like to see Viviana cry; tried like hell to keep her from doing so, no matter the cost. While he was terribly happy his gift of the impromptu maternity shoot had gone off so well with her, he was also horribly confused over her reaction at the end.

Mind fuck fit the bill pretty damned well.

Clearing his throat, Anton pulled Viviana into his embrace, hoping it'd quell her crying. Her hands fisted into the T-shirt he previously pulled on after Scarlett had said she got the shots she wanted. Viviana, on the other hand, still wore very little, though he had managed to pull the button down over her shaking shoulders.

"Did I do something wrong?" he asked.

Viviana shook her head frantically, staring up with wide, brown eyes brimming with shimmering wetness. "Oh, no.

No, you did so well. So good. I just realized … It was really overwhelming, and I'm sorry, I didn't mean to cry. Please don't think badly. It's nothing like that."

Her words only served to confuse Anton further. "But—"

"Thank you for allowing me to photograph you," Scarlett said quietly, keeping a respectable distance from the embracing couple. She'd been silent while she packed equipment, and Anton was grateful for her extending them privacy. "Especially together. It was incredibly touching to witness, and I believe your child is very lucky to be born to such an amazing set of parents who are so clearly in love."

Wiping away the remaining streaks from her cheeks, Viviana took a breath and moved just enough to regard the photographer. "Thank you for coming, even with Anton's demands about transportation and all that ridiculousness."

He snorted above his wife's head. "You know why I did that, baby."

"Still ridiculous," Viviana said.

Scarlett smiled, obviously amused by the exchange. "Believe it or not, but his request is not the oddest I've had. I was more than happy to accommodate it, though, and I'm pleased that I did. This shoot is one of the most emotional I've been allowed to participate in. Your reaction isn't so unusual or uncommon—not with the couples I photograph—but I've never been able to catch it before. It usually happens when the session is over, or I am gone, and by then the moment is lost. Thank *you* for giving me that."

"The pictures," Anton said, surprised to find his voice was gruff from something unknown clanging around in his insides. He didn't want to be rude, but the moments shared between him and Viviana on camera were not for public display.

The photographer seemed to understand what Anton was implying without him even needing to spell it out. "You will have full rights to all the photographs when I'm finished. Some people don't mind displaying their intimacy while others find it very hard and too private. Either way, I respect and understand. I will keep the negatives and put them in a safe place for my own collection. With your permission, I would love to keep one for private display in my studio."

"Which one?" Anton asked.

Scarlett shrugged one shoulder. "I think you know which one."

The final one, he thought. The one with a single, silvery tear slipping down over the high cheekbone of his wife while their gazes were locked. Anton had been so confused about the tear, the way Viviana's face had relaxed with the weight of some strange realization as the air seemed to freeze around them. Regarding him honestly, holding him with those eyes of hers that always reflected the beauty of an old soul, and humming with sweetened, untarnished love that always dripped over his being like liquid silk, that photo was sure to be beautiful.

And entirely terrifying, Anton added silently.

It would, in effect, be a very open showcase of *them*.

Anton had never allowed anyone that private access to the love he had for Viviana.

So yes, it frightened him.

"I think any photo would be fine, right?" Viviana asked, staring up at him.

Anton didn't know how to respond. He knew his wife didn't see their love and devotion the same way he did—something untouchable and untainted that needed to be constantly protected and coveted from the outside world. She didn't mind sharing it openly.

"Fine," he repeated with a smile.

"Thank you," Scarlett replied, winking at Viviana.

Raising up on her toes, Viviana kissed Anton soundly before allowing him to help her pull her arms through the sleeves in the shirt and button up the front. The gentle movements of his son beneath his palms had Anton's heart singing with a divine rhythm beating thoroughly from pure affection alone. He so loved feeling the child, knowing he helped create that innocent little life just waiting to be born.

"Yeah, we're nearly done, Demyan."

"Shush your mouth. That'd be all we need is to go home and find out everybody somehow knows his name, Anton."

Scarlett, already making the slow trek back to the lodge with her small bit of equipment, didn't seem to hear Anton's slip of his son's name.

"All is good," he murmured. "Besides, I was thinking about having it inked on my wrist when we went back."

"But people might *see*."

"Probably not," Anton said with a wiry grin. "I tend to keep my arms covered up pretty well."

"Not when you work out."

Ah, she had a point there. "Never mind, we'll talk about it later. For now, I have one more surprise for my wife."

"Oh?" she asked, voice lighting up with curiosity and amusement. "You don't have to give me anything."

"Yes, I do." Anton placed a quick peck to Viviana's mouth to quiet her up and keep her from arguing further. "Do you know a lot of men give their wives something when the baby is born? A gift for a gift, kind of thing?"

"Sure, but—"

"This is mine to you, Vine. You're not going to want jewelry or some fancy new car to show off. I know that ... I know *you*," he added, enjoying the sight of her smile growing. "The only thing we really need is to be together. Yes, having you here helps if that sit-down happens, and it's a nice break for us both before the baby comes, but it's still all for you. Quiet, love, breakfast in bed, and flowers on the floor in the morning. When do I ever get to do that stuff for you, really?"

Viviana didn't seem to know what to say. Anton wasn't exactly a romantic man, but his wife didn't have a great deal of romantic notions, either. They simply didn't need to because they hadn't ever found a time when those things were needed to keep their feelings and desires alive between them. So, when he did get to bring her home flowers, or take her away like he had, it left a profound effect on them both. It happened not because feelings were fading, but because they wouldn't ever let them.

Sighing, Anton reached up to cup Viviana's cheek, swiping away a bit of moisture still left on her pretty skin. "Maybe this was the solution to a problem I was looking for. Trying to figure out why on earth this woman I love so much would keep things hidden that she knew were important to me; hating it when my wife felt she was undesirable and wouldn't want to be loved; fighting with you. That's not us, and I wanted to show you *us* again, baby.

"I didn't have it planned, nor did I provoke you into an argument the night I brought you here, but that was the moment I figured it out," Anton said with a shrug. "There was something going so wrong. We were linking up here and there but we weren't connecting. It fucking sucked like nothing else and it was screwing me up something awful. You told me to say something, remember?"

Viviana swallowed roughly, but nodded all the same. "Yeah."

"I don't say things—I *do*. I can tell you a million and one times a day that I love you but it's not going to be the same as when you let me show you."

"Okay."

Anton bit the inside of his cheek, surveying the expression his wife sported with clearer eyes. That look falling over her pretty face like a curtain dropping to hide the darkness from clouding up a window was the same one Scarlett had captured on her final shot. It was their vulnerability, her weakness, a strength he could understand, and above all else, a final wholeness.

Connection.

Love.

The realization of why Viviana had started shedding those tears suddenly made a great deal of more sense to Anton. Lust and desire were obvious human needs, things people who cared for each other in a romantic sense would always share. Viviana and Anton didn't have a problem mingling with those things together, despite the brief pauses from the pregnancy. Attraction ignited between the two like a flame to gasoline, and he was content to feed those flames every damned day of their life.

Love, however, could be found over and over again.

"That was it, wasn't it?" Anton asked gently. "Why you started with the crying, because you love me."

"Yeah." Viviana sniffed a quiet laugh, dropping her eyes out of sight. "Odd, right? I've always loved you, it's not something I should be surprised about. It shouldn't take the air right out of my chest, or knock me out of my mind. I *know* I'm in love with you, so *why?*"

Anton really didn't have an answer for that; Viviana didn't seem to mind, though. Instead of speaking, he was graced with the memory of the first time he realized that he too had been so in love with his girl. A girl he always knew he loved, but the shock-and-awe factor of the weight coming down on his heart had still been oh so dumbfounding.

"It's good to be reminded," Viviana told him, her hand coming to splay open to Anton's middle. "So thank you, again, for reminding me."

Anton grinned, taking in her life and love. "Anytime, baby."

• • •

Viviana was lost in the sight of flickering lights dancing along the mouth of the trail as they came to the edge of the forest. From the lake's small dock to the front steps of the lodge, tiny tea lights had been randomly placed and lit. Some were in bunches on the sides of the stairs, others lined down the pathway, and a few were scattered in the grass and gravel. With not a lick of wind in the area, they all burned bright and beautiful.

Daylight was beginning to dim, so the lambent, yellow

glow of tiny flames gave the area a particularly romantic and peaceful quality, even more so than what its natural ambiance held. A quiet hum of the Americana blues music Viviana loved wafted from inside the lodge.

Sounding as emotional as she did sinful, the female's melodic tenor sang of earlier years, of seeing beauty in the backdrop, and of finding love in the dangers of life. The melody crawled over the area like a thick, slow moving fog intent on covering every inch it could reach with its passion and soul. The not so hidden meaning of the lyrics resonated straight to Viviana's heart.

The artist currently singing was a particular favorite of Viviana's. She had no doubt Anton knew it, too. After all, he said it first: he *knew* her.

Following the still flickering candles with her blurred, watery gaze, Viviana was quick to notice the lights in the lodge had been dimmed and smoke puffed from the chimney for the first time since they arrived. It wasn't cold enough for them to need to use it, but she distinctly remembered asking her husband if it would be safe to use it one night, maybe. Anton hadn't given her a real reply.

Now, she knew why.

Even the forest seemed to hold its life at bay as Viviana blinked at the spectacle before her, disbelief and wonder coloring up the love and happiness she was already feeling. She was struck speechless. Starry-eyed and overcome, she tried to speak, but couldn't.

Anton fingered the collar of his shirt she wore, saying nothing and letting the amazement seep in a little further into her blood and bones. How on earth did he find time for this? There had to be at least three hundred tea lights glowing. And where were the other three people who had just been here, anyway?

Seemingly reading her mind, Anton finally gave her some clarity. "Scarlett has two early morning sessions booked in New York tomorrow, so I asked the guys to make sure she arrived back in plenty of time to get some decent rest."

Without really saying it, Anton had also just told Viviana that Rory and Joe wouldn't be back for several hours, likely well after midnight.

"How?" she managed to ask.

Anton stepped behind Viviana's form, saying nothing. Viviana wondered if he would tell her at all, but she forgot those thoughts the moment his fingertips wove into her hair and trailed tenderly in a back and forth motion on her skin. When his warm smell danced along her flesh, she sighed.

"The guys helped a lot—I owe them big. They're probably the only two men who have a personal viewing to our daily lives. They eat with us, sleep in our home occasionally, keep to the shadows, and help me to protect you. In a way, they know us, too. Rory, especially, was more than happy to help."

Wringing her hands and suddenly feeling unsure and nervous as to what she should do next, Viviana found herself lost to the movement of the swaying flames. In every way that counted, she was overwhelmed. From the fast pace of her heart, to the unknown emotions swirling around in her chest, to the choked sensation holding back her air. Anton caught her totally off guard and she didn't know how to react about at all.

It was lovely, amazingly thoughtful, and Viviana was so grateful.

As his arms wrapped around her trembling figure, his hands lacing over her stomach, and his chin rested to her shoulder, Anton grew silent. It seemed like he wasn't even breathing for a second, like he was absorbing the shock from her, too.

"This is …" Viviana couldn't find the words, but her heart was filled, pumping out love by the gallon as slivers of tears escaped from her eyes. "Thank you."

"No, I don't want to hear that. Not right now." When his arms tightened, pulling her closer, Viviana sank into his hug as a quiet sob broke free from her throat. Grazing his hand affectionately over her swelled middle, palm pressing down protectively, Anton placed a kiss to the side of her throat.

"Thank *you*, baby. Your body, your love, your life—those are the things you share with me. Every single day you share those things and the only thing you ask in return is for me to show you that I love you, too."

Viviana was straight spun. Her heart was beating to the tune of his heartfelt words, while her soul was twisting to reach out and find his. Laying her arms over his to feel more of his heat and have more of their skin touching, she let the topsy-turvy emotional waves wash over her freely.

Anton took a deep breath, smiling against her hair. "There's nothing in the world that I could give to repay you for carrying my child. I know that sometimes you think he makes you crazy and terrible, but for me, he makes you amazing and beautiful. This is my first child—my *son*—and the greatest woman in the world is giving him to me. A woman whom I love more than what should be possible. And without even knowing him, I already love him. That's pretty damned incredible to me. Also, I lied."

At that moment, Viviana didn't care what he did wrong. She forced herself to speak, but her words still came out breathless. "About what?"

"The things I said I didn't get for you." It took her a moment to understand what Anton was getting at, but he continued before she had the chance to refute his offerings. When his finger trailed along her neck where a chain would rest, a shiver rolled over her shoulders, causing him to chuckle deeply in response. "Well, the jewelry, of course. I think had I bought you another car—"

"I don't need another car," she grumbled half-heartedly.

"Oh, I know."

The distinct sound of his sharp inhale as Anton leaned down to graze his mouth along the shell of Viviana's ear echoed. Something wonderful and wicked was beginning to rouse in her body. Beneath the yoga shorts she had slipped back on, her sex was already throbbing, wet, and hot. She didn't know if that had been her husband's intention, but he was sure as hell working her up to it quickly enough.

"But," Anton added, popping the word from his mouth. "I was looking into a private jet last month. If I wanted to take my family out of the country for a vacation, I couldn't do it publicly due to my lack of a passport because of those weapons charges."

"You bought a jet for me?" Viviana asked, trying to wrap her mind around that little tidbit of information. Nope, she still couldn't do it. "That's insane."

"*Us*. And no, not yet, it should go through next month sometime. Fly to Jamaica to smoke some of the best grass we can find, hmm? England, maybe, so I can see my son standing on the steps of a palace like the prince he is. I intend to see you sprawled out on a white sand beach, baby, looking like fucking sin in not a thing but your skin."

Jesus Christ, Viviana wasn't getting enough oxygen.

The quietest click of beads hitting together caught her attention, but the nip of Anton's teeth to her jaw made it all disappear. At the same time, something cool slid around Viviana's neck and she reached up automatically to touch the item.

The smooth globes under her fingertips ranged in size from small, to medium, to large depending on how high or low she felt along the three stranded ropes of pearls. Looking down to where the long strands reached below the hollow of her neck, Viviana lifted up the ropes enough to see the pearls were a pretty gray. At the base of the back of her neck, Anton's hands touched down with the faintest of grazes before something slightly heavier than the jewelry itself rested against her skin. While keeping her one hand on the pearls, she reached back to feel the diamond encased clasp that held the links together.

Viviana still couldn't speak. Anton filled the silence for her.

"Pearls are the queen of gems, and it's often said they are the chosen gem of queens. So, it's most appropriate that I give my queen her first pair at one of the most beautiful times in her life. I thought about giving you these after Demyan was born, but I think now is better, no?"

Only a faint nod answered him back. Anton laughed low, running his fingers tentatively along her new accessory before he spoke again. "From the day he is born, and on that same day every month until his first birthday, there will be flowers delivered to our home. For the first year, they will include letters. For every year after, you will receive flowers on his birthday."

She felt the air leave her lungs in a shaky puff. "You didn't—"

"Oh, I'm not finished yet. Some of these things have been in the works for a while. This," he said, touching her pearls, "... for example. Others, like the lodge, tonight, and Scarlett, were last minute thoughts that somehow managed to come together for me. Somebody is looking out for us, Viviana. Or just you."

"The only thing I did was get pregnant, Anton."

"You don't really believe that, do you?"

No, Viviana didn't, but making sense of his worship of her would be a heck of a lot easier if it was that simple. If she was any other normal woman with a regular husband who didn't have the means and mode to buy things eighteen years' worth of flowers, pearls that probably cost more than a house, a jet, and—wait, he did say there was more ...

"That old bookstore in Little Odessa you visit every couple of months to stock up your collection?"

Viviana turned around in his arms, surprised he even knew about that. It wasn't that she kept it from him, but Anton wasn't exactly a huge reader unless it was something dealing with weapons. Although he would act as her pillow while she read. A hard pillow.

"How did you know?"

Anton smiled down at her, the mischief in his blue eyes lighting up his whole face as he traced her bottom lip with his finger. "You kept leaving piles of books in our bedroom until you had a whole stack in the corner. It's not like I have a bookshelf sitting around, Vine. Where did you think that came from, anyway? It didn't just magically appear. While I ordered that, I wondered where in the hell you were getting all of those books from. Joe offhandedly mentioned the bookstore you frequented, so I went from there."

Viviana was scared to ask, but she did anyway. "And?"

"Did you know Mr. Lander's wife is sick?"

Viviana nodded, remembering the man speaking about it. He'd been terribly sad because the bookstore had been for his wife—built over fifty years earlier in the beginning of their marriage, it was her dream to own and run one successfully because she loved to read.

"Well, I didn't," Anton said, frowning. "I should have. Harold's wife was a good friend of my grandmother Anna. Nicoli's wife. Sometimes in the midst of running in the new world, I forget about those who helped run the old one, however it was that they did it. Sandra helped my grandmother once or twice before Nicoli came into the picture, back when her first husband was beating the living hell out of her on a nightly basis."

"Small world."

"Yeah, I guess. I thought I should go in and say hello to him one afternoon after I realized that was the place you were buying all your books from. Harold told me about Sandra, which just …"

"Hurt?" Viviana asked softly.

Anton frowned again. "Nicoli would have done anything for Sandra because of what she did for my grandmother. In fact, he did—they almost lost the bookstore a few years before he died and he cleared their debt no questions asked. He didn't want a damned thing in return, either. It had nothing to do with the Bratva, just him being a friend because he had the ability to do so for someone his wife had once loved."

"That was pretty great of him."

"It was." Sighing, Anton leaned down and kissed the tip of her nose. "So, I guess it was ironic that it also happened to be the place my wife found comfort, too. Especially because

Harold needs to sell the place to help pay for his wife's hospital stays and treatments. Again, the new world and the old one intermingling. It wasn't expected of me to help, or even to consider it, but it wouldn't have felt okay with me had I not. They'll be able to enjoy their last couple of years together, without worrying about money, or stress, or their business.

"I visited Sandra, too—she's in the same hospital as Daniil, coincidentally. It's crazy, her and Harold, I mean. Years later and they're so in love, even sick and dying and losing each other in one way or another."

"A lot like your mom and dad," Viviana said, feeling a sentimental smile take hold of her cheeks.

"Yeah, that, too. A lot like what I thought of us in fifty, maybe sixty years, too."

"Did you buy me the bookstore?"

Anton smirked sinfully, the sight making Viviana's insides swirl with desire. "Yep. I know you want to finish school eventually, and I'm sure you will, but Demyan is going to put a slow to that for a while. This bookstore … it's not mine. You're also not one to sit in the house and do nothing but be a housewife—you need to feel like you're doing something, Vine. It has to be something you enjoy, also. I sincerely hope the bookstore will give you that, and the ability to keep our son closer all the while."

"I …"

Seemingly seeing her difficulty of creating speech, Anton held her close, tucking her face into his chest as arms enclosed her frame. "So, tonight, we'll do whatever you want to do. Dance, love, relax—whatever, Vine. We'll try to come back here at least once a year, and I'm not going to use it as a safe place when I need you out of state, just a getaway for our family. I know you how much you've come to like it. Nicoli gave it to Daniil, he gave it to me, and eventually, I'll give it to Demyan, too."

God, Viviana wished her mind would come up with something appropriate to say. Something as heartfelt as his, something to make her seem grateful for the time, extravagance, and beauty of his words, gifts, and love— anything at all. But, nope. Nothing came. Speechless again, the only thing Viviana could do was cry. Anton let her.

"Thank you for giving me our child, Viviana."

Chapter Twelve

There was a man in Anton's bedroom.

Viviana was downstairs reorganizing all the cupboards in the kitchen, of course, but still.

There was a man in his *bedroom*.

Anton was twitchy. Or his trigger finger was.

"Boy, you better quit glaring at those stairs like you expect them to fall in on themselves." Clarissa kept her eyes on her dusting while scolding. "I thought your week away would have rid some of that tension of yours."

Anton appreciated how Viviana had managed to bring their maid out of her introverted shell. Before, Clarissa addressed him as sir, no matter how many times he asked her not to. She had always been properly respectful and kept her distance. Now, she was more like family, and she didn't let Anton get away with a single fucking thing.

"There's a man in my bedroom."

"That's the fourth time you've muttered that in the last twenty minutes. He's been up there for an hour. Is it really bothering you that badly?"

Yes, Anton thought petulantly. There was nothing he hated more than the thought of another male even coming near the marital bed he shared with his wife. Anton didn't know where that little issue of his stemmed from, but it had his blood fucking boiling. Irrational? Maybe. That didn't make the problem any less real.

"Well, how about I call your mother and let her verbally smack you back into this century. Or better yet ..." Clarissa said lightly, cocking a brow at her boss, "I could go in the kitchen and tell your pregnant wife that while she's been fretting and nesting for the last week, you're sitting here being jealous over the man who is painting your bedroom mural instead of helping her."

Goddamn it.

"You wouldn't call Sasha," Anton replied, not wanting to call Clarissa on whether or not she'd tell Viviana. She probably would.

"Try me. Go help your wife and leave the poor painter alone, Anton."

Sighing heavily, he crossed his arms and glared at the stairs for a while longer.

Perhaps Anton wouldn't have been so agitated about the man if his week hadn't been so damned stressful. While the week long getaway to Vermont had been beneficial for him and Viviana in more ways than one, it had also left things on hold back in New York. Too many things. Nobody would or could do a whole hell of a lot on the business side of things if the boss wasn't around to give the okay.

Well, the boss hadn't been answering calls unless they weren't for business, so shit didn't get done. Now, Anton was backed up to the nuts. It was making him freaking crazy for Christ's sake. He really needed to give Erik and Ivan a little more leeway with their positions and stop taking so much of the responsibility himself—that was all there was to it.

It certainly didn't help that Anton was still worrying about the possibility of one of his guys making plans to kill him. He had been pushing that to the side of his mind, though, attempting to see it from a different perspective. Unfortunately, he had only been able to see it from his own and he hadn't yet confessed his suspicions to anyone else.

The annoying little issue that was Tatiana seemed to die, thank God. Since he'd been back, there was no random appearances, no attempt for contact. Nothing. Anton was grateful, but he was suspicious, too.

So, there were those things, and then there was Sergei.

The stupid, Russian fool.

The Jersey Pakhan still wasn't taking calls. Or better yet, he wasn't refusing a sit-down. After all, he couldn't refuse one if he wasn't asked to have one. Sergei had been playing this game for far too long, and Anton was goddamn well sick of it. Anton assumed because of Boris asking around about Tatiana, that it must have got the other man's panties in a twist over something.

It made Anton nervous.

A good face to face should always happen after something happens to mix the blood between bosses in a bad way.

"What do you mean?" Anton asked, trying to forget his mafia problems for a while.

Clarissa rested her duster against her thigh. "Pardon me?"

"You said she was nesting. What in the hell does that mean?"

It wasn't like he'd ever heard of it before. What did nesting have anything to do with her reorganizing every freaking inch of their kitchen ... and the bathrooms, and their walk-in closet, and the baby's room—four times in a week? If you added that into the sudden urge to clean Viviana had, Anton wondered when in the hell she found time to study for her exams coming up the following week.

"*Nesting*, Anton. Didn't you read those books she gave to you?"

Anton stared at Clarissa like she'd grown a second head. Viviana didn't say he had to read the books just that he should. So, he didn't ... well, most of them. "They don't have guns in them."

"You're a riot. Really. The birth should be fun for you."

"Why?"

"You're just like your grandfather. You have two places your mind goes—family, and *the* family. That's it. If it isn't about guns and money, or wives and homes, you don't want to hear it."

Anton didn't think that was a bad thing. "Fine. I'm going to go ask Viviana what nesting means."

Clarissa huffed, blowing a curl out of her eye in the process. "You men ... I swear. She probably doesn't even know she's doing it, Anton. It's getting close to the end, or at least her body and mind thinks it is. It's like her subconscious way of getting her ready for the baby. She's cleaning every speck of dirt and dust out of this house, making things easier for herself once he's here, and tiring herself out so she can sleep a good ten hours every night."

Anton had to give Clarissa credit, what she said made a lot of sense. He hadn't even considered that was Viviana's motherly instincts coming out to play, but given her sudden need to have a list of things for him to do when he returned home from the club, well ... yeah.

"Huh."

Turning back to stare in the direct vicinity of the man in his bedroom, Anton wished the painter would hurry the hell up and get out. It was still plucking at his nerves like someone was using them as an instrument, and not in a good way.

"The painter isn't even bothering your bed, Anton. He's just painting the wall in the baby's cubby. Now stop being bitter for no reason and make yourself useful. Perhaps you could—"

"Go help Vine, Anton," he said under his breath.

Everybody always needed to pick at Anton's jealousy. As if he could help it, honestly.

"You said it, not me."

The quiet, bluesy melodies singing through the kitchen had Anton smiling as he made his way in that direction. Viviana had her head stuck in the cupboards beside the sink, her hips swaying to the beat as the lyrics rolled off her tongue. Anton didn't get to hear his wife sing as often as he liked—she had a beautiful voice, even if she didn't think so.

Also, Anton wondered where she got that love for blues from. Nicoli had once enjoyed the tone, emotion, and soul to the music and had several favorite bars he liked to frequent to hear it sung live, but his daughter didn't know that.

"Nicoli used to love that noise, too," Anton said, coming up behind his wife.

Viviana must have heard his approach, or knew he had been watching, as she didn't start in fright. "It's not noise. You like it."

Resting his hands to those still swinging hips of hers,

Anton moved to the tune of the beat, feeling Viviana press her backside into his groin as she danced. It wasn't long before he was peppering kisses up the side of her silky, soft neck and one of her hands were weaving into the hair at the nape of his.

Time didn't much matter to Anton when they were like this. It was far too easy for him to get lost in the rocking sway of her shoulders, the smell of floral perfume, and the heat of her skin on his. With Anton's nose skimming behind her ear, her back melting into his front, he decided the best music in the room was her soft, contented sigh.

"What, are you suddenly in the mood to dance, Anton?"

Laughing low, he spun Viviana around so she could face him. "With you, always."

"Well, I have a lot of work to finish in here, so ..."

"We've got a little while to get it done."

Her lips curved with a playful smile. "Three weeks."

Yes, only three. Their son would make his debut exactly on his due date, according to the doctor. Viviana had her appointment three days earlier and they were pleased the insulin seemed to be working to her favor, and Demyan's. After the doctor checked Viviana's cervix—something that made Anton cringe and rage at the same time—she wasn't showing any signs of delivering soon. Not wanting to risk her going overdue, they set up an appointment for her to be at labor and delivery early in the morning on July fifth to be induced.

Anton couldn't believe May had already passed them by and that June was there and leaving just as quickly.

"How are you feeling?" he asked.

"Good. The pressure from this morning is finally gone."

"And the pain?"

"Better," she said.

Eyeing her speculatively, Anton wondered if Viviana was just saying that to appease his worry. She'd woken up around four in the morning out of breath, tears filling her eyes, and with what she described as a horrible ache in her hips. An early morning phone call to the doctor said it was likely just the weight of the baby settling into an uncomfortable spot and to walk until he repositioned himself.

So, Viviana had been on her feet all day. Anton didn't like that.

While Anton loved seeing his wife pregnant, glowing, and so full of life like she was, he also knew it was taking a hell of a lot out of her body. Pregnancy was not an easy thing to get through, he'd come to learn. Not that he didn't have respect for his wife before, but she had it from him in the bucketful now.

"Come on, go sit down and let me finish putting this away for you." Leaning down, he caught her silken mouth with his. "Please?"

Her tongue swept along his bottom lip before slipping in to join his. Anton reveled in the taste of her kiss, the way her lips pressed harder, and her heat started a stirring in his groin. Fuck, how he loved his wife. Viviana fisted his T-shirt to bring him closer. Anton braced his hands to the counter and kissed his wife a little longer.

He could fight to get her to sit down in a minute.

"How about I go lay down in bed, and after you finish putting the rest of this stuff away, you can come join me?" Viviana nipped his jaw.

Anton froze. "No."

Oh, the slap of rejection that colored her cheeks a bright pink had him backtracking instantly.

"Shit, that's not at all what I meant and you know it, baby. The painter is still up there finishing the last bit of the mural and the room probably reeks of fumes. We'll sleep in the guestroom tonight."

Viviana glanced down at where his fingers were squeezing into her sides. "Why do you have a death grip on me?"

Anton loosened his hold. "I don't."

"Yes, you do."

"No—"

"You do that whenever someone gets too close to me."

"Viviana, it's just you and me here."

Something wicked curved Viviana's pretty, pink lips up into a grin. A grin that said she knew exactly what was going on with him. Apparently Anton hadn't been hiding it well enough. "There's a man in our bedroom."

Anton scowled, letting the lie roll off his tongue before he could stop it. "It's not bothering me that bad."

"Really? Well, I'll just go up and say hello, then. After all, he is using that special paint that doesn't give off as much smell. He's got two fans working and the windows open. I'll be fine for a minute or ... five."

"Fuck that you will."

Without even considering his actions, Anton picked Viviana up abruptly and sat her backside firmly on the kitchen counter. He leveled her with a stare that gave away every single one of his feelings when it came to what she just suggested. Those doe-eyes of hers only blinked back mirth at his jealous flare.

"My wife will *not* be in our bedroom alone with any man that isn't me, Viviana."

"Ever?" she asked.

Anton's hands slapped the counter. "*Vine.*"

"Some people think you're scary when you're mad. I think it's cute."

Cute. Great, Anton thought.

Rubbing circles into his quickly throbbing temples, Anton stepped between his wife's opened legs and met her gaze once more. "Please don't go up there."

"You know I wouldn't, Anton."

There was nothing Anton was more grateful for than Viviana's understanding. Some might have called his jealousy irrational, and sure, he knew it kind of was. Viviana never gave him any reason to be worried—she was as true and loyal to him as she would ever be. She was crazy, foolishly in love with him, too, no matter his ridiculousness at times.

Maybe the jealousy stemmed partly from his upbringing,

and a little more from his job. A lot of men in his business only thought of women as toys to be used and discarded. The ones they wanted to keep for themselves, they kept locked away on a shelf to be admired. Trophies, as it were.

Anton never wanted his wife to be seen as his trophy, but allowing his desire and love for her to be written out clear as day was a double-edged sword. Yes, he spoiled her to the nines and back, gave her whatever the hell she wanted whenever she wanted it, but he also let her do as she pleased. Viviana didn't stray out of line, and she *never* strayed from him.

To the men in their world, she was an enigma. A woman who didn't need to be taught or reminded what was expected of her, who didn't socialize outside of the people closest to her husband without first knowing it was okay, and a woman who had yet to have even a shred of impropriety blemish her reputation.

His wife—the *boss's* wife.

It wouldn't be abnormal for other men to watch Viviana, and want her, too. Or, they wanted to see if there was something hidden going on beyond what they could see. Mafia wives were one thing, but Anton's wife was something else entirely.

Anton hadn't expected all of those things from Viviana— nothing beyond her loyalty and love—but she gave it anyway.

Viviana sighed. "Don't worry. I'll stay down here with you until he leaves."

"Thank you," he mumbled.

"However ..."

Her tiny hands grabbed at his sweats, pulling him into her and the counter. Anton hadn't stumbled in years, but when his wife's fingers slipped beneath the cotton of his workout pants and boxer-briefs without any indication she planned on doing it, his knees damned near buckled.

"Fuck ... Vine, wait—"

"Nope." She hushed a soothing sound, dragging her teeth against his cheek. "Be extra quiet, okay?"

Anton fucking choked on his tongue, when those soft, nimble fingers of Viviana's wrapped around his length and squeezed. Whenever he was close to her, his cock was always semi-hard and ready to go, so it only took a few slow, tight strokes of her fist around his length to get the blood rushing straight down to his groin. Already steel-hard, the vein in his shaft throbbing to the beat of his heart, Anton swallowed the groan bubbling up in his chest.

"Clarissa and the pa-paint—"

Viviana clicked her tongue, biting down to his jaw sharply and causing Anton to hiss from the sting. Now it was his wife in control—teasing his body with talented squeezes of her grip in just the right spots on his length, rolling the tip of her thumb over the crest of his cock, scratching lightly with fingernails over tender flesh as she slid her hand back down.

"It's a good thing I love my man," Viviana whispered.

Her tongue snaked out and struck his lips with heat and wetness. Burying his mouth into her chest, clenching his teeth to hide the moans threatening to fall, Anton shuddered against the sweet smell of his wife and her body. Sparks were bursting behind his closed lids as she stroked him faster, her grip turning snugger.

It should have surprised Anton how fast his cock started to ache with the want for release, but it didn't. His wife had been in too much pain that morning for him to even consider sex, and he'd been too damned busy for the last couple of days and coming home late.

Viviana kissed the top of Anton's head, her free hand coming to tangle into his hair as her fingernails scraped along his scalp soothingly. Precum spread under her wandering fingers every time she reached the head of his member, the sticky fluid lubricating sensitive nerves as his body jolted into her embrace like the sudden jerks of his hips.

"Jesus, Vine, don't make me come like this ... I want to be inside of you," he growled.

Viviana laughed breathlessly, her legs tightening to his waist at the same time her fingers clasped painfully tight around his throbbing dick. Effectively, she rooted him in place. "No, I think I want to feel my husband's come all over my fingers."

When she tugged once, then twice, on his cock, Anton grabbed hard to her thighs and compelled the moans of pleasure bubbling up in his throat to go away. Realizing his wife wasn't about to stop in her drive to make him come in his pants, Anton relaxed into the sensations curling his groin with a burning bliss, allowing the pressure to build. Higher it went with every stroke. Tighter it coiled with every squeeze.

"Faster—fuck, please go faster."

She hummed her agreement low and throaty, the noise reverberating straight to his groin.

"It's a good thing I love you," she said again.

Her fingernails in his hair dragged down over his neck and beneath his shirt. The pain registered, but barely. Viviana could leave a dozen marks on his skin and he wouldn't care. Anton loved them. Especially when she marked them over his tattoos.

"Love my man foul-mouthed with his quick temper. Love him when he's jealous and possessive. Love him when he's downright *bad*."

There was no denying the orgasm tightening through his stomach and balls. Muffling the groan against her skin, Anton panted as his cock spilled warm come into Viviana's hand. The jolt of electricity that bit through his flooding veins had him struggling to stay upright.

Anton needed to find some solid ground, he wished the color would come back to his blurred vision for a moment, and he wanted his lungs to work again. Viviana let him have his moment to recover, trailing her hand up and down his tense back slowly and calmingly. Eventually, Viviana pulled her hand from the confines of his sweatpants and leaned over the kitchen sink to turn on the tap. Clearing his throat to rid the thickness that had built up, Anton stayed silent while she washed her hands before drying them on his shirt.

"I'm a towel, huh?" Anton asked, amused.

"The dishtowel is over on the island. I'm super comfortable right now. I didn't realize how much my feet were hurting until I sat down and they stopped."

Yeah, that's why Anton wanted her to cool it for a while. Unfortunately, his pretty wife was too damned stubborn to hear a thing he said, so Viviana needed to notice those things on her own. Ignoring the stickiness coating his softening cock, Anton released his hold and reached down to massage her calves and ankles with both hands for a few, quiet minutes. Those happy, soft moans of pleasure she gave in response was all he needed to continue.

"Go chill out on the couch—get a movie going. I'll be in after I clean up."

"Get new pants, too."

Anton chuckled. "That means I'll have to go see the painter in our bedroom, baby."

"Don't kill him, Anton. I want that mural finished today."

• • •

With her legs elevated, back melting into plush pillows, and the television humming with an old mafia movie sure to make Anton guffaw, Viviana was comfortable and content. She was wondering where in the hell her husband disappeared to. It had been a good half hour since Anton went upstairs to change and clean up, so she was starting to worry for the painter's health.

The poor man, he really had no idea of just how possessive Anton was over the space he was currently painting. Of course, she could hear the quiet conversation coming down from the stairwell, so it was more than likely Anton found a momentary friendship in the painter.

When Demyan kicked a particularly tender spot under her rib, Viviana cursed low and pushed back on the little foot with two of her fingers. That didn't seem to work, so she repositioned herself on the couch until the baby calmed down. While she enjoyed her pregnancy, she would sure be pleased to see it come to an end.

Viviana was ready to have her body back to herself and a baby boy in her arms.

The cell phone on the coffee table ringed with a vibrating jingle. It was Anton's phone, and he had everyone's numbers programmed with certain songs or tunes, so it wasn't one she recognized. Snatching up the device, Viviana realized she didn't recognize the number on the screen, either.

Unsure if she should answer the call, Viviana dropped it back down to the coffee table. "Anton, you've got—"

"Pick that up for me, Vine. It might be important. I'll be down in a moment."

Rolling her eyes, she was quick to pick up the phone again. "Hello?"

"Viviana. What a pleasant surprise to hear your voice."

Instantly, Viviana sat up on the couch. She didn't recognize the man, but by accent alone, she knew he was Russian and his voice somehow felt familiar to her memory. He also seemed to know her. Covering the phone's speaker with her thumb, she called to Anton once more, a little more forceful the second time. Her husband's footsteps upstairs followed her request quickly and Viviana went back to the call.

"Good evening," she replied politely. "I can't say we're on level ground, though. Forgive me, I don't have a clue who you are, and I wouldn't want to be rude."

The man's laughter was scratchy and gruff, but he seemed to enjoy her confusion. That didn't settle well with Viviana at all. "Unfortunately we never had the pleasure of meeting at your husband's birthday party last October. I would have been so honored to meet the daughter of Nicoli Avdonin, well, before Anton broke my nose, that is."

Oh shit. The caller was Sergei. The Jersey Pakhan Anton had been attempting to make contact with for weeks.

Viviana's eyes widened just as Anton slid into the living room sporting a worried expression. It was too late, though. She had already picked up the call and it would be the worst thing she could do to just hand it over without speaking to the man. To some, it may seem like she had shunned Sergei even if that wasn't the case. That could lead to a dangerous situation, as Viviana's word was taken just as seriously as Anton's, which was why she often chose to keep her mouth shut.

Bad blood, they already had more than enough of it between their families.

I'm sorry, Viviana mouthed to Anton.

He wouldn't even know what for, or why, but Viviana felt like she had to say it anyway.

"Put it on speaker," Anton said.

Viviana did what he asked, but two fingers to her lips to signal for him to be quiet.

"Sergei," she finally responded into the phone, managing to keep the shake out of her words. "This is a surprise."

"I'll say." Anton practically spat the words through his clenched teeth, though they were barely breathed at all. "Perfect timing."

"Is it?" Sergei asked. "I had heard your husband was very interested in speaking with me, but I've been terribly busy. Surely you understand, Viviana. He must have been expecting my call, wasn't he?"

The tension drawing Anton's jaw tight was worrisome. As he sat down on the couch, Viviana reached out and cupped his cheek with her hand, hoping to calm his anger a little. His own hand found the crest of her swelled stomach and rubbed back and forth gently.

"I'm sure he was," Viviana said. "We've also been busy, so it isn't too hard to believe our communication lines might have been mixed up, no?"

Viviana's words were an offer to give Sergei an excuse for ignoring Anton, but it was also a way for her to say his disregard was forgiven. By anyone else's standards, they would think the conversation was confusing. Viviana knew between her, Anton, and the man on the phone, everyone understood her veiled implication perfectly.

Sergei chuckled into the receiver. "So I heard. You must be awfully close to having that baby of yours."

"Ours," Viviana corrected instantly, not bothering to keep the bite out of the word. She didn't like how he referred to Demyan as only her baby, as if maybe he didn't belong to Anton at all. That was not only offensive, but a prick move she thought may have only been intended to bother her. "And yes, just three more weeks, if he doesn't come early on his own."

"*He?*" Sergei asked, surprising coloring his tone. "Well, this is news to me. I hadn't heard the child was a boy. Another little prince for the Avdonin family, how wonderful. Anton must be overjoyed."

"Sure he was. Just the same as before we knew the baby was a boy."

Viviana didn't hear Sergei's response to her as she was too busy rolling her eyes in Anton's direction and making a chatter motion with her hand.

"Shh," Anton said with a smile and a shake of his head.

She barely caught the end of Sergei's next sentence as her mind was distracted by Anton. "… if you agree, that is."

"Pardon me?" Viviana asked.

"Didn't you hear my request?"

Viviana frowned. This was why she didn't like to pick up Anton's phone unless she knew who was calling and why. "No, I'm sorry. Anton just came back in from the backyard so I was telling him you're on the phone. Would you like to—"

Sergei's chuckling stopped her from saying more. "No, my dear. What I would like is for you to answer my question and then I will speak with your husband. I'm sure he has much to say to me, but I want a guarantee first."

Something painful lodged in Viviana's throat. While the rest of their conversation had been laced with innuendos regarding Bratva business, that one was a hell of a lot more frank.

"What kind of guarantee, Sergei?"

"A dinner, how does that sound?"

Viviana chanced a glance at Anton, noticing his unease. "I don't set those up, I have never before, and I'm sure you're very aware of that."

"Of course," Sergei replied. "That is not what I'm asking for here."

"A dinner, then? I think it still stands with Anton that Belov Bratva aren't welcomed in Brighton Beach after the unfortunate incident at his birthday."

"That would be precisely the point of this dinner, Viviana. Anton owes me words, as I owe him. It's not a proper thing to be leaving blood to spoil for long, and I believe we've waited more than long enough. Having you there would—"

"Me?" Viviana interrupted, flinching at the same time. "I hadn't realized you expected me to show up, too. I don't think—"

"Are you refusing, Viviana?"

"No," Viviana rushed to say. Now, she was in particularly dangerous waters. The last thing Anton would ever want was her in the middle of a sit-down, especially when she was pregnant. "But as I said before, I'm terribly close to my due date and one doctor doesn't believe I'll make it that long. Traveling to Jersey isn't the best option for me when I'm supposed to be resting my days away."

It wasn't a total lie. The gestational diabetes put a great strain on Viviana and the baby, never mind the worries for the doctors. It put her at risk for other prenatal issues and they did order her to rest, not stress. Other than her exercise, Viviana was expected to keep her days calm and get a full night's sleep.

"Funny. I heard you just arrived back from the Avdonin family lodge. Shaftsbury, Vermont is a much farther drive than New Jersey, Viviana."

"That trip was meant to be relaxing, Sergei, and it was. In fact, I slept the entire drive there and back. I can't say I would do the same if I knew I was heading to Jersey. Forgive me, but your family hasn't exactly given me the warmest welcome into this world, regardless of who my father is. I do think Nicoli would have been sorely disappointed if he were alive for this phone call. How obliging would he have been to bring a woman in on business?"

"That was one of his oldest tricks, my dear."

Viviana stilled. "Pardon me?"

"Women keep things calm, they keep it safe. I picked up a thing or two from Nicoli myself over the years. And you're very right, he wouldn't have been happy to have his tricks played back on him. If Jersey is too far for you, I'm more than happy giving Anton the call of shots on where, when, and how."

"No heat," Viviana said suddenly. In other words, *no guns*. It was a highly unusual request, but one she would demand on anyway if he was so persistent in having her at a sit-down. "I'm the one asking for that, Sergei."

"Unfortunate that you don't trust me, but the request is certainly doable. Anything else, Viviana?"

A slow smile crept over her lips as she darted another look in her husband's direction. If the rage in his eyes wasn't clear, the clenched fists in his lap certainly were. Why should Viviana be the only woman? Why should Anton be the only man who worried because his wife wasn't safe in a Russian sit-down? The answer was pretty obvious to Viviana. He shouldn't.

"Yes, there is something else," she finally said, reaching out to squeeze Anton's thigh encouragingly. "Tatiana—bring her. I insist on it."

This time it was Sergei who stuttered. "I don't think—"

"Are you refusing?" Viviana asked, throwing his words back at him.

Please do, she thought. It would give Viviana every reason to hang up the phone until a more suitable arrangement could be found. She knew Anton would be the one to answer the call next, though. In no way would he agree to her being at their meeting.

"No, of course not," Sergei said quickly. "It's just ... well, I don't think you or my daughter would be pleased is all."

"Maybe not. But it isn't only you and my husband who have things to smooth over, now is it?"

Chapter Thirteen

"He knew we were in Vermont," Anton said.

The boss didn't miss the two gazes lifting to meet his at that statement. For the most part, Ivan and Erik had been agreeable to coming over to Anton's house for an emergency meeting, and they had stayed quiet as he explained the unexpected phone call from Sergei. Anton had finally laid most everything bare for them. They needed to hear what he thought, the things that had been happening, and where he thought they should go from there. Yes, they had been very quiet. Now, though, both men seemed ready to burst.

"There were only a select few who knew where we were," he added.

"Boss ..." Erik started, his face drawn with worry.

Anton's index finger tapped to his desk. "Unfortunately, there are a lot of guys who know of the lodge in Vermont. It wouldn't be a huge stretch to think they put two and two together."

"But it wouldn't be like them," Ivan said.

"Truth." Anton sighed, leaning back in his chair and crossing his arms behind his head as he lifted his boots up to rest on the desk. "This is ... It's fucking downright horrible. Asking Viviana to come in on a sit-down, really. That was dirty pool and I let him know it."

"Understandably smart, though." Erik shook his head with disgust. "Your wife is probably the only human being on this earth you wouldn't draw a gun for. She hates them, so you keep them out of her sight. You'd never hurt her, so you're not going to risk bringing one into a situation where it might do just that. Clearly he knows this shit."

"But how?" Anton dropped his boots down as he leaned forward in the chair, cocking a brow. "*How*, Erik? How many people understand and know me or Vine like that? How many people know it would piss me off and worry me like crazy?"

"Not many," Erik said. "I mean, we do, but ..."

As Erik trailed off, Anton relaxed back into his chair again. By the widening of Erik's eyes, the boss knew at least his one spy had understood what his words truly meant. While Anton didn't believe Erik or Ivan had any hand in some of the things happening to Viviana, he wanted them to realize how it looked on both of them.

Anton was starting to wonder if that was the perpetrator's goal. Did someone want him tearing his own Bratva apart so they could move in when he was least expecting it?

"Boss, you gotta know—"

"Do I?" Anton asked.

Ivan canted his head, a knowing expression dawning on his features. "I had been wondering if you were going to bring it up. I thought you'd come to me first and test the waters. You wouldn't even let me get close enough to the sit-down with the Italian for me to hear a thing. You weren't being shy about it, Anton."

"Actually, I went to Daniil first, but I was starting to seriously consider it after Conrad."

Ivan nodded. "And what did Daniil say?"

"He told me what I already knew. He might as well have called me a goddamned idiot for even considering it."

"Good old Daniil," Ivan said with a grin.

Erik just seemed confused. "Wait, so we're good?"

Anton shrugged. "Yeah, but don't you see what it looks like? Somebody wanted me to go for the throat first and ask questions later. Suddenly Sergei is calling me up making it seem like he's all for a sit-down, and his witchy daughter dropped off the radar. He thinks he's talking in riddles, but he's being a little too clear in my opinion."

"Smart on Vine to ask for Tati's presence," Erik said.

"I don't want my wife within a hundred miles of that bitch," Anton muttered.

Ivan coughed, appearing mighty uncomfortable. "Vine

asked for her. She has to show, Anton."

"But Vine doesn't have to stay." Erik shot a pointed look Anton's way. "Rory and Joe can leave with her not long after we all arrive. She's been having a lot of that false labor, right?"

"On and off, yeah."

"Use that as an excuse. Where'd you agree to have it all go down?"

"Brooklyn, but outside of my territory in Brighton Beach. In two weeks. I have the choice in restaurant, so we'll make sure it's cleared out except for us. I want to arrive second, but I'll have the bulls there checking every one of his people for weapons. I think ... Shit, what if Little Odessa is what it's all about, huh? Does that fucker have such a hard-on for my territory he's willing to start a war over it?"

"Brighton Beach is where we've always been," Erik said.

Ivan jerked his thumb at his counterpart in agreement. "And it's never been an issue before."

"But Sergei has no business being in Jersey," Anton said for them both. "What he does have is a major Cosa Nostra family edging in on his heels at times. More than once he's had issues with the Italians in Jersey because he's greedy as hell and won't leave their shit alone. Getting rid of the Avdonin Bratva here would be a cherry on his pie. He'd get the safe territory, the business, the already set guys—*my* fucking guys," he added angrily.

"They'd cut their throats before working for him," Ivan replied. "They're your brothers, not his."

"So which one of my brothers is working with the bastard, then?" Anton asked scathingly. "Which one of them wants to kill me?"

• • •

Viviana groaned, shifting in the bed to find a more comfortable spot. That didn't come, and instead, she kicked the blankets off her legs and blinked fully awake, frustrated. It took her ten seconds to realize Anton wasn't in the bed with her.

That wasn't unusual. Especially if she considered the phone call from Sergei earlier. It was likely Anton had shut himself away in his library, on the phone with whoever to get the things set up that he needed to. Viviana knew he'd be back in the bed with her by morning, waking her up like he always did.

Unfortunately, sleeping in the guestroom without her husband was irksome. Anton had been right when he said the paint in their bedroom would leave fumes. Their bedroom was a much more personal, safe feeling space, and Viviana didn't think sleep would find her again until Anton was back at her side.

Deciding to find him so he could help her get back to sleep, she got out of the bed and worked an annoying kink out of her neck. It was only then that she could hear the soft voices murmuring down the hallway outside of the guestroom. Because the bedroom door was open, any noise from the upstairs traveled, no matter how low they spoke.

Anton must have left his office door open, too.

Viviana's heart stuttered. He'd promised her once that no face to face business would happen in their home.

"I can't believe you actually thought it was us, though."

Viviana recognized the voice immediately as belonging to Ivan. Erik's familiar, deep laughter followed the statement. At least if their unexpected guests were Anton's closest men, and friends, she could attribute the meeting to the phone call from Sergei. She would overlook it as it wasn't uncommon for them to be there and the day had been unusual as it was.

What Viviana wouldn't overlook were Anton's next words.

"Look to your sides first, right? If somebody was looking to kill me, why not either of you?"

Panic welled like a hard ball of poison in Viviana's gut. It left a bad taste in her mouth. The god-awful nausea that had finally given her a rest for the last couple of months returned with a vengeance, threatening to make her lose her lunch all over the floor.

Someone was trying to hurt her husband? Why hadn't Anton told her?

"At first I thought the photographer and slashed tires were just something to pick at Vine, but hell, she didn't even know about the second issue."

Slashed tires? When had that happened?

Anton continued, not missing a beat. "It didn't seem like she was meant to, either. It's clear the threats were meant for me, you know? Look how close they can get to her, kind of thing. As if they were baiting me or some shit. My guys know how close I keep her bulls—they could work around it like nothing. It's someone outside of our loop that would have trouble getting that close. So, which guy is working with Sergei? That's what we need to figure out."

"You should have brought this up to us way sooner," Ivan said, frustration coloring his tone. "Two weeks might not be enough. That dinner could just be the final trap. Especially if he thinks you're wrapped up in worrying about us, your wife, and whatever else."

"You could always refuse it," Erik said. "Use the baby's upcoming birth as an excuse to hold it off."

"You know what that would mean, man. Gives Sergei every damned right to say Anton needs to get culled. Doesn't matter if she's in labor and he says not happening. It's still a refusal after he already agreed. Technically Sergei's forgiven for his refusal. There's no saying the asshole would do the same for Anton."

Anton grunted his agreement with Ivan. "I'd like to finish it, to be honest. What if Tatiana decides bothering me isn't enough anymore and she decides to try to take another bite out of Vine?"

Just the mention of Tatiana Belov's name sent Viviana's rage spinning. That woman was nothing but trouble. Had she been bothering Viviana's husband?

"I don't want to have to worry about someone from Jersey

coming into my home after the baby is here, trying an attempt on me because I refused a sit-down, either. I've been trying my damnedest to keep this from my wife as it is. She doesn't need to worry about this shit right now. The baby is enough."

"You haven't told her anything?" Erik asked, sounding flabbergasted.

"Very little. Certainly not to this extent."

You have now, Viviana thought sadly.

What was she to do with the information now that she had it?

Viviana didn't know.

While she wanted to be angry with him for hiding the dangerous situation they were currently in, Viviana was only panicked. She suspected that was Anton's worst fear, even beyond someone hurting him. It wasn't unlike her husband not to tell her business things because she wouldn't want to know, anyway.

This was so different, though.

"And what if she wakes up one morning to nothing more than a broadcast like her mother did, huh?" Ivan asked.

That was a loaded question. One that stabbed at her heart and soul with a million little razor sharp knives. Anton might have had his fears, but he wasn't the only one. Viviana certainly had hers, too.

"Not going to happen," Anton said sharply. "Ever."

How could he be so sure?

• • •

Anton rested back to the headboard to catch his breath and brought his wife closer to his side with one arm. Not bothering to make any attempt to leave his sweaty grasp, Viviana laid a soft kiss to his arm as his hand rubbed up her naked side.

After falling into bed around three in the morning once Erik and Ivan were gone, Anton was woken up by his wife not a couple of hours later. It wasn't like her to be up so early, never mind wanting to fuck like they had, given the new pressure and pain she'd been experiencing in the mornings. Anton had no idea what came over Viviana, but he sure as hell wasn't about to complain.

Their coupling had been rough—rougher than he liked given her stage of pregnancy. But even when he tried to slow them down, to take her softer, Viviana wouldn't have it. Anton wasn't one to deny his wife, especially not of that.

"Jesus Christ," he mumbled into the palm of his hand. Even though his body was still humming from her high, his mind was downright exhausted. Three hours of sleep wasn't new to Anton, but he could use a bit more. "Thanks for the wake-up call, baby."

Viviana giggled, but even the sound felt off. "Yeah, I guess."

"Hey," he said into her hair. The grip he had on her tightened momentarily. "What's wrong?"

"Hmm?" Viviana turned just enough to lean up and press her silken mouth to the underside of his jaw. "Nothing, just thinking about Sergei."

"Don't fret over that idiot. He's not even a blip on my radar. We'll get that dinner done and move on."

Anton was lying through his teeth, but concerning his wife just wasn't okay with him. What he wanted her doing was focusing on the end of her pregnancy, their son, and her health. He was the boss, so he'd handle the Bratva issues. There was no way she was going to be brought into the crossfire of Sergei's nonsense, so he didn't think she had any need to be properly informed.

"Actually," he said, thinking about his conversation the night before with his spies. "I think you might just show, and then go. You haven't been feeling terribly great lately, so it's not a stretch to think you might not feel well that day. Just stay long enough to say hello, forgive Tatiana if you want, and then Rory will escort you home and Joe will follow. Business as usual."

"Forgive her if I want," she repeated dully.

"It'd be better if you did, or at least say you do, but it's not expected. You did ask for her, though, so you have to be respectful about whatever you choose to do."

Viviana snorted. "When am I ever not? Can I claw her eyes out after?"

"No," Anton said, laughing. That'd surely be a sight. He bet Viviana would give Tatiana one hell of a run for her money. "Not while you're pregnant with my child, anyhow."

"Yeah, but making her swallow a few teeth would sure make me feel a heck of a lot better."

"My God. You know there's nothing there, right? Her and me, I mean. That's not ... It's just not there, baby. You don't have to be jealous."

"I'm not jealous, Anton." Strangely, he believed her. Viviana shrugged under the weight of his arm resting around her shoulders. "Why should I be ... of *Tatiana*? I have exactly what she doesn't. Everything she thought should have been hers is mine. I have your life, your son, and your love. Even if she was nothing more than your whore, which she isn't, she still wouldn't have any of those things. So no, I'm not jealous of that girl. On the other hand, I do wonder if she is envious of me."

"I have no doubt of that."

Viviana sighed. "Exactly. Tatiana has defied her father, you, and God knows how many others just to hurt me once. That was before we were married, before Demyan, and she only managed to sling words. This time might be different. At this dinner, she's going to see me pregnant, happy, and protected, all because of you. Again, all that she doesn't have and everything she wanted. So it brings me back to safety, I guess. You made it clear you don't want her in any way so would she hurt me, or worse your baby, because of her resentment? Is she that crazy over you?"

Anton stayed silent, letting his wife's words sink in as he considered them. It wasn't that what she said didn't make sense, because it did, but he wondered why Viviana had asked for Tatiana's presence at all.

"You asked for her to be there, Vine. If you were worried about all of this, why ask at all?"

"I also asked for no guns."

"And I'll make sure that's adhered to as best I can," Anton said, still feeling confused. "You won't take a step into any establishment unless it is weapon free."

Viviana felt tense in his arms. "You don't need a gun to kill someone."

"She won't have any chance to be alone with you."

"I know."

"Then what?" Anton asked.

"I want this done," she said so low he strained to hear. "Put an end to it, however you have to. I don't want to worry about her or her goddamned family after it's over. I don't want to think if she can't hurt me, she'll go to the next best thing."

"You're worried she'll try to hurt Demyan."

"Or you. To me, that's just as bad."

"You know that'd never—"

"No, I don't," Viviana interrupted coolly. "But if I didn't have them to worry about, it'd be one less thing for me to consider."

It was only then that her hidden meanings were starting to dawn on Anton. Viviana never asked him for anything in regards to business. She didn't like to have her hands in his pots, so to speak. This was entirely different, especially if she was asking what he thought she was asking.

"Come on, Vine …"

"I want it *done*," she repeated thickly. "Please."

"On your head, though? You want that on your mind, bloodying up your hands, too?"

"Please?"

"Stop it," Anton said, practically spitting the words. "Fuck, just don't say that shit. I'll handle it."

"Before or after one of us is dead?"

Anton was out of the bed before he had blinked.

Grabbing the cotton sleep pants he'd kicked off earlier in his haste to be with his wife, he tugged the article of clothing on and avoided Viviana's stare. With the sheet wrapped tightly around her frame, Viviana turned and watched him from under her lashes.

"You don't know what that means, baby."

"I do," she murmured.

"No, you don't. *Really*," Anton said, raking his fingers through his hair. "Once you've done that, you've done it. You're dirty, then. No amount of soap and water is going to wash that filth off of you, Vine. It doesn't go away. *Ever*."

"This isn't about money, or disrespect, or greed, Anton."

"Stop trying to justify it to yourself. If you have to do that, you shouldn't be making the call for it."

"I'm not justifying the request. I'm not making any calls. And I'm not just anyone asking you for it. This isn't you being the boss, it's me being your wife and asking you as my husband. Can it be done?"

Anton blinked out of his haze, meeting Viviana's determined eyes with his own. "Anything can be done, but that doesn't mean it needs to be."

"I think this does. I can't wake up some morning and you not be here. Why do I keep getting this horrible feeling that's exactly what's going to happen every time I think about that family?"

Another blazing understanding slammed down on Anton. He hadn't thought much of it the night before, but the door to the guestroom had been left open, and they hadn't exactly been quiet during their discussion. A little too much vodka had made Anton forget his wife was sleeping just down the hall a few steps from his office instead of the other side of the upstairs like she usually would.

In fact, he'd went to their bedroom first looking for her. *Shit.*

"Did you eavesdrop on my meeting last night?" he asked.

Viviana didn't look away as she said, "I didn't eavesdrop. I *woke* up."

Instantly, Anton knew he should apologize for hiding the things he had. "I'm ..."

"Don't bother giving your excuses to me," Viviana said, her gaze narrowing. The coldness in her tenor surprised him more than her words. "But given how you treated me for an entire week after I made the mistake of keeping something important from you, I wasn't about to do it again. I suppose you didn't see it the same way, huh?"

"No, I did. What I didn't want was you having this crap on your mind right now. If I had to handle something, I didn't want it on your conscience, too."

"Well, it is now, Anton. And I'm asking you to finish it."

Anton let his emotions simmer as Viviana moved across the bed. With her bare legs dangling over the edge, she reached up and fisted his sleep pants with one hand, using the other to keep the sheet tight to her chest.

"I'm not mad," she told him quietly. "Not with you, anyway."

"Nobody's going to hurt me," he said.

"But they're going to *try*."

"Hit them first, is that what you're saying?"

Viviana shrugged one shoulder. "You've got the call on when, where, and how. Use it."

Anton released a shaky exhale, nodding subtly. "Did you hear what I said about Tatiana, too?"

"That she was bothering you," she replied, calmer than she probably felt. "How?"

"It was only twice. She didn't cross any lines, so I overlooked it."

"That's not what I asked, Anton."

Chewing on the inside of his cheek, Anton said, "When I bought your pearls, she showed up at the jeweler's. A week or so later, she showed up at the coffee shop I frequent."

"She has no need to be in Brooklyn," Viviana noted quietly.

"I know, and I've considered that. I had someone check

up on her, to make sure she wasn't trying to get close to any of my guys. She came back clean, or so it seemed."

Bleakly, Viviana nodded her assent. "I still don't trust her."

"Me, either."

He couldn't help but remember how tightly Viviana had held him that morning, how sharp her teeth had felt nipping into his jaw, and the way she somehow pulled him deeper with every cry. Their lovemaking had been frantic, rushed, and desperate. At first Anton hadn't known why, but he supposed now he did.

"That's what this was for you, huh?"

Viviana cleared her throat, looking away. "What?"

"Me and you this morning. Like you weren't going to have me again."

"No, more like I didn't want to forget. Like every other day, you have to leave. Are you going to be back, Anton? That's my new question. Do I get a new promise to go along with it, too?"

Smacking his lips, Anton could still taste the hot and heady flavor of his wife lingering on his mouth. Viviana's fingers shadowed along his thigh over his cotton pants, keeping his nerves awake and aware of her body's closeness and the heat it caused. Already, his own body was reacting to her and her innocent touch.

"I'll handle it."

"Will you?" Viviana asked, her stare flicking up to seek out his.

"Yeah, but I won't tell you."

Bloody hands, Anton thought. She'd never have them on his watch.

Chapter Fourteen

Two weeks later, Anton found himself calm and waiting as he fixed the knot on his tie in the master bath's mirror. Things had fallen seamlessly together for the dinner with the Jersey Bratva family. A little too easily, maybe. Anton was going to make sure that after tonight, his family, his Bratva, and his wife wouldn't have one more thing to worry about when it came to the Belovs.

"What do you think?"

Anton turned at Viviana's voice, his eyes widening and a low whistle of appreciation falling from his lips. The thigh-high, black dress she wore was tight enough to show off every beautiful curve of her body. And despite being pregnant, Viviana still had her curves and a swaying walk that memorized him if he watched for too long. Black peep-toes with a four inch stiletto heel clicked-clacked against the hardwood floor as she came a little closer, waiting for him to speak.

The sleeves of the V-neck dress stopped at her wrists, effectively covering the scarring she rarely ever noticed anymore. A slight shimmer to the fabric glittered under the lights in their master bath. Her black hair fell in silky, sleek waves and the sharp cut of her bangs only served to shadow her gaze to a demure effect. Not that her eyes needed shadowing. Viviana's features were flawless with her high cheekbones accentuated with blush, full lips painted a striking red, and her dark eyes lined with heavy, black strokes of kohl.

Holy sweet, good goddamn, he thought.

"Is it good?" Viviana asked. "Or too much?"

"No, no way," Anton said quickly. "Definitely *not* too much, baby. God, you're beautiful. You're killing me here. Look at you."

With one hand held out, Anton spun Viviana in a small

circle, taking an inventory of her figure in a dress he'd never seen before. While his wife always dressed appropriately and looked amazing, it wasn't often she went to this extent.

"You trying to prove a point or something, Viviana?"

"Nope. Just thought it'd be a while before I'd get to dress up like this again. The next few months are going to be what? Spit up, formula, poo, no sleep, and *joy*." Viviana laughed a tinkling sound, her hand falling to her stomach. "He's not going to give me much of a break to be your pretty wife, so, why not?"

Leaning down, Anton kissed the corner of her mouth, mindful of the lipstick she'd carefully applied. "You're always going to be my pretty wife, Vine."

"Yes, but will I always look the part? That's the real question."

Anton hummed dismissively, dragging his hand down to the swell of her hip. "Yeah, always."

"So …" Viviana smile turned into a thin frown. "What's the plan tonight?"

"Nothing you need to concern yourself with. You'll stay no longer than five or ten minutes, and then go. The only ones aware you're going to be leaving are me, Ivan, and Erik. That way, it'll be a last minute thing no one expected. I don't want you there for longer than necessary. The less people who know you're leaving, the better. It'll seem unplanned, which is better for us all."

"That's not what I meant, Anton. I mean about handling—"

"You don't get to ask about that," he said calmly.

"But you are going to deal with it, right?"

Anton stared at his reflection in the mirror, his eyes immediately drawn to the woman at his side and the swell of her midsection. Yeah, he was going to handle the Belovs. It wouldn't be pretty. Actually, it'd be downright messy. Erik's ability to bribe certain city officials was going to come in mighty handy when it came time to handle the cleanup.

"Smile, baby, that's all you need to worry about. Just

smile." Anton glanced down at his watch, seeing the time. "It's nearly five, so we need to go."

"Joe and Rory aren't escorting us?" she asked.

"They already left. Two other bulls are at the restaurant helping them check Sergei, his guys, and Tatiana when they arrive."

The wooden box on the bath's counter caught his eye for a second. Luckily, as Anton nearly forgot about the object in the presence of his wife. Viviana had that effect on him every damned time. She made his mind muddle up something fierce.

"Also, before I forget." Anton snatched up the box, opening it up to expose a small handgun resting in a holster. "You're wearing this, no arguments."

Viviana stared at the weapon with barely contained disgust. "But if I'm leaving and there's no risk for me, why do I need it?"

Anton shrugged. "Because you're pregnant with my child and I'm asking you to. It'll be hidden on your thigh, I know you can shoot it, and it's just a precaution."

"Joe and Rory—"

"Stop arguing with me on this. It's important you have a gun on you."

"We're being checked at the restaurant, too, Anton."

"There's not a soul in that room who would dare put their hands between your legs. Not with me standing right there. That dress is too tight for it to be hidden elsewhere, and as you asked for no heat, they won't expect you to have one on anyway."

Bending down, Anton said nothing as he clasped the holster around her thigh and tightened it to fit. Viviana didn't fight with him as he tugged on the Velcro to insure it wasn't going to slip down.

"Comfortable?"

Viviana shuddered. "No. I know it's there. So, no."

"Vine, listen to me," he whispered pleadingly. Glancing up, Anton could see the tension in her face, the unease in her eyes. His fingers skimmed the insides of her thighs, hoping to will some of her discomfort away. "Do not take this off until I say it's okay to do so. Please."

"Do you honestly think I need it?"

"I know what I'm doing tonight. I know what Ivan and Erik are doing. I know what my brothers will do when I ask them to do it. What I don't know is who has been working with Sergei, or who would hurt you if given the chance. Could someone be waiting outside of the restaurant when you leave?" Anton asked rhetorically, ignoring the wince Viviana responded with. "Yeah, baby, they could. Rory and Joe aren't going to be inside so they can also keep their guns, but they don't know why they aren't allowed inside. They, like everybody else, think you're going to be there start to finish. Just ... do this for me."

Over the last two weeks, Anton had provided his wife whatever information she wanted. When she asked about the tires, he told her the truth. When she wanted to surmise on who was going behind Anton's back, he talked it out with her. While it wasn't easy, and there was a lot he didn't want her to know for the sake of her own sanity, he told her anyway.

If she had the will to ask, she had the will to know.

Anton made no apologies for keeping it from her initially and Viviana didn't ask for one.

"Okay," Viviana finally said with a small nod.

• • •

As far as Viviana was concerned, the differences between her and Tatiana Belov were obvious. She was an olive hue to Tatiana's milk and cream complexion. Dark eyes to a slate-blue. Viviana had been born with an Italian set of morals and the Russian girl had been brought up spoiled by her Bratva roots. And while they were both exceptionally beautiful in their own rights, Viviana was not ugly in her heart.

There was no hatred in Viviana's stare as she stood across

from Tatiana.

Tatiana, however, did not hide her contempt in the slightest.

Viviana ignored the burning gaze from Tatiana as Anton removed the fur coat from her shoulders and handed it to a man waiting. The article was dubiously checked, as was the suit jacket her husband removed. She stood in silence, watching as Anton stood off to the side and allowed Sergei's men to check him for weapons.

A pen was drawn out of his pants pocket and Anton scoffed. "Really? You're worried about that?"

"Boss?" the man asked, turning to Sergei expectantly.

Sergei waved off the item and the pen was handed back to Anton like nothing was amiss. When the unknown man turned on Viviana, ready to check her as well, Anton growled under his breath.

"Do not put hands on my wife without asking for permission."

"Touchy," Tatiana said dryly.

"Shush." Sergei admonished his daughter with a single look. "Kain, you know better. Anton, may he check her?"

Anton nodded, his eyes flicked away from the man, dismissive and bored. "Touch her skin and I will remove your fingers."

Viviana managed not to shiver as Kain's hands skimmed her waist. There wasn't a place on her body she could hide a gun, other than the spot Anton had put the small revolver, so to her the act of being frisked was nothing more than a show. Something to make her uncomfortable. And it did.

When Kain's hand unexpectedly roamed over her midsection, Viviana flinched.

Anton didn't miss the distress for a second. Without warning, Viviana found herself pushed backwards at the same time Kain was lifted from the floor. His back slammed down to a table. The room went deafeningly quiet as silverware, wine glasses, and a chair toppled over in Anton's aggression. The warning that shouted from Anton's mouth in Russian was nothing compared to his clenched fists as he pulled Kain up from the table just long enough to slam him back down.

It only took a brief moment before people started to move around them. Fortunately, no weapons or guns meant there wasn't much anyone could do but watch and wait it out. Viviana caught sight of nothing as Ivan tugged her to the side, his arm wrapping to her shoulders and turning her back to the action.

"Shh," he said quietly in her ear. "Let him make his point."

"You dare to touch my child?" Anton shouted. "Do you think she's hiding something there, you fucking fool?"

"I apologize," Kain said in a gasp of breath.

"Louder, so my wife will hear it, too." Another slam of Kain's back hitting the table resounded. Viviana bit her lip to keep from asking Anton to stop. She understood he was only doing it to keep anyone else's hands from touching her again. "Now!"

"I apologize for touching your child, Pakhan."

Viviana was allowed to turn around just in time to see Kain moving off the table. Anton was wiping his hands on his dress shirt, seemingly disgusted that he had touched the man at all.

"I think I've had enough of my wife being handled, Sergei," Anton muttered bitingly. "The next one of your men who do it will apologize with their life. Are we clear?"

"Funny, my daughter didn't have the slightest issue being checked by your men," Sergei replied.

"My wife is not your daughter." Anton tipped his chin up, offering Tatiana a baleful look and a cruel sneer. "Viviana is accustomed to my hands, not just any man's. Can Tati say the same?"

Sergei turned red but Viviana beat him to the verbal punch.

"Anton, no more." It was quiet and forceful, but the statement was enough to level out the emotions running high in the room. Viviana took a step out of Ivan's hold and laid her hand to Anton's arm gently. "Apologize. That was uncalled for."

Anton glanced down at her, his brow cocking as the corner of his mouth lifted with the ghost of a grin.

"Acting like a *principessa*." His Russian roughened up the Italian word, and Viviana snorted under her breath when he added, "Not the time, baby."

"A lady, not a Cosa Nostra princess. Apologize. For me?"

"Sergei, my wife assumes I've offended your daughter," Anton said, not taking his eyes off Viviana. His smirk grew when the Jersey Pakhan stayed silent. "My wife forgets it was Tatiana who called her a Russian whore months ago."

"I didn't forget, I forgave. There's a difference."

Anton ticked two of his fingers under her chin, winking as he leaned down to kiss her cheek. "True, my merciful little wife," he said, turning back to the others. "My apologies, Sergei. Are you happy with the restaurant, and did it meet your requirements?"

Sergei, looking unhappily at his daughter who studied her manicure with the falsest fascination, sighed. "Well enough. The employees were fine with letting my men check the floors and backrooms so long as your men were with them. The owner closed before supper to extend us privacy. It works."

"Any feds following?"

"They trailed after my daughter's bulls when we switched cars an hour away. You?" Sergei asked.

"The same, though it took us … What, three switches, Vine?"

"Three too many," Viviana said under her breath. She hated switching cars, but the meeting wasn't one anyone wanted overheard or recorded, so she dealt with it. "May we sit, now? I'm not feeling well, and I'm not to be on my feet for long."

"Yes, sit."

Sergei wasted no time prodding his daughter into a chair at a ready-set table. Anton pulled out a seat for Viviana, his mouth coming down to graze along her neck as she sat. She couldn't help but notice the acidic gaze of Tatiana had turned on her once again.

Viviana met the girl's hatred head on, unbothered and not willing to give her the rise she so clearly wanted.

A lady, she reminded herself silently.

Jealousy was an ugly, horrible color to wear.

The dozen of men in the room wandered to designated spots as Sergei waved for the man closest to them to sit down at the next table, and Anton waved for Ivan and Erik to sit as well.

"Your Sovietnik couldn't join?" Anton asked.

"His thoughts on this dinner did not match mine," Sergei said cryptically.

"Unfortunate," Ivan stated to Anton's right.

"Yes, well, he'll come around, I'm sure." Sergei smiled, but the expression didn't stick with Viviana as true. "Shall we eat?"

"Vine?" Anton's hand came to rest on her stomach at the question. Viviana smiled, ignoring the tender ache in her lower back as she straightened a little further in her chair.

"Let's eat."

• • •

Anton watched for the third time as Viviana hid her scowl by tipping up her glass of water and rubbed her lower back with her free hand. Already, she'd been at the dinner for much longer than he anticipated she would be, so it was just about time for her to take her leave. If she was uncomfortable or in pain, it was even more of a reason to get her home and in their bed.

"Hey, are you okay?" Anton asked.

All the movement at the table stopped at his question.

Viviana set her glass to the table and shook her head. "Just … my lower back is starting to act up again."

"Pregnancy will do that." Tatiana observed Viviana from

the other side of the table with an almost dismissive quality. Anton bit back his retort. The comment might have been easy to overlook if her next one wasn't so scathing. "After all, you can't expect to blow up like a balloon and not have some issues, right?"

Viviana's jaw ticked. "Have you been pregnant before, Tati? I didn't realize you had personal experience in the work of bearing a child."

"God, no." Tatiana scoffed with a roll of her blue eyes. "I would never allow my body to go through that kind of hell."

"I'd be pleased to have a grandchild eventually," Sergei said, keeping his eyes down on his plate as he wiped his mouth. Anton knew Tatiana was Sergei's only child. The one son he did have died in infancy, regrettably. "Never say never, my dear."

"If I get any say, it damn well will be never."

Sergei dropped his napkin to the table. "Wonderful."

Anton ignored the exchange, his attention fully diverted to his wife. He wasn't sure if she was faking the discomfort, or if she was really experiencing it. It wasn't unusual and considering the heels she wore, her back could very well be bothering her. The doctor appointment they went to the day before said she didn't appear to be close to delivering, despite being one week off from her due date.

"Vine?" he asked again, a little more forcefully. She didn't have to answer for Anton to see the obvious anxiety filling up her gaze. The small smile she offered him didn't quite reach her eyes, either. Lowering his voice, he leaned into her side to only she would hear him. "How long?"

Viviana all but brushed his concern off. "Since this morning, but nothing is regular or too bothersome. It's just a back ache, Anton."

Anton straightened in his chair, tossing Ivan a look over his wife's shoulder. "Viviana needs to go home. Immediately."

Sergei's fork clattered to his plate. "But—"

"But nothing," Anton interrupted firmly. "She's in pain

and she's diabetic. What she needs right now is rest, not stress. Considering she only has one more week to do so, I'd like for her to be calm and comfortable. Has my wife not met your desires for this dinner, Sergei?"

"Tatiana?" Sergei asked instead, glancing his daughter's way.

The blonde flicked her wrist dismissively. "I'm sure we're good, right, Vine?"

Viviana huffed out a breath of air. It was the first show of frustration she had shown towards the other woman all evening.

"Sure," Viviana said dully. "Just fine."

Anton stood and Sergei followed immediately. "May I walk her out, Anton?"

That hadn't exactly been in his plans, but Anton couldn't see the harm. Unless Viviana didn't agree, that was. "Vine, you good?"

She nodded. "Yes, of course."

Helping Viviana to stand, he couldn't help but notice how hard her stomach seemed to be under his palm. She shook off his second voice of concern with a roll of her eyes. Anton took a moment to say goodbye, kissing her mouth and letting her wipe the red stain the kiss left behind on his lips.

"Love you, hmm?" he whispered.

Viviana grinned as Sergei offered his hand for her to take. "Like crazy."

Anton didn't watch Sergei walk his wife through the restaurant, but he make sure Boris followed close behind. Knowing it would probably be his only chance to get Tatiana in private, he turned back to the table and sat down, meeting the girl's unbidden, vile gaze.

"I can't help but wonder …" Tatiana lips curved with a spiteful grin as she regarded Anton. "After she's had that child of yours, will she still be so pretty? Will you still pant at her feet like her puppy dog? Who do you think your first whore will be, Anton, someone you know, or someone you don't? Do you think she'll cry?"

Anton took her words for what they were worth: absolutely nothing.

"How much does it bother you, Tati?" he asked back quietly. "Enough that you had to hire a photographer to watch her at our home? Did you want to punish yourself so much that you had to have proof she was mine, that she was pregnant, safe, and happy? Was that it?"

Tatiana leaned back in her chair, a perfectly shaped brow lifting in her contemplation. "Why would I want to watch your wife, Anton?"

The arrogant smugness in her tone couldn't be hidden. It prickled at Anton's nerves like nothing else. "That's not a denial."

"Oh, he's good-looking *and* quick," Tatiana quipped.

"Your reason—it's jealousy. It always has been. It was jealousy that made you come to my club after Vine and I were engaged, because in your crazy head, I couldn't have possibly found a woman to tie me down. It was jealously that made you check up on me weeks ago. My wife was right, Tati. She is not the one between you who feels envy, because she already has everything you don't. But, slashing her tires, photographing her at home, that's a whole other ballgame. Do you hate me that badly? Is your father truly stupid enough to go along with it?"

"Not you. *Her.* Sergei doesn't give a shit about her, he just wanted what should have been his so he let me be."

"You're a liar. You know, you're the only fucking female I've met that makes me want to go out and catch myself a felony, Tati. Whatever crazy plan you might have had for us, it wasn't going to be. We sparked but it sure as fuck wasn't in a good way. You need to let it go."

"So you say," she responded lightly.

That only pissed Anton off more. "You are crazy, huh? You know what my father taught me about women like you?"

"What's that?"

"You're just a dog digging for your bone. A *bitch*, that's

what he would have called you. No good for nothing."

Anton pulled that pen from his pocket, tapping it to the tabletop. If Kain had thought to pull the cap off the top of it, he might have noticed how the tip had been sharpened down and a razor's blade inserted into the tip. Messy, but effective.

"And good for nothing animals just need to be put the fuck down so they don't cause anybody else anymore harm. I think you've caused my wife enough, so your time is running out."

Tatiana smiled a cruel sight, tipping up her jaw to him. "I suppose he never warned you about when the bitch bites back, though, did he?"

Ivan cleared his throat, tossing his napkin to the table. The man has stayed silent during the entire exchange, much to Anton's surprise and gratitude. "I think we're almost finished here."

Tatiana laughed under her breath, her mouth pulling into an ugly sneer. "Oh no, we're far from done. Have you been going crazy, Anton? Have you figured it out, yet?"

"Figured out what, Tati?" he asked, distracted by the sight over her shoulder.

Behind Tatiana, Anton noticed the owner of the restaurant was standing in one of the doorways that led to the kitchen. That was his signal. The few employees were making their way out of the back. They knew Viviana was out of the restaurant, so they had five minutes before all hell would break loose in the kitchen. Hell came in the form of fire, after all. The owner of the restaurant had been looking to refurbish the place, anyhow.

It was just another win-win in Anton's eyes.

"You haven't, have you?" Tatiana asked cockily. "You have no idea just how close I've gotten to you."

"Not close enough," Anton replied indifferently.

He snapped his fingers at the only brigadier whose presence he requested at the dinner. As Boris walked back past the table, Anton tossed him the pen in one fluid motion. Ivan glanced at his boss and gave a single nod to say he too was ready.

Sergei wouldn't make it back to the table alive.

Tatiana wouldn't leave it with breath still in her lungs.

It'd be a full contact brawl and the fire that followed would burn the building down in ten minutes flat. Anton and his guys would be blocks away when the fire department arrived on scene. Erik had already worked his magic on the official side. A detective, one fire marshal, and three cops picked up those bribes like they were candy. Dirty, the whole fucking city was full of dirt.

"You should have stayed out of her life, Tatiana," Anton said. "I warned you once."

"I didn't need to do anything. You already put him there."

He didn't have time to dissect what she implied. With the sound of Sergei returning from the front of the restaurant, Anton held out two fingers for Boris to see down at his side. Ivan slipped the butter knife off the side of the table at the same time Erik grabbed the nearly empty wine bottle and began walking towards the kitchen. What actions could be witnessed were all innocent enough ...

Until they weren't.

When Sergei hit the floor behind him with a painful shout and the Jersey men reached for the guns that wouldn't be in their pockets, Anton stood. Finally, fear lit up Tatiana's blue eyes, but something else stared back, too. Something that chilled him to the core.

"You're already too late," Tatiana said. "I hope you said goodbye."

Whatever that meant, Anton would kill her for it, too.

Chapter Fifteen

"Fuck," Anton spat. "Stop moving, Ivan."

Something lodged in Anton's throat, choking him up as he pressed his hand flat and hard against Ivan's midsection. Tears crawled freely over his cheeks. Anton hadn't even realized he was crying until the salty taste of his tears fell to his bruised lips. It was just a little too much for Anton to see his friend in the state he was.

"Hey, hey." Ivan clasped Anton's face, smearing streaks of blood over his cheeks. The coldness seeping from Ivan's skin to Anton's was enough to make him shiver. "Shit, look at you, huh? Kain sure did a fucking number on you."

Anton shook Ivan's worry off as he was in a much worse state. "I'm fine. Just smacked me good in the mouth."

"Yeah, with a *chair*," Ivan said, laughing bleakly.

Anton's shoulder slammed into the back of the driver's seat as Erik took a turn a little too sharply. When Ivan groaned in pain, Anton cussed low again.

"Easy, Erik." Boris reached up between the front seats to smack the man driving in the back of the head. "We need to make it to the clinic with him alive, dumbass."

Erik apologized repeatedly.

Anton's hold on Ivan's stomach loosened, slipping in the slick, warm blood that pumped out from under his fingers. The fluid was thick, coating his hands and soaking to stain everything it touched with a morbid dark cherry color. Never had the smell of blood turned him nauseated before, but when it was coming out of the body of his best friend like it was, killing him with every drop that spilled, Anton couldn't help but want to be sick.

"Anton, it ... it's all right." Even Ivan didn't seem to believe his own words. "Calm down."

No, it wasn't. That was the sad truth. Anton could only

shake his head above his friend.

Ivan was losing blood much too fast, and they still had another fifteen minutes before they'd arrive to the clinic they used when shit like this happened. They couldn't just drive up to any ER and take Ivan in because doctors and nurses were required to report gunshot wounds to police. The particular clinic they were going to would keep quiet for a hefty price, and hopefully, they'd save Ivan while they were at it. Anton couldn't take the chance it would be linked back to the fire at the restaurant they had left only ten minutes before, so he took the risk of a longer drive to a safe place.

Anton's shoe skidded on the puddle of Ivan's blood that had gathered on the floor. Feeling his hold on the wound slip again, Anton's frustration grew. He needed to keep as much pressure on the damage as he could to keep Ivan from bleeding out.

Boris leaned over Ivan's laid out body and slammed his hands into Anton's chest, pushing him backwards. "Move, Boss. Jesus." Ivan coughed, blood spilling heavily from the injury as Anton's hands fell from his middle only long enough for Boris's to replace them with his own. "I've got it. Take a second. He'll be okay."

Anton ignored the crimson wetness smeared over his hands, soaking through his clothes. Leaning against the SUV's back door, his fist pressed to his forehead as he fought off the urge to beat the shit out of something … anything.

It shouldn't have been like that.

It wasn't supposed to go down like that.

Where had that gun come from, anyway?

The fight that ensued after Boris had taken Sergei down was nothing more than a blur to Anton's mind. He vaguely remembered getting his hands around Tatiana's throat. That hadn't taken him long, not when he had to worry about the five other Jersey Bratva in the room. The ache in his neck brought back a memory of something heavy that had slammed down on his back.

And then there was one loud pop.

Anton knew the sound of a gun firing off. That particular sound would follow him forever, he knew.

Everything that came after that one gunshot had been a lot more violent, a lot messier. It had also been quick. The one with the gun—who was he?

"How'd we miss that shit, huh?" Anton asked, his voice cracking.

"I don't know, Boss," Boris mumbled, keeping his eyes down on Ivan.

"We checked them all," Ivan stated, his voice too calm and his eyes starting to glaze. "Honest to God, we fucking check—"

"Shut up. Stop talking. You're bleeding, so you can't talk right now."

Erik snorted in the front seat. "Ivan, you're giving Anton a heart attack back there."

"Fucking thought it was us who was going to off you," Ivan said with a snort. "Idiot. Why would I ever off *you*, huh?"

"Shut up," Anton repeated weakly.

Anton wouldn't have minded their joking so much if he wasn't so concerned about Ivan. He knew they were only trying to calm him down, but the deathly pale shade taking hold of Ivan's skin and the coolness of the man's body in Anton's lap said more than anything else could. It didn't help that there was pain written all over his best friend's features and the blood just kept on coming.

"What'd he do, hit a fucking vein, or what?" Erik asked.

Boris swallowed nervously, meeting Anton's gaze before he shook his head. "Hit something."

"As long as he didn't hit my goddamned bowels or stomach we'll be okay."

"Shit, shit, shit." Anton squeezed his eyes shut, still trying to figure out what had gone wrong. "How'd we manage to miss that?"

"I told you ..." Ivan trailed off with another cough and red saliva saturated his lips. Anton's heart stopped for a moment. If his friend was spitting up blood, it was more than likely the bullet had hit something internally.

"Fuck! Stop talking!" Anton shouted.

"No," Ivan growled back. "Listen to me. We checked him. Every one of those men were checked. Who checked *him*, Anton?"

Anton didn't know because he hadn't been there. He wanted to arrive second. He had trusted the men who were there to do their jobs properly. The only odd man out in the equation was Boris. That was only because Anton had faith his brigadier had nothing to do with whatever betrayal the Jersey Pakhan had planned, never mind his ability to kill someone with just about anything in his hands.

"I don't know," he said frantically. "I wasn't ... I don't—"

"*Joe*," Boris breathed, his head snapping up as his eyes landed on Anton. "Joe checked that fucker. I think Rory was going to but he took Tatiana instead, or maybe Joe told him to. I wasn't close enough to hear, but ..."

Anton wasn't listening anymore. Several realizations slammed into his mind like pieces of a puzzle. It was painful, and terrifying, and heart wrenching all at once. He'd made a horrible, terrible mistake. They'd overlooked what was right in front of their faces.

The photographer should have been chased away if Joe had done his job that day. Joe was the only one with Viviana's car when her tires were slashed and he'd made a phone call to Rory after saying the other man's phone wasn't working. Tatiana had been in trouble with a Russian, according to Boris's sources.

I didn't need to do anything. You already put him there.

Tatiana told him, but Anton hadn't listened.

It was always someone close. Unfortunately, Anton had mistakenly thought the target was only on him. That couldn't have been more wrong. How much closer could a person get to Viviana than one of her bulls?

"Pull over!"

"We're five minutes away," Erik said, turning to look over

his shoulder. "You sure you want to get out now?"

Anton met Ivan's gaze and he could tell by the water gathering there that the other man had figured it out, too. There were two more cars behind them; the other vehicles of Anton's Bratva that had needed to be removed from the restaurant before the officials arrived. One of them would work. He had to get home, now.

"I'm sorry," Anton whispered. "Ivan, I'm so sorry."

"Don't. I'll—" Ivan stopped up short, swallowing the words instead. "It'll be fine."

Would it?

• • •

"Well, crap." Rory tossed his cell phone into the passenger seat with disgust, rubbing at his forehead, exasperated. "Damn, that sucks."

"What's wrong?" Viviana asked.

She didn't like that he suddenly seemed more quiet and nervous than usual. Rory was the more upbeat of her two bulls, the constantly smiling one. He always tried to find the humor in situations and he kept Viviana talking when she grew too quiet. Maybe it was their closeness in age that helped their friendliness along.

From the back seat, she barely made out his shrug in the darkness of the SUV. "Nothing for you to worry about, Vine."

"Yeah, that's not going to happen. I just left a sit-down—"

"A *dinner*." Rory leveled her with a look in the mirror. "Nothing more."

"Call a spade a spade. Regardless, you can't tell me we're on the best terms with Jersey right now. So, I'll ask again, what's wrong?"

"Change in plans." With those words, Rory took an exit onto the highway that Viviana wasn't expecting him to. They should have kept going straight to return back to Brighton

Beach. This new direction would eventually lead them towards Connecticut. "Joe called and said there was some issue. Boss wants you out of town. I guess he'll meet us at the lodge in Vermont before morning."

Viviana instantly wanted to know about what the issue was, but something else prickled at the back of her mind. "Anton isn't using the lodge as a safe house, anymore."

Rory glanced up into the rear view mirror. "Huh?"

"The lodge, it's not a safe house. Why would he want me going there if something happened? Besides, our home is closer, Rory. Take me home and Anton can take me wherever the hell he wants."

Besides, her back was hurting something fierce and Viviana had the strangest urge to lay down and sleep. The ache in her back was starting to travel around her sides and through her front, also. She was beginning to wonder if it might be something more. The sensations were no more intense than the false labor was. She'd been terribly stressed out over the last day regarding the Jersey sit-down, so it could have been just that manifesting itself, too.

Viviana wasn't all too concerned about it. Or she was trying not to be.

"Sorry," Rory said, checking over his shoulder before changing lanes. "I don't make the rules, Vine. I just follow orders. Boss called Joe, that's all I know."

But that didn't make sense, either. Anton usually contacted Rory first because Viviana was almost always with him when she was traveling with a bull. And if it was so serious that she suddenly needed to leave town, where in the hell was her husband? Dallying around with his guys?

"This is fucking ridiculous," Viviana said, huffing angrily. "I need to go home and go to bed!"

"Whoa." Once more, Rory met her gaze in the mirror, clearly bothered by her show of temper. "Seriously, what's the matter?"

Viviana clamped her mouth shut. Even she didn't know what to make of her outburst. It wasn't like she had much of a reason to be angry, but her emotions were suddenly rolling in their own mess of a turmoil. She didn't know what to think of it, but she hadn't been able to really settle or feel normal since leaving the restaurant.

Calm one second and bordering on tears the next, Viviana felt like a hot mess on the inside. She hadn't experienced emotional currents like that since she first found out about the pregnancy.

What she really wanted was Anton, a hot bath, and bed.

It didn't have to be in that order, either.

Rest. Her body was demanding it.

"Vine?" Rory asked again, warily watching her in the mirror.

"I think maybe I'm …" She trailed off, not knowing how exactly to express her confusing thoughts. If she really considered it, Viviana knew she'd been feeling off for the last couple of days. Mostly, she'd been ignoring it, not even mentioning her restlessness to Anton. Distracted by the lights of other cars on the highway, Viviana felt exhausted.

There was no question in her mind, she didn't need or want to go back to Vermont. Not tonight, and not anytime soon. The drive was too long and she was too close to her due date. Anton knew this.

"Can I just call Anton and be sure that's what he wants, please?"

Rory offered her one his cashmere smiles. "Go for it. It's not like I want to drive half the night away, either. Maybe he'll be cool with us finding a random hotel and bunkering down for the night."

Unfortunately, Anton didn't pick up when Viviana called the first time. He also didn't pick up the second, or third. It wasn't uncommon for Anton to turn his cell on silent if he was handling an issue, so Viviana didn't think much of it. It did annoy the hell out of her, though.

Frustrated, Viviana settled back into the rear seat of the SUV and said, "Well, I guess we're driving."

Rory snorted under his breath. "Guess so."

Not twenty minutes later, Viviana's cell phone rang in her lap. The tune was unfamiliar and the number on the screen certainly wasn't Anton's. In fact, she didn't recognise it at all. She wasn't even sure if she should answer it. The last time she picked up an unknown number, it led to a sit-down with Sergei and his vile daughter.

Viviana decided to pick up the call, anyway. "Hello?"

"Vine? Oh, Jesus Christ." Anton breathed heavily into the receiver. "Thank God."

Instantly, her heart rate exploded at the fear saturating his voice. "Anton? Where is your phone?"

"Baby ... what car are you in?"

"Rory's. Why?"

"Where is Joe?" he asked.

Viviana blinked, unsure of what that had anything to do with his panic. "What's wrong? Did something happen?"

"Viviana, where is Joe?"

"Why?"

"Vine!"

"Trailing us like he always does," she said weakly. "Anton, what's wrong? Why didn't you pick up your phone and whose number is this?"

"Someone's," he replied vaguely. "Mine must have dropped out in the other car. I hope it did, anyway. Listen to me, this is important. I'm halfway to Brighton. What road are you on right now?"

The heart in her chest that was beating out of control might as well have stopped altogether. "What?"

"I'm about fifteen minutes away from our house. How close are you? Tell Rory to keep driving, baby. Whatever you do, do not stop that car."

"But Joe said you didn't want us going to Brighton because—"

The choked sound that escaped Anton had Viviana's tears welling. "You're not on your way home?"

"No," Viviana said in a whisper. "We're ... Rory, where are we?"

"Close to crossing over into Connecticut."

"Did you hear that?" she asked Anton.

"Yeah, I did. Okay, keep driving. Just ... keep fucking driving, Vine."

"But—"

"And tell Rory not to pick up his phone," he interrupted. "Especially not for Joe."

Finally, an understanding began to dawn on Viviana. Dread crept up her spine as the dull ache in her back increased. There would be no reason for Rory not to pick up any calls from Joe. He was her protector just as much as Rory was. Anton trusted the two men with her life—expressed that very sentiment many times.

But, had he been wrong?

It was only then that she considered the way Sergei had tipped his head in Joe's direction as he led her out of the restaurant. She had thought the action was only meant to be respectful, a way of acknowledging the bull, but now ... Viviana didn't think it was that all at.

Oh God.

"Is it Joe? Is he the one we missed in this?"

Anton went silent over the line before he cussed severely. "Give Rory your phone."

"Anton—"

"Give it to him!"

With shaking hands, Viviana handed the phone up to the bull. Rory placed the phone to his ear with one hand, keeping the other on the steering wheel and his eyes on the road.

"Yeah, Boss?" Viviana stayed silent, noticing how Rory's fingers tightened their grip momentarily. "No way, I'd have *known* ..."

"And you think I wouldn't?" she heard Anton roar.

Viviana sunk into the seat, swallowing the bile threatening to rise.

"But ... shit, Joe said—" Rory cut off, listening intently before his gaze in the mirror flicked up to stare out the back window. "He got shot? There weren't supposed to be any guns inside! Goes to show Jersey was planning something, I suppose. Is he all right?"

"Who?" Viviana asked, her heart jumping into her throat.

Rory ignored her. "I can't not answer him if he calls, Boss. He'll know. Hell, he must know the dinner turned sour if Tatiana isn't picking up her calls for him. How long before he puts two and two together and figures out you know, too, huh?"

If Tatiana wouldn't be able to pick up her phone that could only mean ...

Viviana shook off the thought. She wouldn't finish it even in the privacy of her own mind. She knew what she asked for, and she more than understood what it meant. What she wouldn't do now was overthink and fret about it. Anton wouldn't tell her—that's what he said. The reason was obvious: she couldn't know for sure if it was him if he didn't admit it. She didn't want to know anyway.

"How far away are you?" Rory asked quietly. "Yeah, speed it up, then. Traffic isn't too bad. We're not far from Columbus Park. Will that work, you think?"

"Will what work?"

Again, Viviana's question was disregarded.

"Damn it, Boss," Rory mumbled, his gaze slipping down in the mirror to meet Viviana's. "You know I would. You don't even have to ask. Jen fucking loves her like nothing else and I just ... yeah, okay, it'll be fine, don't worry. Keep driving, that's all. And I'm sorry I didn't know."

Without another word, the phone was handed back. Viviana slipped it up to her ear and hid her face from Rory's view by looking out the window. Tears had started to slip out of the corners of her eyes, snaking lines down her cheeks.

"It's bad, right?" she asked.

Viviana swore she could hear the vehicle he was in speed up. "Not if I can help it, baby. How are you feeling?"

"I don't think that's impor—"

"It is to me," he interjected strongly. "I always tell you that you muddle me up. When I need to think, you make me go into a different place. This … It's not even the same. Talk to me for a minute, this phone is almost dead. I need to hear you talk, that's all."

"I'm scared." Anton released a shaky breath into the phone, choking off another sound. Was her husband crying? That only served to send another round of Viviana's own tears falling. "Anton, it's okay."

"Don't worry about it," he said too flippantly for it to feel true. "With Ivan and all, I just couldn't handle it."

Ivan? Was he the one who was hurt? "Is he okay?"

"I don't know. Maybe, maybe not. That's not important."

Viviana disagreed. "It is. You talk to *me*."

Anton sighed. "I missed it, Vine. I dropped the ball and if he dies, that's on me. What will I tell Eva, huh? I'm sorry, but I might as well have held the gun? Three little girls with no father. I fucked that up so bad."

"Not you." Viviana searched for the right words to soothe him, but she knew there weren't any that would work. None but the truth, anyway. "You can't be on everyone and be everywhere all at once, Anton."

"I should have *known*."

"And now we'll fix it."

Anton fell silent.

"Anton?" Viviana asked, worried the call had cut out.

"Fix it," he said. "But what if this is something I can't fix, Vine?"

"You haven't failed me yet."

Anton didn't refute her claim because he couldn't. What Viviana said was absolutely true, and despite her fear over the situation and the danger she knew she was in, she had to have faith it would be okay. Even if it didn't seem like it, and even with her mind suddenly shutting down and her heart racing out of control, she had to find that familiar trust she had always had in her husband.

"It'll be okay," Viviana told Anton. "It will."

"Ivan said that, too. He's probably choking to death on his own blood right now."

"Stop that. That's not what you or I need or want to hear, Anton."

"Tell Boss I'm slowing down a little to give him a bit more time to catch up," Rory said.

Viviana's worry grew when Anton replied, "Heard him. Good plan."

She hated that this was what the situation was reduced to: a plan. Not a good one, or one that may work, or even one she understood. No, just a plan. Two words Viviana didn't have a thing to correlate them to.

Faith, she reminded herself.

A faint beep sounded over the phone. "What was that?" Viviana asked.

Anton huffed, the sound filled with frustration. "The goddamn phone is dying. Of course it's dying, because nothing tonight could go as it should have. Everything has to be a crapshoot in one way or another."

His panic manifesting the way it was certainly wasn't helping her to stay calm.

"Anton, *please* stop."

"I'm sorry," her husband rushed to say. "Jesus, Vine, I'm so sorry. I'm not accustomed to you being on the other end of the phone in these situations, okay? I just ..." Trailing off, Anton swore and she heard the vehicle's engine roar on the other end of the call. "I love you. I have to hang up the call, turn the phone off, and save the power. I'll call back when I'm close enough to see Joe's SUV."

Again, her pulse picked up to a dangerous rate. "Please don't hang up on me."

Anton released a harsh breath. "I'm sorry. This won't take long. I promise."

"But what if something goes bad?"

"I'd say we're already at bad. If I don't make it in time, and Rory can't handle it, you certainly can, Viviana."

Yes, because the gun was still safely hidden on her thigh in its holster.

"I didn't tell you to take it off," Anton said.

"No," she whispered hopelessly.

"So use it."

Chapter Sixteen

Anton's grip on the steering wheel rhythmically tightened and loosened as he covered miles on the highway. With the car cruising at a speed far beyond the limit, Anton wasn't concerned in the least about being pulled over by highway patrol.

After hanging up on his wife, he'd all but turned silent again. There were no noises he wanted to hear other than her voice, just to say she was safe, but even that couldn't be afforded then.

With no one else traveling in the car with him, Anton was left to his own thoughts.

The tears that had fallen on his cheeks were long dried, now. The slow building rage bubbling like a rolling boil inside his stomach only grew in size and strength with every passing second. Even his skin seemed to crawl with his fury.

How fucking *dare* Joe?

How dare he betray his Bratva, his boss, and his life like he had?

Joe's disloyalty would go far beyond just Viviana and Anton. In effect, it would affect his entire brotherhood. It would serve as a painful reminder that while they lived in a modern world with different expectations from the old world, there were still laws the Bratva needed to uphold.

Bratva men lived their life by a strict code of the Vor. Raised with the code's beliefs instilled in them, none could deny there would only be one punishment acceptable for the bull's indiscretion and choices.

Death.

Joe was vetted Vor, just the same as Anton had been.

There was no doubt in the boss's mind that the bull knew where this would lead. After all, it was the road he'd chosen to travel and so Joe must have chosen the consequences just as well. But how could he possibly be so goddamned stupid?

That was Anton's question. It was one he likely wouldn't get the chance to ask, but it was on his mind nonetheless.

Growing up, the notions of the Vor had been repeated to Anton until the words became more of a prayer than an understanding. They were words that had shaped him, hardened him, and *made* him. Words he, like Joe, had chosen to accept and live his life by.

Show no emotion, never touch the floors with your bare hands, forsake your family for your brotherhood, and never deny your Vor status. Own no property, marry no woman, create no children, and accept nothing from police.

Anton blinked at the streams of light coming from the front of his car, surprised at the harshness in some of those customs he had been taught. Not all men chose to live with no wife, or children, but some did. Boris, for example, had never taken a wife, he didn't have kids, and the brigadier didn't own a thing that someone else would take from him. Others, like Ivan, chose to follow the code to his own advantage and disregard what didn't benefit him.

How many of those rules had Anton broken?

How many had his grandfather and father broken?

He'd shed tears over his friend's state, and shown his fear for his wife's danger. It wasn't the first time Anton had let his emotions get the best of him, and it likely wouldn't be the last. He struggled to remember the few times he'd witnessed the same faults in Nicoli or Daniil when he was growing up.

With Daniil it had been rare. Locked behind closed doors when no one could see or hear, when only Sasha would listen, not speak.

With Nicoli, it had been even rarer.

Once, Anton thought. When Nicoli confessed who Viviana really was. He had seen his grandfather's stony façade break only then. She had been more than just Anton's weakness.

As the world changed, so did the strict principles of the Vor's code. The same things that had been expected decades ago were no longer acceptable. Marriage and family were now common occurrences with Bratva men. But, there were things that would never change in the code, too.

Loyalty. Honor. *Respect*.

Yes, Joe would answer for his misdeeds with his life, but Anton wouldn't grieve for the man's blatant disregard of their thieves' creed.

The Bratva would, however. They always did. Anton would let his men have their regret for a fallen brother. It was only proper. He didn't care a bit about Joe, though.

Anton only wanted the bull *dead*.

• • •

Viviana was jerked out of her panicked thoughts by the cell phone jingling in the front seat.

Rory cussed as he plucked up the phone before his gaze slid to meet hers in the rear view mirror. "It's Joe."

The bull had yet to call Rory, and they'd been driving a little while. The tension only seemed to rise higher in the SUV at the thought of simply picking up the call. Rightfully so, as picking up the call was not only stupid, in Viviana's opinion, but dangerous as well.

What other choice did they have?

Ignoring it might only tip Joe off.

She couldn't help but wonder if the other bull already was, considering the time. How long could that sit-down with the Jersey family really go on? Surely not for hours. If Joe was in contact with Tatiana in some way, would he have been trying to call her all this time?

"Gotta pick it up," Rory said. "We're maybe two minutes away from Columbus Park, anyway. Boss can't be too far behind, now."

Viviana nodded. It was all she could offer, really. She had no idea what Columbus Park had anything to do with the plan they didn't speak about. "Sure, whatever."

"Keep quiet, okay?"

"Okay."

The call rang a fourth time before Rory answered it. "Yeah?"

Needing to do something with her hands, Viviana drummed her fingers uselessly against her stomach. The baby had been unusually quiet for the last few hours. He normally moved around like crazy. Minus the occasional twinge from her back ache, or the balling up sensation in her lower abdomen, Viviana was content to ignore the baby's lack of movement.

It was just another sign that she could be in the early stages of labor.

Viviana didn't even want to consider the possibility.

If she was … Oh God, if she was what would that mean?

It wasn't the right time. It wasn't safe.

So, Viviana settled back in the seat and purposely snubbed the warning signs.

Rory's quiet tenor in the front seat drew in her attention. "No way, Boss hasn't called. Jersey must be taking him for a roll or some nonsense. Fucking Sergei …"

Viviana rolled her eyes, fighting off the urge to snort. Fucking Sergei was an understatement. She sincerely hoped he liked his place in hell, if that's where he was sent.

"I haven't slowed down, Joe; I have no interest in driving any longer than necessary tonight. I'm tired … What in the fuck are you bitching about? No, I didn't … No, she's sleeping. Probably going to wake up and need to piss soon. I don't know! It's a woman thing, like a pregnancy thing or some shit. It's not like she's real pleased about driving to Vermont tonight, okay? If she's gotta stop to use the bathroom, I'll let her do it.

"I told you, I'll wake her up soon and ask," Rory said, sounding almost bored. "Well if you're so worried about Boss, why don't you fucking call him, then? Jesus."

Rory hung up the phone with no notice, tossing it to the passenger seat.

"Won't that make him angry?" Viviana asked.

Rory shrugged. "Probably, but he's used to me doing that. He'll call back in thirty seconds."

Viviana frowned, wringing her hands nervously in her lap. How far away was Anton, now? The gun at her thigh felt like it was searing into her skin. She was all too aware of its presence and the fact that she may need to use it. She hadn't fired a gun in … years. Well before Roman had been murdered, anyway.

It didn't matter, though, because Viviana wouldn't ever forget how.

She could still hear her dad's words in her ear …

"I don't want to."

"Stop your whining, Vine. Get a better grip on the gun, or you'll break your damned wrist," Roman muttered. "It's got a mighty kickback because it's a high calibre revolver."

"But, Dad, I don't need—"

"What …" her father interrupted, shooting her a pointed look, "just because you're a girl, you can't learn to handle a weapon? Is that it?"

"I shouldn't have to," Viviana argued.

"You're gonna learn to shoot a gun whether you like it or not. Now, hold it tight or your mother will kick my ass when she finds out I had to take you to the ER for x-rays."

"But—"

Roman didn't give her the chance to argue again. Before Viviana could get another word out, her father's large hand was covering hers still holding the gun. He pulled her arm up and aimed at the glass bottles lined up on the fence. Forcing her thumb up to pull back the hammer, Viviana felt the gun click in her hand. Then, his trigger finger was pressing back on hers.

It wasn't a hair trigger by any means. She hadn't known what to expect. When the gun went off, it vibrated her whole body. Viviana swore her teeth rattled. The revolver recoiled hard and fast but her father's steady, strong grip kept it from slamming back on her too hard. A noise she didn't recognize escaped from her throat. Something unknown welled in her stomach. Fear maybe, but a little bit of excitement, too.

"Ouch." She whined under her breath, feeling a deep ache start in her wrist.

Roman chuckled. "Yeah, it's not going to feel real great until you get used to it. Try it again."

Viviana didn't have the patience to argue a second time, but she wasn't entirely sure she was ready to shoot the heavy gun again, either.

"You afraid of it?" Roman asked.

"No."

"Is it the girl thing, again?"

Viviana scowled. "No."

She didn't sound the least bit convincing.

Roman sucked air between his teeth, rocking back on his heels. "It's real simple, baby girl. Someday you might have to know and I want you to be able to take the shot and get it right the first time. You're going to have just the one when they come at you. Make it count. You being a female won't make any difference when the bullet hits them. And don't you blink about it when it does.

"Now," he said with a nod. "Do it again."

She did.

Strangely, the memory of Roman helped to settle Viviana momentarily. It wasn't that she never thought of him, because she did, but most times it brought on more grief than it did happiness.

As Rory predicted, his cell phone rang less than a minute after he'd hung it up. Once more, he allowed it to ring several times before finally answering the call.

"What, Joe? I'm busy here," Rory said.

Viviana had to give her younger bull some credit. He didn't break his character while speaking to Joe. Rory kept his tone the same as he always would, pretending his frustration was rising like usual, and didn't give any hint that he knew what was really going on.

Whether or not it was working on Joe was another story.

Viviana couldn't help but feel her fear flare up again. Her breathing turned shallow and her heart was beating out of control. Clammy, her hands were useless extremities laying lifeless in her lap. She didn't know what, if anything, there was she could do.

She wished she could be more like Rory, capable of pretending everything was fine.

Even though it so clearly wasn't.

"Take the lead, then," she heard Rory say. "If I'm going to slow for you, just take it. I'm going the goddamn speed limit, man. Precious cargo and all that jazz." Silence was a brief passing in the car before Rory snorted. "Sure, whatever. Did you call—no? Well don't complain, Joe. If he wanted ..."

Rory trailed off as the phone sitting in Viviana's lap started to ring with that loud, unfamiliar chime. Her wide eyes met his in the rear view mirror, panicked and unsure. Viviana couldn't not answer Anton's call, but she also knew Joe thought she was sleeping, too.

"Nothing, man. That's not her phone," Rory said quickly. Viviana hid the phone in her hand and bunched it up inside her fur coat. The ringing's sound was muffled slightly, but given the way her bull's lips were drawn thin and tight, his hand grasping tighter to the steering wheel, she knew Joe didn't believe him. "Do you hear anything? I sure don't ... Nah, I told you that she's fucking sleeping. Why would she call him? What are you so concerned about, anyway? Fuck this, Joe, I'm calling—"

"No!"

The shout was so loud Viviana flinched inwardly. Rory held the phone away from his ear, shock and anger flitting over his features. They could still hear Joe's irate voice buzzing in the phone's speaker.

Viviana swallowed the lump forming in her throat. The phone in her own hand had stopped ringing.

Please call back, she begged hopelessly.

Now, more than ever, she needed to talk to her husband. Even if it was useless conversation and mundane words. Even if they ignored the obvious and pretended like what was happening didn't exist. Viviana needed that, she didn't care.

Like Joe hadn't just roared at him, Rory kept calm as he placed the phone back to his ear and began speaking. "Listen, I don't know what the hell is wrong with you, but if you shout at me like that again, I'll pistol whip your fucking ass." Rolling his eyes, Rory huffed and said, "Sure you would, asshole. Thanks for waking Vine up with your nonsense. I have to go."

Again, the phone was turned off and tossed uncaringly to the seat.

Viviana tried like heck not to notice, but she couldn't help it: Rory's hands were trembling.

"Can you call Boss back?" Rory asked quietly. Worry had pitched his tone a little higher than normal. "Be fast about it, Vine."

Apparently Rory had reason to worry. Viviana turned to look over her shoulder just in time to see the SUV behind them speed up at an alarming rate. The vehicle loomed close enough to the back of theirs that she could make out the shape of the man driving. Tailgating was one thing, but what Joe was doing was just downright dangerous.

If they had to stop suddenly, where would Joe be?

Right inside their trunk. That's where.

"Holy crap he's close," Viviana said.

"He's being an idiot," Rory muttered low. "Trying to make a point."

He hit the gas and the force of their SUV lurching forward sent Viviana falling back into the seat with wide eyes. It was only then that she noticed her seatbelt was unbuckled, so she made quick work of fixing that issue.

Viviana pulled out the phone to call Anton, but she didn't have to. He was already calling her back. Pressing the on button, she didn't even need to put the phone up to her ear to hear his fear. Anton was calling her name loud and clear through the speaker, over and over. Her heart clenched at the thought of him worrying about why she hadn't picked up his first call.

But hadn't he said he wouldn't call until he could see Joe?

"Anton?" Silence covered the phone. "Hey, it's okay. I'm here."

"Damn it, baby. Why didn't you answer me?" he asked sharply.

"Rory was on the phone with Joe."

"Oh." All of the fight left his voice with the one word.

"How close is he?" Rory asked.

"Close enough to see his taillights," Anton said. Viviana relayed the information. "Far enough with my lights turned off so he won't notice me."

Viviana glanced out at the pitch-black darkness surrounding their vehicle. There weren't any streetlights and the area they were driving through was dense with forest. How could he even see where he was driving?

"Is that safe?" she dared to ask.

"Safer than him noticing me," Anton replied. "How are you doing?"

Viviana bit the inside of her cheek, willing the unannounced tears to stop welling. "Good."

"Really? Because it's been a rough day."

"Okay, so I'm a little tired. Terrified, too."

Anton took her confession in stride, or he seemed to. "I promise a hot bath, a warm bed, and me as soon as we get home."

Clearing her throat, she smiled at his offerings. "We might have to put that off, though."

"No way. Rest and relax, that's what you need to do."

And birth a baby, she thought. Maybe.

"There's a turn off for a private access into Columbus Park coming up. I'm taking it," Rory stated from the front seat.

Viviana's heart lurched into her throat as her stomach dropped. "Why?"

"Because I need to get closer," Anton said. "Somehow. That'll probably help."

As Rory turned on his blinker to signal he was making a turn, the stress and tension in the SUV turned up a notch or two. Anton went quiet on his end of the phone and Viviana forced herself not to turn around and look out the back window. She didn't want to know how close Joe was to their vehicle.

As the car started to turn into the dark, dirt road, Rory's phone began ringing again. Rory tossed the phone a glance, but didn't move to pick it up.

"Just a little detour," he said under his breath. "Keep following, asshole."

Soon enough, Joe's call stopped ringing through.

The road was bumpy, jostling Viviana with every pothole the tires hit. She tried to see beyond the rows and rows of trees lining either side of their SUV. She couldn't make out much, but she did notice there was a slight ditch on the left side. The embankment wasn't overly deep, and was more than likely just a water runoff for a lake or something.

The darkness and unknown area didn't bother Viviana, though. What did bother her was the silence on the other end of her phone. "Anton?"

"I'm just turning in the road, too," he said quietly.

Viviana took a deep breath, willing it to calm her raging emotions. "Okay, should I—"

She didn't get to ask if she should hang up her phone. She did manage to hear Rory's low cuss before something slammed into the back of their SUV with a force that sent their vehicle swerving off to the side. Viviana's shoulder rammed into the door and the sharp sting of agony ricocheted through her side. Her cry of pain and surprise fell on deaf ears as the phone slipped from her grasp and hit the floor with a dull thud.

Shocked, she realized Joe had driven his vehicle into the back of theirs.

Totally terrified and unsure what Joe was trying to do,

Viviana only wanted to get the phone off the floor and back into her hands. She needed Anton. Their SUV sped up as a slight bump knocked their vehicle from behind again. The second hit wasn't nearly as hard as the first one, but it was still enough to send the terror skyrocketing. Dread crawled over Viviana's skin as she tried to catch her breath and calm down enough to think.

Rory still hadn't spoken a word from the front.

Viviana wrangled with her belt to try and grab the fallen phone. She couldn't reach it from her spot without unbuckling the seatbelt but that didn't stop her from trying. Anton's shouts from the phone echoed up from the floor. When she couldn't grab it, a sob escaped her chest.

"*Don't* unbuckle, Vine! You might need it."

Sitting back and knowing Anton must have been in a terrible panic, Viviana dug her hands into the soft leather of the seat and closed her eyes. That gun on her thigh burned a little more. Viviana didn't want to think about using it, or needing to.

Tears fell over her cheeks, gathering on her trembling lips.

Good God, Anton could not see her like this.

Rory seemed to notice her state as his quiet, calm voice brought her out of a meltdown. "Hey, what's the name of that boy of yours, huh?"

Somehow, Viviana managed a short laugh. Was this really the right time to be discussing her son's name? She knew her bull was only attempting to cool her fear, and surprisingly, it worked.

"What?"

"The baby's name," he said again. "Jen won't leave me alone about it. You're close enough, so what's his name going to be? My bet was on Daniil or Anton."

Viviana licked her lips. "Wrong, well, sort of. Can't tell you anyway, Anton would have a fit."

Rory scoffed, but the sound didn't ring true. The car was going dangerously fast, hitting the bumps and divots in the road with more force than before. The pain in her shoulder was dulled, but it still hurt something fierce.

"Sure you can," Rory said, lifting his gaze to meet hers in the mirror. "Come on, Vine, what if I never find out? I'm kind of like his guard, too, right, so I should know. Boss will get over it. It's not like I'll tell anyone, promise."

Sure, Rory finished up his statement with an offhanded comment about Anton, but Viviana hadn't missed his words right before that.

What if I never find out?

Was that how he thought this situation was going to end?

"Rory ..."

The hard profile of the man in the front seat turned just enough for her to see the softness he always held in his gaze. "I meant to thank you, by the way."

"For what?"

Rory chuckled, his grip on the steering wheel tightening as their SUV sped up impossibly faster. "For Jen, I guess. Boss never would have let me date the girl because she works at one of his joints. You've been good for him, more than he knows. Good for a lot of people. So, thanks."

Viviana didn't know what to say.

Rory didn't give her the chance to figure it out. "His name?"

She could still hear Anton calling for her from the forgotten phone on the floor.

Faith, Viviana reminded herself.

It would be all right. It had to be.

As Joe's vehicle bumped into theirs again, she closed her eyes.

"You'll find out when he's born just like everybody else."

It was the last thing Viviana said before she felt their vehicle drop off the side of the embankment.

Chapter Seventeen

"No …"

Anton felt something painful expand and burst in his chest as he caught the faint outline of the SUV his wife was in drop out of sight. The lights of the SUV dimmed before blinking out completely as the taillights disappeared.

The phone at his ear crackled with static as Viviana's piercing scream echoed through the receiver. He could hear glass shattering and the metal of the car crunching under whatever weight it slammed into.

His heart beat a staccato rhythm. Anton couldn't even manage to breathe. The embankment wasn't large, maybe only fifteen or twenty feet deep. Even so, it was more than big and deep enough to roll a vehicle. Enough to hurt a passenger, or knock them out. Enough to kill a person if they weren't buckled in, or God forbid if a tree went through a window. Anton wasn't even trying to think about the speed Rory had been traveling when Joe knocked them over the ditch. An accident at that rate of speed was more than enough to do serious damage.

Joe's SUV stopped at the same time Anton's car did. The bull was getting out of the car, a gun firmly seated in his palm as his form strode along the dirt road.

Unfortunately, Anton was quite a ways behind and he had a bit of a run to catch up. He didn't dare take the chance of going further and having Joe draw his gun out on him. Sure, Anton had a weapon of his own, but it wouldn't make a difference if the bull shot him dead while he was still behind the wheel of a moving vehicle.

Besides that, Anton still wasn't sure if Joe had seen him or if he didn't know that he was following behind at all. It was more likely that Joe assumed this would be the best place and time to make his move on Viviana when Rory chose to drive into the dirt road. Anton had been hoping to get a little closer to the man's vehicle before Rory stopped, but Joe hadn't given him the chance.

Anton was stuck frozen. Lightheaded with blurred vision, he was suddenly dizzy and lost. There was no noise on the phone he held to his ear. No crying, no words. The sounds of the car crashing into ground had all but stopped, too. There was just … nothing. Dead silence, but the phone hadn't cut out the call.

"Vine," he whispered, knowing his wife wasn't going to answer him back.

Dread clawed through his cold veins. As Anton blinked at the headlights flooding over the shadow of Joe who was still staring down the embankment, he couldn't help but let his mind run wild. His wife and unborn son had just been in an accident. A man with a gun and thoughts intent on killing them was less than maybe thirty feet away.

Anton was much farther than that.

Watching in a horror induced haze as Joe came to the edge of the embankment and looked over, Anton didn't know what to do. The lights from SUV Joe had been driving lit up the road, trees, and the bull enough to give Anton a decent view of what he was dealing with. When Joe lurched forward, slipping off the edge of the ditch to jump down the embankment, Anton finally sprung back to life. Adrenaline pumped through his blood as he slammed his car into park and flung open the driver's side door.

The warm air felt like a slap in the face as he hit the ground running.

Anton was an athlete. There wasn't much he couldn't do in the physical sense. But his physicality didn't matter a single bit in the situation he found himself in because he was much too far away. Anton simply wasn't fast enough, he couldn't be. He knew he wouldn't make it to his wife in nearly enough time to save her from Joe's wrath or his gun. The only thing he could hope for was Rory being awake and capable of using his own weapon, or Viviana being able to use hers.

"Oh God, Viviana! *Vine!*"

He shouted into the phone again and again, but still, nothing answered him back.

Anton didn't falter in his run when the first gunshot rang out in the darkness.

• • •

Viviana jerked awake at the loud bang. Glass shattered around her face, littering shards into her hair. She struggled to remember what had happened and why her shoulder hurt so goddamned badly. Groaning, she didn't focus too long on the muffled noise that sounded just out of reach.

Oddly, she felt slightly off balance.

Viviana turned her head to the side, wiping off the glass fragments from her face. Something warm and wet smeared on her cheeks from the touch. The coppery taste of blood lingered on her mouth. Sparing a glance out the broken window beside her, Viviana realized the vehicle she was in had slammed into the trunk of a tree.

But hadn't a window just broken? Wasn't there a bang?

A bang that reminded her of something … something frightening.

Like a gun, maybe.

Was it a gunshot?

What was that bang?

What was that noise?

Who was yelling?

With a thick throat and no voice, Viviana looked to her right. That window was broken, too, and her eyes blurred as she attempted to see through the darkness. A shape was there—*someone* was out there, shouting.

The person reached through the window, trying to grab her, but she was too far away for them to reach. By the shape of his form, she knew he was a man.

"Anton?"

Ouch. Talking hurt worse than breathing. Viviana's throat

felt scratchy and raw.

"Fucking door!"

No, it couldn't be her husband. Anton's voice was deeper, with silken tenors and a deep baritone bass. This was nothing like the soothing, familiar voice of her husband. This person was angry. Viviana's whole body flinched as she heard something slam into the car door. The man's foot, likely.

Had the door been crushed shut when they wrecked?

At the memory of the SUV rolling off the embankment, Viviana was flooded with the rest of her forgotten mind. No, it certainly wasn't Anton outside of the vehicle.

It was Joe.

Had he shot into the car already?

That would certainly explain the bang that brought her back into consciousness.

"Rory," Viviana said hoarsely as Joe once again struggled to open the door.

Why wasn't he just shooting her? Why was he trying to get inside the car?

Where was Anton? He hadn't been far behind, or so she thought.

"Rory," she said again, louder the second time. The bull in the front seat didn't answer Viviana back. In the darkness, she couldn't see a thing but the glow of the dashboard's clock, anyway.

"Fuck this," she heard Joe mutter.

The telltale click clack of a gun resounded outside the car.

It took Viviana less than a second to reach down between her legs with her shaking hands, fumbling to find the small handgun she knew should have been at her thigh.

By the grace of fucking God, it was.

At the same time Viviana's arm lifted with the gun in hand, aimed at the figure outside the window, she watched with clearing vision as Joe raised his into it. Viviana didn't have to think about her next move. There was no sadness or guilt over her choice, she didn't even hesitate. This man would not take her life, he would not hurt her child.

Instead, she remembered Roman.

Get a better grip on that gun.

You only get the one.

Make it count.

Don't you blink about it, girl.

The trigger pulled back smooth and easy under her finger. Viviana watched as the blaze and smoke from her gun clouded the car with a burst of light and gray. The scent of gunpowder choked her lungs at the same time a sob ripped past her lips. Joe fell back with a painful shout of shock, his gun dropping into the car with a clatter as his body hit the ground.

Relief never felt so good, but Viviana didn't have a clue if he was going to be able to get back up or not. She didn't have the time to sit there and think it all over, either. Groping to unbuckle the belt that was keeping her confined, she somehow managed to find the latch. Bits of sharp glass scratched against her skin as she released the buckle.

Viviana just started to crawl over the backseat as she heard Anton's voice outside the broken window.

• • •

"Viviana!"

The second gunshot exploded into the night just as Anton propelled his body over the side of the embankment.

Fortunately, he'd been able to hear every word Joe shouted in English and Russian as he tried futilely to get inside the car. It must have been too dark for Joe to properly see inside the car, so the first shot had been nothing more than a failed attempt to shoot Viviana through the window. The bull's words had echoed up to the dirt road Anton had been running down. It somehow urged him to move a hell of a lot faster, even though he had been able to tell by Joe's words that Viviana was still alive.

The second gunshot might as well have stopped his heart straight up.

Anton landed on hard earth, a sting radiating up his left ankle as he hit down.

Only one headlight in the SUV had survived the impact. It gave off just enough light for Anton to make out the wreckage. It was clear by the dents that now covered the black vehicle from the roof to the wheel wells that it had in fact rolled when it fell into the deep ditch. Every window was broken out, and it rested on the two passenger side tires while the driver's side were a good half of a foot in the air.

Rage flooded Anton's body as he noticed the form sprawled out near the back of the SUV. Joe lay on the ground, clearly wounded as the rich color of crimson slipped down around his neck, soaking into the ground. Joe's hands clutched up near his throat as his boots dug into the earth and the sweet music of his choking reached Anton's spot.

Viviana had one hell of an aim, Anton thought.

The small handgun he gave her wasn't that high of a calibre, but it would stop a man in his tracks if used correctly. Clearly his wife had used it correctly.

Fuck, was he ever grateful.

"Viviana?" Anton called her name again, ignoring the pain in his ankle as he moved closer to the SUV.

"I-I'm here … Please get me out of here, please. The door won't open."

The beautiful sound of his wife's voice, strained but alive, was the only thing needed to make Anton move. "Oh, baby. I'm coming. It's okay."

He crossed the space, jumping over the small creek of water in one fluid swoop, and made it to the side of the SUV in seconds. Viviana's hands came out of the window at the same time his went in.

For a single moment, Anton just needed to touch Viviana. To feel the warmth of her flesh, hear the sounds of her breaths, and see the life blinking back in her brown eyes. Anton simply needed to know she was there—okay, healthy, alive. That was all. Even in the darkness of the SUV he could see where she'd bruised up her cheek in the accident. A few scratches dotted up the side of her jaw, glass littered the black strands of her hair, and blood was smudged on her brow and hands.

Anton didn't give a shit about the blood on her mouth when he kissed her through the broken window. The tears making rivulets down her cheeks smeared onto his. Anton shushed tenderly against her lips, feeling the trembling in her shoulders as he wrapped his arms around her.

"The baby?" he asked.

Viviana sobbed brokenly, but shook her head. "Everything's fine, I promise. Please just get me out of this car. I can't breathe in here."

Anton didn't waste any time doing what she asked. The door had been crushed shut, but the window was more than big enough to get her out. Being mindful of the shards of glass still around the opening he pulled Viviana out from the back. Cradling her to his chest, Anton stood there holding his wife for long enough to tell her over and over that she was okay. Viviana buried her face into his neck and started to cry low, with hiccupping sniffles that wracked her form all over.

"Shh," he said against her hair. "It's all right, I've got you."

"Vivi-viana … Vine?"

Anton felt the air he'd been holding in release. Rory had survived the car rolling over and Joe coming down on them, too. Somehow. Anton hadn't checked the other bull, but he was more concerned over getting his wife out first.

"Rory, you okay?" Anton asked loudly.

Anton listened as glass was brushed off, Rory groaned painfully, and then the man's head popped out of the driver's side window. He had one hell of a bump on his forehead, a bloodied up lip, and few scrapes and bruises. The accident had only knocked him out, luckily. But that bump was a good sign he might be concussed, too.

Rory clamoured out of the broken window, landing to the ground with a thump. The man sat there, head in his hands, and stared at the ground, saying nothing.

The gurgling coming from three feet away reminded

Anton of Joe.

And his wife in his arms.

Viviana tried to look in Joe's direction, but Anton wouldn't let her. The last thing she needed was to see the damage she'd caused.

"Rory, I need you to get up. Can you do that?" Anton asked.

Anton had very little time left with Joe.

"What's that, Boss?"

By the slight slur in Rory's words, it was obvious he likely was concussed.

Anton set Viviana to the ground. She shook her head frantically, trying to keep her grip on his shirt, but something stopped her and she let out an awful howl of pain. Instantly, Anton was checking over his wife to find what the problem was. Pushing down the mink fur over her right shoulder, he found it.

"Shit." Anton breathed heavily at the sight of Viviana's shoulder, bruised, swollen, and out of place. His fingers ghosted along the joint. "Okay, it's not too bad."

Yeah, that was a lie. It was going to hurt like hell.

"Ow." Viviana whined with wetness in her eyes. "That doesn't look good."

"Yeah, yeah I know. Probably hurts a lot. Just popped out, that's nothing severe that I can't fix. Did you hit it?"

"Twice," Viviana said with a wince.

"This is going to hurt, but it'll be quick. On three, take a breath. When it hurts, let it out. Okay?"

Viviana nodded, but Anton could see her fear. Holding her left side to his chest, Anton wrapped his left arm around her shaking frame, then used his right to grab firmly to her arm just above her elbow. Keeping her steady so she couldn't squirm, he counted back quickly and when her sharp inhale echoed, he clenched his eyes shut and slipped her shoulder back into joint.

Nothing could have muffled the agonizing scream she let loose.

Nothing.

Over and over, Anton apologized. Clasping her face between his palms, he kissed away the fresh round of tears.

Viviana's shout must have been enough to wake Rory from his stupor because the young man was stumbling over. Just coming up behind Anton's wife, the bull spared a glance at his former counterpart still choking on blood three feet away.

"Damn, you get him?" Rory asked.

Anton shook his head over Viviana's shoulder but said nothing else. It was enough. Rory seemed to get the point, clearing his throat and leaving the rest of the words unsaid. There was no need to remind Viviana, and she still hadn't tried to look again so she must not have wanted to know, either.

"Here, Boss, I'll take her." Rory held his arms out before jerking his chin up at the embankment. "It's not too high. How far is the car?"

"Three minute run behind Joe's SUV. Get her settled and come back with the gas can in the back of my car."

Rory didn't argue and neither did Viviana.

Anton waited until they were rounding the top of the embankment before he moved over to Joe. He kneeled down beside the man's head, ignoring the blood that soaked through his pants. Joe was still clutching for dead life at the bullet wound in his throat. Blood pumped out around his fingers with every beat of his heart. A bluish tint had started to color Joe's skin and lips. Blood vessels were beginning to burst in his eyes while capillaries had expanded and bulged in his face.

It was hard fucking work to suffocate while you bled out, then choke on the same blood you were losing. Yes, hard work indeed. Anton felt nothing while Joe struggled for life and breath. If anything, Anton was enjoying it. With wide eyes filled with horror, Joe watched as his boss said nothing. More than anything, Anton wanted to chuckle at the bull's plight.

No amount of pressure on the injury would save him. No medical intervention would help him, now. No, Joe was too far gone and there was no doubt in Anton's mind that the man on the ground knew it, too.

"Viviana did this to you. Can you believe that? Hell, I bet you didn't expect this, Joe. Did you think I wouldn't protect my wife every way that I could?" Anton asked darkly. "Of course I would, Joe. Of course she would carry a weapon. Of course I would take that risk. She's my wife, and unlike you, I love her."

Anton reached out with both hands, forcing the bull to remove his hands from the gunshot wound at his throat. The gurgling and choking became louder instantly and blood spurted. Anton refused Joe access to put pressure back on his injury.

In a flash, Anton squeezed Joe's throat with one hand, letting go of the hands he'd been holding down at the same time. With his other hand, Anton pinched Joe's nose so he couldn't receive air for his airways through there, either. Blood spit out from Joe's mouth while he scratched, clawed, and fought weakly against Anton's hold.

"I'm going to watch you die," Anton said with a smile. "Poetic justice, in my opinion. Your betrayal very well could have cost me my best friend, my wife, and my son. I don't appreciate that. When you're dead, I'll put you in that SUV you caused to wreck, and light your ass on fire. It'll probably be blamed on one of my enemies when they do manage to find you. Who knows how long that will take? I don't care so long as you are dead."

Joe suffocated a little more, his eyes widening as the bluish hue to his lips spread outwards along his mouth. The life was starting to blink from Joe's eyes. There was no more air for him to breathe with the blood filling his air passages.

He was drowning in his own blood.

No, Anton didn't care a bit.

Chapter Eighteen

Viviana listened as the beautiful music of her baby boy's heartbeat filled the master bathroom. Coming out of a handheld fetal heart rate monitor, the noise was similar to the clatter of hooves on the ground. Resting her head back against the vanity's mirror, she sighed.

"His heart rate is normal. Everything sounds fine," Sasha said, watching the heart rate number light up on the Doppler. "You're not contracting at any real length or severity, so I don't think you have to worry about him coming for at least another couple of days. Some women have this for several days before active labor starts. I'd say this is early, if at all. Very, very early. You can still do whatever you normally would and have no worries so long as you're comfortable."

When Sasha moved to take the Doppler away, Viviana shook her head, feeling her own heart speed up at the prospect of losing that sound. "Please don't. Not yet."

Sasha offered her an understanding smile. "Okay. We can do that. It's not like it's going to hurt him."

There was definitely some benefits to having a nurse as your mother-in-law. Viviana hadn't wanted to drag Sasha from Daniil's side when they finally returned home, but she knew they didn't have much of a choice. Taking Rory into an Emergency Room wouldn't be a smart option if they wanted to keep a low profile about the accident, and Viviana had only suffered a few minor bruises and scrapes.

What she had been more concerned about was the baby.

Now, she was worrying about Anton.

Standing in the doorway of the bathroom, her husband was stoic and silent with his arms crossed over his chest. Blood had stained his clothes and skin, but Anton hadn't made a move to clean it off yet. In fact, he hadn't done a whole hell of a lot but stick close to her since they returned home.

Viviana understood his need to be close, but Anton wasn't speaking much, either.

It probably didn't help that there seemed to be an underlying tension rolling thick between Sasha and Anton. They barely looked at one another, which wasn't something Viviana was used to. In fact, Sasha hadn't even said hello to her son when she arrived.

"Is that good?" Sasha asked, bringing Viviana from her thoughts.

"Huh?" Glancing down at the Doppler, Viviana smiled. "Yeah, that's great. Thanks for coming to help."

"I think I'll stay for a little while longer and keep an eye on Rory downstairs." Sasha shrugged as she wiped the gel from her daughter-in-law's stomach before helping her to fix her dress. "But, say nothing about it ... literally."

Anton coughed. "You know we wouldn't, Mom."

Those were the first words he had spoken in an hour. Viviana was surprised he spoke at all, really. Clearly Anton was struggling with something, but he was battling it alone. She wished he wouldn't.

Sasha sighed heavily, packing up the kit she'd brought along. "Keep your arm in that sling," she told Viviana. "Keep pressure off of it."

Viviana's shoulder was still aching something awful, but it wasn't anything she couldn't handle. While she knew popping it back into place would hurt, she hadn't expected it to hurt quite that much. It was almost like bone smashing into bone. There was nothing to soften the blow and she wished she could just forget about it.

"Other than that ..." Sasha continued, plucking up some gauze and peroxide, "let's get to work on cleaning some of these scrapes and getting the rest of this glass out of your hair, huh?"

"I'll do it." Anton took a step into the bathroom, his gaze flashing to his wife and then his mother. "It's fine."

"Anton, I'm not going to hurt her."

"I didn't—" Furrowing his brow and clenching his fists at his sides, Anton released a shaky breath before shaking his head. "I can do it. She'll need to get out of those clothes, take a shower, and whatever else. I'd be more comfortable taking care of it myself."

"And what about Viviana, son? I don't know what happened tonight, but perhaps she might need some time to adjust and absorb it all before …" Sasha trailed off, glancing away with a guilty expression when Anton scowled. "I'm sorry," she added quickly.

"I didn't intend for her to be hurt!"

"I'm not," Viviana said, wanting to reassure Sasha's fear.

Sasha acted as if her daughter-in-law hadn't said a thing. "I don't mean her physical state. Emotionally she might need a minute alone. You could give it to her, that's all I meant."

"And what about *me*, Mom?" Anton asked. "Do you think it was easy for me to be there, to feel it, or to see it? Why are you angry with me right now?"

Sasha dropped the first aid kit to the counter, sadness clouding her features. "Did I say I was angry with you, Anton?"

"Then why argue with me?"

Viviana begged her mind to catch up to speed and figure out something to say or do to stop her husband and his mother from snapping at one another like they were. It wasn't often, if at all, that it happened. Anton had a great deal of respect for his parents. Whatever this was seemed to be laced with something else Viviana couldn't possibly understand.

"I'm sorry I screwed up," Anton told Sasha. "God, Ma, I'm so fucking sorry. I didn't know, okay?"

"You think playing with guns and being what you are makes you so infallible. Like nothing's ever going to hurt you, Anton. You're not even in the same world anymore. I can't count the times I said this to your father and asked him to stop. Don't bring this home to me, don't hurt me with it. You're doing the same damned things he did! Did nothing I ever tell you reach your ears? Open your eyes."

"They are!" he shouted. "Do you think I wanted this, really?"

"It's all you've ever—"

"I didn't want this, Ma," Anton interrupted, shoving his clenched fist into his chest.

"You've been pulling these stunts since you were fourteen-years-old. Your father's been doing it for a lot longer. Every time one of you does something like this, it kills me. I've been cleaning this crap up for years; I'm sick of it. And you have the nerve to say you didn't want this? Don't start that with me, Anton. Get out and let me clean up another mess for the Bratva. God knows I'm used to it by now."

"No."

"Excuse me?" Sasha asked, her eyes snapping back to her son's.

"I said no. I didn't want this, Ma," he repeated, voice thick. "I was young and stupid. I didn't see it the same way then that I do now, but it was already too late. And when I did see ..." Anton tossed his wife a glance, blinking away the water in his eyes before looking back to his mother. "When I did see what else I wanted, there was nothing I could do about it. I was already in the brotherhood and you know they weren't going to let me have what I wanted if I wasn't *this*."

Viviana felt the wetness of her tears slide over her bruised cheek and she made quick work of wiping it away. While Anton's angry confession was confusing at best, she'd gotten the gist of what he meant. His initiation into the Bratva might have been a mistake brought on by bad choices, but his decision to go further in the mafia lifestyle was firmly connected to his wife and the desire he had to have her.

"And I'm good at doing it," Anton said with a shrug. "But like it always has, things happen that I can't control, and I have to make the best of it. I'm sorry I didn't do what you wanted me to do growing up, but this is my life now. I'm perfectly fine with it. I don't regret it, none of it. I didn't realize you were so disappointed in me."

Sasha drummed her fingers on the counter, avoiding eye contact. "I never said that."

"Right now, you don't have to."

Viviana bit her lip, watching the war battle between Anton and his mother. Reaching out, she laid her hand to her mother-in-law's arm reassuringly. "It is okay, Sasha. We just ... It's been a rough night. Just give us a few minutes. If I need anything, I'll get Anton to ask you back up."

"If you're sure?"

Viviana nodded. "I'm sure."

Grabbing the clean pile of facecloths she'd placed to the counter, Sasha made her move to leave the bathroom but stopped at her son's side. "Not disappointed, just afraid. You, like your father used to do, frighten me with this. I told you not to be the same and you're not listening."

"And she's not you, Ma," Anton said. "So it's not the same."

When Sasha was gone, Anton stared at the closed door in silence.

"What was that?" Viviana asked. Somehow she felt as if she'd been privy to a moment she shouldn't have been.

"Something she's been needing to say for years, I imagine. I'm sure she's told Daniil a few times, but never me. Until tonight. I guess you could say this isn't a first for Sasha, and it bothers her to be reminded."

"A different time might have been better," Viviana said.

Anton turned around to face her, his expression pensive. "When I was seventeen, she had to reset my nose, splint my wrist, and dig a bullet out of my shoulder. Daniil might have gotten away with saying it was just a normal fight if it weren't for the bullet. I caused an issue with a bull, and nearly got myself killed over it. They couldn't take me into the hospital because of the bullet wound. The doctor they used to use was on call and Daniil was worried about infection."

"So Sasha did it?"

Anton hummed indifferently, but a darkness clouded his

eyes. "Cried the whole time. Wouldn't look me in the face. Screamed at Daniil for hours after. I'd never seen her like that. I don't know, maybe that was the first time she couldn't pretend I wasn't going to be just like them."

There was a sadness coating his words and hanging heavily around the edges of the room. Viviana didn't know what, if anything, she could say to help her husband or make him feel better. Some things had to work out on their own, after all.

"She is proud of you," Viviana said after a brief moment. "She told me."

"Not right now," Anton murmured.

"Hey, come here."

She didn't have to tell him a second time. Viviana found herself wrapped in her husband's warm, safe embrace. A puff of air blew over her hair, the action filled with frustration and exhaustion. Being mindful of her shoulder, Anton held her tighter, kissing the top of her head.

"I'm sorry, Vine. So sorry. I can't even give you a minute alone because I can't be away from you. I'm fucking horrible right now, I know."

"No, never. Not horrible, just mine."

Viviana felt his mouth curve with a smile against her hairline. "Yeah, that, too."

Her cheek ached from the bruise when she smiled, too. The little scrapes dotting her face and hands were beginning to sting as well. Fatigue was starting to set into her body and mind. More than anything, Viviana wanted to rest. She wanted to relax with Anton close, as he was the only person who could give her the best sense of protection, love, and comfort.

Anton's hand shadowed along the side of her stomach. "When the SUV dropped off—"

"Don't," she interjected, shivering. "Please don't."

Nodding to her request, Anton reached over and turned on the tap for the sink. "Let's get you cleaned up. I think I promised my wife something, so I better get on that, huh?"

Viviana struggled to remember what it was he had

promised. "Oh yeah, what's that?"

"A hot bath, bed, and me," he said with a smirk. "Unless you're interested in something different ..."

Viviana laughed. She wasn't going to dwell on the night they had, just move forward. Or at least try.

"Never," she replied. "You're perfect."

It wasn't a lie.

• • •

Anton rested his hip against the counter, willing his thoughts and emotions to take a back seat for a damned minute so he could think. Viviana had long since fallen asleep, but he just couldn't do the same. His insides were torn up in a multitude of ways he couldn't begin to explain, starting with his mother who still hadn't left, yet.

Apparently she didn't trust him to wake Rory up every hour on the hour to make sure the bull was okay.

Sasha moved effortlessly through his kitchen, grabbing the honey for her tea and a teaspoon to stir it with. "Something on your mind, Anton?"

"I'm sorry, Mom," he said a little stiffly.

"Oh, it's not Ma, now? You know, you only call me that when you're pissed off about something. I'd love to know who you picked that up from. I'd smack them one, I swear it." Anton pretended to ignore her quiet rant. He'd called her that for years, but she was right, only when he was in a mood. Her gaze flicked in his direction but it was back to her cup just as quickly. "Sorry for what?"

Shame was a horrible emotion to experience and Anton was feeling it tenfold. The lift of his mother's brow as she stared up over the rip of her cup had him feeling like he was sixteen and stupid all over again. Sasha always did know how to make him feel reprimanded without ever saying a word.

"For cussing at you, yelling like I did, and whatever. I had a hard night and let it spill over onto you. I didn't mean anything by it. I know it worries and bothers you to think about somebody getting hurt. I shouldn't have called you here tonight like I did, but Vine was—"

Sasha cut him off with a roll of her eyes and an indignant huff. "Who else were you going to call, huh? And that's just as much my grandchild as it is your son, so I'm not going to ever say no. It's just when you call me like that, frantic and freaking out ... you remind me of them. I don't want to do that again, Anton. I lived it once, it was enough. I don't think your wife needs a front row seat to it, either, speaking from my own experiences here."

"I don't."

"Hmm?"

Anton crossed the kitchen, grabbing his own cup out of a cupboard and finding the coffee in another. If he was going to have this conversation with Sasha, he needed a little more caffeine to do it. Liquor wasn't exactly an option, but he wished it was.

"I don't give her a front row seat. She's never brought into it like you're thinking she must be. I've never let her see anything since we've been married. She wouldn't have been there tonight had she not picked up Sergei's fucking call. You said I didn't remember what you told me, but I do."

"And then I see her like that."

"I didn't want it to happen," Anton said, readying his coffee but forgoing sugar and milk. "It shouldn't have, but I trusted the wrong person and didn't know until it was too late. She was supposed to be safe tonight, at home waiting for me like she always is, not in the middle of ... that."

"She could have died, Anton. Your son—"

"Is fine," he said shortly. "I handled it."

"Will you every time?"

"Didn't Dad?" Anton asked back.

Sasha flinched. Guilt flooded Anton like a crushing wave. "You're just like him, you know."

"I don't know, I think he had a calmer head in situations like these."

Her scoff was playful, but it didn't ring quite so true. "So you thought. But you are, like him, I mean. You love and you hate, that's just what you do and there isn't any in-between. Unfortunately there's a very thin line amongst the two and when you're doing one or the other, your behavior is the same. Intense actions, full-throttle emotions, and anything in the way is nothing more than fodder to the plan. Love and hate, do you even know the difference?"

"Yes, now," he replied immediately. "But I don't have regrets or make excuses for this, Mom. I am who I am and I'm okay with it. I just want you to be, too."

"I want you *alive*!"

There it is, Anton thought. The crux of the matter his mother always considered but never quite spoke much about. The thing she feared when he was six and she pulled him out of his bed in the middle of the night to hide him in the closet when an unhappy man of Daniil's came into their home. The same thing she worried about when Nicoli died and he stepped up to bat.

Now, there were just two more people for her to think about and relate that fear to.

"Don't you know why I wanted to clean Vine up, Mom?" Anton asked, frustration coloring his tone.

"Because clearly you didn't trust me—"

"*No*," Anton said angrily. "Because you've done it enough. Because I still remember the way you cried when you did it for Dad, or me. Because I know you hated it, but you're right, who the fuck else was I going to call? Yeah, I could have taken her into some hospital and took the risk of it being on record, but I wanted you and so did she. So yeah, I'm sorry I dredged up your old memories and disappointed you tonight, but the bottom line is pretty damned simple. She's upstairs, breathing. My son still has a heartbeat and his first day on earth coming up soon. So be pissed off at me, hate the lifestyle I live if you want, I don't care.

"I don't have regrets or make excuses," he repeated, picking up his coffee and turning on his mother. "Not a one.

But I apologize, and that's more than Dad ever did. That's what you told me to do. I fucking remember. I'll give her one every single time, and I'll mean it, too."

Sasha's gaze traveled past Anton to the wall behind him. He thought maybe she'd argue with him, but instead she surprised him with something completely off topic. "How's Ivan?"

Anton swallowed his sadness, wishing he hadn't told his mother about his lawyer's plight. It was just one more person for her to fret about. "It's going to be touch and go for a couple of days. He lost a lot of blood. Boris was there, though, so they had a compatible blood type on hand."

"Lucky him. Eva must be out of her mind."

"Yeah." But that was about all he knew.

Sasha waved at the clock on the wall. "I need to go wake Rory up. You should check on Vine, and get some sleep. It won't be very long before you can't sleep at all."

"I don't get enough as it is," Anton said, joking half-heartedly.

"And whose fault is that?"

"Enough of that. I don't want to fight with you again, Ma."

Sasha's lips quirked up into the hint of a smile. As she walked past, her hand came up to pat his bare shoulder, directly over his star tattoo. Anton knew his mother was aware of what wearing those stars meant and the importance the marking was to his status as a high ranking Vor. She'd rarely ever acknowledged it before, and in fact, he couldn't remember a time she had touched them or looked at them since he had the ink done.

"No fighting," she said softly. "But you were right."

Shocked, Anton asked, "About what?"

"She's not like me. I'd have made your father sleep on the couch for a week after something like this."

Anton smirked. "She likes me close."

"You must be doing something right, then. Goodnight, Anton."

"Night, Ma."

• • •

Viviana fumbled for the gun, her hands shaking and heart pounding. The bloody taste in her mouth was thick. She could see Joe outside the SUV, cursing her, trying to get in through the broken window to grab her. She was terrified and the gun wasn't where it should be.

Where was the gun?

The air around her felt light and heavy at the same time while Viviana only felt sluggish.

What was wrong with her?

Again, she frantically searched for the gun.

Something cool, heavy, and metal met her fingers on the floor of the SUV. She was quick to pluck up the missing weapon, pull back the hammer, and aim it out the window. There was no waiting, no worrying, and no thinking.

Just aim and fire.

Boom.

But the face in the window wasn't a man she would ever shoot.

It was already too late.

"Vine?"

A gasp sucked into Viviana's lungs as her eyes flew open. Sweaty, sore, and tired, her body seemed to weigh a hundred pounds more than what it actually did. The blurriness in her vision wouldn't disappear no matter how many times she tried to blink it away. Her pulse raced in the darkness.

"Wake up, baby. It was just a dream, that's all."

At Anton's voice, Viviana's tears began to fall. The soft shushing he started to hum as his arms enveloped her from behind did little to settle the panic raging a war through her insides. She couldn't breathe, and he held her tighter. Painful sobs burst from Viviana's lips like popping bubbles.

"Viviana, hey, it's okay … come on, look at me, everything's fine," Anton whispered.

Turned in the bed under his hands, Viviana could finally see his face. The hard lines of Anton's profile was softened from the small lamp behind him. Concern wrote heavy lines in his furrowed brow. Those striking blue eyes of his scanned her face as his thumb rolled over her cheekbone gently.

Seeing Anton reminded her that it had been just a dream, but it still didn't help what Viviana could remember. It didn't help to take away the realization of what she had done. *Move forward*, Viviana told herself. That's what she wanted to do. So why couldn't she do it?

"We're home," he said quietly, but firmly. "In our bed. Feel the sheets, huh?" Viviana nodded, but it felt bleak and unsure. Under the soft sheets, their legs tangled together, rooting her to the spot. Anton continued speaking when she didn't. "The room smells like your perfume, me, and us."

Viviana's fingers found purchase against Anton's bare chest before balling into shaking fists. Squeezing her eyes shut, she willed away the image of Joe falling back. She didn't want to hear the sound of his pain as the bullet hit him.

Where had she shot him?

Had it been quick?

No, Viviana didn't think so. She could still hear him struggling for air, the morbid gurgles of his suffocation as he died just feet away. It hadn't been quick at all, or easy.

"Hey, hey, hey." Anton all but chanted the words into Viviana's ears. "Open your eyes, Vine. We're home. We finally finished the baby's room the way you wanted it. You're going to visit Daniil tomorrow. You're five days off from your due date. Sasha is still downstairs. Rory is fine, too. Home," he repeated tenderly. "Stop holding your breath, you need to breathe."

Hadn't she been?

Anxiety clashed with memories, shoving Viviana's fears straight to the surface all over again. Nausea washed over her like a tidal wave. Bile threatened to rise in her throat. She was still trembling something fierce.

Oh God, what had she done?

Viviana's hands itched and twitched. They felt sticky and gummed up with something she couldn't see.

"Open your eyes!"

Viviana's eyes flew open at the command, meeting Anton's. Immediately he had her rolled to her back, fitted between her thighs as his hands clasped her face and kept her head tilted up enough to meet his stare head on.

"Where are we?" he asked.

"Home," she said.

Anton nodded. "And?"

"In b-bed. Just a dream. I'm sorry, I'm sorry."

"No, no, no." Anton shook his head, rolling his thumbs over her cheekbones with the lightest flutters. Warmth and love skimmed the places on her skin that he touched. "It's okay. It happens."

Despite Anton not putting any pressure down on her body, Viviana's chest felt like a massive weight was resting on it. She couldn't get enough air, or clear her mind enough to think. She'd never had an anxiety attack quite so bad before.

Viviana swallowed down the sick feeling and focused on her husband.

"You want to talk about it?"

"Not really." God, even her voice sounded feeble.

Anton didn't seem to be very pleased with that. "You'll go back to sleep and it'll happen again, I know it."

"I don't want to think about … *that*."

"Killing somebody," Anton said, acting as if he didn't notice her flinch. "You'd rather just dream it over and over, then?"

"Do you?"

"Sometimes, but they're not nightmares anymore."

"But they were."

"When I was younger, sure." Anton didn't seem to like admitting that fact, as the frown he sported deepened. "The first time was the worst. I didn't sleep well for months, but I got over it. The second time was easier and the dreams didn't last as long. The panic attacks lessened over time. Then, they went away, too."

"How?"

Anton shifted his gaze away. "I'm not you, baby. It's not the same."

"Indulge me, please."

"Okay." Discomfort was thinning Anton's mouth into a hard line as he said, "So I thought about it a lot. Let myself replay what happened. I stopped trying to justify why it happened, why I had to do it, and why it shouldn't have occurred at all. Excuses and regrets stopped playing a part, I just accepted what I did. Sometimes I talked it out with Daniil, or Nicoli, depending on my mood or the severity. I didn't want them seeing me struggle over something I assumed they thought would come easy to me."

"They didn't think that?"

Anton offered one of his smiles, but it didn't feel as true as it usually would. "No, but they let me be to work it out the way I needed and wanted to. Because I'm not them, either."

Viviana didn't know what to say, so instead she relaxed into Anton's hand rubbing comfortingly along her side and the warmth of his body pressing into hers. The clean, masculine scent of her husband helped to calm her a bit more in the darkened bedroom.

"My hands feel so dirty." At the confession, Viviana felt the need to hide her hands down at her sides, but she kept her grip on Anton. He was her solid ground—the stability she needed. "Like I need to wash myself again."

Anton grunted his disapproval. "But what'd you do wrong, huh? Nothing. Killed somebody who was going to kill you. No one was there to save you but yourself."

"You're justifying it."

"You're not me. This isn't even remotely the same." When Viviana went to argue, Anton's severe expression stopped her. "He'd have killed you and not even cared. Do you think he was considering Demyan when he aimed that gun through the window? No. Not to be nasty and make you feel worse, but this wouldn't even stick in court as a homicide and that's what matters, anyway."

"That's not all that matters!"

Anton sighed. "No, you're right. It's not, but it is important. If the outside world wouldn't consider you a murderer, then why are you, Viviana?"

The statement stilled her into silence.

She didn't have a valid retort.

"That's not fair," Viviana muttered.

"It's how I see it. You'll figure out how you want to deal with it, eventually. But for now ..." Anton said with a shrug, "what do you need me to do for you?"

Viviana didn't even have to think about that question. She knew what she needed and wanted from her husband. It was the same thing she always took from him willingly, fully, and totally. It was the very best way they connected and the one way he always left her feeling complete.

Titling her mouth up, she kissed his jaw, feeling the stubble scratch against her sensitive lips. Flicking out her tongue to lick Anton's freshly cleaned skin, the taste of him lingered along her taste buds. Anton shuddered at the suggestive contact, his hands coming to rest on her hips to fist the fabric of her sweatpants.

She could feel the hesitation in his grip.

"Is it okay?"

Viviana laughed lightly, her stress falling away. "I was told to do whatever I normally would, remember? Besides, I haven't felt anything in a while so it was likely nothing."

Anton didn't need more prompting.

He took his sweet time undressing her, kissing the small scratches she'd sustained in the accident, whispering quiet and loving against her skin, and letting his hands roam tenderly up and down her humming body. When Viviana was naked and begging against silky sheets, Anton took her soft and slow until her flesh slicked up under their heat, her nerves sizzled, and her thoughts began to blur. Loved her beautifully long, until sleep was edging around her senses. Made her forget about the memories plaguing threatening dreams.

That was exactly what she had needed from him.

And Anton always did it so well.

Chapter Nineteen

Anton groaned, stretching in the bed and feeling his spine crack. Clearly his body was still a little stiff from the stress of what happened with Joe and Jersey a couple of nights before.

"That sounded healthy," Viviana said.

"Ugh. It hurt, but it kind of didn't. I need a massage."

"One with a happy ending?"

Anton's eyes popped open, leveling on his wife with a playful glare. She simply stuck her tongue out in response. He liked their mornings the very best. Sheets that always smelled like them, sunlight filtering in through opened curtains, and whispered words in bed. Yeah, it was his favorite time of day with his wife.

"Are you offering?" Anton asked. He wasn't about to deny a single one of her happy endings. Viviana gave the best ones.

"Sorry, not today."

The wince that drew her lips into a thin line had Anton's concern making an appearance. It was only then he noticed her odd position on the other side of the bed. With the body pillow bunched up and two regular pillows tossed on top, Viviana was half curled over the fluffy mountain with her stomach resting into the mound. Also, her hair was damp and she'd changed out of the clothes she went to bed in the night before.

How long had she been awake?

It was completely abnormal for Viviana to be up before Anton. Usually he was the one waking her up with murmurs, promises, and love.

"So, what are you doing today?" Viviana asked, bringing him out of his musings.

"I have business at the club. Why?"

"Is it terribly important?"

Now, Anton was just more confused. "Vine, business is always important. Especially after the mess with Jersey. You know this."

That was an understatement. Anton had a lot of explaining to do and he was deflecting a great deal of it as much as he could. The remaining New Jersey Bratva had questions, and they wanted a face to face with him and his guys as soon as possible. Anton agreed, but he wanted them to have a little bit of time to cool down first. Erik had been the one to remind Anton that Sergei said it himself, his Sovietnik hadn't been in agreement about the dinner. That must be a good thing for Anton's Bratva, somehow. At least he was trying to look at it that way.

Other than that, there was also the issue of the fire at the restaurant. They hadn't been provided with a great deal of time to clean up, and while one detective and a fire marshal was on his payroll, that didn't mean everybody included in the investigation would be.

The feds were finally starting to whisper according to Erik's informants.

Anton didn't like that at all.

They all needed to be careful with just about anything they did for a while.

"No, I know it's important. I just meant, could you take the day off?" she asked quieter.

Rolling his neck back and forth to work out the kinks, Anton pushed himself up in the bed to sit. Skidding her hand towards his, Viviana caught his grasp and intertwined their fingers with a light squeeze. Love flooded his veins at the act. It was the simplest things with them, he knew. Easy actions, small words, and being together was as easy as breathing.

Hell, if she wanted him to take a day …

Anton's thought process dropped off the radar when Viviana gripped his hand tighter against the sheets. Pain flitted over her features, darkening her eyes before she hid her face from his view into the mound of pillows.

"Vine?"

All that answered him back was one low, painful moan. Her other arm had come to wrap around the base of her midsection as she swayed her hips back and forth. Taking another inventory of the position Viviana was in, Anton vaguely remembered seeing the same thing in one of those labor and delivery books she'd asked him to read. He'd skipped most of it, but having a photographic memory when it came to visual stuff certainly helped him along in other spots.

This was one of those times.

Clearly his wife was in labor.

Finally, Anton realized what was happening but it didn't make him jump into action like he thought it would. Instead, he was frozen.

"How long?" he asked.

"Since three," Viviana said, her voice muffled by the pillows.

"*This morning?*"

"Oh, don't yell." Viviana turned to glower at him. "It's just a goddamned contraction, Anton."

Just a contraction. *Right.* The doctors had been so positive they would have to induce her.

Anton spluttered over his thoughts that all rushed out at once. "But, but … Why didn't you wake me up?"

"Because it was going to go on for hours whether you were up with me or not. I'm fine. I took a bath to relax, I've been timing them. Everything is just fine. Calm down."

"I am calm!"

"Uh-huh," she mumbled, scoffing. "Whatever, yelling at me over there like you are."

Anton hadn't meant to yell, but his nerves were starting to come out to play.

Holy shit, he was about to be a father.

Anton scrambled to Viviana's side, kissing up her cheek with quick pecks until she graced him with one of her beaming smiles. "You're okay, really?"

"They're getting stronger and longer. Coming quicker, too,

so it's probably a good time to get up and get going."

"Have you called Mom?"

"Sasha said she'd be here by eight. It's only seven-thirty, so you have time to grab a shower if you want."

Anton sighed, rubbing his wife's back as the overwhelming emotions rammed into him over and over.

"Vine, are you sure you're okay?"

"I'm finally getting scared," Viviana said, sighing into the pillow. "But that's okay."

Well, it would be, but it was going to hurt a whole hell of a lot getting there.

• • •

Anton sat back in the recliner, holding the swaddled bundle of a sleeping new child in his arms. Subconsciously he rocked the baby boy back and forth, a gentle shushing falling from his lips as he stared down at his son.

Demyan was so beautiful. So amazingly perfect. Much, much more than Anton had expected. Demyan was also tinier than Anton thought he would be, even though he'd seen newborns before. Soft like the most expensive silks. A peaches and cream complexion, all clear and healthy with a tinge of pink around his cheeks. Ten tiny toes and ten tiny fingers. A nose that sloped more like his mother's and cheekbones that near matched his father's.

Demyan had squalled and screeched like the doctor was the worst person alive for taking him out of his warm, comfy home. Those cries had been the best thing Anton ever heard. Despite everything that had happened during the pregnancy, the baby was healthy, happy, and strong with lungs to match and an attitude already beginning to form.

Sure, Demyan had been a little scary looking at first, but he was incredible.

Tufts of black hair peeked out from the top of the blue swaddling blanket. A single tiny fist had managed to work its way out from the tight wrapping. Demyan pursed his pink lips against his hand. Hesitantly, Anton traced a shaky line below the baby's fanned out lashes. He just wanted to touch him because his son seemed so unreal. How could anything that remarkable have come partly from him?

Amazing couldn't even begin to describe his child.

Love wasn't a good enough word.

How was it possible for someone to fall so instantaneously in love with something else?

"You okay?"

Anton glanced up at his wife's tired voice. Viviana sat up in her bed, rubbing away the sleep in her eyes. She'd done remarkably well. Better than Anton thought she would fair during birth. Her labor had gone on for hours as she said it would, a total of twenty-one hours. None of which she complained, though she did cry when the pain became more severe. That only served to break his heart because there wasn't a damned thing he could do to help her.

But she still did it.

Good God, his heart was swelled, tied, and knotted a million times over with love, pride, and gratitude for his wife.

"Yeah, I'm good." Giving his son all of his attention once more, Anton knew he was more than just good. "God, he looks just like you, Vine."

"Some," Viviana said. "That mouth is all yours, his hair is a blue-black like yours, and those eyes …"

Seemingly at the sound of his mother's voice alone, Demyan woke up with a little cry. Cloudy blue eyes most newborns were known for stared up at Anton, unfocused and unsure. Had he sported brown eyes like his mother, he would have been born with dark eyes, but no, somehow he took that blue hue from his father.

Anton wondered how rare that was.

"Are you going to share him any, or what?"

Anton chuckled. "Not yet."

"Share him with me at least?" she asked.

"Shhh," he soothed, cradling the baby a little closer to his chest. Immediately the baby began to root for something he surely wasn't going to find at his father's breast. When Demyan couldn't find what he needed, the high pitch squalls began. "He doesn't want me." Anton tried not to sound whiney, not wanting to let his son go, but he failed miserably. "I guess I don't have much of a choice but to share, huh?"

Viviana grinned and waved her husband over.

"Nope. First me, and then the world. Poor you."

Yes, poor him indeed.

Anton wanted to keep his son just for him, but there was a whole hallway of people waiting to meet Demyan. They still hadn't announced his name, not even to Sasha when she met the child earlier.

Daniil would be the first to know.

That was Anton's gift to his father. The last one he could give, anyway.

"Fine, I'm going," Anton told his son when the cries turned desperate. "Let's go get you your mother, little man."

Viviana winced as she resituated herself on the bed. Birthing an almost ten pound boy was no easy feat, and she'd done it without any pain medication to help her along. Again, Anton had been awestruck of the ability and strength his wife had.

Passing the still angrily screeching Demyan to his mother, the baby shouted a little louder. His face turned into Viviana's chest. His little mouth pursed before the suckling action started up again, his tiny fists balling as Viviana undid the swaddling blanket. It wasn't long before the cries were quieted completely, finally finding the one thing he wanted. Lucky for them all that Demyan took right to breastfeeding. He didn't seem to have a lick of trouble latching on or staying there.

Sitting up on the edge of the bed, Anton ghosted the tips of his fingers along his son's arm, enjoying the silky smoothness and the warmth of the baby. He couldn't seem to get enough of physically feeling his son. He'd waited so long to meet him, to see, and know him, that now it all felt a little surreal.

Nine months had been way, way too long but they were worth every damned minute.

Watching Viviana stare warmly down at the breastfeeding infant, Anton was reminded of the first time she'd laid eyes on Demyan. Tears had fallen over her cheeks when they placed him on her chest wrapped in that fluffy, clean towel. There had been much too much movement and activity going on around them. A nurse trying to clean the child, a doctor readying to prep the cord for cutting, and another nurse attempting to hand Anton scissors.

There was just too fucking much.

So he stopped them. Asked them to be quiet. Demanded they give his wife one second just to look, to feel, to know her son. It hadn't been the doctors and nurses who made this child, wanted him so badly, or fought like they had for him. No, that had been just Anton and Viviana.

She needed that moment and he gave it to her.

"Hey, come here," Viviana said, reaching out to tug on Anton's T-shirt.

Leaning forward, Anton caught his wife's sweet mouth with his own. Swiping his tongue along the seam of her lips, she granted him access to her mouth with a wide smile. Anton poured every ounce of affection, devotion, and pride he had for his wife into the languid, affectionate kiss.

"So in love with you," he murmured into her mouth.

"Yeah?"

Anton nodded, letting his hand cup the back of Demyan's head as he said, "Yeah, like crazy. So, so much right now, Vine. More than ever. You're just … you and him amaze me."

"Ready to show the world this boy of yours, then?" Viviana asked with a tender smile.

"Let's just start with Daniil. The rest can wait."

• • •

When Daniil had first been readmitted into the hospital five months earlier, Anton and Viviana changed their choice in hospital for the birth accordingly. Neither of them wanted to drive their newborn son from one end of Brooklyn to the other so soon after coming into the world, never mind Anton's desire to have his wife rest as much as possible. So, being born in the same hospital as his grandfather was currently in had its benefits for Demyan.

Convincing the nurses that he would be fine to walk from one end of the hospital to the other with his father and grandmother was a whole different matter altogether. Anton hadn't let that argument go on for long. His son was perfectly healthy, a nine on the Apgar scale. Daniil wasn't suffering from any virus, so there wasn't a valid medical excuse for the baby not to be in the same room as his grandfather.

The nurses still tried to refuse.

The doctor on call in the maternity ward hadn't had an effective reason to decline the visit, but it was clear he wasn't all too comfortable agreeing with it, either.

Anton simply walked on by and let their rebuttals fade into the background.

Demyan was his son, so it was his choice. Well, his and Viviana's. She didn't mind, but she did voice her sadness about not being able to come along. Having just given birth to her first child only a few hours before, Viviana was still bleeding a little too heavily and it was a cause for concern. The doctor wanted her lying down more than sitting upright, let alone walking and standing for any great length of time.

Standing outside of Daniil's hospital room, Anton went through the usual checklist of questions for the safety of his father's health. Had he been sick recently? Was he feeling feverish? Had he spent time with anyone who was sick or feverish? The answers were all the same: no. Finally, the doctor gave the okay.

Sasha's hands fluttered over the baby. Already, she was devoted to spoiling Demyan as often and as much as she could possibly get away with. Anton's mother made the perfect grandmother as far as he was concerned.

"Look at my grandbaby." Sasha cooed over the wrapped up baby boy. "He's so perfect and pretty."

Anton rolled his eyes. "Pretty, Ma?"

Sasha tossed him a baleful look. "He's a baby. He can be pretty for a little while. Let him be a baby, not a little boy already. Besides, look at him."

"You spent half of the morning with him."

"Yes, but you wouldn't let me hold him very much."

Oddly, that was true. It wasn't that he didn't trust anyone, he did. Anton just … Damn, he didn't want to put his son down. Viviana had him for nine months so now it was his turn. People would have to deal with it. Even so, he knew his mother didn't fall into that category of people.

"Can I?" Sasha asked, holding out her arms.

Anton hesitated. "I wanted to take him in."

"Anton, stop being a helicopter."

What in the hell did that even mean?

"You can do it, Ma. I just haven't really been far from him since he was born this morning. I didn't know if you wanted me to wait for a minute, but I was hoping to see Daniil when he met him."

Carefully, he allowed his mother to take the sleeping, happy, freshly fed Demyan. With the fluffy blue blanket pulled back from his face, his head of black hair stood out against his light features. All over again, Anton was stunned at how thunderstruck simply looking at his child made him.

"Pretty amazing, isn't it?" Sasha asked.

He didn't even have to ask what she meant. "Yeah. I used to just correlate love to Vine, or you, or Dad, or the things in life that made me feel good. Those were the kinds of loves I felt."

"It's not even the same." Sasha pushed back a few tendrils of the baby's hair from his forehead. "This is a whole other ballgame, Anton. They don't just change your circumstance, they change who you are. It's instant, and it gets bigger and better with every new thing."

"Something like that," he agreed.

Sasha smirked, reaching out with one hand to smack her son lightly. "Something. Act like you don't want to admit it, then. He reminds me so much of you, it's out of this world."

"I thought he looked like Viviana."

"Sure, but he's got a whole lot of his Papa, too. Your mouth, for sure. Especially when he's squawking."

"Thanks," Anton said with a short laugh.

"He's got her almond shaped eyes, though."

"But *blue* eyes."

"Lucky," Sasha said. "I thought those would be lost for sure."

Anton didn't want to admit how proud that made him. A boy tended to take after their mother, so to know his son had an equal amount of both parents in his features was a pretty cool thing.

For a short time, he was lost watching his mother standing there just holding Demyan. Anton knew there was a period in his life where she worried about him, worried that he may never get to this particular point in his life. She had wished so badly for him to find peace and happiness in the situation he was forced upon. Anton wanted her to know that he had. Demyan would do that, in one way.

The birth of something new would help to heal the loss of something loved.

But that didn't mean they wanted to say goodbye, either.

"You ready?" he asked softly. "I'm sure Dad is going crazy in there without you. This is probably the longest you've been away from him for months."

Sasha sniffed but hid the water in her eyes with a quick blink and a slow smile. "I love your father."

Confusion settled in his heart. "I know."

"So, no, Anton, I'm not ready."

Grief ripped apart Anton's soul. The harsh reality of his father's situation was one they couldn't ignore. While he had seemed to turn a new leaf during the beginning of the pregnancy, Daniil had only gone slowly downhill since then. Just last week they had inserted a feeding tube as his appetite was all but lost and his weight had dramatically lessened over the last month. The slightest cold or cough would send his father to the grave.

Cancer was a horrible, murderous disease, no matter which kind it was.

Daniil had fought his battle hard, and Anton was proud of his father despite the odds he had been given. He was even proud when his father chose to stop fighting because that in itself was a decision that had to have been a war. And when it would have been so easy to just let go, Daniil had held on for the one thing in life he had yet to meet: Demyan.

It wasn't just them saying goodbye, Daniil was saying it, too.

"Okay," Sasha said, wiping away the one tear that had escaped. "Let's meet your grandfather, sweet child."

Anton pushed open the door to Daniil's private room, holding it open for his mother to walk in with the baby safely cradled in her capable hands. Instantly, his eyes were drawn to his father's across the room.

Frail and weak, Daniil didn't look like he once had. Sickness had grayed his once healthy tone, turning him gaunt and older than he truly was. Shadowed bruises dotted his small arms and blue veins were visible on his translucent, thin skin. Tiredness and fatigue wrote heavy lines on his features and sickness left hallows where muscle had once filled him out. A portacath was inserted into his upper chest, providing all the fluids and medication he needed without doing damage to his weakened veins. The feeding tube was inserted through his left nostril.

But above his sickness and state, Daniil only looked back to his son with a smile. One that was filled with love, pride, and hope. There was no sadness in his gaze, no grief in his happiness.

"Finally," Daniil said with a wave. The remote in his hand was tossed to the side, forgotten. "Bring that boy to me. I've been waiting for hours!"

"Sorry." Anton let the door shut behind him before

turning back to his father. "I wanted to make sure Vine was settled."

Sasha walked across the room as Daniil asked, "And how is she? Good, yeah?"

"Great. She did awesome, but she's tired. It was fucking amazing, honestly."

"My God. That mouth of yours." Sasha's narrowed gaze flashed with a warning. "Little ears here, Anton."

Daniil rolled his eyes at his wife, arms outstretched to take the tiny bundle of blue from her grasp. With his one hand supporting Demyan's head and the other holding his back, Daniil pulled up his legs and rested the baby down to look at him. Once more, Anton watched as someone else fell in love with his son at first glance.

"Oh, he's a *sokrovishche*." Daniil professed his adoration over his grandson again, his face lighting up with a little more life. Yes, Demyan was a treasure indeed. "Look at this *malysh* of yours. My God, he's like a little you, Anton."

"He really is, huh?" Sasha smiled. "Just like our baby. Black as night and light like cream. He's even got those eyes, too. So beautiful. He's precious. Big, too."

"Nine pounds, ten ounces," Anton informed quietly. "He's going to be tall. Twenty-three inches long."

"Healthy?" Daniil asked, glancing up from the baby.

"Like a horse. Eats like nothing else. Sleeps a couple of hours at a time so far. He's great."

Sasha crawled up on the bed beside her husband, settling in at his side before gently pushing open the blanket around Demyan a little more. They shared a secret smile and then Sasha laid her cheek to Daniil's shoulder. Strangely, the sight of his parents so close together, delighted, ecstatic, and whispering over his new son seemed like a private moment he was intruding on. Anton hadn't expected to feel like that at all.

Anton briefly wondered if he was taking a leap into the past staring at them. Was that how they sat together and fawned over his birth, too? Had they been so enamoured staring down at their first child like he did for Demyan?

"How does it feel?" he heard Daniil ask.

Anton cleared his throat, willing the thickness rising there to leave. "Like falling in love."

"Yeah, don't I know that," Daniil said in a whisper. "I remember looking down at you and thinking I couldn't have possibly created something so innocent and beautiful. How you ever came from me, I didn't know. I thought Sasha was the most amazing thing to ever walk the earth just for giving you to me."

"And Nicoli sat in the corner with him for hours, fussing and cooing over him like he was the new father," Sasha added. "Rocked you to sleep that first night and the nurses had to come in and tell him visiting hours were over."

Anton laughed. He couldn't imagine his step-grandfather being so smitten over a baby, never mind him. But, it wasn't too hard to believe. They'd always shared a different kind of bond than Anton had with others.

"Oh, your grandpapa Nicoli would have adored you, my little man," Daniil said, his gaze back down on Demyan. "Yes, I bet he would have."

"Are you going to do a bris?" Sasha asked.

Anton didn't miss how his mother avoided his look when she asked. His and Viviana's choice to forgo a stricter religious life and live theirs how they pleased was sometimes a hot button with his mother. Daniil never cared, but Sasha had always followed her Jewish beliefs and customs.

A bris, or Brit Milah, was the ceremony at which a Jewish baby boy was circumcised on the eighth day of his life on earth. The child was held by his sandek, or godfather, during the ceremony, presented with his Hebrew name, and blessed. Usually a meal would follow to celebrate the tradition and child.

"We talked about it," Anton said.

"And?"

"Sasha," Daniil chided quietly. "Let them be. She's not even Jewish."

"I'm just curious, Daniil. Mind your manners."

Anton sighed. "We're going to do it, Ma. It'd be customary for me to ask you or Dad to be his sandek but Vine thought it'd be nice if it was Ivan instead."

"That'd be fine." Sasha was pleased, clearly. "I'm sure he'll be happy."

"So …" Daniil said, tilting his head down to the baby. "What's this boy's name, hmm?"

Oddly, Anton didn't blurt out the name like he assumed he would. They'd kept it so private and now that it was time to share, he was suddenly nervous. Would the name fit his boy as well as he thought it did? Would his parents approve of the different style and American ring?

"Anton?" Daniil asked again with a raised brow. "My grandson's name?"

"Demyan," he answered, surprised to hear the quaver in his own voice. "His name is Demyan Anton Nicoli Avdonin."

Sasha beamed up at her son. "I like that. It's new. My money was on the namesake, though."

"Mine wasn't," Daniil said with a conspiring grin at the baby.

"Why's that?" Anton asked, honestly curious.

"It's obvious. You two have never been traditional so there wasn't any way either of you were going to give this child a simple name." Lifting Demyan up from his resting spot, Daniil held him high and stared up at the sleeping child with pure adoration and affection. "It's a good name, Anton. I have no doubt he will own and carry it well."

"You think?"

"Absolutely. He has you for a papa, after all," Daniil replied, not taking his attention away from the baby. "Welcome to this world, Demyan. I'm so happy I was able to meet you on your journey. I hope you find all that you need and want from this life, beautiful boy, and so much more."

Chapter Twenty

"Mmm, but I don't want to go."

Viviana laughed, leaning forward to press a soft kiss to Anton's mouth to quiet up his complaining. He took five days away from being boss and spent every single one of them with her and Demyan. She was grateful that he had taken that time with him, but now he needed to get back to his work.

After three days of being in the hospital, both Viviana and Demyan were released to go home. The first night alone with a newborn had surely been the hardest. They woke up to the sounds of him choking only to find Demyan had swallowed his own saliva down the wrong hole. That had been terrifying, never mind the fact that the poor baby cried until he turned himself red all over. He hadn't slept nearly as well at home as he did in the hospital. Anything new was just as scary as it was exciting.

Clarissa was there to help, thank God, and Sasha made an effort to come over once a day to check on things, but being new parents was definitely a learning curve.

"Let me take him with me, Vine."

"What are going to do, huh?' she asked teasingly, poking Anton's chest. "Breastfeed him?"

"That's why we bought those bottles that were forty dollars apiece, baby."

Sure, that was true enough, but Demyan took just fine to the breast. They didn't need to bottle feed him. Viviana wasn't going to confuse her son by starting to pump and feed with bottles. She didn't mind the late nights with several feedings, or the cluster feedings before bed. No, none of that bothered her a bit.

She loved her son. Adored him to the moon and back. He was her little prince.

"Go, Anton. We'll be here when you get back."

Anton frowned. "But will you be okay?"

Viviana wasn't offended by him asking. Essentially, it would be her first day alone with Demyan. Someone else had always been around to help if she was unsure about something, but even Clarissa was out of the house running errands for most of the morning and afternoon.

"I'll be fine," Viviana said. "Call me when you … Wait, what are you doing today?"

Anton shrugged. "Business, like usual. A meeting with the guys. Nothing too big."

Viviana's smile dissipated. He seemed awfully nonchalant for it just being simple business. Anton had yet to mention a thing to her about Joe, or what came after, and he didn't say a thing about the dinner or the mysterious fire at the restaurant she had seen on the news. Six dead, three of which had been identified while the other three bodies were still waiting for confirmation.

Tossing a peek to her son out of the corner of her eye, Viviana noted he was still snug tight in a Moses basket. The baby was content and sleeping. Now, she had to consider him every time Anton left the house as well. Would Anton be back for Demyan, too?

"Vine, hey," Anton murmured. "What's wrong?"

"Just your guys, right?" she asked.

"Who else would I need to handle right now?"

"Jersey, maybe."

Understanding dawned on Anton's features. "That's not happening for another month or more. They've got their own mess to handle, and I don't think they plan on coming back on us for anything. I did what was necessary. That was all. I didn't break any rules, especially since Sergei was already planning to come in on me. They'd have done the same."

"They tried, Anton. It failed. Someone very well might be pissed off and looking for their revenge."

"The new Pakhan is going to clean house, starting with his own. It's not your business to be worrying about it, anyway.

You're not Bratva, you're a wife."

"Of a Bratva *boss*," she said a little hotly. "So yes, I get to worry, Anton."

"Please don't do this with me right now. I don't want to leave and you be angry."

Viviana took a cleansing breath, hoping it would help her rising anger. At times her emotions still ran hot and cold. It didn't help that Viviana was tired and she knew Anton was, too. Despite her not needing him to get up with their son in the middle of the night, several times, he did anyway. Anton never complained. Instead he crawled into bed beside her, buried his face into her neck while she fed Demyan, and kept her awake with words and teasing kisses.

Anton was a great husband, and an even greater father. Actions spoke much louder than words and Anton was full of them, on both accounts. His mornings were spent fawning over Demyan and lavishing the same attention he had always showered on his wife. His evenings, when the baby slept, were spent at her side, with her in his arms as they relaxed together.

Viviana couldn't have picked a better man to be her partner and lover in life.

Fighting with Anton was the last thing she wanted to do. He didn't deserve it.

"I'm sorry," Viviana said. "But I do worry. I can't help it."

"So, you're not angry with me?"

"No, I'm not angry, but you seem to forget the spot I'm in here, too."

"Come here," he said huskily, grasping her wrists and pulling her into his warm chest. "Don't be pissy, Viviana. I never forget, thank you very much, but it is what it is. What are we going to do about it?"

"Nothing," she mumbled.

"Exactly, nothing. I'll be home around supper, like I always am. I'll kiss you to sleep, like I always do."

"Hmm, well, that does sound nice. Especially now that you get to do it several times over in the night."

"Don't tease me." Anton's chuckles rocked their bodies. "The doctor said six weeks for healing, remember? I don't know if I can last that long."

Viviana gasped in mock indignation. "How will you ever survive, Anton?"

"I'll manage ... with many painfully cold showers."

She snorted under her breath before tiling her head up to kiss the underside of his chin. Viviana knew he didn't really mind about the six weeks of abstinence. Her body was still swollen, tender, and healing. It would be for a while. Sitting down could be an effort at times. Sex was the last thing on her mind.

That didn't mean they couldn't have any physical contact, though, and Anton was the first to feed into that however he could. It could be as simple as his arms around her waist, his fingers in her hair, or his kiss on her hand. It did matter, she liked him close, and he gave it to her as often as possible.

And God, every time he did, Viviana yearned and burned for more.

"Six weeks is long, but I think you'll be okay," she told him.

Anton smirked, offering her a cheeky wink. "The wait will be worth it. And besides that, we got something good from it."

The sleeping baby caught both their eyes. Demyan was still cuddled in his blankets, his fist stuck up by his lips like it usually was. She couldn't believe how much he'd taken after his father in his appearance. But, it was more than just appearance, too. Viviana had noticed her son calmed easier in the arms of his father. Anton's voice, especially when he was speaking Russian, soothed the boy's fussing. Demyan preferred the blue swaddling blanket his father had held him wrapped in for most of their stay at the hospital, probably because it smelled like Anton.

Already there was a bond between the two that was remarkable to witness.

Viviana smiled as she said, "We made something amazing,

Anton."

"We sure did."

"All right, you better get going."

"Still don't want to," Anton muttered unhappily.

"Sooner you leave, the quicker it'll be over." Viviana's suggestion seemed to work as Anton's shoulders relaxed slightly. "I'll be okay with him, I promise."

"I know you will, Vine. It's me who's having the meltdown here. Ten bucks says I'm home before supper."

"Twenty says you don't make it until noon," she said, just to tease.

Anton grinned. "Oh, you're on."

• • •

Hollers welcomed Anton into his office at Seven Lights. Waving his hands in the air and giving his three favorite guys a bow, Anton grinned at the affection they showed his return. Not all of his men were there, but the most important ones were.

Erik, Boris, and Ivan.

The only ones he'd wanted to see without a prearranged meeting.

Erik reached out to cuff his shoulder while loud congratulations were expressed.

"He lives another day!" Erik leered.

Ivan laughed and said, "Oh, the new daddy is in the house."

"Birth is as bad as they say, yeah?" Boris asked.

Anton chuckled. "It wasn't that bad, actually."

"Liar."

Anton's gaze found his best friend's instantly, a relieved smile overtaking him as he regarded Ivan. His lawyer was pale, tired looking, and probably weak, but he seemed a hell of a lot better than he had the last time Anton was with him.

At least now he fucking looked alive.

Crossing the room, Anton met Ivan before he could stand

from his spot on the couch. Ivan didn't need to get up to greet him, not in Anton's opinion. The man deserved more than that for the bullet he took. The quiet embrace between the two men lasted long enough for Anton to feel the strength in the hold.

"Does he look as much like you as I've heard?" Ivan asked.

Anton shrugged as he pulled away. "Quite a bit. He took after her, too. He's got a good mix of us both."

Ivan had yet to see Demyan, and actually, today was his first day away from his own home and family since the night over a week before that nearly took his life. Anton and Viviana had received a steady stream of visitors to their house since they arrived home from the hospital. Most were Bratva, a few had been his wife's friends from school, and others were their mutual friends, people like Jen. Anton didn't mind the visitors, but he liked privacy more. He was happy the guests were finally beginning to slow.

"Blue eyes, too?" Ivan asked.

"Just like his Papa," Erik said as he sat down. Ivan winced at the jostle of movement on the couch. "Sorry, man."

"It's all right, but you don't weigh as much as a horse, so don't act like it," Ivan replied easily.

Anton sat down behind his desk, relaxed back into the familiar chair, and propped his boots up on the oak top. Comfort and familiarity seeped into his blood like a drug, but he felt different sitting there, more so than he usually would. It was almost like something was missing. His mind was there where it needed to be. Ready to talk business, the new shipment coming in at the end of the month, and the issue of Jersey, but an odd sentiment prickled at him.

Or maybe his heart was simply elsewhere.

Like at home, with his wife and son.

Shit, now he just wanted to call Viviana.

Anton sighed away the melancholy. "So, anything new?"

"It's only been five days, Boss," Boris said, exhaling a heavy puff of cigar smoke.

"Eight," Anton corrected. "I haven't been properly caught up on anything since the sit-down. Someone needs to fix that shit immediately. I hate being out of the loop."

"You were the one who turned your phone off."

"True."

"I received an interesting call," Ivan said, offering something new to the conversation. "I was surprised he didn't call you directly, or his wife, for that matter."

Anton raised a brow. It wasn't like Ivan to be vague. "Who?"

"Who else has that ample amount of stupidity? The Don, of course. Wanting to wish Viviana congratulations from him and his wife on the birth of her first child. Maybe it was just his way of being respectful, but Conrad didn't wait to get on the phone with me after Demyan's birth was announced in the Times."

"Wait, my son's birth was in the motherfucking Times?"

"A baby boy born to a former Cosa Nostra Don's daughter and the current Bratva mob prince?" Boris asked over the tip of his cigar. Scoffing, he rolled his eyes, "I'm surprised they didn't plaster those titles on him just for good measure and call him New York underground royalty. You're goddamn right they had that announcement in the Times, Boss. What would they call him, anyway? The Russian Don?"

Anton stared at his brigadier, wondering where on earth the man had gotten that from. It was funny, but it wasn't. Anton was just trying to decide if he wanted to be offended or not. Somebody else who didn't know Boris well enough probably would have taken it offensively.

"Jesus, Boris, you're an idiot," Ivan said through his laughter. "If I was close enough, and it didn't hurt to get up, I'd smack the shit outta you."

"Demyan can't be the Don," Anton finally said, deciding he wasn't all too offended. It was all for shits and giggles, anyway. Something to lighten up the room, get the guys loose and ready to talk. "Couldn't ever be, he's *Russian*. Looks like a Russian, too."

"I heard they're taking 'em even if they're only half, now," Boris replied with a teasing smirk.

"Yeah, but the bloodline can't be disputed, and it needs to come from the father's side. My child doesn't have a lick of Italian from me." Anton grinned smugly, catching the freshly cut cigar Boris tossed over the desk. "He gets just enough from his mother to color him up. Even with that, Demyan's perfect."

"So says the father he came from," Erik said with a snort. "You wait till he turns into you. Wrecking every vehicle you could get your hands on, getting kicked off the baseball team for handing out ecstasy in the locker room, and running with girls whose daddies were one step away from putting a bullet in your ass. You might not think he's so perfect, then, boy. God knows Daniil was ready to lay a well-deserved licking down on you more than once for the stunts you pulled growing up."

Anton's arm ached at the reminder. No, he had managed not to take a bullet in his backside, but the one that all but lodged in his shoulder had been a wakeup call of sorts. A few months later he was in Barbados with Viviana. The rest was history.

"Ah, you old fool," Boris mumbled around his cigar. "Erik, you ran those women just as hard. We overlooked Anton's issues because he eventually grew up. When did you manage to? How many wives now? Three?"

"Four." Anton had to point out the correct number just to poke the bear.

"*Mne vse ravno*," Erik said with a wink. "I'm only in it for the *pizda*."

Ivan shook his head in disbelief. "Oh! The pussy, he says. Because you need to be married to get that."

Anton guffawed. "Don't let your wife hear you say that. You won't be getting any more *pizda* for a while, you perverted fucker."

"Anyway." Ivan whistled low, bringing their attention and

laughter to him. "Back to the call from Conrad. It didn't last too long, but it was enough."

Erik grumbled under his breath, looking more disgusted by the second. "Ugh. Fucking Italians, man. Can we just be done with that family and move on? I've had enough. Wasn't getting rid of their good for nothing boss a huge red flag that we don't want their friendship? We've got our own issues with New Jersey. We don't need to be slumming it with Cosa Nostra, too."

"I agree," Anton said. "What'd you tell him, Ivan?"

It wasn't that Anton didn't appreciate the call, he just wondered if there was more behind Conrad's motives. Hadn't the Don been the one to say each boss should keep to their own territories? The last thing he wanted, or needed, was to have issues with the Italians. Anton mulled it all over as he found his favorite Zippo and worked on lighting up his cigar.

Things were finally starting to smooth out a little in his life. Couldn't it stay that way?

Fuck, Anton hoped so.

"Didn't tell him nothing he might have wanted to hear," the lawyer responded. "Gave him a thank you on your behalf, as I should."

"And as my Sovietnik?"

Ivan smirked wickedly. "Told him to keep his distance."

"Good." Anton sighed, relived that was one less thing he'd have to handle. "We don't need that trouble."

Both Boris and Erik agreed.

"What else?" Anton flicked his Zippo between his forefinger and thumb, hearing the clink, clack of metal as the top popped open and then closed again. No one spoke. "You're telling me there's nothing?"

"Nothing hugely important that needs attention," Ivan said, sounding bored. "It's been quiet. That's not a bad thing."

"Vegas is finally saying yes to my proposition with the last gun shipment," Boris said.

There was something Anton could talk about. He'd been

working for years to get his guns leaking into certain parts of the States. Vegas was just one of them, but it was a big fucking one. Getting his weapons out of the States was an easy feat, but working into an already booming illegal marketplace was tough.

"Just like that? No dividends for them?"

"There's always something," the brigadier replied. "Give it time. This is the first deal you've worked with a Vegas guy, so give him what he wants. It'll pay off in the long run, I promise you that."

"Well, shit," Anton mused, leaning back in his chair as smoke curled high to the ceiling.

"And the shipment coming in at the end of the month ..."

Anton flicked Boris with a sharp look. That shipment was over five-point-two million in illegal substance they couldn't afford to lose. It would be even worse if the authorities picked up on it and trailed to back to him. "What about it?"

Erik made a noise under his breath. "Take a pill, Anton. Calm your nerves."

"There's a crapload of money we're going to make on that boat," Ivan muttered.

Anton jerked his thumb in his lawyer's direction. "Truth."

"Viktor let me know they had a little issue a week ago," Boris started to explain.

"Oh, yeah? What kind now?"

Fucking Viktor, Anton thought. That goddamned brigadier was causing him more issues than he wanted to admit. If Viktor wasn't causing some kind of shit, he was starting it somewhere else.

"Guess the load isn't going to be as big as they thought. Viktor said the guys screwed up on the weigh in, but we paid just as much for the original. What was he supposed to do about it, he asked. I didn't know what to tell him. I'm not the boss, you know?"

The room went silent for a good minute. Anton inhaled a burning drag from his cigar, letting the harsh smoke tumble around in his lungs before he exhaled it to the air. He needed to seriously think about what he'd just been told before he reacted to it.

Runners didn't screw up a weigh in on shipments. That was the crux of the matter. Sure, they'd skim a little here and there to make a couple of thousand in profit above their original price, but that wasn't anything to the grand scheme of things. It was expected, really. Runners wanted their money to come in clean, just like the traffickers did. Striking bad deals, or making mistakes that would cost them future ones, wasn't in the repertoire.

The only plausible explanation was that someone else had skimmed off quite a bit of the drug shipment for themselves, or they were planning to. Quick money, even if the product still needed to be checked for quality and control. It didn't matter to the thief who took it, they'd sell it just as easy and wouldn't give a shit about the rest.

"That's going to be an issue," Anton said quietly. "One he's going to have to answer for, somehow. I don't care how, Boris, but it better be fucking good or I'll see him in a grave. Mark my words, I'll do it."

Boris kept his face a mask of calm, but Anton could see the war fighting in the older man's eyes. The two brigadiers had been friends for many years and tended to stick together. However, when Viktor fell out of Anton's favor the year before because he smacked around Viviana, Boris had started to create a little distance from his friend.

You don't bite the hand that feeds you, after all.

"Do what you gotta do, Boss," Boris stated. "He knows how this goes."

"If I find out he did something and make the call to cull him, are you going to give him warning?" Anton asked.

"It's not my call to make."

"Good answer." Anton wasn't quite finished, though. He wanted to make sure exactly what side his brigadier was on. "And what if I make the call to you?"

Boris cringed. "I'd rather you didn't."

"But?" Anton asked.

"I'd do it. Business as usual," Boris said dully. "What else?"

Exactly, Anton thought. The life wasn't easy, but they lived it nonetheless. *What else?*

Anton leaned back in his chair, propping his boots up on the desk once more. "Anything else?"

Looks were shared between the men in the room, but nothing was amiss. Apparently it truly had been quiet, for the most part. Damn, Anton didn't want to get his hopes up for things settling down but it was sure seeming like that was going to be the case. There were such things as miracles, after all.

"Just that prince of yours," Ivan said with a smile. "I've got to get over there soon."

"Want to see a picture?"

Three grown men might as well have turned into children right before Anton's eyes. Laughing, he pulled out his cell phone and brought up the picture files. It wasn't long before he found the one he'd taken early that morning. It had automatically become his favorite in the bunch, and damn, he'd taken quite a few of his son in just the short span of five days. Regarding the photo before he turned the phone to show the guys, Anton was reminded of that odd feeling he started out the morning with.

The one that told him to go back home for a little while longer.

Sunlight had just started to filter in through the bedroom windows, illuminating the photo with natural light. Viviana was rolled to her side on their bed, sleeping with one arm laying up along her son's back to hold him close. Demyan was curled in the sheets with his mother, that tiny fist of his up against his mouth while his other hand was grasping tight to a lock of his mother's hair. He wasn't sleeping, though. Those blue eyes of his were wide open, staring up into his mother's face with an awestruck amazement only a baby could have.

People could say newborns didn't have in-depth

understanding of emotions all they wanted, Anton knew they were wrong. Demyan had love already. He just did. And like his father, all that love he felt revolved around Viviana.

When Demyan had started up his fussing that morning, Anton knew the baby couldn't be hungry or dirty. Viviana just fed, cleaned, and laid him down in his bed not thirty minutes before. She had just managed to fall back asleep, too. Anton wanted her to get some more sleep. Getting up six times a night for thirty to forty minutes each time with their son was tiresome; she needed the extra rest.

So, when even Anton couldn't get the baby to fall back to sleep, he thought maybe ... maybe his son was just like him even straight from the womb. Perhaps all he wanted was the thing he loved the very most. The touch, closeness, smell, and sight of all that love. When he placed Demyan beside his sleeping mother, and a tiny little fist shot out to snag Viviana's lock of hair, Anton wasn't surprised to find out he was right.

"What do you want to do today, Boss?" Boris asked, bringing Anton from his musings.

Anton glanced around the room. Things were good. Great, even. He didn't need to be here.

"I owe my wife twenty bucks."

Chapter Twenty-One

Anton stared at the grave.

It was standard size, but the hole in the ground seemed larger than normal. Like maybe it was ready to suck him up and swallow him whole, too. The black marble headstone was meticulous in detail and design, the inscriptions clean and clear. Everything had gone along perfectly without a single bump in the plans of the funeral.

The day was sunny, warm, and summer hung thick in the air.

Just as his father would have wanted.

Slowly, every progression and battle won in Daniil's fight against cancer had been lost. In a short two week span, Anton's father had slipped away a little more. If it wasn't his organs failing, his lungs wouldn't catch air. The hospital wanted to keep people out to preserve what time Daniil might have had left, but the man didn't want that at all.

He wanted everybody.

Anton had to respect his father for that.

Goodbyes weren't easy. But he'd said each one with a smile.

Anton missed him already.

Demyan had been born early on the morning of July third. Daniil said his final goodbye exactly two weeks later, thirty minutes before the time when Demyan had entered the world. It wasn't nearly enough time. It *wasn't*.

He said his hello, Anton reminded himself silently.

Anton's throat ached from holding back the sobs threatening to rise. He'd long since clenched his teeth shut like a goddamned steel trap to keep himself from crying. His fists shoved firmly in his pockets kept the shaking of his hands contained. The slow, rhythmic breathing he'd somehow managed to find helped to stop his breaths from turning ragged with anxiety and sorrow.

The tears were a losing battle. They leaked from his eyes freely, rolling down his cheeks in streaks of shining wetness, and dropping to the lapels of his suit jacket. The fedora tilted low to hide his face kept others from seeing the emotion.

It didn't matter, though, because Anton could still feel it.

Good God, the grief was painful. Something awful that left him feeling raw, broken, and lost from the inside out. His soul was being ripped apart for his mother's sadness, his family's loss, and his own heartache. Anton wasn't accustomed to being so emotionally disabled like he currently was.

Nothing had ever had quite the effect on him like the death of his father had.

Once more, Anton stared down into the grave. The casket resting deep into the freshly dug earth still shined with newness. Nothing had soiled it, yet. No dirt was blockading his father in for the rest of eternity. Anton could still see the peace on Daniil's face as he lay in his silk lined resting place, peace overtaking the sickness that had plagued him for too long.

There was no pain for Daniil now.

There was no cancer, no more hospitals, treatments, and worry.

Just peace.

Somehow, Anton needed to keep reminding himself of that.

His father was better, now. Finding comfort in a new place. Receiving health in a healed soul. Looking down, watching them. Because even the bad guys had souls. Surely Daniil's hadn't been so tainted that he would be denied heaven. He might not have lived his life according to the law, or the way the temple would have told him to, but he lived it how he wanted and needed. He'd been a good father and husband, taught love, respect, and honor to his only child, and left Anton with a legacy to carry on.

No, he hadn't been that bad of a man.

Sighing heavily, Anton peered under the rim of his fedora. The crowd of mourners had all but gone, now. Even Sasha had said her final goodbyes a while ago, coming to stand beside her son for his support and comfort while she did so. She was holding a dinner at her home later to celebrate her husband's life.

Not his death, Anton thought, again needing the reminder. *Don't mourn his death. Remember his life.*

It was starting to become a mantra of sorts.

Anton wished to all hell it would start to help.

It wasn't.

Viviana hadn't been able to make it through all of the readings at the gravesite before Demyan began to stir with his fussiness and desire to feed. With a soft kiss to his cheek, a squeeze of her hand around his, and an apology, she'd left his side for the first and only time that day to return to their SUV and take care of their son.

Not surprisingly, Anton felt alone.

That sensation didn't last for long when a form saddled up beside his. The well-dressed man wasn't familiar to the Russian boss. Anton had been fortunate enough to recognize every face that stared back at him and gave their apologies and sentiments for his father's passing. Giving the man a second glance, Anton noticed the shining badge down at his hip where his hands were tossed into his pockets.

A federal agent had made face at Daniil's funeral.

A federal fucking agent.

Could they get any lower?

What business, or right, did they have to intrude on his family's grief and pain?

Indignant anger burrowed hard and fast into Anton's heart, pumping through his veins with every beat. His teeth clenched harder for a whole different reason. He needed to force his hands deeper into his pockets just to keep from throttling the man in his sudden flare of rage and disbelief.

"Leave," Anton said under his breath. The agent said nothing, simply tipped his head up to the sun and blinked in the brightness. "I said—"

"November sixth and into the early morning hours of the seventh of last year, where were you, Mr. Avdonin?"

Anton felt his spine crack as he stood a little straighter. That date was one he wouldn't ever forget. It was the day Viviana had nearly been killed by a bomb that was placed by her Uncle Sonny. Those early morning hours of the seventh was when Anton killed Sonny for that goddamned bomb. That day had been filled with nothing but pain, but there had also been a little joy, too. They'd found out about Demyan.

"In the hospital with my wife. A bomb nearly killed her. Check her records."

"I don't doubt *she* was there," the agent replied. "Three weeks ago, the car trailing you lost your vehicle, where were you then?"

"With my *wife*."

"Where with your wife?"

Anton growled low, grinding his teeth to stop from cutting out at the agent with a verbal attack. That wasn't something he wanted to do at his father's funeral. "None of your business."

The agent gave a condescending smile from the side. "You've always been so careful, Anton. Your business and your boys have been one of the hardest for our team to infiltrate. Very little evidence, if any at all, and what is left surely wouldn't be enough to take us back to you."

Anton scowled under his fedora. What was the man's point?

"So? You decided to impose your unwanted, and uninvited, presence at my father's funeral just to say I've got the upper hand on you? Thanks, but I didn't need that memo. Feel free to get the fuck out of this cemetery before I have someone remove you."

"Had," the agent responded dully.

"Excuse me?"

"Had. As in the upper hand is gone, Boss. Somewhere along the lines, you started to fuck up. Messy isn't like you. I was almost disappointed."

Anton stared at the man, his brain running a million miles a minute to try and figure out when, if it had happened at all, that he had managed to miss something in his disputes and issues over the last year. Nothing came to his mind. Nothing that would be a cause for concern.

Of course, Anton knew they would suspect him in the death of Sonny, never mind the recent deaths of the Belovs. But suspecting and having hard evidence were two very diverse things. It meant the difference between a life sentence and his freedom, after all. Anton wasn't about to make those kinds of errors.

Staring at the agent, Anton was quick to notice the man seemed young. Maybe around his age. Was this some new agent trying to get his name in the papers and bigger in his boss's eye by taking a swing at a mob boss?

Anton wasn't standing for that shit. "Listen, I've got a lawyer. Feel free to—"

"Oh, we will," the agent interrupted calmly. "Soon, probably. Did you know there was a single bullet shell found in the ruins of the Primo Delight restaurant that burned down three weeks ago? I heard you got along quite well with the owner. The Belovs, you were good friends with them, too, right? There wasn't a single body in the restaurant that showed a gunshot wound, and there was no weapon recovered. I noticed your lawyer seemed to be in a little pain today. How's he fairing in life?"

Anton swallowed the spiteful retort that wanted out. "Is that all you've got on me? A shell with no gun to place it to, connections to a dead boss who probably deserved what he got, and my lawyer? Come on, that's ridiculous. No judge would even look at the arrest warrant. Try again."

"No, that's not all. I haven't seen you smoking cigarettes in a while, either."

That was random. Anton frowned away from the man. "That's a crime, now? Jesus, my wife considers that a battle won."

"Does she? Hmm." The agent hummed disparagingly. "Well, I'm sure she won't be pleased to know you were smoking the night Sonny Carducci was killed, will she? Tossed those butts straight to the ground, you did. When we did a standard angle test with lasers to find out where the shot had been taken from, guess what it led us to?"

Anton's heart leaped into his throat. Had he tossed his cigarettes out the window? Having a felony conviction in his past for illegal weapons meant Anton's DNA was in the system, as were his fingerprints.

"Again, that proves nothing."

"I disagree."

Anton refused to let his panic show. "Are you here to arrest me?"

Now it was the agent's turn to scowl. "No, unfortunately. You're right, we're not quite there, yet. But we will be, Anton. That's what I'm here to tell you. I hope you're ready, you have a lot to answer for."

Anton allowed his calm, cool, and confident mask to take its rightful place. "And how long will that take?" he asked, cockily. "It's already been nine months since the first crime you suggest I may have committed. You haven't come for me yet, so what do you really have? Suspicions, but no hard proof. Show me the reports. Show me the cigarettes. Show me the missing gun that wasn't used in a crime that by all accounts, wasn't even a crime to begin with, just an unfortunate event. Show me these things. Worry me. Go ahead."

The agent's jaw flexed angrily.

"You can't," Anton murmured, turning back to stare into the grave. "Or you're waiting for something that's not here, yet. It doesn't matter either way. I'm not easily frightened. You need means and motive, and you don't have it, do you? Again, how long will it take your investigation to come up with something a judge will consider worthy? Two years, maybe four? Long enough for my son to know my name, for my wife to see our anniversary a couple of times over. Too long for me to care."

"You do." The agent sighed. Anton hated that he did, but he wouldn't give the man the satisfaction of seeing it. With a nod at the grave the agent said, "My sympathies for your loss."

Anton nearly choked on his outraged anger at the man's gall.

"Go to hell and rot there, asshole."

• • •

Viviana was buckling a sleeping Demyan into his car seat as a hand came to rest on her waist. She didn't start in fright from the unexpected approach. She knew her husband's woodsy scent anywhere. Finishing up her job of securing the baby's harness, she sighed into the warm touch of Anton's fingers trailing lightly up her side. Without turning her around, he leaned over her form and skimmed the side of her neck with his nose and mouth.

"He good?" Anton asked.

"Yep. For a little while, anyway. Are you?"

Anton sucked air through his teeth, the sound filled with stress. "I will be, eventually."

The day had been hard for Anton. Viviana knew that for a fact. He hadn't even wanted to get out of bed that morning, and that just wasn't like him. She understood he was in pain and grieving, just the same as his mother, and even Viviana, in her own way. Things wouldn't have quite the same feel without Daniil around.

Viviana just wanted to see the sadness leave her husband's eyes.

"Did you say goodbye?"

She felt Anton shrug behind her as she placed the baby's bag into the back seat. "I'm never going to say goodbye, Vine. Not like that. I can't without feeling like I'm losing him all over again. Once was enough."

"I know," she whispered.

THE LIFE

Finally, she felt his strong grip prodding her to turn. Sexy and dark in his black suit, Anton had kept her sadness and tears at bay for most of the day by keeping her mind distracted on him. Now, though, with the water in his blue eyes staring back, she found it near impossible to stop from letting the floodgates of tears open.

Instead, she choked back the sorrow in her heart and asked, "Who was that?"

"Hmm?"

"That man you were talking with a little while ago. I didn't recognize him."

Anton's jaw ticked, his nostrils flared. "No one important."

Viviana stared the lie straight in the face. Why wouldn't he want to tell her who the man was? "You sure?"

"Of course. So, do you have enough diapers and whatnot to do Demyan a little while?"

"A few hours, why?"

Anton smiled faintly. "I wanted to drive."

"Drive?"

"Yeah, drive. Think. Take my son to a lake and dip his feet into one for the first time. I don't know, something to give me a happy memory of this day instead of just ... this," he said with a wave at himself. Viviana could see exactly what he meant by his words. Anton was wrought with tension. There was pain edging the corners of his mouth down and anguish warring in his gaze. Even his voice didn't hold the same strong tenor it usually did. "Can we?"

Viviana trailed her fingers along his shirt beneath his jacket, feeling the rock solid muscles lining his abdomen clench under her touch. He seemed to calm by her hand, though, so she kept the same tender strokes going as she talked.

"We can do whatever you want, Anton. The dinner isn't until six tonight, so we've got a while. It's not like we need bottles and Demyan has enough pampers to do him for a little trip. Let's go."

"Go," he echoed softly.

"Want me to drive?" she asked.

Anton blinked down at her, a sliver of wetness coating his bottom lashes. The sight all but broke her heart, but she didn't acknowledge the tears. He wouldn't want her to. "Nah, baby. I just want to hold your hand, and drive."

"Okay. We can do that, too."

• • •

Throaty blues crawled from the speakers of their Mercedes-Benz. Viviana had opened the doors to the SUV and turned the music up to a level that wouldn't bother the baby but was loud enough to fill the area with its heart and soul.

Resting back to the front of the SUV, she smiled as Anton supported Demyan's head and body with his arm before dipping the baby's bare feet into the cold water of the lake. Instantly, like a shock to his little body, Demyan jerked at the new sensation.

He didn't cry, though.

Anton laughed, dipping his own hand into the water before bringing his wet fingers up to trace along Demyan's cheeks. "Cold, little man? Yeah, Papa's not even sorry. Just the look on your face was worth it."

Viviana was going to take pictures of the moment, but Anton asked her not to. Not everything had to be captured, he said. They took enough photos on a day to day basis. Some of his best memories growing up were never photographed or videotaped.

When Viviana thought back to her own raising, she had to agree.

"Bring him to me so I can dry his little toes before they freeze," Viviana said, still grinning at the happiness on her husband's face.

"It's the end of July, Vine. He's not going to catch a cold."

"He's just a baby, Anton."

"You're being a helicopter."

The snort Viviana released was indelicate. "You wouldn't even know what that meant if I didn't tell you, smartass."

"You love it," Anton said with a grin over his shoulder

"Whatever you say, Boss."

Anton shot her a look as he stood, sending her insides pitching up to a fever. He'd long forgone his coat and rolled up the sleeves of his dress shirt to his elbows. The new ink on his flesh caught her eye. Like Anton wanted, he had his son's name tattooed, written with script in black along his wrist. What had surprised her more was the matching design on his other wrist with her name.

You're the only people on this earth who can bar me down and make me want to stay, he'd said. Appropriate, then, that he tattooed them both on his wrists as if they were handcuffs to hold him barred for the rest of his life.

Anton raked his fingers through his hair, the style standing up like it'd been windswept.

And he looked happier.

That's all Viviana wanted to see in Anton. Just some genuine happiness.

"Come here."

Anton rolled his eyes at her demand. "Vine, he's fine."

"No, I just want you to come over here for a minute. I know he's okay."

Slowly, Anton made his way over. Nuzzling his face down close to his son's, the smile creeping over his cheeks was a sweet relief. Demyan's little hands were clasping Anton's neck like he wanted to draw him closer.

"Here, bossy pants," Anton said when he was standing in front of Viviana. "Dry his feet up and put his socks back on."

Instead of doing what he asked, Viviana reached out and fisted his shirt, pulling him close enough for her to kiss his mouth. Intense couldn't adequately describe the way her body, heart, and soul reached out to need and want the man in front of her. It was like an urge that beat upwards from her middle and forced its way out with no warning.

Viviana didn't have to think about it. She knew it would

always be like that between them.

"Hey," he said, his tone turning deeper. "That was unexpected. Nice, but unexpected."

"Love you."

"God, do I ever love you," Anton replied, smirking.

The squirming baby boy resting against Anton's chest in his arm stilled momentarily. Glancing down at her son, Viviana beamed at the child. Something amazing, indeed. He brightened up just about everything he came I contact with. She thought of what it would be like to see him older, growing, and loving.

How would Demyan grow? Would he be like his father, only sharing his love carefully and privately? Would he be strong and handsome, chasing girls until one finally settled him down? Would he be Bratva, or just a boy?

Viviana couldn't wait to find out.

"Are you always going to be here, Vine?" Anton asked quietly.

"Huh?" Viviana didn't know what to say to that. Anton's hand cupped her face, his thumb rolling along her cheekbone as she stared into his eyes. "Of course I'm going to be here. Why ask that?"

"What if ..." Anton's gaze darted down to Demyan. "What if I mess something up someday with this life of ours? Would you be still be here, then?"

Viviana didn't even hesitate. "Yes."

"You know, you never did tell me what Nicoli wrote to you in that letter."

"I don't think he meant for you to know."

Anton shrugged. "Maybe. Would you tell me if I asked, though?"

She ticked two of her fingers under his chin to make him look up again. "Maybe."

"Was there anything important for me?" Anton asked.

Viviana's grin grew, matching the one taking over his features as Anton watched their son. "He hoped you made me live."

"Do I?"

Yeah, he really did. No one could do it better.

"Every single day of our life, Anton."

ABOUT THE AUTHOR

Bethany-Kris is a Canadian author, lover of much, and mother to three very young sons, one cat, and two dogs. A small town in Eastern Canada where she was born and raised is where she has always called home. With her boys under her feet, a snuggling cat, barking dogs, and a spouse calling over his shoulder, she is nearly always writing something ... when she can find the time.

Find Bethany-Kris at:
Her website www.bethanykris.com,
or on Facebook at www.facebook.com/bethanykriswrites,
on her blog at www.bethanykris.blogspot.ca,
or on Twitter - @BethanyKris.

Sign up to Bethany-Kris's New Release Newsletter here:
http://eepurl.com/bf9lzD

MORE BY BETHANY-KRIS

The Russian Guns
The Arrangement
The Life
The Score
Demyan & Ana
Shattered

Filthy Marcellos
Filthy Marcellos: Lucian
Filthy Marcellos: Giovanni
Filthy Marcellos: Dante

Watch for more at www.bethanykris.com

THE LIFE

Bethany-Kris

www.ingramcontent.com/pod-product-compliance
Lightning Source LLC
Chambersburg PA
CBHW031337020726
47499CB00005B/1306